THE NOVELS AND TALES OF HENRY JAMES

New York Edition

VOLUME X

THE SPOILS OF POYNTON

A LONDON LIFE

THE CHAPERON

HENRY JAMES

NEW YORK

CHARLES SCRIBNER'S SONS

PREFACE

IT was years ago, I remember, one Christmas Eve when I was dining with friends: a lady beside me made in the course of talk one of those allusions that I have always found myself recognising on the spot as "germs." The germ, wherever gathered, has ever been for me the germ of a "story," and most of the stories straining to shape under my hand have sprung from a single small seed, a seed as minute and wind-blown as that casual hint for "The Spoils of Poynton" dropped unwitting by my neighbour, a mere floating particle in the stream of talk. What above all comes back to me with this reminiscence is the sense of the inveterate minuteness, on such happy occasions, of the precious particle — reduced, that is, to its mere fruitful essence. Such is the interesting truth about the stray suggestion, the wandering word, the vague echo, at touch of which the novelist's imagination winces as at the prick of some sharp point: its virtue is all in its needle-like quality, the power to penetrate as finely as possible. This fineness it is that communicates the virus of suggestion, anything more than the minimum of which spoils the operation. If one is given a hint at all designedly one is sure to be given too much; one's subject is in the merest grain, the speck of truth, of beauty, of reality, scarce visible to the common eye — since, I firmly hold, a good eye for a subject is anything but usual. Strange and attaching, certainly, the consistency with which the first thing to be done for the communicated and seized idea is to reduce almost to nought the form, the air as of a mere disjoined and lacerated lump of life, in which we may have happened to meet it. Life being all inclusion and confusion, and art being all discrim- ination and selection, the latter, in search of the hard latent

v

value with which alone it is concerned, sniffs round the mass as instinctively and unerringly as a dog suspicious of some buried bone. The difference here, however, is that, while the dog desires his bone but to destroy it, the artist finds in *his* tiny nugget, washed free of awkward accretions and hammered into a sacred hardness, the very stuff for a clear affirmation, the happiest chance for the indestructible. It at the same time amuses him again and again to note how, beyond the first step of the actual case, the case that constitutes for him his germ, his vital particle, his grain of gold, life persistently blunders and deviates, loses herself in the sand. The reason is of course that life has no direct sense whatever for the subject and is capable, luckily for us, of nothing but splendid waste. Hence the opportunity for the sublime economy of art, which rescues, which saves, and hoards and " banks," investing and reinvesting these fruits of toil in wondrous useful "works" and thus making up for us, desperate spendthrifts that we all naturally are, the most princely of incomes. It is the subtle secrets of that system, however, that are meanwhile the charming study, with an endless attraction, above all, in the question — endlessly baffling indeed — of the method at the heart of the madness; the madness, I mean, of a zeal, among the reflective sort, so disinterested. If life, presenting us the germ, and left merely to herself in such a business, gives the case away, almost always, before we can stop her, what are the signs for our guidance, what the primary laws for a saving selection, how do we know when and where to in-tervene, where do we place the beginnings of the wrong or the right deviation? Such would be the elements of an en-quiry upon which, I hasten to say, it is quite forbidden me here to embark: I but glance at them in evidence of the rich pasture that at every turn surrounds the ruminant critic. The answer may be after all that mysteries here elude us, that general considerations fail or mislead, and that even the fondest of artists need ask no wider range than the logic of the particular case. The particular case, or in other words his relation to a given subject, once the relation is established, forms in itself a little world of exercise and agitation. Let him hold himself perhaps supremely fortunate if he can meet half the questions with which that air alone may swarm.

So it was, at any rate, that when my amiable friend, on the Christmas Eve, before the table that glowed safe and fair through the brown London night, spoke of such an odd matter as that a good lady in the north, always well looked on, was at daggers drawn with her only son, ever hitherto exemplary, over the ownership of the valuable furniture of a fine old house just accruing to the young man by his father's death, I instantly became aware, with my "sense for the subject," of the prick of inoculation; the *whole* of the virus, as I have called it, being infused by that single touch. There had been but ten words, yet I had recognised in them, as in a flash, all the possibilities of the little drama of my "Spoils," which glimmered then and there into life; so that when in the next breath I began to hear of action taken, on the beautiful ground, by our engaged adversaries, tipped each, from that instant, with the light of the highest distinction, I saw clumsy Life again at her stupid work. For the action taken, and on which my friend, as I knew she would, had already begun all complacently and benightedly further to report, I had absolutely, and could have, no scrap of use; one had been so perfectly qualified to say in advance: " It's the perfect little workable thing, but she'll strangle it in the cradle, even while she pretends, all so cheeringly, to rock it; wherefore I'll stay her hand while yet there's time." I did n't, of course, stay her hand — there never *is* in such cases "time"; and I had once more the full demonstration of the fatal futility of Fact. The turn taken by the excellent situation — excellent, for development, if arrested in the right place, that is in the germ — had the full measure of the classic ineptitude; to which with the full measure of the artistic irony one could once more, and for the thousandth time, but take off one's hat. It was not, however, that this in the least mattered, once the seed had been transplanted to richer soil; and I dwell on that almost inveterate redundancy of the wrong, as opposed to the ideal right, in any free flowering of the actual, by reason only of its approach to calculable regularity.

If there was nothing regular meanwhile, nothing more so than the habit of vigilance, in my quickly feeling where interest would really lie, so I could none the less acknowledge afresh that these small private cheers of recognition made the spirit easy and the temper bland for the confused whole. I "took" in fine, on the spot, to the rich bare little fact of the two related figures, embroiled perhaps all so sordidly; and for reasons of which I could most probably have given at the moment no decent account. Had I been asked why they were, in that stark nudity, to say nothing of that ugliness of attitude, "interesting," I fear I could have said nothing more to the point, even to my own questioning spirit, than " Well, you'll see!" By which of course I should have meant " Well, *I* shall see " — confident meanwhile (as against the appearance or the imputation of poor taste) that interest would spring as soon as one should begin really to see *anything*. That points, I think, to a large part of the very source of interest for the artist: it resides in the strong consciousness of his seeing all for himself. He has to borrow his motive, which is certainly half the battle; and this motive is his ground, his site and his foundation. But after that he only lends and gives, only builds and piles high, lays together the blocks quarried in the deeps of his imagination and on his personal premises. He thus remains all the while in intimate commerce with his motive, and can say to himself — what really more than anything else inflames and sustains him — that he alone has the *secret* of the particular case, he alone can measure the truth of the direction to be taken by his developed data. There can be for him, evidently, only one logic for these things; there can be for him only one truth and one direction — the quarter in which his subject most completely expresses itself. The careful ascertainment of how it shall do so, and the art of guiding it with consequent authority — since this sense of " authority " is for the master-builder the treasure of treasures, or

PREFACE

at least the joy of joys — renews in the modern alchemist something like the old dream of the secret of life.

Extravagant as the mere statement sounds, one seemed accordingly to handle the secret of life in drawing the positive right truth out of the so easy muddle of wrong truths in which the interesting possibilities of that " row," so to call it, between mother and son over their household gods might have been stifled. I find it odd to consider, as I thus revert, that I could have had none but the most general warrant for " seeing anything in it," as the phrase would have been; that I could n't in the least, on the spot, as I have already hinted, have justified my faith. One thing was " in it," in the sordid situation, on the first blush, and one thing only — though this, in its limited way, no doubt, a curious enough value : the sharp light it might project on that most modern of our current passions, the fierce appetite for the upholsterer's and joiner's and brazier's work, the chairs and tables, the cabinets and presses, the material odds and ends, of the more labouring ages. A lively mark of our manners indeed the diffusion of this curiosity and this avidity, and full of suggestion, clearly, as to their possible influence on other passions and other relations. On the face of it the " things " themselves would form the very centre of such a crisis; these grouped objects, all conscious of their eminence and their price, would enjoy, in any picture of a conflict, the heroic importance. They would have to be presented, they would have to be painted — arduous and desperate thought; something would have to be done for them not too ignobly unlike the great array in which Balzac, say, would have marshalled them : *that* amount of workable interest at least would evidently be " in it."

It would be wrapped in the silver tissue of some such conviction, at any rate, that I must have laid away my prime impression for a rest not disturbed till long afterwards, till the year 1896, I make out, when there arose a question of my contributing three " short stories " to " The Atlantic Monthly "; or supplying rather perhaps a third to complete a trio two members of which had appeared. The echo of the situation mentioned to me at our Christmas Eve dinner awoke again, I recall, at that touch — I recall, no doubt, with true humility, in view of my renewed mismeasurement of my charge. Painfully associated for me had " The Spoils of Poynton " remained, until recent re-perusal, with the awkward consequence of that fond error. The subject had emerged from cool reclusion all suffused with a flush of meaning; thanks to which irresistible air, as I could but plead in the event, I found myself — as against a mere commercial austerity — beguiled and led on. The thing had " come," the flower of conception had bloomed — all in the happy dusk of indifference and neglect; yet, strongly and frankly as it might now appeal, my idea would n't surely overstrain a *natural* brevity. A story that could n't possibly be long would have inevitably to be " short," and out of the depths of that delusion it accordingly began to struggle. To my own view, after the " first number," this composition (which in the magazine bore another title) conformed but to its nature, which was not to transcend a modest amplitude; but, dispatched in instalments, it felt itself eyed, from month to month, I seem to remember, with an editorial ruefulness excellently well founded — from the moment such differences of sense could exist, that is, as to the short and the long. The sole impression it made, I woefully gathered, was that of length, and it has till lately, as I say, been present to me but as the poor little " long " thing.

It began to appear in April 1896, and, as is apt blessedly to occur for me throughout this process of revision, the old, the shrunken concomitants muster again as I turn the pages. They lurk between the lines; these serve for them as the barred seraglio-windows behind which, to the outsider in the glare of the Eastern street, forms indistinguishable seem to move and peer; " association " in fine bears upon them with its infinite magic. Peering through the lattice from without inward I recapture a cottage on a cliff-side, to which, at the earliest approach of the summer-time, redoubtable in London through the luxuriance of still other than " natural " forces, I had betaken myself to finish a book in quiet and to begin

another in fear. The cottage was, in its kind, perfection;
mainly by reason of a small paved terrace which, curving
forward from the cliff-edge like the prow of a ship, overhung
a view as level, as purple, as full of rich change, as the ex-
panse of the sea. The horizon was in fact a band of sea;
a small red-roofed town, of great antiquity, perched on its
sea-rock, clustered within the picture off to the right; while
above one's head rustled a dense summer shade, that of a
trained and arching ash, rising from the middle of the terrace, brushing the parapet with a heavy fringe and covering
the place like a vast umbrella. Beneath this umbrella and
really under exquisite protection " The Spoils of Poynton "
managed more or less symmetrically to grow.

I recall that I was committed to begin, the day I finished
it, short of dire penalties, " The Other House "; with which
work, however, of whatever high profit the considerations
springing from it might be too, we have nothing to do here
—and to the felt jealousy of which, as that of a grudging
neighbour, I allude only for sweet recovery of the fact,
mainly interesting to myself I admit, that the rhythm of the
earlier book shows no flurry of hand. I " liked " it—the earlier book: I venture now, after years, to welcome the sense
of that amenity as well; so immensely refreshing is it to be
moved, in any case, toward these retrospective simplicities.
Painters and writers, I gather, are, when easily accessible to
such appeals, frequently questioned as to those of their productions they may most have delighted in; but the profession
of delight has always struck me as the last to consort, for
the artist, with any candid account of his troubled effort—
ever the sum, for the most part, of so many lapses and com-
promises, simplifications and surrenders. Which is the work
in which he hasn't surrendered, under dire difficulty, the best
thing he meant to have kept? In which indeed, before the
dreadful *done*, doesn't he ask himself what has become of
the thing all for the sweet sake of which it was to proceed
to that extremity? Preference and complacency, on these
terms, riot in general as they best may; not disputing, however, a grain of which weighty truth, I still make out, be-

tween my reconsidered lines, as it were, that I must—my opera-box of a terrace and my great green umbrella indeed aiding—have assisted at the growth and predominance of Fleda Vetch.

For something like Fleda Vetch had surely been latent in one's first apprehension of the theme; it wanted, for treatment, a centre, and, the most obvious centre being "barred," this image, while I still wondered, had, with all the assurance in the world, sprung up in its place. The real centre, as I say, the citadel of the interest, with the fight waged round it, would have been the felt beauty and value of the prize of battle, the Things, always the splendid Things, placed in the middle light, figured and constituted, with each identity made vivid, each character discriminated, and their common consciousness of their great dramatic part established. The rendered tribute of these honours, however, no vigilant editor, as I have intimated, could be conceived as allowing room for; since, by so much as the general glittering presence should spread, by so much as it should suggest the gleam of brazen idols and precious metals and inserted gems in the tempered light of some arching place of worship, by just so much would the muse of "dialogue," most usurping influence of all the romancingly invoked, be routed without ceremony, to lay her grievance at the feet of her gods. The spoils of Poynton were not directly articulate, and though they might have, and constantly did have, wondrous things to say, their message fostered about them a certain hush of cheaper sound—as a consequence of which, in fine, they would have been costly to keep up. In this manner Fleda Vetch, maintainable at less expense—though even she, I make out, less expert in spreading chatter thin than the readers of romance mainly like their heroines to-day—marked her place in my foreground at one ingratiating stroke. She planted herself centrally, and the stroke, as I call it, the demonstration after which she could n't be gainsaid, was the simple act of letting it be seen she had character.

For somehow—that was the way interest broke out,

once the germ had been transferred to the sunny south window-sill of one's fonder attention — character, the question of what my agitated friends should individually, and all intimately and at the core, show themselves, would unmistakeably be the key to my modest drama, and would indeed alone make a drama of any sort possible. Yes, it is a story of cabinets and chairs and tables; they formed the bone of contention, but what would merely "become" of them, magnificently passive, seemed to represent a comparatively vulgar issue. The passions, the faculties, the forces their beauty would, like that of antique Helen of Troy, set in motion, was what, as a painter, one had really wanted of them, was the power in them that one had from the first appreciated. Emphatically, by that truth, there would have to be moral developments — dreadful as such a prospect might loom for a poor interpreter committed to brevity. A character is interesting as it comes out, and by the process and duration of that emergence; just as a procession is effective by the way it unrolls, turning to a mere mob if all of it passes at once. My little procession, I foresaw then from an early stage, would refuse to pass at once; though I could keep it more or less down, of course, by reducing it to three or four persons. Practically, in "The Spoils," the reduction is to four, though indeed — and I clung to that as to my plea for simplicity — the main agents, with the others all dependent, are Mrs. Gereth and Fleda. Fleda's ingratiating stroke, for importance, on the threshold, had been that she would understand; and positively, from that moment, the progress and march of my tale became and remained that of her understanding.

Absolutely, with this, I committed myself to making the affirmation and the penetration of it my action and my "story"; once more, too, with the re-entertained perception that a subject so lighted, a subject residing in somebody's excited and concentrated feeling about something — both the something and the somebody being of course as important as possible — has more beauty to give out than under any other style of pressure. One is confronted obviously thus with the question of the importances; with that in particular, no doubt, of the weight of intelligent consciousness, consciousness of the whole, or of something ominously like it, that one may decently permit a represented figure to appear to throw. Some plea for this cause, that of the intelligence of the moved mannikin, I have already had occasion to make, and can scarce hope too often to evade it. This intelligence, an honourable amount of it, on the part of the person to whom one most invites attention, has but to play with sufficient freedom and ease, or call it with the right grace, to guarantee us that quantum of the impression of beauty which is the most fixed of the possible advantages of our producible effect. It may fail, as a positive presence, on other sides and in other connexions; but more or less of the treasure is stored safe from the moment such a quality of inward life is distilled, or in other words from the moment so fine an interpretation and criticism as that of Fleda Vetch's — to cite the present case — is applied without waste to the surrounding tangle.

It is easy to object of course " Why the deuce then Fleda Vetch, why a mere little flurried bundle of petticoats, why not Hamlet or Milton's Satan at once, if you 're going in for a superior display of ' mind ' ? " To which I fear I can only reply that in pedestrian prose, and in the " short story," one is, for the best reasons, no less on one's guard than on the stretch; and also that I have ever recognised, even in the midst of the curiosity that such displays may quicken, the rule of an exquisite economy. The thing is to lodge somewhere at the heart of one's complexity an irrepressible *appreciation*, but where a light lamp will carry all the flame I incline to look askance at a heavy. From beginning to end, in " The Spoils of Poynton," appreciation, even to that of the very whole, lives in Fleda; which is precisely why, as a consequence rather grandly imposed, every one else shows for comparatively stupid; the tangle, the drama, the tragedy and comedy of those who appreciate consisting so much of their relation with those who don't. From the presented reflexion of this truth my story draws, I think, a certain assured appearance of roundness and felicity. The " things "

PREFACE

are radiant, shedding afar, with a merciless monotony, all
their light, exerting their ravage without remorse; and Fleda
almost demonically both sees and feels, while the others but
feel without seeing. Thus we get perhaps a vivid enough
little example, in the concrete, of the general truth, for the
spectator of life, that the fixed constituents of almost any
reproducible action are the fools who minister, at a particular
crisis, to the intensity of the free spirit engaged with them.
The fools are interesting by contrast, by the salience they
acquire, and by a hundred other of their advantages; and the
free spirit, always much tormented, and by no means always
triumphant, is heroic, ironic, pathetic or whatever, and, as
exemplified in the record of Fleda Vetch, for instance, "successful," only through having remained free.

I recognise that the novelist with a weakness for that
ground of appeal is foredoomed to a well-nigh extravagant
insistence on the free spirit, seeing the possibility of one in
every bush; I may perhaps speak of it as noteworthy that
this very volume happens to exhibit in two other cases my
disposition to let the interest stand or fall by the tried spon-
taneity and vivacity of the freedom. It is in fact for that
respectable reason that I enclose "A London Life" and
"The Chaperon" between these covers; my purpose having been here to class my reprintable productions as far as
possible according to their kinds. The two tales I have just
named are of the same "kind" as "The Spoils," to the
extent of their each dealing with a human predicament in
the light, for the charm of the thing, of the amount of
"appreciation" to be plausibly imputed to the subject of it.
They are each—and truly there are more of such to come
— "stories about women," very young women, who,
affected with a certain high lucidity, thereby become char-
acters; in consequence of which their doings, their sufferings or whatever, take on, I assume, an importance. Laura
Wing, in "A London Life," has, like Fleda Vetch, acuteness and intensity, reflexion and passion, has above all a
contributive and participant view of her situation; just as
Rose Tramore, in "The Chaperon," rejoices, almost to

insolence, very much in the same cluster of attributes and advantages. They are thus of a family — which shall have also for us, we seem forewarned, more members, and of each sex.

As to our young woman of " The Spoils," meanwhile, I briefly come back to my claim for a certain definiteness of beauty in the special effect wrought by her aid. My problem had decently to be met — that of establishing for the other persons the vividness of their appearance of comparative stupidity, that of exposing them to the full thick wash of the penumbra surrounding the central light, and yet keeping their motions, within it, distinct, coherent and "amusing." But these are exactly of course the most "amusing" things to do; nothing, for example, being of a higher reward artistically than the shade of success aimed at in such a figure as Mrs. Gereth. A character she too, absolutely, yet the very reverse of a free spirit. I have found myself so pleased with Mrs. Gereth, I confess, on resuming acquaintance with her, that, complete and all in equilibrium as she seems to me to stand and move there, I shrink from breathing upon her any breath of qualification; without which, however, I fail of my point that, thanks to the " value " represented by Fleda, and to the position to which the elder woman is confined by that irradiation, the latter is at the best a " false " character, floundering as she does in the dusk of disproportionate passion. She is a *figure*, oh definitely — which is a very different matter; for you may be a figure with all the blinding, with all the hampering passion in life, and may have the grand air in what shall yet prove to the finer view (which Fleda again, *e. g.*, could at any time strike off) but a perfect rage of awkwardness. Mrs. Gereth was, obviously, with her pride and her pluck, of an admirable fine paste; but she was not intelligent, was only clever, and therefore would have been no use to us at all as centre of our subject — compared with Fleda, who was only intelligent, not distinctively able. The little drama confirms at all events excellently, I think, the contention of the old wisdom that the question of the personal will has more than all else to say to the verisimilitude of these exhibitions. The will that rides the crisis quite most triumphantly is that of the awful Mona Brigstock, who is *all* will, without the smallest leak of force into taste or tenderness or vision, into any sense of shades or relations or proportions. She loses no minute in that perception of incongruities in which half Fleda's passion is wasted and misled, and into which Mrs. Gereth, to her practical loss, that is by the fatal grace of a sense of comedy, occasionally and disinterestedly strays. Every one, every thing, in the story is accordingly sterile *but* the so thriftily constructed Mona, able at any moment to bear the whole of her dead weight at once on any given inch of a resisting surface. Fleda, obliged to neglect inches, sees and feels but in acres and expanses and blue perspectives; Mrs. Gereth too, in comparison, while her imagination broods, drops half the stitches of the web she seeks to weave.

If I speak of classifying I hasten to recognise that there are other marks for the purpose still and that, failing other considerations, " A London Life " would properly consort, in this series, with a dozen of the tales by which I at one period sought to illustrate and enliven the supposed " international " conflict of manners; a general theme dealing for the most part with the bewilderment of the good American, of either sex and of almost any age, in presence of the " European " order. This group of data might possibly have shown, for the reverse of its medal, the more or less desperate contortions of the European under American social pressure. Three or four tried glances in that direction seemed to suggest, however, no great harvest to be gathered; so that the pictorial value of the general opposition was practically confined to one phase. More reasons are here involved than I can begin to go into — as indeed I confess that the reflexions set in motion by the international fallacy at large, as I am now moved to regard it, quite crowd upon me; I simply note therefore, on one corner of the ground, the scant results, above all for interesting detail, promised by confronting the fruits of a constituted order with the fruits of no order at all. We may strike lights by opposing order to order, one sort to another sort; for in that case we get the correspondences and equivalents that make differences mean something; we get the interest and the tension of disparity where a certain parity may have been in question. Where it may *not* have been in question, where the dramatic encounter is but the poor concussion of positives on one side with negatives on the other, we get little beyond a consideration of the differences between fishes and fowls.

By which I don't mean to say that the appeal of the fallacy, as I call it, was not at one time quite inevitably irresistible; had it nothing else to recommend it to the imagination it would always have had the advantage of its showy surface, of suggesting situations as to which assurance seemed easy, founded, as it felt itself, on constant observation. The attraction was thus not a little, I judge, the attraction of facility; the international was easy to do, because, as one's wayside bloomed with it, one had but to put forth one's hand and pluck the frequent flower. Add to this that the flower *was*, so often, quite positively a flower — that of the young American innocence transplanted to European air. The general subject had, in fine, a charm while it lasted; but I shall have much more to say about it on another occasion. What here concerns us is that "A London Life" breaks down altogether, I have had to recognise, as a contribution to my comprehensive picture of bewildered Americanism. I fail to make out to-day why I need have conceived my three principal persons as sharers in that particular bewilderment. There was enough of the general human and social sort for them without it; poor young Wendover in especial, I think, fails on any such ground to attest himself — I need n't, surely, have been at costs to bring him all the way from New York. Laura Wing, touching creature as she was designed to appear, strikes me as a rare little person who would have been a rare little person anywhere, and who, in that character, must have felt and judged and suffered and acted as she did, whatever her producing clime.

The great anomaly, however, is Mrs. Lionel; a study of a type quite sufficiently to be accounted for on the very scene of her development, and with her signs and marks easily mistakeable, in London, for the notes of a native luxuriance. I recall the emphasis, quite the derision, with which a remarkably wise old friend, not American, a trenchant judge who had observed manners in many countries and had done me the honour to read my tale, put to me: " What on earth possessed you to make of your Selina an American, or to make one of your two or three Americans a Selina? — resembling so to the life something quite else, something which hereabouts one need n't go far to seek, but failing of any felicity for a creature engendered *là-bas*." And I think my friend conveyed, or desired to convey, that the wicked woman of my story was falsified above all, as an imported product, by something distinctly other than so engendered in the superficial " form " of her perversity, a high stiff-backed angular action which is, or was then, beyond any American " faking." The truth is, no doubt, that, though Mrs. Lionel, on my page, does n't in the least achieve character, she yet passes before us as a sufficiently vivid image, which was to be the effect designed for her—an image the hard rustle of whose long steps and the sinister tinkle of whose multiplied trinkets belie the association invoked for them and positively operate for another. Not perhaps, moreover, as I am moved to subjoin, that the point greatly matters. What matters, for one's appreciation of a work of art, however modest, is that the prime intention shall have been justified — for any judgement of which we must be clear as to what it was. It was n't after all of the prime, the very most prime, intention of the tale in question that the persons concerned in them should have had this, that or the other land of birth; but that the central situation should really be rendered — that of a charming and decent young thing, from wheresoever proceeding, who has her decision and her action to take, horribly and unexpectedly, in face of a squalid " scandal " the main agent of which is her nearest relative, and who, at the dreadful crisis, to guard against

PREFACE

personal bespattering, is moved, with a miserable want of effect, to a wild vague frantic gesture, an appeal for protection that virtually proves a precipitation of her disgrace.

Nobody concerned need, as I say, have come from New York for that; though, as I have likewise intimated, I must have seen the creation of my heroine, in 1888, and the representation of the differences I wished to establish between her own known world and the world from which she finds herself recoiling, facilitated in a high degree by assured reference to the simpler social order across the sea. I had my vision (as I recover the happy spell) of her having "come over" to find, to her dismay, what "London" had made of the person in the world hitherto most akin to her; in addition to which I was during those years infinitely interested in almost any demonstration of the effect of London. This was a form of response to the incessant appeal of the great city, one's grateful, one's devoted recognition of which fairly broke out from day to day. It was material ever to one's hand; and the impression was always there that no one so much as the candid outsider, caught up and involved in the sweep of the machine, could measure the values revealed. Laura Wing must have figured for me thus as the necessary candid outsider—from the moment some received impression of the elements about me was to be projected and embodied. In fact as I remount the stream it is the particular freshness of that enjoyed relation I seem to taste again; the positive fond belief that I had my right oppositions. They seemed to ensure somehow the perfect march of my tolerably simple action; the straightness, the artful economy of which—save that of a particular point where my ingenuity shows to so small advantage that, to anticipate opprobrium, I can but hold it up to derision—hasn't ceased to be appreciable. The thing made its first appearance in "Scribner's Magazine" during the summer of 1888, and I remember being not long before at work upon it, remember in fact beginning it, in one of the wonderful faded back rooms of an old Venetian palace, a room with a pompous Tiepolo ceiling and walls of ancient pale-green damask, slightly shredded and patched, which, on the warm mornings, looked into the shade of a court where a high outer staircase, strikingly bold, yet strikingly relaxed, held together one scarce knew how; where Gothic windows broke out, on discoloured blanks of wall, at quite arbitrary levels, and where above all the strong Venetian voice, full of history and humanity and waking perpetual echoes, seemed to say more in ten warm words, of whatever tone, than any twenty pages of one's cold pale prose.

In spite of all of which, I may add, I do penance here only for the awkwardness of that departure from the adopted form of my recital which resides in the picture of the interview with young Wendover contrived by Lady Davenant in the interest of some better provision for their poor young friend. Here indeed is a lapse from artistic dignity, a confession of want of resource, which I may not pretend to explain to-day, and on behalf of which I have nothing to urge save a consciousness of my dereliction presumably too vague at the time. I had seen my elements presented in a certain way, settled the little law under which my story was to be told, and with this consistency, as any reader of the tale may easily make out for himself, interviews to which my central figure was not a party, scenes revolving on an improvised pivot of their own, had nothing to do with the affair. I might of course have adopted another plan — the artist is free, surely, to adopt any he fancies, provided it *be* a plan and he adopt it intelligently; and to that scheme of composition the independent picture of a passage between Lady Davenant and young Wendover might perfectly have conformed. As the case stands it conforms to nothing; whereas the beauty of a thing of this order really done as a whole is ever, certainly, that its parts are in abject dependence, and that even any great charm they may individually and capriciously put forth is infirm so far as it does n't measurably contribute to a harmony. My momentary helplessness sprang, no doubt, from my failure to devise in time some way of giving the value of Lady Davenant's appeal to the young man, of making it play its part in my heroine's history and consciousness, without so awkwardly thrusting the lump sum on the reader.

Circumventions of difficulty of this degree are precisely the finest privilege of the craftsman, who, to be worth his salt, and master of *any* contrived harmony, must take no tough technical problem for insoluble. These technical subterfuges and subtleties, these indirectly-expressed values, kept indirect in a higher interest, made subordinate to some general beauty, some artistic intention that can give an account of itself, what are they after all but one of the nobler parts of our amusement? Superficially, in "A London Life," it might well have seemed that the only way to picture the intervention on Laura Wing's behalf of the couple just named was to break the chain of the girl's own consciousness and report the matter quite straight and quite shamelessly; this course had indeed every merit but that of its playing the particular game to which I had addressed myself. My prime loyalty was to the interest of the game, and the honour to be won the more desirable by that fact. Any muddle-headed designer can beg the question of perspective, but science is required for making it rule the scene. If it be asked how then we were to have assisted at the copious passage I thus incriminate without our privilege of presence, I can only say that my discovery of the right way should—and would—have been the very flower of the performance. The real "fun" of the thing would have been exactly to sacrifice my comparative platitude of statement—a deplorable depth at any time, I have attempted elsewhere to signify, for any pretending master of representation to sink to—without sacrificing a grain of what was to be conveyed. The real fun, in other words, would have been in not, by an exceptional collapse of other ingenuity, making my attack on the spectator's consciousness a call as immediate as a postman's knock. This attack, at every other point, reaches that objective only through the medium of the interesting girl's own vision, own experience, with which all the facts are richly charged and coloured. That saturates our sense of them with the savour of Laura's sense—thanks to which enhancement we get intensity. But from the chapter to which I have called attention, so that it may serve perhaps as a lesson, intensity ruefully drops. I can't say worse for it—and have been the more concerned to say what I do that without this flaw the execution might have appeared from beginning to end close and exemplary.

It is with all that better confidence, I think, that the last of my three tales here carries itself. I recapture perfectly again, in respect to "The Chaperon," both the first jog of my imagination and the particular local influence that presided at its birth—the latter a ramshackle inn on the Irish coast, where the table at which I wrote was of an equilibrium so vague that I wonder to-day how any object constructed on it should stand so firm. The strange sad charm of the tearful Irish light hangs about the memory of the labour of which this small fiction—first published in two numbers of "The Atlantic Monthly" of 1891—was one of the fruits; but the subject had glimmered upon me, two or three years before, in an air of comedy comparatively free from sharp under-tastes. Once more, as in the case of its companions here, the single spoken word, in London, had said all—after the manner of that clear ring of the electric bell that the barest touch of the button may produce. The talk being of a certain lady who, in consequence of early passages, had lived for years apart from her husband and in no affluence of good company, it was mentioned of her that her situation had improved, and the desert around her been more or less brought under cultivation, by the fact of her having at last made acquaintance with her young unmarried daughter, a charming girl just introduced to the world and thereby qualified for "taking her out," floating her in spite of whatever past damage. Here in truth, it seemed to me, *was* a morsel of queer comedy to play with, and my tale embodies the neat experiment. Fortunately in this case the principle of composition adopted is loyally observed; the values gathered are, without exception, gathered by the light of the intense little personal consciousness, invoked from the first, that shines over my field and the predominance of which

PREFACE

is usurped by none other. That is the main note to be made about "The Chaperon"; except this further, which I must reserve, however—as I shall find excellent occasion—for an ampler development. A short story, to my sense and as the term is used in magazines, has to choose between being either an anecdote or a picture and can but play its part strictly according to its kind. I rejoice in the anecdote, but I revel in the picture; though having doubtless at times to note that a given attempt may place itself near the dividing-line. This is in some degree the case with "The Chaperon," in which, none the less, on the whole, picture ingeniously prevails; picture aiming at those richly summarised and fore-shortened effects—the opposite pole again from expansion inorganic and thin—that refer their terms of production, for which the magician has ever to don his best cap and gown, to the inner compartment of our box of tricks. From *them* comes the true grave close consistency in which parts hang together even as the interweavings of a tapestry. "The Chaperon" has perhaps, so far as it goes, something of that texture. Yet I shall be able, I think, to cite examples with still more.

HENRY JAMES.

CONTENTS

THE SPOILS OF POYNTON

THE
SPOILS OF POYNTON

I

Mrs. Gereth had said she would go with the rest
to church, but suddenly it seemed to her she should n't
be able to wait even till church-time for relief: breakfast was at Waterbath a punctual meal and she had
still nearly an hour on her hands. Knowing the
church to be near she prepared in her room for the
little rural walk, and on her way down again, passing
through corridors and observing imbecilities of decoration, the æsthetic misery of the big commodious
house, she felt a return of the tide of last night's
irritation, a renewal of everything she could secretly
suffer from ugliness and stupidity. Why did she
consent to such contacts? why did she so rashly
expose herself? She had had, heaven knew, her
reasons, but the whole experience was to be sharper
than she had feared. To get away from it and out
into the air, into the presence of sky and trees, flowers
and birds, was a necessity of every nerve. The flowers
at Waterbath would probably go wrong in colour
and the nightingales sing out of tune; but she remembered to have heard the place described as possessing those advantages that are usually spoken of as
natural. There were advantages enough it clearly
did n't possess. It was hard for her to believe a
woman could look presentable who had been kept

awake for hours by the wall-paper in her room; yet none the less, as she rustled in her fresh widow's weeds across the hall, she was sustained by the consciousness, which always added to the unction of her social Sundays, that she was, as usual, the only person in the house incapable of wearing in her preparation the horrible stamp of the same exceptional smartness that would be conspicuous in a grocer's wife. She would rather have perished than have looked *endimanchée*.

She was fortunately not challenged, the hall being empty of the other women, who were engaged precisely in arraying themselves to that dire end. Once in the grounds she recognised that, with a site, a view, that struck the note, set an example to all inmates, Waterbath ought to have been charming. How she herself, with such elements to handle, would have taken the fine hint of nature! Suddenly, at the turn of a walk, she came on a member of the party, a young lady seated on a bench in deep and lonely meditation. She had observed the girl at dinner and afterwards: she was always looking at girls with reference, apprehensive or speculative, to her son. Deep in her heart was a conviction that Owen would in spite of all her spells marry at last a frump; and this from no evidence she could have represented as adequate, but simply from her deep uneasiness, her belief that such a special sensibility as her own could have been inflicted on a woman only as a source of anguish. It would be her fate, her discipline, her cross, to have a frump brought hideously home to her. This girl, one of the two Vetches, had no beauty, but

4

Mrs. Gereth, scanning the dulness for a sign of life, had been straightway able to classify such a figure as for the moment the least of her afflictions. Fleda Vetch was dressed with an idea, though perhaps not with much else; and that made a bond when there was none other, especially as in this case the idea was real, not imitation. Mrs. Gereth had long ago generalised the truth that the temperament of the frump may easily consort with a certain casual prettiness. There were five girls in the party, and the prettiness of this one, slim, pale and black-haired, was less likely than that of the others ever to occasion an exchange of platitudes. The two less developed Brigstocks, daughters of the house, were in particular tiresomely "lovely." A second glance, a sharp one, at the young lady before her conveyed to Mrs. Gereth the soothing assurance that she also was guiltless of looking hot and fine. They had had no talk as yet, but here was a note that would effectually introduce them if the girl should show herself in the least conscious of their community. She got up from her seat with a smile that but partly dissipated the prostration Mrs. Gereth had recognised in her attitude. The elder woman drew her down again, and for a minute, as they sat together, their eyes met and sent out mutual soundings. "Are you safe? Can I utter it?" each of them said to the other, quickly recognising, almost proclaiming, their common need to escape. The tremendous fancy, as it came to be called, that Mrs. Gereth was destined to take to Fleda Vetch virtually began with this discovery that the poor child had been moved to

5

flight even more promptly than herself. That the poor child no less quickly perceived how far she could now go was proved by the immense friendliness with which she instantly broke out: "Is n't it too dreadful?"

"Horrible — horrible!" cried Mrs. Gereth with a laugh; "and it's really a comfort to be able to say it." She had an idea, for it was her ambition, that she successfully made a secret of that awkward oddity her proneness to be rendered unhappy by the presence of the dreadful. Her passion for the exquisite was the cause of this, but it was a passion she considered she never advertised nor gloried in, contenting herself with letting it regulate her steps and show quietly in her life, remembering at all times that there are few things more soundless than a deep devotion. She was therefore struck with the acuteness of the little girl who had already put a finger on her hidden spring. What was dreadful now, what was horrible, was the intimate ugliness of Waterbath, and it was of that phenomenon these ladies talked while they sat in the shade and drew refreshment from the great tranquil sky, whence no cheap blue plates depended. It was an ugliness fundamental and systematic, the result of the abnormal nature of the Brigstocks, from whose composition the principle of taste had been extravagantly omitted. In the arrangement of their home some other principle, remarkably active, but uncanny and obscure, had operated instead, with consequences depressing to behold, consequences that took the form of a universal futility. The house was bad in all conscience, but it might have passed if they had only let it alone. This saving mercy was beyond them; they had smothered it with trumpery ornament and scrapbook art, with strange excrescences and bunchy draperies, with gimcracks that might have been keepsakes for maid-servants and nondescript conveniences that might have been prizes for the blind. They had gone wildly astray over carpets and curtains; they had an infallible instinct for gross deviation and were so cruelly doom-ridden that it rendered them almost tragic. Their drawing-room, Mrs. Gereth lowered her voice to mention, caused her face to burn, and each of the new friends confided to the other that in her own apartment she had given way to tears. There was in the elder lady's a set of comic water-colours, a family joke by a family genius, and in the younger's a souvenir from some centennial or other Exhibition, that they shudderingly alluded to. The house was perversely full of souvenirs of places even more ugly than itself and of things it would have been a pious duty to forget. The worst horror was the acres of varnish, something advertised and smelly, with which everything was smeared: it was Fleda Vetch's conviction that the application of it, by their own hands and hilariously shoving each other, was the amusement of the Brigstocks on rainy days.

When, as criticism deepened, Fleda dropped the suggestion that some people would perhaps see something in Mona, Mrs. Gereth caught her up with a groan of protest, a smothered familiar cry of "Oh my dear!" Mona was the eldest of the three, the one Mrs. Gereth most suspected. She confided to her

7

young friend how it was her suspicion that had brought her to Waterbath; and this was going very far, for on the spot, as a refuge, a remedy, she had clutched at the idea that something might be done with the girl before her. It was her fancied exposure at any rate that had sharpened the shock, made her ask herself with a terrible chill if fate could really be plotting to saddle her with a daughter-in-law brought up in such a place. She had seen Mona in her appropriate setting and had seen Owen, handsome and heavy, dangle beside her; but the effect of these first hours had happily not been to darken the prospect. It was clearer to her that she could never accept Mona, but it was after all by no means certain Owen would ask her to. He had sat by somebody else at dinner and afterwards had talked to Mrs. Firmin, who was as dreadful as all the rest, but redeemingly married. His heaviness, which in her need of expansion she freely named, had two aspects: one of them his monstrous lack of taste, the other his exaggerated prudence. If it should come to a question of carrying Mona with a high hand there would be no need to worry, for that was rarely his mode of proceeding.

Invited by her companion, who had asked if it were n't wonderful, Mrs. Gereth had begun to say a word about Poynton; but she heard a sound of voices that made her stop short. The next moment she rose to her feet, and Fleda could then see her alarm to be by no means quenched. Behind the place where they had been sitting the ground dropped with some steepness, forming a long grassy bank up which

8

Owen Gereth and Mona Brigstock, dressed for church but making a familiar joke of it, were in the act of scrambling and helping each other. When they had reached the even ground Fleda was able to read the meaning of the exclamation in which Mrs. Gereth had expressed her reserves on the subject of Miss Brigstock's personality. Miss Brigstock had been laughing and even romping, but the circumstance had n't contributed the ghost of an expression to her countenance. Tall, straight and fair, long-limbed and strangely festooned, she stood there without a look in her eye or any perceptible intention of any sort in any other feature. She belonged to the type in which speech is an unaided emission of sound, in which the secret of being is impenetrably and incorruptibly kept. Her expression would probably have been beautiful if she had had one, but whatever she communicated she communicated, in a manner best known to herself, without signs. This was not the case with Owen Gereth, who had plenty of them, and all very simple and immediate. Robust and artless, eminently natural yet perfectly correct, he looked pointlessly active and pleasantly dull. Like his mother and like Fleda Vetch, but not for the same reason, this young pair had come out to take a turn before church.

The meeting of the two couples was sensibly awkward, and Fleda, who had perceptions, and these now more and more roused, took the measure of the shock inflicted on Mrs. Gereth. There had been intimacy — oh yes, intimacy as well as puerility — in the horse-play of which they had just had a glimpse.

The party began to stroll together to the house, and Fleda had again a sense of Mrs. Gereth's quick management in the way the lovers, or whatever they were, found themselves separated. She strolled behind with Mona, the mother possessing herself of her son, her exchange of remarks with whom, however, remained, as they went, vividly inaudible. That member of the party in whose intenser consciousness we shall most profitably seek a reflexion of the little drama with which we are concerned drew a yet livelier impression of Mrs. Gereth's intervention from the fact that ten minutes later, on the way to church, still another pairing had been effected. Owen walked with Fleda, and it was an amusement to the girl to feel sure this was by his mother's direction. Fleda had other amusements as well: such as noting that Mrs. Gereth was now with Mona Brigstock; such as observing that she was all affability to that young woman; such as reflecting that, masterful and clever, with a great bright spirit, she was one of those who impose, who interfuse themselves; such as feeling finally that Owen Gereth was absolutely beautiful and delightfully dense. This young person had even from herself wonderful secrets of delicacy and pride; but she came as near distinctness as in the consideration of such matters she had ever come at all in now embracing the idea that it was of a pleasant effect and rather remarkable to be stupid without offence — of a pleasanter effect and more remarkable indeed than to be clever and horrid. Owen Gereth at any rate, with his inches, his features and his lapses, was neither of these latter things. She herself was prepared, if she should ever marry, to contribute all the cleverness, and she liked to figure it out that her husband would be a force grateful for direction. She was in her small way a spirit of the same family as Mrs. Gereth. On that flushed and huddled Sunday a great matter occurred; her little life became aware of a singular quickening. Her meagre past fell away from her like a garment of the wrong fashion, and as she came up to town on the Monday what she stared at from the train in the suburban fields was a future full of the things she particularly loved.

II

THESE were neither more nor less than the things
with which she had had time to learn from Mrs.
Gereth that Poynton overflowed. Poynton, in the
south of England, was this lady's established, or
rather her disestablished, home: it had recently
passed into the possession of her son. The father of
the boy, an only child, had died two years before, and
in London, with his mother, Owen was occupying
for May and June a house good-naturedly lent them
by Colonel Gereth, their uncle and brother-in-law.
His mother had laid her hand so engagingly on Fleda
Vetch that in a very few days the girl knew it was
possible they should suffer together in Cadogan Place
almost as much as they had suffered together at
Waterbath. The kind soldier's house was also an
ordeal, but the two women, for the ensuing month,
had at least the relief of their confessions. The great
drawback of Mrs. Gereth's situation was that, thanks
to the rare perfection of Poynton, she was condemned
to wince wherever she turned. She had lived for
a quarter of a century in such warm closeness with
the beautiful that, as she frankly admitted, life had
become for her a true fool's paradise. She could n't
leave her own house without peril of exposure. She
did n't say it in so many words, but Fleda could see
she held nothing in England really comparable to
Poynton. There were places much grander and

richer, but no such complete work of art, nothing that would appeal so to those really informed. In putting such elements into her hand destiny had given her an inestimable chance; she knew how rarely well things had gone with her and that she had enjoyed an extraordinary fortune.

There had been in the first place the exquisite old house itself, early Jacobean, supreme in every part; a provocation, an inspiration, the matchless canvas for a picture. Then there had been her husband's sympathy and generosity, his knowledge and love, their perfect accord and beautiful life together, twenty-six years of planning and seeking, a long, sunny harvest of taste and curiosity. Lastly, she never denied, there had been her personal gift, the genius, the passion, the patience of the collector — a patience, an almost infernal cunning, that had enabled her to do it all with a limited command of money. There would n't have been money enough for any fumbler, she said with pride, but there had been money enough for her. They had saved on lots of things in life, and there were lots of things they had n't had at all, but they had had in every corner of Europe their swing among the demons of Jews. It was fascinating to poor Fleda, who had n't a penny in the world nor anything nice at home, and whose only treasure was her subtle mind, to hear this genuine English lady, fresh and fair, young in the fifties, admit with gaiety and conviction that she was herself the craftiest stalker, who had ever tracked big game. Fleda, with her mother dead, had n't so much even as a home, and her nearest chance of one was that there was some appearance her sister would become engaged to a curate whose eldest brother was supposed to have property and would perhaps allow him something. Her father paid some of her bills but did n't like her to live with him; and she had lately, in Paris, with several hundred other young women, spent a year at a studio, arming herself for the battle of life by a course with an impressionist painter. She was determined to work, but her impressions, or somebody's else, were as yet her only material. Mrs. Gereth had told her she liked her because she had an extraordinary *flair;* but under the circumstances a *flair* was a questionable boon: in the dry spaces in which she had mainly moved she could have borne a chronic catarrh. She was now much summoned to Cadogan Place and before the month elapsed was kept to stay, to pay a visit of which the end, it was agreed, should have nothing to do with the beginning. She had a sense partly exultant and partly alarmed of having quickly become necessary to her imperious friend, who indeed gave a reason quite sufficient for it in telling her there was nobody else who understood. From Mrs. Gereth there was in these days an immense deal to understand, though it might freely be summed up in the circumstance that she was wretched. Fleda was thus assured she could n't completely know why till she should have seen the things at Poynton. She could perfectly grasp this connexion, which was exactly one of the matters that, in their inner mystery, were a blank to everybody else.

The girl had a promise that the wonderful house

should be shown her early in July, when Mrs. Gereth would return to it as to her home; but even before this initiation she put her finger on the spot that in the poor lady's troubled soul ached hardest. This was the misery haunting her, the dread of the inevitable surrender. What Fleda had to sit up to was the confirmed appearance that Owen Gereth would marry Mona Brigstock, marry her in his mother's teeth, and that such an act would have incalculable bearings. They were present to Mrs. Gereth, her companion could see, with a vividness that at moments almost ceased to be that of sanity. She would have to give up Poynton, and give it up to a product of Waterbath — that was the wrong that rankled, the humiliation at which one would be able adequately to shudder only when one should know the place. She did know Waterbath and despised it — she had that qualification for sympathy. Her sympathy was intelligent, for she read deep into the matter: she stared, aghast, as it came home to her for the first time, at the cruel English custom of the expropriation of the lonely mother. Mr. Gereth had apparently been a very amiable man, but Mr. Gereth had left things in a way that made the girl marvel. The house and its contents had been treated as a single splendid object; everything was to go straight to his son, his widow being assured but a maintenance and a cottage in another county. No account whatever had been taken of her relation to her treasures, of the passion with which she had waited for them, worked for them, picked them over, made them worthy of each other and the house, watched them, loved them, lived with them. He appeared to have assumed she would settle questions with her son and that he could depend on Owen's affection and Owen's fairness. And in truth, as poor Mrs. Gereth enquired, how could he possibly have had a prevision — he who turned his eyes instinctively from everything repulsive — of anything so abnormal either as a Waterbath Brigstock or as a Brigstock Waterbath? He had been in ugly houses enough, but had escaped that particular nightmare. Nothing so perverse could have been expected to happen as that the heir to the loveliest thing in England should be inspired to hand it over to a girl so exceptionally tainted. Mrs. Gereth spoke of poor Mona's taint as if to mention it were almost a violation of decency, and a person who had listened without enlightenment would have wondered of what fault the girl had been or had indeed not been guilty. But Owen had from a boy never cared, never taken the least pride or pleasure in his home.

"Well then if he does n't care —!" Fleda exclaimed with some impetuosity; stopping short, however, before she completed her sentence.

Mrs. Gereth looked at her rather hard. "If he does n't care?"

Fleda cast about; she had not quite had a definite idea. "Well — he 'll give them up."

"Give what up?"

"Why those beautiful things."

"Give them up to whom?" Mrs. Gereth more boldly stared.

"To you of course — to enjoy, to keep for yourself."

"And leave his house as bare as your hand? There's nothing in it that is n't precious."

Fleda considered; her friend had taken her up with a smothered ferocity by which she was slightly disconcerted. "I don't mean, naturally, that he should surrender everything; but he might let you pick out the things to which you're most attached."

"I think he would if he were free," said Mrs. Gereth.

"And do you mean, as it is, that she'll prevent him?" Mona Brigstock, between these ladies, was now nothing but "she."

"By every means in her power."

"But surely not because she understands and appreciates them?"

"No," Mrs. Gereth replied, "but because they belong to the house and the house belongs to Owen. If I should wish to take anything she would simply say, with that motionless mask, 'It goes with the house.' And day after day, in the face of every argument, of every consideration of generosity, she would repeat, without winking, in that voice like the squeeze of a doll's stomach, 'It goes with the house — it goes with the house.' In that attitude they'll shut themselves up."

Fleda was struck, was even a little startled by the way Mrs. Gereth had turned this over — had faced, if indeed only to recognise its futility, the notion of a battle with her only son. These words led her to take a sounding she had not thought it discreet to take before: she brought out the idea of the possibility, after all, of her friend's continuing to live at Poynton. Would they really wish to proceed to extremities? Was no good-humoured graceful compromise to be imagined or brought about? Could n't the same roof cover them? Was it so very inconceivable that a married son should for the rest of her days share with so charming a mother the home she had devoted more than a score of years to making beautiful for him? Mrs. Gereth hailed this question with a wan compassionate smile: she replied that a common household was in such a case just so inconceivable that Fleda had only to glance over the fair face of the English land to see how few people had ever conceived it. It was always thought a wonder, a "mistake," a piece of overstrained sentiment; and she confessed she was as little capable of a flight of that sort as Owen himself. Even if they both had been capable they would still have Mona's hatred to reckon with. Fleda's breath was sometimes taken away by the great fierce bounds and elisions which, on Mrs. Gereth's lips, the course of discussion could take.

This was the first she had heard of Mona's hatred, though she certainly had not needed Mrs. Gereth to tell her that in close quarters that young lady would prove secretly mulish. Later Fleda perceived indeed that perhaps almost any girl would hate a person who should be so markedly averse to having anything to do with her. Before this, however, in conversation with her young friend, Mrs. Gereth furnished a more vivid motive for her despair by asking how she could possibly be expected to sit there with the new pro-

prietors and accept — or call it, for a day, endure —
the horrors they would perpetrate in the house. Fleda
argued that they would n't after all smash things
nor burn them up; and Mrs. Gereth admitted when
pushed that she did n't quite suppose they would.
What she meant was that they would neglect them,
ignore them, leave them to clumsy servants — there
was n't an object of them all but should be handled
with perfect love — and in many cases probably wish
to replace them by pieces answerable to some vulgar
modern notion of the "handy." Above all she saw
in advance with dilated eyes the abominations they
would inevitably mix up with them — the maddening
relics of Waterbath, the little brackets and pink vases,
the sweepings of bazaars, the family photographs and
illuminated texts, the "household art" and household
piety of Mona's hideous home. Was n't it enough
simply to contend that Mona would approach Poynton
in the spirit of a Brigstock and that in the spirit of a
Brigstock she would deal with her acquisition? Did
Fleda really see *her*, Mrs. Gereth demanded, spending
the remainder of her days with such a creature's
elbow halfway down her throat?

Fleda had to declare that she certainly did n't and
that Waterbath had been a warning it would be
frivolous to overlook. At the same time she privately
reflected that they were taking a great deal for granted and that, inasmuch as to her knowledge Owen
Gereth had positively denied his betrothal, the ground
of their speculations was by no means firm. It struck
our young lady that in a difficult position Owen conducted himself with some natural art; treating this

domesticated confidant of his mother's wrongs with a simple civility that almost troubled her conscience, so deeply she felt she might have had for him the air of siding with that lady against him. She wondered if he would ever know how little really she did this and that she was there, since Mrs. Gereth had insisted, not to betray but essentially to plead and protect. The fact that his mother disliked Mona Brigstock might have made him dislike the object of her preference, and it was detestable to Fleda to remember that she might have appeared to him to offer herself as an exemplary contrast. It was clear enough, however, that the happy youth had no more sense for a motive than a deaf man for a tune; a limitation by which, after all, she could gain as well as lose. He came and went very freely on the business with which London abundantly furnished him, but he found time more than once to say to her "It's awfully nice of you to look after poor Mummy." As well as his quick speech, which shyness made obscure — it was usually as desperate as a "rush" at some violent game — his child's eyes in his man's face put it to her that, you know, this really meant a good deal for him and that he hoped she would stay on. With a person in the house who, like herself, was clever, poor Mummy was conveniently occupied. Fleda found a beauty in the candour and even in the modesty which apparently kept him from suspecting that two such wiseheads could possibly be occupied with Owen Gereth.

III

THEY went at last, the wiseheads, down to Poynton, where the palpitating girl had the full revelation. "*Now* do you know how I feel?" Mrs. Gereth asked when in the wondrous hall, three minutes after their arrival, her pretty associate dropped on a seat with a soft gasp and a roll of dilated eyes. The answer came clearly enough, and in the rapture of that first walk through the house Fleda took a prodigious span. She perfectly understood how Mrs. Gereth felt — she had understood but meagrely before; and the two women embraced with tears over the tightening of their bond — tears which on the younger one's part were the natural and usual sign of her submission to perfect beauty. It was not the first time she had cried for the joy of admiration, but it was the first time the mistress of Poynton, often as she had shown her house, had been present at such an exhibition. She exulted in it; it quickened her own tears; she assured her companion that such an occasion made the poor old place fresh to her again and more precious than ever. Yes, nobody had ever, that way, *cared*, ever felt what she had achieved: people were so grossly ignorant, and everybody, even the knowing ones as they thought themselves, more or less dense. What Mrs. Gereth had achieved was indeed a supreme result; and in such an art of the treasure-hunter, in selection and comparison refined to that point, there was an element of creation, of personality. She had commended Fleda's *flair*, and Fleda now gave herself up to satiety. Preoccupations and scruples fell away from her; she had never known a greater happiness than the week passed in this initiation.

Wandering through clear chambers where the general effect made preferences almost as impossible as if they had been shocks, pausing at open doors where vistas were long and bland, she would, even had n't she already known, have discovered for herself that Poynton was the record of a life. It was written in great syllables of colour and form, the tongues of other countries and the hands of rare artists. It was all France and Italy with their ages composed to rest. For England you looked out of old windows — it was England that was the wide embrace. While outside, on the low terraces, she contradicted gardeners and refined on nature, Mrs. Gereth left her guest to finger fondly the brasses that Louis Quinze might have thumbed, to sit with Venetian velvets just held in a loving palm, to hang over cases of enamels and pass and repass before cabinets. There were not many pictures — the panels and the stuffs were themselves the picture; and in all the great wainscoted house there was not an inch of pasted paper. What struck Fleda most in it was the high pride of her friend's taste, a fine arrogance, a sense of style which, however amused and amusing, never compromised nor stooped. She felt indeed, as this lady had promised her she should, both a respect and a compassion she had not known before; thus the vision of the coming surrender could but fill her with

an equal pain. To give it all up, to die to it — that
thought ached in her breast. She herself could imagine clinging there with a clutch indifferent to dignity.
To have created such a place was to have had dignity
enough; when there was a question of defending it
the fiercest attitude was the right one. After so intense
a taking of possession she too was to give it up; for
she reflected that if Mrs. Gereth's remaining would
have offered her an apology for a future — stretching
away in safe years on the other side of a gulf —
the advent of the others could only be, by the same
law, a great vague menace, the ruffling of a still
water. Such were the emotions of a hungry girl
whose sensibility was almost as great as her oppor-
tunities for comparison had been small. The museums
had done something for her, but nature had done
more.

If Owen had not come down with them nor joined
them later it was because he still found London
jolly; yet the question remained of whether the jollity
of London were not merely the only name his small
vocabulary yielded for the jollity of Mona Brigstock.
There was indeed in his conduct another ambiguity
— something that required explaining so long as his
motive did n't come to the surface. If he was in love
what was the matter? And what was the matter still
more if he was n't? The mystery was at last cleared
up: this Fleda gathered from the tone in which, one
morning at breakfast, a letter just opened made Mrs.
Gereth cry out. Her dismay was almost a shriek:
"Why he 's bringing her down — he wants her to see
the house!" They flew, the two women, into each

other's arms and, with their heads together, soon
made out the reason, the baffling reason why nothing
had yet happened, to be that Mona did n't know, or
Owen did n't, whether Poynton would really please
her. She was coming down to judge; and could anything in the world be more like poor Owen than the
ponderous probity that had kept him from pressing
her for a reply till she should have learned if she ap-
proved what he had to offer her? That was a scruple
it had naturally been impossible to impute. If only
they might fondly hope, Mrs. Gereth wailed, that
the girl's expectations would be dashed! There was
a fine consistency, a sincerity quite affecting, in her
arguing that the better the place should happen to
look, the better it should express the conceptions
to which it owed its origin, the less it would speak to
an intelligence so primitive. How could a Brigstock
possibly understand what it was all about? How,
really, could a Brigstock logically do anything but
hate it? Mrs. Gereth, even as she whisked away
linen shrouds, persuaded herself of the likelihood on
Mona's part of some bewildered blankness, some
collapse of admiration that would prove disconcerting to her swain — a hope of which Fleda at least
could see the absurdity and which gave the measure
of the poor lady's strange, almost maniacal disposition
to thrust in everywhere the question of "things," to
read all behaviour in the light of some fancied relation to them. "Things" were of course the sum of the
world; only, for Mrs. Gereth, the sum of the world
was rare French furniture and oriental china. She
could at a stretch imagine people's not "having," but

she could n't imagine their not wanting and not missing.

The young couple were to be accompanied by Mrs. Brigstock, and with a prevision of how fiercely they would be watched Fleda became conscious, before the party arrived, of an amused diplomatic pity for them. Almost as much as Mrs. Gereth's her taste was her life, though her life was somehow the larger for it. Besides, she had another care now: there was some one she would n't have liked to see humiliated even in the person of a young lady formed to foster his never suspecting so much delicacy. When this young lady appeared Fleda tried, so far as the wish to efface herself allowed, to be mainly the person to take her about, show her the house and cover up her ignorance. Owen's announcement had been that, as trains made it convenient, they would present themselves for luncheon and depart before dinner; but Mrs. Gereth, true to her system of glaring civility, proposed and obtained an extension, a dining and a spending of the night. She made her young friend wonder against what rebellion of fact she was sacrificing in advance so profusely to appearance. Fleda was appalled after the first hour by the rash innocence with which Mona had accepted the responsibility of observation, and indeed by the large levity with which, sitting there like a bored tourist in fine scenery, she exercised it. She felt in her nerves the effect of such a manner on her companion's, and it was this that made her want to entice the girl away, give her some merciful warning or some jocular cue. Mona met intense looks, however, with eyes that might have been blue beads, the only ones she had — eyes into which Fleda thought it strange Owen Gereth should have to plunge for his fate and his mother for a confession of whether Poynton were a success. She made no remark that helped to supply this light; her impression at any rate had nothing in common with the feeling that, as the beauty of the place throbbed out like music, had caused Fleda Vetch to burst into tears. She was as content to say nothing as if, their hostess afterwards exclaimed, she had been keeping her mouth shut in a railway-tunnel. Mrs. Gereth contrived at the end of an hour to convey to Fleda that it was plain she was brutally ignorant; but Fleda more finely discovered that her ignorance was obscurely active.

Mona was not so stupid as not to see that something, though she scarcely knew what, was expected of her that she could n't give; and the only mode her intelligence suggested of meeting the expectation was to plant her big feet and pull another way. Mrs. Gereth wanted her to rise, somehow or somewhere, and was prepared to hate her if she did n't: very well, she could n't, would n't rise; she had already moved at the altitude that suited her and was able to see that since she was exposed to the hatred she might at least enjoy the calm. The smallest trouble, for a girl with no nonsense about her, was to earn what she incurred; so that, a dim instinct teaching her she would earn it best by no fond overflow, and combining with the conviction that she now definitely held Owen, and therefore the place, she had the pleasure of her honesty as well as of her security.

Did n't her very honesty lead her to be belligerently
blank about Poynton, inasmuch as it was just Poynton that was forced upon her as a subject for effusive-
ness? Such subjects, to Miss Brigstock, had an air
almost of indecency; so that the house became uncanny to her by the very appeal in its name — an
appeal that somewhere in the twilight of her being,
as Fleda was sure, Mona thanked heaven she *was*
the girl stiffly to draw back from. She was a person
whom pressure at a given point infallibly caused to
expand in the wrong place instead of, as it is usually
administered in the hope of doing, the right one.
Her mother, to make up for this, broke out universally, pronounced everything "most striking," and
was visibly happy that Owen's captor should be so
far on the way to strike: but she jarred upon Mrs.
Gereth by her formula of admiration, which was that
anything she looked at was "in the style" of something else. This was to show how much she had
seen, but it only showed she had seen nothing; everything at Poynton was in the style of Poynton, and
poor Mrs. Brigstock, who at least was determined to
rise and had brought with her a trophy of her journey, a "lady's magazine" purchased at the station,
a horrible thing with patterns for antimacassars,
which, as it was quite new, the first number, and
seemed so clever, she kindly offered to leave for the
house, was in the style of a vulgar old woman who
wore silver jewelry and tried to pass off a gross
avidity as a sense of the beautiful.

By the day's end it was clear to Fleda Vetch that,
however Mona judged, the day had been determin-

ant. Whether or no she felt the charm she felt the challenge: at an early moment Owen Gereth would be able to tell his mother the worst. Nevertheless when the elder lady, at bedtime, coming in a dressing-gown and a high fever to the younger one's room, cried out "She hates it; but what will she do?" Fleda pretended vagueness, played at obscurity and assented disingenuously to the proposition that they at least had a respite. The future was dark to her, but there was a silken thread she could clutch in the gloom — she would never give Owen away. He might give himself — he even certainly would; but that was his own affair, and his blunders, his innocence, only added to the appeal he made to her. She would cover him, she would protect him, and beyond thinking her a cheerful inmate he would never guess her intention, any more than, beyond thinking her clever enough for anything, his astute mother would discover it. From this hour, with Mrs. Gereth, there was a flaw in her frankness. Her admirable friend continued to know everything she did: what was to remain unknown was her general motive.

From the window of her room, the next morning before breakfast, the girl saw Owen in the garden with Mona, who strolled beside him under a listening parasol but without a visible look for the great florid picture hung there from so far back by Mrs. Gereth's hand. Mona kept dropping her eyes, as she walked, to catch the sheen of her patent-leather shoes, which resembled a man's and which she kicked forward a little — it gave her an odd movement — to help her see what she thought of them. When Fleda came

down Mrs. Gereth was in the breakfast-room; and
at that moment Owen, through a long window, passed
in alone from the terrace and very endearingly kissed
his mother. It immediately struck their guest that
she was in their way, for had n't he been borne on a
wave of joy exactly to announce, before the Brigstocks
departed, that Mona had at last faltered out the
sweet word he had been waiting for? He shook
hands with his friendly violence, but Fleda contrived not to look into his face: what she liked most
to see in it was not the reflexion of Mona's big boot-
toes. She could bear well enough that young lady
herself, but she could n't bear Owen's opinion of her.
She was on the point of slipping into the garden
when the movement was checked by Mrs. Gereth's
suddenly drawing her close, as if for the morning
embrace, and then, while she kept her there with the
bravery of the night's repose, breaking out: "Well,
my dear boy, what *does* your young friend there
make of our odds and ends?"

"Oh she thinks they're all right!"

Fleda immediately guessed from his tone that he
had not come in to say what she supposed: there was
even something in it to confirm Mrs. Gereth's belief
that their danger had dropped. She was sure moreover that his tribute to Mona's taste was a repetition
of the eloquent words in which the girl had herself
recorded it; she could indeed hear with all vividness the probable pretty passage between the pair.
"Don't you think it's rather jolly, the old shop?"
"Oh it's all right!" Mona had graciously remarked;
and then they had probably, with a slap on a back,

run another race up or down a green bank. Fleda knew Mrs. Gereth had n't yet uttered a word to her son that would have shown him how much she feared; but it was impossible to feel her friend's arm round her and not become aware that this friend was now throbbing with a strange intention. Owen's reply had scarcely been of a nature to usher in a discussion of Mona's sensibilities, but Mrs. Gereth went on in a moment with an innocence of which Fleda could measure the cold hypocrisy. "Has she any sort of feeling for nice old things?" The question was as fresh as the morning light.

"Oh of course she likes everything that's nice." And Owen, who constitutionally shirked questions — an answer was almost as hateful to him as a "trick" to a big dog— smiled kindly at Fleda and conveyed that she'd understand what he meant even if his mother did n't. Fleda, however, mainly understood that Mrs. Gereth, with an odd wild laugh, held her so hard as to hurt her.

"I could give up everything without a pang, I think, to a person I could trust, I could respect." The girl heard her voice tremble under the effort to show nothing but what she wanted to show, and felt the sincerity of her implication that the piety most real to her was to be on one's knees before one's high standard. "The best things here, as you know, are the things your father and I collected, things all that we worked for and waited for and suffered for. Yes," cried Mrs. Gereth with a fine freedom of fancy, "there are things in the house that we almost starved for! They were our religion, they were our life, they

were *us!* And now they're only *me* — except that
they're also *you*, thank God, a little, you dear!"
she continued, suddenly inflicting on Fleda a kiss
intended by every sign to knock her into position.
"There is n't one of them I don't know and love —
yes, as one remembers and cherishes the happiest
moments of one's life. Blindfold, in the dark, with
the brush of a finger, I could tell one from another.
They're living things to me; they know me, they
return the touch of my hand. But I could let them
all go, since I have to so strangely, to another affection, another conscience. There's a care they want,
there's a sympathy that draws out their beauty.
Rather than make them over to a woman ignorant
and vulgar I think I'd deface them with my own
hands. Can't you see me, Fleda, and would n't you do
it yourself?" — she appealed to her companion with
glittering eyes. "I could n't bear the thought of such
a woman here — I *could* n't. I don't know what she'd
do; she'd be sure to invent some deviltry, if it should
be only to bring in her own little belongings and horrors! The world is full of cheap gimcracks in this
awful age, and they're thrust in at one at every turn.
They'd be thrust in here on top of my treasures,
my own. Who'd save *them* for me — I ask you who
would?" and she turned again to Fleda with a dry
strained smile. Her handsome high-nosed excited
face might have been that of Don Quixote tilting at
a windmill. Drawn into the eddy of this outpouring
the girl, scared and embarrassed, laughed off her
exposure; but only to feel herself more passionately
caught up and, as it seemed to her, thrust down the

fine open mouth (it showed such perfect teeth) with which poor Owen's slow cerebration gaped. "*You* would, of course — only you, in all the world, because you know, you feel as I do myself, what's good and true and pure." No severity of the moral law could have taken a higher tone in this implication of the young lady who lacked the only virtue Mrs. Gereth actively esteemed. "*You* would replace me, *you* would watch over them, *you* would keep the place right," she austerely pursued, "and with you here — yes, with you, I believe I might rest at last in my grave!" She threw herself on Fleda's neck, and before that witness, horribly shamed, could shake her off, had burst into tears which could n't have been explained but which might perhaps have been understood.

IV

A WEEK later Owen came down to inform his mother he had settled with Mona Brigstock; but it was not at all a joy to Fleda, aware of how much to himself it would be a surprise, that he should find her still in the house. That dreadful scene before breakfast had made her position false and odious; it had been followed, after they were left alone, by a scene of her own making with her extravagant friend. She notified Mrs. Gereth of her instant departure: she could n't possibly remain after being offered to Owen so distinctly, before her very face, as his mother's candidate for the honour of his hand. That was all he could have seen in such an outbreak and in the indecency of her standing there to enjoy it. Fleda had on the prior occasion dashed out of the room by the shortest course and, while still upset, had fallen on Mona in the garden. She had taken an aimless turn with her and they had had some talk, rendered at first difficult, thoroughly thankless, by Mona's apparent suspicion that she had been sent out to spy, as Mrs. Gereth had tried to spy, into her opinions. Fleda was wise enough to treat these opinions as a mystery almost awful; which had an effect so much more than reassuring that at the end of five minutes the young lady from Waterbath suddenly and perversely said: "Why has she never had a winter garden thrown out? If ever I have a place

33

of my own I mean to have one." Fleda, dismayed, could see the thing — something glazed and piped, on iron pillars, with untidy plants and cane sofas; a shiny excrescence on the noble face of Poynton. She remembered at Waterbath a conservatory where she had caught a bad cold in the company of a stuffed cockatoo fastened to a tropical bough and a waterless fountain composed of shells stuck into some hardened paste. She asked Mona if her idea would be to make something like this conservatory; to which Mona replied: "Oh no, much finer; we haven't got a winter garden at Waterbath." Fleda wondered if she meant to convey that it was the only grandeur they lacked, and in a moment she went on: "But we *have* got a billiard-room — that I *will* say for us!" There was no billiard-room at Poynton, but there would evidently be one, and it would have, hung on its walls, framed at the "Stores," caricature-portraits of celebrities taken from a "society paper."

When the two girls had gone in to breakfast it was for Fleda to see at a glance that there had been a further passage, of some high colour, between Owen and his mother; and she had turned pale in guessing to what extremity, at her expense, Mrs. Gereth had found occasion to proceed. Hadn't she after her clumsy flight been pressed upon Owen in still clearer terms? Mrs. Gereth would practically have said to him: "If you'll take *her* I'll move away without a sound. But if you take any one else, any one I'm not sure of as I am of her — heaven help me, I'll fight to the death!" Breakfast this morning at Poynton had been a meal singularly silent, in spite

of the vague little cries with which Mrs. Brigstock
turned up the underside of plates and the knowing
but alarming raps administered by her big knuckles
to porcelain cups. Some one had to respond to her,
and the duty assigned itself to Fleda, who, while
pretending to meet her on the ground of explanation,
wondered what Owen thought of a girl still indeli-
cately anxious, after she had been grossly hurled at
him, to prove by exhibitions of her fine taste that she
was really what his mother pretended. This time
at any rate their fate was sealed: Owen, as soon as
he should get out of the house, would describe to
Mona the extraordinary display made to him, and
if anything more had been wanted to "fetch" her,
as he would call it, the deficiency was now made up.
Mrs. Gereth in fact took care of that — took care
of it by the way, at the last, on the threshold, she
said to the younger of her departing guests, with an
irony of which the sting was wholly in the sense, not
at all in the sound: "We have n't had the talk we
might have had, have we? You 'll feel I 've neglected
you and you 'll treasure it up against me. *Don't*,
because really, you know, it has been quite an accident,
and I 've all sorts of information at your disposal. If
you should come down again (only you won't, ever
— I feel that!) I should give you plenty of time to
worry it out of me. Indeed there are some things I
should quite insist on your learning; not permit you
at all, in any settled way, *not* to learn. Yes indeed,
you 'd put me through, and I should put you, my
dear! We should have each other to reckon with and
you 'd see me as I really am. I 'm not a bit the vague

35

mooning easy creature I dare say you think. However, if you won't come you won't; *n'en parlons plus*. It *is* stupid here after what you're accustomed to. We can only, all round, do *what* we can, eh? For heaven's sake don't let your mother forget her precious publication, the female magazine with the what-do-you-call-'em?—the greasecatchers. There!"

Mrs. Gereth, delivering herself from the doorstep, had tossed the periodical higher in air than was absolutely needful — tossed it toward the carriage the retreating party was about to enter. Mona, from the force of habit, the reflex action of the custom of sport, had popped out, with a little spring, a long arm and intercepted the missile as easily as she would have caused a tennis-ball to rebound from a racket. "Good catch!" Owen had cried, so genuinely pleased that practically no notice was taken of his mother's impressive remarks. It was to the accompaniment of romping laughter, as Mrs. Gereth afterwards said, that the carriage had rolled away; but it was while that laughter was still in the air that Fleda Vetch, white and terrible, had turned on her hostess with her scorching "How *could* you? Great God, how *could* you?" This lady's perfect blankness was from the first a sign of her smooth conscience; and the fact that till indoctrinated she didn't even know what Fleda meant by resenting her late offence to every susceptibility gave our young woman a sore scared perception that her own value in the house was the mere value, as one might say, of a good agent. Mrs. Gereth was generously sorry, but was still more surprised — surprised at Fleda's not having liked to be shown off to Owen as the right sort of wife for him. Why not, in the name of wonder, if she absolutely *was* the right sort ? She had admitted on explanation that she could see what her young friend meant by having been laid, as Fleda called it, at his feet; but it struck the girl that the admission was only made to please her and that Mrs. Gereth was secretly surprised at her not being as happy to be sacrificed to the supremacy of a high standard as she was happy to sacrifice her. She had taken a tremendous fancy to her, but that was on account of the fancy — to Poynton of course — taken by Fleda herself. Was n't this latter fancy then so great after all ? Fleda felt she could pronounce it great indeed when really forgiving for the sake of it what she had suffered and, after reproaches and tears, asseverations and kisses, after practical proof that she was cared for only as a priestess of the altar and a view of her bruised dignity which left no alternative to flight, accepting the shame with the balm, consenting not to depart, taking refuge in the thin comfort of the truth at least brought home to her. The truth was simply that all Mrs. Gereth's scruples were on one side and that her ruling passion had in a manner despoiled her of her humanity. On the second day, when the tide of emotion had somewhat ebbed, she said soothingly to her companion: "But you *would*, after all, marry him, you know, darling, would n't you, if that girl were not there ? I mean of course if he were to ask you," Mrs. Gereth had thoughtfully added. Yet she made the strangest free reach over all such preliminaries.

"Marry him if he were to ask me? Most distinctly not!"

The question had not come up with this definiteness before, and Mrs. Gereth was clearly more surprised than ever. She marvelled a moment. "Not even to have Poynton?"

"Not even to have Poynton."

"But why on earth?" Mrs. Gereth's sad eyes were fixed on her.

Fleda coloured; she hung fire. "Because he's too stupid!" Save on one other occasion at which we shall in time arrive she never came nearer to betraying to Mrs. Gereth that she was in love with Owen. She found a vain charm in reflecting that if Mona had not been there and he had not been too stupid and he verily had asked her, she might, should she have wished to keep her secret, have found it possible to pass off the motive of her conduct as a mere passion for his property.

Mrs. Gereth evidently thought in these days of little but things hymeneal; for she broke out with sudden rapture in the middle of the week: "I know what they'll do: they *will* marry, but they'll go and live at Waterbath!" There was positive joy in that form of the idea, which she embroidered and developed: it seemed so much the safest thing that could happen. "Yes, I'll have you, but I won't go *there!*" Mona would have said with a vicious nod at the southern horizon: "we'll leave your horrid mother alone there for life." It would be an ideal solution, this ingress the lively pair, with their spiritual need of a warmer medium, would playfully punch in the ribs of her ancestral home; for it would not only prevent recurring panic at Poynton — it would offer them, as in one of their gimcrack baskets or other vessels of ugliness, a diurnal round of felicity that Poynton could never give. Owen might manage his estate just as he managed it now, and Mrs. Gereth would manage everything else. When in the hall, on the unforgettable day of his return, she had heard his voice ring out like a call to a terrier she had still, as Fleda afterwards learned, clutched frantically at the conceit that he had come, at the worst, to announce some compromise; to tell her she would have to put up with the girl yes, but that some way would be arrived at of leaving her in personal possession. Fleda Vetch, whom from the earliest hour no illusion had brushed with its wing, now held her breath, went on tiptoe, wandered in outlying parts of the house and through delicate muffled rooms while the mother and son faced each other below. From time to time she stopped to listen; but all was so quiet she was almost frightened: she had vaguely expected a sound of contention. It lasted longer than she would have supposed, whatever it was they were doing; and when finally, from a window, she saw Owen stroll out of the house, stop and light a cigarette and then pensively lose himself in the plantations, she found other matter for trepidation in the fact that Mrs. Gereth did n't immediately come rushing up into her arms. She wondered if she ought n't to go down to her, and measured the gravity of what had occurred by the circumstance, which she presently ascertained, that the poor lady had retired to her room and wished not

39

to be disturbed. This admonition had been for her
maid, with whom Fleda conferred as at the door of a
death-chamber; but the girl, without either fatuity
or resentment, judged that, since it could render Mrs.
Gereth indifferent even to the ministrations of disinterested attachment, the scene had been tremendous.

She was absent from luncheon, where indeed Fleda
had enough to do to look Owen in the face: there
would be so much to make that hateful in their common memory of the passage in which his last visit had
terminated. This had been her apprehension at least;
but as soon as he stood there she was constrained to
surprise at the practical simplicity of the ordeal — a
simplicity that was altogether his own simplicity, the
particular thing that, for Fleda Vetch, some other
things of course aiding, made almost any direct relation with him pleasant. He had neither wit nor tact
nor inspiration: all she could say was that in his
presence, uncontrolled as it might be, the alienation
these charms were usually depended on to allay
did n't occur. On this occasion for instance he did
so much better than "carry off" an awkward remembrance: he simply did n't have it. He had clean
forgotten she was the girl his mother would have
fobbed off on him; he was conscious only of her being
there as for decent service — conscious of the dumb
instinct that from the first had made him regard her
not as complicating his intercourse with that personage, but as simplifying it. Fleda found it beautiful
that this theory should have survived the incident of
the other day; found it exquisite that whereas she
was aware, through faint reverberations, that for her

kind little circle at large, who did n't now at all matter, her tendency had begun to define itself as parasitical, this strong young man, who had a right to judge and even a reason to loathe her, did n't judge and did n't loathe, let her down gently, treated her as if she pleased him — in fact evidently liked her to be just where she was. She asked herself what he did when Mona denounced her, and the only answer to the question was that perhaps Mona did n't denounce her. If Mona was inarticulate he was n't such a fool then to marry her. That he was glad Fleda was there was at any rate sufficiently shown by the domestic familiarity with which he said to her: "I must tell you I 've been having an awful row with my mother. I 'm engaged to be married to Miss Brigstock."

"Ah really ?" cried Fleda, achieving a radiance of which she was secretly proud. "How very exciting!"

"Too exciting for poor Mummy. She won't hear of it. She has been slating her fearfully. She says she's a regular barbarian."

"Why she's lovely!" Fleda exclaimed.

"Oh she's all right. Mother must come round."

"Only give her time," said Fleda. She had advanced to the threshold of the door thus thrown open to her and, without exactly crossing it, she threw in an appreciative glance. She asked Owen when his marriage would take place, and in the light of his reply read that Mrs. Gereth's wretched attitude would have no influence at all on the event, absolutely fixed when he had come down and distant by only three months. He liked Fleda's seeming to be

41

on his side, though that was a secondary matter; for what actually most concerned him was the line his mother took about Poynton, her declared unwillingness to give it up.

"Naturally I want my own house, you know," he said, "and my father made every arrangement for me to have it. But she may make it devilish awkward. What in the world's a fellow to do?" This it was that Owen wanted to know, and there could be no better proof of his friendliness than his air of depending so utterly on Fleda Vetch to tell him. She questioned him, they spent an hour together, and, as he spoke of the force of the concussion from which he had rebounded she found herself scared and depressed by the material he seemed to offer her to deal with. It *was* devilish awkward, and it was so in part because Owen had no imagination. It had lodged itself in that empty chamber that his mother hated the surrender because she hated Mona. He didn't of course understand why she hated Mona, but this belonged to an order of mysteries that never troubled him: there were lots of things, especially in people's minds, that a fellow didn't understand. Poor Owen went through life with a frank dread of people's minds: there were explanations he would have been almost as shy of receiving as of giving. There was therefore nothing that accounted for anything, though on its own free lines it was vivid enough, his picture to Fleda of his mother's all but express refusal to move. That was what it came to; for didn't she refuse to move when she as good as declared that she would move only with the furniture? It was the furniture he would n't give up; and what was the good of Poynton pray without the furniture? Besides, the furniture happened to be his, just as everything else happened to be. The furniture — the word, on his lips, had somehow to Fleda the sound of washing-stands and copious bedding, and she could well imagine the note it might have struck for Mrs. Gereth. The girl herself, in this interview with him, spoke of the contents of the house only as "the works of art." It did n't, however, in the least matter to Owen what they were called; what did matter, she easily guessed, was that it had been laid upon him by Mona, been made in effect a condition of her consent, that he should hold his mother to the strictest accountability for them. Mona had already entered upon the enjoyment of her rights. She had made him feel that Mrs. Gereth had been liberally provided for, and had asked him strikingly enough what room there would be at Ricks for the innumerable treasures of the big house. Ricks, the sweet little place offered to the mistress of Poynton as the refuge of her declining years, had been left to the late Mr. Gereth a considerable time before his death by an old maternal aunt, a good lady who had spent most of her life there. The house had in recent times been let, but it was amply furnished, it contained all the defunct aunt's possessions. Owen had lately inspected it, and he communicated to Fleda that he had quietly taken Mona to see it. It was n't a place like Poynton — what dower-house ever was? — but it was an awfully jolly little place, and Mona had taken a tremendous fancy to it. If there were a few things at Poynton that were Mrs. Gereth's peculiar property she must of course take them away with her; but one of the matters that became clear to Fleda was that this transfer would be now wholly subject to Miss Brigstock's approval. The special business she herself thus became aware of being charged with was that of seeing Mrs. Gereth safely and singly off the premises.

Her heart failed her, after Owen had returned to London, with the ugliness of this duty — with the ugliness indeed of the whole close contest. She saw nothing of Mrs. Gereth that day; she spent it in roaming with sick sighs, in feeling, as she passed from room to room, that what was expected of her companion was really dreadful. It would have been better never to have had such a place than to have had it and lose it. It was odious to *her* to have to look for solutions: what a strange relation between mother and son when there was no fundamental tenderness out of which a solution would irrepressibly spring! Was it Owen who was mainly responsible for that poverty? Fleda could n't think so when she remembered that, so far as he was concerned, Mrs. Gereth would still have been welcome to keep her seat by the Poynton fire. The fact that from the moment one accepted his marrying one saw no very different course for him to take — this fact made her all the rest of that aching day find her best relief in the mercy of not having yet to face her hostess. She dodged and dreamed and fabled and trifled away the time. Instead of inventing a remedy or a compromise, instead of preparing a plan by which a scan-

44

dal might be averted, she gave herself, in her sacred solitude, up to a mere fairy-tale, up to the very taste of the beautiful peace she would have scattered on the air if only something might have been that could never have been.

V

"I 'LL give up the house if they'll let me take what I require!"—that, on the morrow, was what Mrs. Gereth's stifled night had qualified her to say with a tragic face at breakfast. Fleda reflected that what she "required" was simply every object that surrounded them. The poor woman would have admitted this truth and accepted the conclusion to be drawn from it, the reduction to the absurd of her attitude, the exaltation of her claim. The girl's dread of a scandal, of spectators and critics, grew less the more she saw how little vulgar avidity had to do with this rigour. It was not the crude love of possession; it was the need to be faithful to a trust and loyal to an idea. The idea was surely noble; it was that of the beauty Mrs. Gereth had so patiently and consummately wrought. Pale but radiant, her back to the wall, she planted herself there as a heroine guarding a treasure. To give up the ship was to flinch from her duty; there was something in her eyes that declared she would die at her post. If their difference should become public the shame would be all for the others. If Waterbath thought it could afford to expose itself, then Waterbath was welcome to the folly. Her fanaticism gave her a new distinction, and Fleda remarked almost with awe that she had never carried herself so well. She trod the place like a reigning queen or a proud usurper; full as it

was of splendid pieces it could show in these days no
ornament so effective as its menaced mistress.

Our young lady's spirit was strangely divided;
she had a tenderness for Owen which she deeply
concealed, yet it left her occasion to marvel at the
way a man was made who could care in any relation
for a creature like Mona Brigstock when he had
known in any relation a creature like Adela Gereth.
With such a mother to give him the pitch how could
he take it so low? She wondered she did n't despise
him for this, but there was something that kept her
from it. If there had been nothing else it would have
sufficed that she really found herself from this moment, between the pair, the sole messenger and
mediator.

"He'll come back to assert himself," Mrs. Gereth
had said; and the following week Owen in fact reappeared. He might merely have written, Fleda
could see, but he had come in person because it was
at once "nicer" for his mother and stronger for his
cause. He did n't like such a row, though Mona
probably did; if he had n't a sense of beauty he had
after all a sense of justice; but it was inevitable he
should clearly announce at Poynton the date at which
he must look to find the house vacant. "You don't
think I'm rough or hard, do you?" he asked of
Fleda, his impatience shining in his idle eyes as the
dining-hour shines in club-windows. "The place at
Ricks stands there with open arms. And then I give
her lots of time. Tell her she can remove everything
that belongs to her." Fleda recognised the elements
of the sort of case the newspapers called a deadlock

in the circumstance that nothing at Poynton belonged to Mrs. Gereth either more or less than anything else. She must either take everything or nothing, and the girl's suggestion was that it might perhaps be an inspiration to do the latter and begin again on a clean page. What, however, was the poor woman in that event to begin with? What was she to do at all on her meagre income but make the best of the *objets d'art* of Ricks, the treasures collected by Mr. Gereth's maiden-aunt? She had never been near the place: for long years it had been let to strangers, and after this the foreboding that it would be her doom had kept her from positively courting abasement. She had felt she should see it soon enough, but Fleda (who was careful not to betray to her that Mona had seen it and had been gratified) knew her reasons for believing that the maiden-aunt's principles had had much in common with the principles of Waterbath. In short the only thing she would ever have to do with the *objets d'art* of Ricks would be to turn them out into the road. What belonged to her at Poynton, as Owen said, would conveniently mitigate the void resulting from that demonstration.

The exchange of observations between the friends had grown very direct by the time Fleda asked Mrs. Gereth if she literally meant to shut herself up and stand a siege, or if it might be her idea to expose herself, more informally, to be dragged out of the house by constables. "Oh I prefer the constables and the dragging!" the heroine of Poynton had readily answered. "I want to make Owen and Mona do everything that will be most publicly odious." She gave

it out as her one thought now to force them to a line
that would dishonour them and dishonour the tra-
dition they embodied, though Fleda was privately
sure she had visions of an alternative policy. The
strange thing was that, proud and fastidious all her
life, she now showed so little distaste for the world's
hearing of the broil. What had taken place in her
above all was that a long resentment had ripened.
She hated the effacement to which English usage
reduced the widowed mother; she had discoursed of
it passionately to Fleda; contrasted it with the beautiful homage paid by other countries to women in that
position, women no better than herself, whom she
had seen acclaimed and enthroned, whom she had
known and envied; made in short as little as possible
a secret of the injury, the bitterness she found in it.
The great wrong Owen had done her was not his
"taking up" with Mona — that was disgusting,
but it was a detail, an accidental form; it was his
failure from the first to understand what it was to
have a mother at all, to appreciate the beauty and
sanctity of the character. She was just his mother
as his nose was just his nose, and he had never had
the least imagination or tenderness or gallantry about
her. One's mother, gracious goodness, if one were
the kind of fine young man one ought to be, the only
kind Mrs. Gereth cared for, was a subject for poetry,
for idolatry. Had n't she often told Fleda of her
friend Madame de Jaume, the wittiest of women,
but a small black crooked person, each of whose
three boys, when absent, wrote to her every day of
their lives? She had the house in Paris, she had the

49

house in Poitou, she had more than in the lifetime
of her husband — to whom, in spite of her appearance, she had afforded repeated cause for jealousy —
because she was to have till the end of her days the
supreme word about everything. It was easy to see
how Mrs. Gereth would have given again and again
her complexion, her figure, and even perhaps the
spotless virtue she had still more successfully retained,
to have been the consecrated Madame de Jaume.
She was n't, alas, and this was what she had at present
a splendid occasion to protest against. She was of
course fully aware of Owen's concession, his willingness to let her take away with her the few things she
liked best; but as yet she only declared that to meet
him on this ground would be to give him a triumph,
to put him impossibly in the right. "Liked best?"
There was n't a thing in the house she did n't like
best, and what she liked better still was to be left
where she was. How could Owen use such an expression without being conscious of his hypocrisy? Mrs.
Gereth, whose criticism was often gay, dilated with
sardonic humour on the happy look a dozen objects
from Poynton would wear, and the charming effect
they would conduce to, when interspersed with the
peculiar features of Ricks. What had her whole life
been but an effort toward completeness and perfection? Better Waterbath at once, in its cynical
sameness, than the ignominy of such a mixture!

All this was of no great help to Fleda, in so far
as Fleda tried to rise to her mission of finding a way
out. When at the end of a fortnight Owen came
down once more it was ostensibly to tackle a tenant

50

on the property whose course with them had not been straight; the girl was sure, however, that he had really come, on the instance of Mona, to see what his mother was up to. He wanted to convince himself that she was preparing her departure, and he desired to perform a duty, distinct but not less imperative, in regard to the question of the perquisites with which she would retreat. The tension between them was now such that he had thus to reconnoitre without meeting the enemy. Mrs. Gereth was as willing as himself that he should address to Fleda Vetch whatever cruel remarks he might have to make; she only pitied her poor young friend for repeated encounters with a person as to whom she perfectly understood the girl's repulsion. Fleda found it of a fine dim inspiration on Owen's part not to have expected her to write to him: he would n't have wished any more than herself that she should have the air of spying on his mother in his interest. What made it of good effect to deal with him in this more familiar way was the sense that she understood so perfectly how poor Mrs. Gereth suffered and that she measured so adequately the sacrifice the other side did take rather monstrously for granted. She understood equally how Owen himself suffered, now that Mona had already begun to make him do things he did n't like. Vividly Fleda apprehended how *she* would have first made him like anything she would have made him do; anything even as disagreeable as this appearing there to state, virtually on Mona's behalf, that of course there must be a definite limit to the number of articles appropriated. She took a

longish stroll with him in order to talk the matter
over; to say if she did n't think a dozen pieces,
chosen absolutely at will, would be a handsome allowance; and above all to consider the very delicate
question of whether the advantage enjoyed by Mrs.
Gereth might n't be left — well, to her honour. To
leave it so was what Owen wished; but there was
plainly a young lady at Waterbath to whom, on his
side, he already had to render an account. He was
as touching in his off-hand annoyance as his mother
was tragic in her intensity; for if he could n't help
having a sense of propriety about the whole matter
he could as little help hating it. It was for his hating
it, Fleda reasoned, that she liked him so, and her
insistence to his mother on the hatred perilously
resembled on one or two occasions a revelation of
the liking. There were moments when, in conscience,
that revelation pressed her; inasmuch as it was just
on the ground of her not liking him that Mrs. Gereth
trusted her so much. Mrs. Gereth herself did n't
in these days like him at all, and she was of course
always on Mrs. Gereth's side. He ended really,
while the preparations for his marriage went on, by
quite a little custom of coming and going; but at no
one of these junctures would his mother receive him.
He talked only with Fleda and strolled with Fleda;
and when he asked her, in regard to the great matter,
if Mrs. Gereth were really doing nothing, the girl
usually replied: "She pretends not to be, if I may
say so; but I think she's really thinking over what
she'll take." When her friend at the great house
asked her in turn what "those monsters" were doing

she could have but one answer. "They're waiting, dear lady, to see what *you* do!"

Mrs. Gereth, a month after she had received her great shock, did something abrupt and extraordinary: she caught up her companion and went over to have a look at Ricks. They had come to London first and taken a train from Liverpool Street, and the least of the sufferings they were armed against was that of passing the night. Fleda's admirable dressing-bag had been given her by her high benefactress. "Why it's charming!" she exclaimed a few hours later, turning back again into the small prim parlour from a friendly advance to the single plate of the window. Mrs. Gereth hated such windows, the one flat glass sliding up and down, especially when they enjoyed a view of four iron pots on pedestals, painted white and containing ugly geraniums, ranged on the edge of a gravel path and doing their best to give it the air of a terrace. Fleda had instantly averted her eyes from these ornaments, but Mrs. Gereth grimly gazed, wondering of course how a place in the deepest depths of Essex and three miles from a small station could contrive to look so suburban. The room was practically a shallow box, with the junction of the walls and ceiling guiltless of curve or cornice and marked merely by the little band of crimson paper glued round the top of the other paper, a turbid grey sprigged with silver flowers. This decoration was rather new and quite fresh; and there was in the centre of the ceiling a big square beam papered over in white, as to which Fleda hesitated about throwing out that it was rather picturesque. She recognised

53

in time that this venture would be weak and that she should, all through, be able to say nothing either for the mantel-pieces or for the doors, of which she saw her companion become sensible with a soundless moan. On the subject of doors especially Mrs. Gereth had the finest views: the thing in the world she most despised was the meanness of the undivided opening. From end to end of Poynton there swung high double leaves. At Ricks the entrances to the rooms were like the holes of rabbit-hutches.

It was all, none the less, not so bad as Fleda had feared; it was faded and melancholy, whereas there had been a danger it would be contradictious and positive, cheerful and loud. The place was crowded with objects of which the aggregation somehow made a thinness and the futility a grace; things that told her they had been gathered as slowly and as lovingly as the golden flowers of the other house. She too, for a home, could have lived with them: they made her fond of the old maiden-aunt; they made her even wonder if it did n't work more for happiness not to have tasted, as she herself had done, of knowledge. Without resources, without a stick, as she said, of her own, Fleda was moved, after all, to some secret surprise at the pretensions of a shipwrecked woman who could hold such an asylum cheap. The more she looked about the surer she felt of the character of the maiden-aunt, the sense of whose dim presence urged her to pacification: the maiden-aunt had been a dear; she should have adored the maiden-aunt. The poor lady had passed shyly, yet with some bruises, through life; had been sensitive and ignorant and exquisite: that too was a sort of origin, a sort of atmosphere for relics and rarities, though different from the sorts most prized at Poynton. Mrs. Gereth had of course more than once said that one of the deepest mysteries of life was the way that — given certain natures — hideous objects could be loved. But it was n't a question of love at present for these; it was only a question of some practical patience. Perhaps a thought of that kind had stolen over her when, at the end of a brooding hour, she exclaimed, taking in the house with a strenuous sigh: "Well, something can be done with it!" Fleda had repeated to her more than once the indulgent fancy about the maiden-aunt — she was so sure she had deeply suffered. "I'm sure I thoroughly hope she did!" was, however, all the more austere of the pilgrims to Ricks had replied.

VI

IT was a great relief to the girl at last to feel sure
that the dreadful move would really be made. What
might happen if it should n't had been from the
first indefinite. It was absurd to pretend that any violence was probable — a tussle, dishevelment, pushes,
scratches, shrieks; yet Fleda had an imagination
of drama, of a "great scene," a thing, somehow, of
indignity and misery, of wounds inflicted and received, in which indeed, though Mrs. Gereth's presence, with movements and sounds, loomed large to
her, Owen remained indistinct and on the whole unag-
gressive. He would n't be there with a cigarette in
his teeth, very handsome and insolently quiet: that
was only the way he would be in a novel, across
whose interesting page some such figure, as she half-
closed her eyes, seemed to her to walk. Fleda har-
boured rather, and indeed with shame, the confused,
pitying vision of Mrs. Gereth with her great scene
left in a manner on her hands, Mrs. Gereth missing
her effect and having to appear merely hot and in-
jured and in the wrong. The symptoms that she
would be spared even that spectacle resided not so
much, through the chambers of Poynton, in an air of
concentration as in the hum of uneasy alternatives.
There was no common preparation, but one day, at
the turn of a corridor, she found her hostess standing
very still, with the hanging hands of despair and yet
56

with the active eyes of adventure. These eyes appeared to Fleda to meet her own with a strange dim bravado, and there was a silence almost awkward before either of the friends spoke. The girl afterwards thought of the moment as one in which her hostess mutely accused her of an accusation, meeting it at the same time, however, by a kind of defiant acceptance. Yet it was with mere melancholy candour that Mrs. Gereth at last sighingly exclaimed: "I'm thinking over what I had better take!" Fleda could have embraced her for this virtual promise of a concession, the announcement that she had finally accepted the problem of knocking together a shelter with the small salvage of the wreck.

It was true that when after their return from Ricks they tried to lighten the ship the great embarrassment was still immutably there, the odiousness of sacrificing the exquisite things one would n't take to the exquisite things one would. This immediately made the things one would n't the very things one ought to, and, as Mrs. Gereth said, condemned one, in the whole business, to an eternal vicious circle. In such a circle, for days, she had been tormentedly moving, prowling up and down, comparing incomparables. It was for that one had to cling to them — for their faces of supplication. Fleda herself could judge of these faces, so conscious of their race and their danger, and she had little enough to say when her companion asked her if the place, all perversely fair on October afternoons, looked like a place to give up. It looked, to begin with, through some effect of season and light, larger than ever, immense, and it brimmed over as with the hush of sorrow, which was in turn all charged with memories. Everything was in the air — each history of each find, each circumstance of each capture. Mrs. Gereth had drawn back every curtain and removed every cover; she prolonged the vistas, opened wide the whole house, gave it an appearance of awaiting a royal visit. The shimmer of wrought substances spent itself in the brightness; the old golds and brasses, old ivories and bronzes, the fresh old tapestries and deep old damasks threw out a radiance in which the poor woman saw in solution all her old loves and patiences, all her old tricks and triumphs.

Fleda had a depressed sense of not, after all, helping her much: this was relieved indeed by the fact that Mrs. Gereth, letting her off easily, did n't now seem to expect it. Her sympathy, her interest, her feeling for everything for which her hostess felt, were a force that really worked to prolong the deadlock. "I only wish I bored you and my possessions bored you," that lady declared with some humour; "then you'd make short work with me, bundle me off, tell me just to pile certain things into a cart and have done." Fleda's sharpest difficulty was in having to act up to the character of thinking Owen a brute, or in having at least to carry off the inconsistency of seeing him when he came down. By good fortune it was her indicated duty, her prescribed function, as well as a due protection to Mrs. Gereth. She thought of him perpetually and her eyes had come to rejoice in his manly magnificence more even than they rejoiced in the royal cabinets of the red saloon.

She wondered, very faintly at first, why he came so often; but of course she knew nothing of the business he had in hand, over which, with men red-faced and leather-legged, he was sometimes closeted for an hour in a room of his own that was the one monstrosity of Poynton: all tobacco-pots and bootjacks, his mother had said — such an array of arms of aggression and castigation that he himself had confessed to eighteen rifles and forty whips. He was arranging for settlements on his wife, he was doing things that would meet the views of the Brigstocks. Considering the house was his own Fleda thought it nice of him to keep himself in the background while his mother remained; making his visits, at some cost of ingenuity about trains from town, only between meals, taking pains to let it press lightly on her that he was there. This was rather a check to her meeting Mrs. Gereth on the ground of his being a brute; the most possible really at last was not to contradict her when she repeated that he was posted — just insultingly posted to watch. He *was* watching, no doubt; but he watched somehow with his head turned away. He knew Fleda to know at present what he wanted of her, so that it would be gross of him to say it over and over. It existed as a confidence between them and made him sometimes, with his wandering stare, meet her eyes as if a silence so pleasant could only unite them the more. He had no great flow of speech, certainly, and at first the girl took for granted that this only exhausted any conceivable statement of the matter. Yet little by little she speculated as to whether, with a person who, like herself, could after all put him at some domestic ease, it was not supposable he would have more conversation if he were not keeping some of it back for Mona.

From the moment she suspected he might be thinking how Mona would judge his chattering so to an underhand "companion," an inmate all but paid in shillings, this young lady's repressed emotion began to require still more repression. She grew impatient of her posture at Poynton, privately pronouncing it false and horrid. She said to herself that she had let Owen know of her having, to the best of her power, directed his mother in the general sense he desired; that he quite understood this and that he also understood how unworthy it was of either of them to stand over the good lady with a note-book and a lash. Was n't this practical unanimity just practical success? Fleda became aware of a sudden desire, as well as of pressing reasons, for the cessation of her long stay. She had not, on the one hand, like a minion of the law, undertaken to see Mrs. Gereth down to the train and locked, in sign of her abdication, into a compartment; neither had she on the other committed herself to hold Owen indefinitely in dalliance while his mother gained time or worked with the spade at a counter-mine. Besides, people *were* saying that she fastened like a leech on other people — people who had houses where something was to be picked up : this disclosure was frankly made her by her sister, now distinctly doomed to the curate and in view of whose nuptials she had almost finished, as a present, a wonderful piece of embroidery suggested, and precisely at Poynton, by an old Spanish altar-cloth. She would have to exert herself still further for the intended recipient of this offering, turn her out for the altar and subsequent straits with more than that drapery. She would go up to town, in short, to dress Maggie; and their father, in lodgings at West Kensington, would stretch a point and take them in. He, to do him justice, never reproached her with profitable devotions; so far as they existed he rather studied to glean from the same supposed harvest. Mrs. Gereth gave her up as heroically as if she had been a great bargain, and Fleda knew she should n't herself miss any imminent visit of the young man's, since the young man was shooting at Waterbath. Owen shooting was Owen lost, and there was scant sport at Poynton.

The first news she had from Mrs. Gereth was news of that lady's having accomplished, in form at least, her dread migration. The letter was dated from Ricks, to which place she had been transported by an impulse apparently as sudden as the inspiration she had obeyed before. "Yes, I've literally come," she wrote, "with a band-box and a kitchen-maid; I've crossed the Rubicon, I've taken possession. It has been like plumping into cold water. I saw the only thing was to do it, not to stand shivering. I shall have warmed the place a little by simply being here for a week; when I come back the ice will have been broken. I did n't write to you to meet me on my way through town, because I know how busy you are and because, besides, I'm too savage and odious to be fit company even for you. You'd say I really go too far, and there's no doubt whatever I do. I'm here, at any rate, just to look round once more, to see certain things done before I enter in force. I shall probably be at Poynton all next week. There's more room than I quite measured the other day, and a rather good set of old Worcester. But what are space and time, what's even old Worcester, to your wretched and affectionate A. G.?"

The day after Fleda received this letter she had occasion to enter a big shop in Oxford Street — a journey she achieved circuitously, first on foot and then by the aid of two omnibuses. The second of these vehicles put her down on the side of the street opposite her shop, and while, on the curbstone, she humbly waited, with a parcel, an umbrella and a tucked-up frock, to cross in security, she became aware that, close beside her, a hansom had pulled up short and in obedience to the brandished stick of a demonstrative occupant. This occupant was exactly Owen Gereth, who had caught sight of her as he rattled along and who, with an exhibition of white teeth that, from under the hood of the cab, had almost flashed through the fog, now alighted to ask her if he could n't give her a lift. On learning her destination to be just over the way he dismissed his vehicle and joined her, not only piloting her to the shop but taking her in: with the assurance that his errands did n't matter and that it amused him to be concerned with hers. She told him she had come to buy a trimming for her sister's frock, and he expressed a joyous interest in the purchase. His joy, always hilarious, was apt to be out of proportion to the case, but it struck her at present as higher-pitched than ever; especially when she had suggested he might find it a good time to buy a garnishment of some sort for Mona. After wondering an instant whether he read the full satiric meaning, such as it was, into this remark, Fleda dismissed the possibility as inconceivable. He stammered out that it was for *her* he should like to buy something, something "ripping," and that she must give him the pleasure of telling him what would best please her. He could n't have a better opportunity for making her a present — the tribute of recognition of all she had done for Mummy that he had had in his head for weeks.

Fleda had more than one small errand in the big bazaar, and he went up and down with her, pointedly patient, pretending to be interested in questions of tape and of change. She had now not the least hesitation in wondering what Mona would think of such proceedings. But they were not her doing — they were Owen's; and Owen, inconsequent and even extravagant, was unlike anything she had ever seen him before. He broke off, he came back, he repeated questions without heeding answers, he made vague and abrupt remarks about the resemblances of shop-girls and the uses of chiffon. He unduly prolonged their business together, giving Fleda a sense of his putting off something particular that he had to face. If she had ever dreamed of Owen Gereth as finely fluttered she would have seen him with some such manner as this. But why should he be finely fluttered? Even at the height of the crisis his mother had n't made him flagrantly nervous, and at present he was satisfied about his mother. The one idea he stuck to was that Fleda should mention something she would let him give her: there was everything in the world in the wonderful place, and he made her incongruous offers — a travelling-rug, a massive clock, a table for breakfast in bed, and above all, in a resplendent binding, a set of somebody's "works." His notion was a testimonial, something of the sort usually done by subscription — and in this case indeed perhaps the Brigstocks would contribute; so that the "works" in especial would be a graceful intimation that it was her cleverness he wished above all to commemorate. He was immensely in earnest, but the articles he pressed upon her betrayed a delicacy that went to her heart: what he would really have liked, as he saw them tumbled about, was one of the splendid stuffs for a gown — a choice proscribed by his fear of seeming to patronise her, to refer to her small means and her deficiencies. Fleda found it easy to chaff him about his exaggeration of her deserts; she gave the just measure of them in consenting to accept a small pin-cushion, costing sixpence, in which the letter F was marked out with pins. A sense of loyalty to Mona was not needed to enforce this discretion, and she was careful not to renew her reference to their beautiful friend. She noticed on this occasion more things in Owen Gereth than she had ever noticed before, but what she noticed most was that he said no word of his intended. She asked herself what he had done, in so long a parenthesis, with his loyalty or at least with his "form"; and then reflected that even had he done

64

something very good the situation in which such a question could come up was already a little strange. Of course he was n't thinking of anything so vulgar as to make love to her; but there was a kind of punctilio for a man known to be engaged.

That punctilio did n't prevent Owen's remaining with her after they had left the shop, nor his hoping she had a lot more to do, nor yet his pressing her to look with him, for a possible glimpse of something she might really let him give her, into the windows of other establishments. There was a moment when, under this pressure, she made up her mind that his tribute would be, if analysed, a tribute to her insignificance. But all the same he wanted her to come somewhere and have luncheon with him: what was that a tribute to ? She must have counted very little if she did n't count too much for a romp in a restaurant. She had to get home with her trimming, and the most she was amenable to in his company was a retracing of her steps to the Marble Arch and then, after a discussion when they had reached it, a walk with him across the Park. She knew Mona would have considered she ought now to take the "penny bus" again; but she had by this time to think for Owen as well as for herself — she could n't think for Mona. Even in the Park the autumn air was thick, and as they moved westward over the grass, which was what Owen preferred, the cool greyness made their words soft, made them at last rare and everything else dim. He wanted to stay with her — he wanted not to leave her: he had dropped into complete silence, but that was what his silence said. What was it he had postponed? What was it he wanted still to postpone? She grew a little scared while they strolled together and while she thought. The indication, all indirect, was too vague to be flagrant, but it was as if somehow he were feeling differently. Fleda Vetch did n't suspect him at first of feeling differently to *her*, but only of feeling differently to Mona; yet she was not unconscious that this latter difference would have had something to do with his being on the grass there beside her. She had read in novels about gentlemen who on the eve of marriage, winding up the past, had surrendered themselves for the occasion to the influence of a former tie; and there was something in Owen's behaviour now, something in his very face, that suggested a resemblance to one of those gentlemen. But whom and what, in that case, would Fleda herself resemble? She was n't a former tie, she was n't any tie at all; she was only a deep little person for whom happiness was a kind of pearl-diving plunge. Happiness was down at the very bottom of all that had lately occurred; for all that had lately occurred was that Owen Gereth had come and gone at Poynton. That was the small sum of her experience, and what it had made for her was her own affair, quite consistent with her not having dreamed it had made a relation — at least what *she* called one — for Owen. The old relation, at any rate, was with Mona — Mona whom he had known so very much longer.

They walked far, to the southwest corner of the great Gardens, where, by the old round pond and the old red palace, when she had put out her hand to him in farewell, declaring that from the gate she must positively take a conveyance, it seemed suddenly to rise between them that this was a real separation. She was on his mother's side, she belonged to his mother's life, and his mother, in the future, would never, never come to Poynton. After what had passed she would n't even be at his wedding, and it was not possible now that Mr. Gereth should mention that ceremony to the girl, much less express a wish that the girl should be present at it. Mona, from decorum and with reference less to the bridegroom than to the bridegroom's mother, would of course not invite any such creature as Miss Vetch. Everything therefore was ended; they would go their different ways; it was the last time they should stand face to face. They looked at each other with the fuller sense of it and, on Owen's part, with an expression of dumb trouble, the intensification of his frequent appeal to any interlocutor to add the right thing to what he said. It struck Fleda at this moment that the right thing might easily be the wrong. At any rate he only said: "I want you to understand, you know — I want you to understand."

What did he want her to understand? He seemed unable to bring it out, and this understanding was moreover exactly what she wished not to arrive at. Bewildered as she was she had already taken in as much as she should know what to do with; the blood also was rushing into her face. He liked her — it was stupefying — more than he really ought: that was what was the matter with him and what he desired her to swallow; so that she was suddenly as frightened

67

as some thoughtless girl who finds herself the object of an overture from a married man.

"Good-bye, Mr. Gereth — I *must* get on!" she declared with a cheerfulness that she felt to be an unnatural grimace. She broke away from him sharply, smiling, backing across the grass and then turning altogether and moving as fast as she could. "Good-bye, good-bye!" she threw off again as she went, wondering if he would overtake her before she reached the gate; conscious with a red disgust that her movement was almost a run; conscious too of the very confused handsome face with which he would look after her. She felt as if she had answered a kindness with a great flouncing snub, but in any case she had got away — though the distance to the gate, her ugly gallop down the Broad Walk, every graceless jerk of which hurt her, seemed endless. She signed from afar to a cab on the stand in the Kensington Road and scrambled into it, glad of the encompassment of the four-wheeler that had officiously obeyed her summons and that, at the end of twenty yards, when she had violently pulled up a glass, permitted her to feel herself all wretchedly ready to burst into tears.

VII

As soon as her sister had been married she went
down to Mrs. Gereth at Ricks — a promise to this
effect having been promptly exacted and given; and
her inner vision was much more fixed on the altera-
tions there, complete now as she understood, than
on the success of her plotting and pinching for Maggie's happiness. Her imagination, in the interval,
had indeed had plenty to do and numerous scenes
to visit; for when on the summons just mentioned it
had taken a flight from West Kensington to Ricks,
it had hung but an hour over the terrace of painted
pots and then yielded to a current of the upper air
that swept it straight off to Poynton and to Waterbath. Not a sound had reached her of any supreme
clash, and Mrs. Gereth had communicated next to
nothing; giving out that, as was easily conceivable,
she was too busy, too bitter and too tired for vain
civilities. All she had written was that she had got
the new place well in hand and that Fleda would be
surprised at the way it was turning out. Everything
was even yet upside down; nevertheless, in the sense
of having passed the threshold of Poynton for the
last time, the amputation, as she called it, had been
performed. Her leg had come off — she had now
begun to stump along with the lovely wooden sub-
stitute; she would stump for life, and what her young
friend was to come and admire was the beauty of

her movement and the noise she made about the house. The reserve of Poynton, as well as that of Waterbath, had been matched by the austerity of Fleda's own secret, under the discipline of which she had repeated to herself a hundred times a day that she rejoiced in cares so heavy as to exclude all thought of it. She had lavished herself, in act, on Maggie and the curate, and had opposed to her father's selfishness a heavenly patience. The young couple wondered why they had waited so long, since everything seemed after all so easy. She had thought of everything, even to how the "quietness" of the wedding should be relieved by champagne and her father — very firmly — kept brilliant on a single bottle. Fleda knew, in short, and liked the knowledge, that for several weeks she had appeared exemplary in every relation of life.

She had been perfectly prepared to be surprised at Ricks, for Mrs. Gereth was a wonder-working wizard, with a command, when all was said, of good material; but the impression in wait for her on the threshold made her catch her breath and falter. Dusk had fallen when she arrived, and in the plain square hall, one of the few good features, the glow of a Venetian lamp just showed on either wall, in perfect proportion, a small but splendid tapestry. This instant perception that the place had been dressed at the expense of Poynton was a shock: it was as if she had abruptly seen herself in the light of an accomplice. The next moment, folded in Mrs. Gereth's arms, her eyes were diverted; but she had already had, in a flash, the vision of great gaps in the other house. The two tapestries, not the biggest pieces but those most splendidly toned by time, had been on the whole its most uplifted pride. When she could really see again she was on a sofa in the drawing-room, staring with intensity at an object soon distinct as the great Italian cabinet that had been in the red saloon. All without looking she was sure the room was occupied by just such other objects, stuffed with as many as it could hold of the trophies of her friend's struggle. By this time the very fingers of her glove, resting on the seat of the sofa, had thrilled at the touch of an old velvet brocade, a wondrous texture she could recognise, would have recognised among a thousand, without dropping her eyes on it. They stuck to the cabinet with dissimulated dread while she painfully asked herself if she should notice it, notice everything, or just pretend not to be affected. How could she pretend not to be affected with the very pendants of the lustres tinkling at her and with Mrs. Gereth, beside her, staring at her even as she herself stared at the cabinet and hunching up the back of Atlas under his globe? She was appalled at this image of what Mrs. Gereth had on her shoulders. That lady was waiting and watching her, bracing herself and preparing the same face of confession and defiance she had shown at Poynton the day she had been surprised in the corridor. It was farcical not to speak; and yet to exclaim, to participate, would give one a bad sense of being mixed up with a theft. This ugly word sounded, for herself, in Fleda's silence, and the very violence of it jarred her into a scared glance, as of a creature detected, to right and

left. But what again the full picture most showed
her was the far-away empty sockets, a scandal of
nakedness between high bleak walls. She at last
uttered something formal and incoherent — she did
n't know what: it had no relation to either house.
Then she felt all her friend's weight, as it were, once
more on her arm. "I've arranged a charming room
for you — it's really lovely. You'll be very happy
there." This was spoken with extraordinary sweetness and with a smile that meant: "Oh I know what
you're thinking; but what does it matter when you're
so loyally on my side?" It had come indeed to a question of "sides," Fleda thought, for the whole place
was in battle array. In the soft lamp-light, with one
fine feature after another looming up into sombre
richness, it defied her not to pronounce it a triumph
of taste. Her passion for beauty leaped back into life;
and was not what now most appealed to it a certain
gorgeous audacity? Mrs. Gereth's high hand was,
as mere great effect, the climax of the impression.

"It's too wonderful what you've done with the
house!" — the visitor met her friend's eyes. They
lighted up with joy, that friend herself was so pleased
with what she had done. This was not at all, in its
accidental air of enthusiasm, what Fleda wanted
to have said: it offered her as stupidly announcing
from the first minute on whose side she was. Such
was clearly the way Mrs. Gereth took it; she threw
herself upon the delightful girl and tenderly embraced her again; so that Fleda soon went on with
a studied difference and a cooler inspection. "Why
you brought away absolutely everything!"

"Oh no, not everything. I saw how little I could get into this scrap of a house. I only brought away what I required."

Fleda had got up; she took a turn round the room. "You 'required' the very best pieces — the *morceaux de musée*, the individual gems!"

"I certainly did n't want the rubbish, if that's what you mean." Mrs. Gereth, on the sofa, followed the direction of her companion's eyes; with the light of her satisfaction still in her face she slowly rubbed her large handsome hands. Wherever she was she was herself the great piece in the gallery. It was the first Fleda had heard of there being "rubbish" at Poynton, but she did n't for the moment take up this false plea; she only, from where she stood in the room, called out, one after the other, as if she had had a list before her, the items that in the great house had been scattered and that now, if they had a fault, were too much like a minuet danced on a hearth-rug. She knew them each by every inch of their surface and every charm of their character — knew them by the personal name their distinctive sign or story had given them; and a second time she felt how, against her intention, this uttered knowledge struck her hostess as so much free approval. Mrs. Gereth was never indifferent to approval, and there was nothing she could so love you for as for doing justice to her deep morality. There was a particular gleam in her eyes when Fleda exclaimed at last, dazzled by the display, "And even the Maltese cross!" That description, though technically incorrect, had always been applied at Poynton to a small but marvellous crucifix of ivory, a masterpiece of delicacy, of expression and of the great Spanish period, the existence and precarious accessibility of which she had heard of at Malta, years before, by an odd and romantic chance — a clue followed through mazes of secrecy till the treasure was at last unearthed.

"'Even' the Maltese cross?" Mrs. Gereth rose as she sharply echoed the words. "My dear child, you don't suppose I'd have sacrificed *that!* For what in the world would you have taken me?"

"A *bibelot* the more or less," Fleda said, "could have made little difference in this grand general view of you. I take you simply for the greatest of all conjurors. You've operated with a quickness — and with a quietness!" Her voice just trembled as she spoke, for the plain meaning of her words was that what her friend had achieved belonged to the class of operations essentially involving the protection of darkness. Fleda felt she really could say nothing at all if she could n't say she took in the risks heroically run, all the danger surmounted. She completed her thought by a resolute and perfectly candid question. "How in the world did you get off with them?"

Mrs. Gereth confessed to the fact of great evasions with a cynicism that surprised her. "By calculating, by choosing my time. I *was* quiet and I *was* quick. I manœuvred, prepared my ground; then at the last I rushed!" Fleda drew a long breath: she saw in the poor woman something much better than sophistical ease, a crude elation that was a comparatively simple state to deal with. Her elation, it was true, was not so much from what she had done as from the way she had done it — by as brilliant a stroke as any commemorated in the annals of punished crime. "I succeeded because I had thought it all out and left nothing to chance. The whole business was organised in advance, so that the mere carrying it into effect took but a few hours. It was largely a matter of money: oh I was horribly extravagant — I had to turn on so many people. But they were all to be had — a little army of workers, the packers, the porters, the helpers of every sort, the men with the mighty vans. It was a question of arranging in Tottenham Court Road and of paying the price. I have n't paid it yet; there 'll be a horrid bill; but at least the thing's done! Expedition pure and simple was the essence of the bargain. ' I can give you two days,' I said; 'I can't give you another second.' They undertook the job, and the two days saw them through. The people came down on a Tuesday morning; they were off on the Thursday. I admit that some of them worked all Wednesday night. I had thought it all out; I stood over them; I showed them how. Yes, I coaxed them, I made love to them. Oh I was inspired — they found me wonderful. I neither ate nor slept, but I was as calm as I am now. I did n't know what was in me; it was worth finding out. I'm very remarkable, my dear: I lifted tons with my own arms. I'm tired, very, very tired; but there's neither a scratch nor a nick, there is n't a teacup missing." Magnificent both in her exhaustion and in her triumph she sank on the sofa again, the sweep of her eyes a rich synthesis and the restless friction of her hands a clear betrayal. "Upon my word," she laughed, "they really look better here!"

Fleda had listened in awe. "And no one at Poynton said anything? There was no alarm?"

"What alarm should there have been? Owen left me almost defiantly alone. I had taken a special time I had reason to believe safe from a descent." Fleda had another wonder, which she hesitated to express: it would scarcely do to ask if such a heroine had n't stood in fear of her servants. She knew more-over some of the secrets of the heroine's humorous household rule, all made up of shocks to shyness and provocations to curiosity — a diplomacy so artful that several of the maids quite yearned to accom-pany her to Ricks. Mrs. Gereth, reading sharply the whole of her visitor's thought, caught it up with fine frankness. "You mean that I was watched — that he had his myrmidons, pledged to wire him if they should see what I was 'up to'? Precisely. I know the three persons you have in mind: I had them in mind myself. Well, I took a line with them — I settled them."

Fleda had had no one in particular in mind and had never believed in the myrmidons; but the tone in which Mrs. Gereth spoke added to her suspense. "What did you do to them?"

"I took hold of them hard — I put them in the forefront. I made them work."

"To move the furniture?"

"To help, and to help so as to please me. That was the way to take them: it was what they had least expected. I marched up to them and looked

76

each straight in the eye, giving him the chance to choose if he'd gratify me or gratify my son. He gratified *me*. They were too stupid!"

She massed herself more and more as an immoral woman, but Fleda had to recognise that another person too would have been stupid and another person too would have gratified her. "And when did all this take place?"

"Only last week; it seems a hundred years. We've worked here as fast as we worked there, but I'm not settled yet: you'll see in the rest of the house. However, the worst's over."

"Do you really think so?" Fleda presently enquired. "I mean does he after the fact, as it were, accept it?"

"Owen — what I've done? I haven't the least idea," said Mrs. Gereth.

"Does Mona?"

"You mean that she'll be the soul of the row?"

"I hardly see Mona as the 'soul' of anything," the girl replied. "But have they made no sound? Have you heard nothing at all?"

"Not a whisper, not a step, in all the eight days. Perhaps they don't know. Perhaps they're crouching for a leap."

"But wouldn't they have gone down as soon as you left?"

"They may not have known of my leaving." Fleda wondered afresh; it struck her as scarcely supposable that some sign shouldn't have flashed from Poynton to London. If the storm was taking this term of silence to gather, even in Mona's breast, it would probably discharge itself in some thunder-burst. The great hush of every one concerned was strange; but when she pressed Mrs. Gereth for the sense of it that lady only replied with her brave irony: "Oh I took their breath away!" She had no illusions, however; she was still prepared to fight. What indeed was her spoliation of Poynton but the first engagement of a campaign?

All this was exciting, but Fleda's spirit dropped, at bedtime, in the quarter embellished for her particular pleasure, where she found several of the objects that in her earlier room she had most admired. These had been re-enforced by other pieces from other rooms, so that the quiet air of it was a harmony without a break, the finished picture of a maiden's bower. It was the sweetest Louis Seize, all assorted and combined — old chastened figured faded France. Fleda was impressed anew with her friend's genius for composition. She could say to herself that no girl in England, that night, went to rest with so picked a guard; but there was no joy for her in her privilege, no sleep even for the tired hours that made the place, in the embers of the fire and the winter dawn, look grey, somehow, and loveless. She could n't care for such things when they came to her in such ways; there was a wrong about them all that turned them to ugliness. In the watches of the night she saw Poynton dishonoured; she had cherished it as a happy whole, she reasoned, and the parts of it now around her seemed to suffer like chopped limbs. To lie there in the stillness was partly to listen for some soft low plaint from them. Before going to bed she had walked about with Mrs. Gereth and seen at whose expense the whole house had been furnished. At poor Owen's from top to bottom — there was n't a chair he had n't sat upon. The maiden-aunt had been exterminated — no trace of her to tell her tale. Fleda tried to think of some of the things at Poynton still unappropriated, but her memory was a blank about them, and in the effort to focus the old combinations she saw again nothing but gaps and scars, a vacancy that gathered at moments into something worse. This concrete image was her greatest trouble, for it was Owen Gereth's face, his sad strange eyes, fixed upon her now as they had never been. They stared at her out of the darkness and their expression was more than she could bear: it seemed to say that he was in pain and that it was somehow her fault. He had looked to her to help him, yet this was what her help had been. He had done her the honour to ask her to exert herself in his interest, confiding to her a task of difficulty but of the highest delicacy. Had n't that been exactly the sort of service she longed to render him? Well, her way of rendering it had been simply to betray him and hand him over to his enemy. Shame, pity, resentment oppressed her in turn; in the last of these feelings the others were soon submerged. Mrs. Gereth had imprisoned her in that torment of taste, but it was clear to her for an hour at least that she might hate Mrs. Gereth.

Something else, however, when morning came, was even more intensely definite: the most odious thing in the world for her would be ever again to meet Owen. She took on the spot a resolve to neglect

no precaution that could lead to her going through
life without that calamity. After this, while she
dressed, she took still another. Her position had
become in a few hours intolerably false; in as few
more hours as possible she would therefore put an
end to it. The way to put an end would be to let her
friend know that, to her great regret, she could n't
be with her now, could n't cleave to her to the point
that everything about them so plainly urged. She
dressed with a sort of violence, a symbol of the manner in which this purpose had been precipitated.
The more they parted company the less likely she
was to come across Owen; for Owen would be drawn
closer to his mother now by the very necessity of
bringing her down. Fleda, in the inconsequence of
distress, wished to have nothing to do with her fall;
she had had too much to do with everything. She
was well aware of the importance, before breakfast
and in view of any light they might shed on the question of motive, of not suffering her invidious expression of a difference to be accompanied by the traces
of tears; but it none the less came to pass, downstairs, that after she had subtly put her back to the
window to make a mystery of the state of her eyes
she stupidly let a rich sob escape her before she could
properly meet the consequences of being asked if she
was n't delighted with her room. This accident
struck her on the spot as so grave that she felt the
only refuge to be instant hypocrisy, some graceful
impulse that would charge her emotion to the quickened sense of her friend's generosity — a demonstration entailing a flutter round the table and a renewed

embrace, yet not so successfully improvised but that Fleda fancied Mrs. Gereth to have been only half-reassured. She had been startled at any rate and might remain suspicious: this reflexion interposed by the time, after breakfast, our young woman had recovered sufficiently to say what was in her heart. She accordingly did n't say it that morning at all. She had absurdly veered about; she had encountered the shock of the fear that Mrs. Gereth, with sharp-ened eyes, might wonder why the deuce (she often wondered in that phrase) she had grown so warm about Owen's rights. She would doubtless at a pinch be able to defend them on abstract grounds, but that would involve a discussion, and the idea of a discus-sion made her nervous for her secret. Until in some way Poynton should return the blow and give her a cue she must keep nervousness down; and she called herself a fool for having forgotten, however briefly, that her one safety was in silence.

Directly after luncheon her friend took her into the garden for a glimpse of the revolution — or at least, said the mistress of Ricks, of the great row — that had been decreed there; but the ladies had scarcely placed themselves for this view before the younger one found herself embracing a prospect that opened in quite another quarter. Her attention was called to it, oddly, by the streamers of the par-lour-maid's cap, which, flying straight behind the neat young woman who unexpectedly burst from the house and showed a long red face as she ambled over the grass, seemed to articulate in their flutter the name that Fleda lived at present only to catch.

"Poynton — Poynton!" said the morsels of muslin;
so that the parlour-maid became on the instant an
actress in the drama, and Fleda, assuming pusillan-
imously that she herself was only a spectator, looked
across the footlights at the exponent of the principal
part. The manner in which this artist returned the
look showed her as equally preoccupied. Both were
haunted alike by possibilities, but the apprehension
of neither, before the announcement was made, had
taken the form of the arrival at Ricks, in the flesh, of
Mrs. Gereth's victim. When the messenger informed
them that Mr. Gereth was in the drawing-room the
blank "Oh!" emitted by Fleda was quite as precipitate as the sound on her hostess's lips, besides being,
as she felt, much less pertinent. "I thought it would
be somebody," that lady afterwards said; "but I
expected on the whole a solicitor's clerk." Fleda
did n't mention that she herself had expected on the
whole a brace of constables. She wondered at Mrs.
Gereth's question to the parlour-maid.

"For whom did he ask?"

"Why for *you* of course, dearest friend!" Fleda
interjected, falling instinctively into the address that
embodied the intensest pressure. She wanted to put
Mrs. Gereth between her and her danger.

"He asked for Miss Vetch, mum," the girl replied
with a face that brought startlingly to Fleda's ear the
muffled chorus of the kitchen.

"Quite proper," said Mrs. Gereth austerely. Then
to Fleda: "Please go to him."

"But what to do?"

"What you always do — see what he wants."

82

Mrs. Gereth dismissed the maid. "Tell him Miss Vetch will come." Fleda saw that nothing was in the mother's imagination at this moment but the desire not to meet her son. She had completely broken with him and there was little in what had just happened to repair the rupture. It would now take more to do so than his presenting himself uninvited at her door. "He's right in asking for you — he's aware that you're still our communicator; nothing has occurred to alter that. To what he wishes to transmit through you I'm ready, as I've been ready before, to listen. As far as *I*'m concerned, if I couldn't meet him a month ago how am I to meet him to-day? If he has come to say 'My dear mother, you're here, in the hovel into which I've flung you, with consolations that give me pleasure,' I'll listen to him; but on no other footing. That's what you're to ascertain, please. You'll oblige me as you've obliged me before. There!" Mrs. Gereth turned her back and with a fine imitation of superiority began to redress the miseries immediately before her. Fleda meanwhile hesitated, lingered for some minutes where she had been left, feeling secretly that her fate still had her in hand. It had put her face to face with Owen Gereth and evidently meant to keep her so. She was reminded afresh of two things: one of which was that, though she judged her friend's rigour, she had never really had the story of the scene enacted in the great awe-stricken house between the intimate adversaries weeks before — the day the elder took to her bed in her overthrow. The other was that at Ricks as at Poynton it was before all

things her own place to accept thankfully a useful-
ness not, she must remember, universally acknowledged. What determined her at the last, while Mrs.
Gereth disappeared in the shrubbery, was that,
though at a distance from the house and with the
drawing-room turned the other way, she could absolutely see the young man alone there with the sources
of his pain. She saw his simple stare at his tapestries,
heard his heavy tread on his carpets and the hard
breath of his sense of unfairness. At this she went to
him fast.

VIII

"I ASKED for you," he said when she stood there, "because I heard from the flyman who drove me from the station to the inn that he had brought you here yesterday. We had some talk — he mentioned it."

"You did n't know I was here?"

"No. I knew only you had had in London all you told me that day to do; and it was Mona's idea that after your sister's marriage you were staying on with your father. So I thought you were with him still."

"I am," Fleda replied, idealising a little the fact. "I'm here only for a moment. But do you mean," she went on, "that if you had known I was with your mother you would n't have come down?"

The way Owen hung fire at this question made it sound more playful than she had intended. She had in fact no consciousness of any intention but to confine herself rigidly to her function. She could already see that in whatever he had now braced himself for she was an element he had not reckoned with. His preparation had been of a different sort — the sort congruous with his having been careful to go first and lunch solidly at the inn. He had not been forced to ask for her, but she became aware in his presence of a particular desire to make him feel that no harm could really come to him. She might upset him, as

85

people called it, but she should take no advantage of having done so. She had never seen a person with whom she wished more to be light and easy, to be exceptionally human. The account he presently gave of the matter was that he indeed would n't have come if he had known she was on the spot; because then, did n't she see? he could have written to her. He would have had her there to let fly at his mother.

"That would have saved me — well, it would have saved me a lot. Of course I'd rather see you than her," he somewhat awkwardly added. "When the fellow spoke of you I assure you I quite jumped at you. In fact I've no real desire to see Mummy at all. If she thinks I *like* it —!" He sighed disgustedly. "I only came down because it seemed better than any other way. I did n't want her to be able to say I had n't been all right. I dare say you know she has taken everything; or if not quite everything at least a lot more than one ever dreamed. You can see for yourself — she has got half the place down. She has got them crammed — you can see for yourself!" He had his old trick of artless repetition, his helpless iteration of the obvious; but he was sensibly different for Fleda, if only by the difference of his clear face mottled over and almost disfigured by little points of pain. He might have been a fine young man with a bad toothache, with the first even of his life. What ailed him above all, she felt, was that trouble was new to him. He had never known a difficulty; he had taken all his fences, his world wholly the world of the personally possible, rounded indeed by a grey suburb into which he had never had occasion to stray.

In this vulgar and ill-lighted region he had evidently now lost himself. "We left it quite to her honour, you know," he said ruefully.

"Perhaps you've a right to say you left it a little to mine." Mixed up with the spoils there, rising before him as if she were in a manner their keeper, she felt she must absolutely dissociate herself. Mrs. Gereth had made it impossible to do anything but give her away. "I can only tell you that on my side I left it to her. I never dreamed either that she would pick out so many things."

"And you don't really think it's fair, do you? You *don't!*" He spoke very quickly; he really seemed to plead.

Fleda just faltered. "I think she has gone too far." Then she added: "I shall immediately tell her I've said that to you."

He appeared puzzled by this statement, but he presently rejoined: "You have n't then said to her what you think?"

"Not yet; remember that I got here only last night." She struck herself as ignobly weak. "I had had no idea what she was doing. I was taken completely by surprise. She managed it wonderfully."

"It's the sharpest thing I ever saw in *my* life!" They looked at each other with intelligence, in appreciation of the sharpness, and Owen quickly broke into a loud laugh. The laugh was in itself natural, but the occasion of it strange; and stranger still to Fleda, so that she too almost laughed, the inconsequent charity with which he added: "Poor dear old

Mummy! That's one of the reasons I asked for you," he went on — "to see if you'd back her up."

Whatever he said or did she somehow liked him the better for it. "How can I back her up, Mr. Gereth, when I think, as I tell you, that she has made a great mistake?"

"A great mistake! That's all right." He spoke — it wasn't clear to her why — as if this attestation had been a great point gained.

"Of course there are many things she hasn't taken," Fleda continued.

"Oh yes, a lot of things. But you wouldn't know the place, all the same." He looked about the room with his discoloured swindled face, which deepened Fleda's compassion for him, conjuring away any smile at so candid an image of the dupe. "You'd know this one soon enough, wouldn't you? These are just the things she ought to have left. Is the whole house full of them?"

"The whole house," said Fleda uncompromisingly. She thought of her lovely room.

"I never knew how much I cared for them. They're awfully valuable, aren't they?" Owen's manner mystified her; she was conscious of a return of the agitation he had produced in her on that last bewildering day, and she reminded herself that, now she was warned, it would be inexcusable of her to allow him to justify the fear that had dropped on her. "Mother thinks I never took any notice, but I assure you I was awfully proud of everything. Upon my honour I *was* proud, Miss Vetch."

There was an oddity in his helplessness; he appeared to wish to persuade her and to satisfy himself that she sincerely felt how worthy he really was to treat what had happened as an injury. She could only exclaim almost as helplessly as himself: "Of course you did justice! It's all most painful. I shall instantly let your mother know," she again declared, "the way I've spoken of her to you." She clung to that idea as to the sign of her straightness.

"You'll tell her what you think she ought to do?" he asked with some eagerness.

"What she ought to do?"

"*Don't* you think it — I mean that she ought to give them up?"

"To give them up?" Fleda cast about her again.

"To send them back — to keep it quiet." The girl had not felt the impulse to ask him to sit down among the monuments of his wrong, so that, nervously, awkwardly, he fidgeted over the room with his hands in his pockets and an effect of returning a little into possession through the formulation of his view. "To have them packed and dispatched again, since she knows so well how. She does it beautifully" — he looked close at two or three precious pieces. "What's sauce for the goose is sauce for the gander!"

He had laughed at his way of putting it, but Fleda remained grave. "Is that what you came to say to her?"

"Not exactly those words. But I did come to say" — he stammered, then brought it out — "I did come to say we must have them right back."

"And did you think your mother would see you?"

"I wasn't sure, but I thought it right to try — to

put it to her kindly, don't you see? If she won't see
me then she has herself to thank. The only other way
would have been to set the lawyers at her."

"I'm glad you did n't do that."

"I'm dashed if I want to!" Owen honestly responded. "But what's a fellow to do if she won't
meet a fellow?"

"What do you call meeting a fellow?" Fleda asked
with a smile.

"Why letting *me* tell her a dozen things she can
have."

This was a transaction that Fleda had after a moment to give up trying to represent to herself. "If
she won't do that—?" she went on.

"I'll leave it all to my solicitor. *He* won't let her
off, by Jove. I know the fellow!"

"That's horrible!" said Fleda, looking at him in
woe.

"It's utterly beastly."

His want of logic as well as his vehemence startled
her; and with her eyes still on his she considered
before asking him the question these things suggested.
At the last she asked it. "Is Mona very angry?"

"Oh dear yes!" said Owen.

She had noted that he would n't speak of Mona
without her beginning. After waiting fruitlessly now
for him to say more she continued: "She has been
there again? She has seen the state of the house?"

"Oh dear yes!" he repeated.

Fleda disliked to appear not to take account of his
brevity, but it was just because she was struck by it
that she felt the pressure of the desire to know more.

What it suggested was simply what her intelligence supplied, for he was incapable of any art of insinuation. Was n't it at all events the rule of communication with him for her to say on his behalf what he could n't say? This truth was present to the girl as she enquired if Mona greatly resented what Mrs. Gereth had done. He satisfied her promptly; he was standing before the fire, his back to it, his long legs apart, his hands, behind him, rather violently jiggling his gloves. "She hates it awfully. In fact she refuses to put up with it at all. Don't you see? — she saw the place with all the things."

"So that of course she misses them."

"Misses them — rather! She was awfully sweet on them." Fleda remembered how sweet Mona had been, and reflected that if that was the sort of plea he had prepared it was indeed as well he should n't see his mother. This was not all she wanted to know, but it came over her that it was all she needed. "You see it puts me in the position of not carrying out what I promised," Owen said. "As she says herself" — he hung fire an instant — "it's just as if I had obtained her under false pretences." Just before, when he spoke with more drollery than he knew, it had left Fleda serious; but now his own clear gravity had the effect of exciting her mirth. She laughed out, and he looked surprised, but went on: "She regards it as a regular sell."

Fleda was silent; yet finally, as he added nothing, she exclaimed: "Of course it makes a great difference!" She knew all she needed, but none the less she risked after another pause an interrogative remark. "I forgot when it is your marriage takes place?"

He came away from the fire and, apparently at a loss where to turn, ended by directing himself to one of the windows. "It's a little uncertain. The date is n't quite fixed."

"Oh I thought I remembered that at Poynton you had told me a day and that it was near at hand."

"I dare say I did; it was for the nineteenth. But we've altered that—she wants to shift it." He looked out of the window; then he said: "In fact it won't come off till Mummy has come round."

"Come round?"

"Put the place as it was." In his off-hand way he added: "You know what I mean!"

He spoke not impatiently, but with a kind of intimate familiarity, the mildness of which made her feel a pang for having forced him to tell her what was embarrassing to him, what was even humiliating. Yes indeed, she knew all she needed: all she needed was that Mona had proved apt at putting down that wonderful patent-leather foot. Her type was misleading only to the superficial, and no one in the world was less superficial than Fleda. She had guessed the truth at Waterbath and had suffered from it at Poynton; at Ricks the only thing she could do was to accept it with the dumb exaltation that she felt rising. Mona had been prompt with her exercise of the member in question, for it might be called prompt to do that sort of thing before marriage. That she had indeed been premature who might say save those who should have read the matter in the full light of results? Neither at Waterbath nor at Poynton had even Fleda's thoroughness discovered all there was — or rather all there was n't — in Owen Gereth. "Of course it makes all the difference!" she said in answer to his last words. She pursued the next moment: "What you wish me to say from you then to your mother is that you demand immediate and practically complete restitution?"

"Yes, please. It's tremendously good of you."

"Very well then. Will you wait?"

"For Mummy's answer?" Owen stared and looked perplexed; he was more and more fevered with so much vivid expression of his case. "Don't you think that if I'm here she may hate it worse — suppose I may want to make her reply bang off?"

Fleda weighed it. "You don't then?"

"I want to take her in the right way, don't you know? — treat her as if I gave her more than just an hour or two."

"I see," said Fleda. "Then if you don't wait — good-bye."

This again seemed not what he wanted. "Must *you* do it bang off?"

"I'm only thinking she'll be impatient — I mean, you know, to learn what will have passed between us."

"I see," said Owen, looking at his gloves. "I can give her a day or two, you know. Of course I did n't come down to sleep," he went on. "The inn seems a beastly hole. I know all about the trains — having no idea you were here." Almost as soon as his entertainer he was struck with the absence of the visible, in this, as between effect and cause. "I mean because in that case I should have felt I could stop over. I should have felt I could talk with you a blessed sight longer than with Mummy."

"We've already talked a long time," smiled Fleda.

"Awfully, have n't we?" He spoke with the stupidity she did n't object to. Inarticulate as he was he had more to say; he lingered perhaps because vaguely aware of the want of sincerity in her encouragement to him to go. "There's one thing, please," he mentioned, as if there might be a great many others too. "Please don't say anything about Mona."

She did n't understand. "About Mona?"

"About it being *her* that thinks she has gone too far." This was still slightly obscure, but now Fleda understood. "It must n't seem to come from *her* at all, don't you know? That would only make Mummy worse."

Fleda knew exactly how much worse, but felt a delicacy about explicitly assenting: she was already immersed moreover in the deep consideration of what might make "Mummy" better. She could n't see as yet at all, could only clutch at the hope of some inspiration after he should go. Oh there was a remedy, to be sure, but it was out of the question; in spite of which, in the strong light of Owen's troubled presence, of his anxious face and restless step, it hung there before her for some minutes. She guessed that, remarkably, beneath the decent rigour of his errand, the poor young man, for reasons, for weariness, for disgust, would have been ready not to insist. His fitness to fight his mother had left him — he was n't in fighting trim. He had no natural avidity and even no special wrath; he had none that had not been taught him, and it was his doing his best to learn the lesson that had made him so sick. He had his delicacies, but he hid them away like presents before Christmas. He was hollow, perfunctory, pathetic; he had been girded by another hand. That hand had naturally been Mona's, and it was heavy even now on his strong broad back. Why then had he originally rejoiced so in its touch? Fleda dashed aside this question, for it had nothing to do with her problem. Her problem was to help him to live as a gentleman and carry through what he had undertaken; her problem was to reinstate him in his rights. It was quite irrelevant that Mona had no intelligence of what she had lost — quite irrelevant that she was moved not by the privation but by the insult. She had every reason to be moved, though she was so much more moveable, in the vindictive way at any rate, than one might have supposed — assuredly more than Owen himself had imagined.

"Certainly I shall not mention Mona," Fleda said, "and there won't be the slightest necessity for it. The wrong's quite sufficiently yours, and the demand you make perfectly justified by it."

"I can't tell you what it is to me to feel you on my side!" Owen exclaimed.

"Up to this time," said Fleda after a pause, "your mother has had no doubt of my being on hers."

"Then of course she won't like your changing."

"I dare say she won't like it at all."

"Do you mean to say you'll have a regular kick-up with her?"

"I don't exactly know what you mean by a regular kick-up. We shall naturally have a great deal of discussion — if she consents to discuss at all. That's why you must decidedly give her two or three days."

"I see you think she *may* refuse to discuss at all," said Owen.

"I'm only trying to be prepared for the worst. You must remember that to have to withdraw from the ground she has taken, to make a public surrender of what she had publicly appropriated, will go uncommonly hard with her pride."

Owen considered; his face seemed to broaden, but not into a smile. "I suppose she's tremendously proud, isn't she?" This might have been the first time it had occurred to him.

"You know better than I," said Fleda, speaking with high extravagance.

"I don't know anything in the world half so well as you. If I were as clever as you I might hope to get round her." Owen waited for more thought; then he went on: "In fact I don't quite see what even you can say or do that will really fetch her."

"Neither do I, as yet. I must think — I must pray!" the girl pursued, smiling. "I can only say to you that I'll try. I *want* to try, you know — I want to help you." He stood looking at her so long on this that she added with much distinctness: "So you must leave me, please, quite alone with her. You must go straight back."

"Back to the inn?"

"Oh no, back to town. I'll write to you to-morrow."

He turned about vaguely for his hat. "There's the chance of course that she may be afraid."

"Afraid you mean of the legal steps you may take?"

"I've got a perfect case — I could have her up. The Brigstocks say it's simply stealing."

"I can easily fancy what the Brigstocks say!" Fleda permitted herself to remark without solemnity.

"It's none of their business, is it?" was Owen's unexpected rejoinder. Fleda had already noted that no one so slow could ever have had such quick transitions.

She showed her amusement. "They've a much better right to say it's none of mine."

"Well, at any rate, you don't call her names."

Fleda wondered if Mona did; and this made it all the finer of her to exclaim in a moment: "You don't know what I shall call her if she holds out!"

Owen gave her a gloomy glance; then he blew a speck off the crown of his hat. "But if you do have a set-to with her?"

He paused so long for a reply that Fleda said: "I don't think I know what you mean by a set-to."

"Well, if she calls *you* names."

"I don't think she'll do that."

"What I mean to say is if she's angry at your backing me up — what will you do then? She can't possibly like it, you know."

"She may very well not like it; but everything depends. I must see what I shall do. You mustn't worry about me."

She spoke with decision, but Owen seemed still unsatisfied. "You won't go away, I hope?"

"Go away?"

"If she does take it ill of you."

Fleda moved to the door and opened it. "I'm not prepared to say. You must have patience and see."

"Of course I must," said Owen — "of course, of course." But he took no more advantage of the open door than to say: "You want me to be off, and I'm off in a minute. Only before I go please answer me a question. If you *should* leave my mother where would you go?"

She blinked a little at the immensity of it. "I have n't the least idea."

"I suppose you'd go back to London."

"I have n't the least idea," Fleda repeated.

"You don't — a — live anywhere in particular, do you?" the young man went on. He looked conscious as soon as he had spoken; she could see that he felt himself to have alluded more grossly than he meant to the circumstance of her having, if one were plain about it, no home of her own. He had meant it as an allusion of a highly considerate sort to all she would sacrifice in the case of a quarrel with his mother; but there was indeed no graceful way of touching on that. One just could n't be plain about it.

Fleda, wound up as she was, shrank from any treatment at all of the matter; she simply neglected his question. "I *won't* leave your mother," she said instead. "I'll produce an effect on her. I'll convince her absolutely."

"I believe you will if you look at her like that!"

She was wound up to such a height that there might well be a light in her pale fine little face — a light that, while for all return at first she simply shone back at him, was intensely reflected in his own. "I'll make her see it, I'll make her see it!" — she rang out like a silver bell. She had at that moment a perfect faith she should succeed; but it passed into something else when, the next instant, she became aware that Owen, quickly getting between her and the door she had opened, was sharply closing it, as might be said, in her face. He had done this before she could stop him, and he stood there with his hand on the knob and smiled at her strangely. Clearer than he could have spoken it was the sense of those seconds of silence.

"When I got into this I did n't know you, and now that I know you how can I tell you the difference? And *she*'s so different, so ugly and vulgar, in the light of this squabble. No, like *you* I've never known one. It's another thing, it's a new thing altogether. Listen to me a little: can't something be done?" It was what had been in the air in those moments at Kensington, and it only wanted words to be a committed act. The more reason, to the girl's excited mind, why it should n't have words; her one thought was not to hear, to keep the act uncommitted. She would do this if she had to be horrid.

"Please let me out, Mr. Gereth," she said; on which he opened the door with a debate so very brief that in thinking of these things afterwards — for she was to think of them for ever — she wondered in what tone she must have spoken. They went into the hall, where she came upon the parlour-maid, of whom she asked if Mrs. Gereth had come in.

"No, miss; and I think she has left the garden. She has gone up the back road." In other words they had the whole place to themselves. It would have been a pleasure, in a different mood, to converse with that parlour-maid.

"Please open the house-door," said Fleda.

Owen, as if in quest of his umbrella, looked vaguely about the hall — looked even wistfully up the staircase — while the neat young woman complied with Fleda's request. Owen's eyes then wandered out of the framed aperture. "I think it's awfully nice here," he struck off. "I assure you I could do with it myself."

"I should think you might, with half your things here! It's Poynton itself — almost. Good-bye, Mr. Gereth," Fleda added. Her intention had naturally been that the neat young woman, releasing the guest, should remain to close the door on his departure. That functionary, however, had acutely vanished behind a swinging screen of green baize garnished with brass nails, a horror Mrs. Gereth had not yet had time to abolish. Fleda put out her hand, but Owen turned away — he could n't find his umbrella. She passed into the open air — she was determined to get him out; and in a moment he joined her in the little plastered portico which had small resemblance to any feature of Poynton. It was, as Mrs. Gereth had said, the portico of a house in Brompton.

"Oh I don't mean with all the things here," he

explained in regard to the opinion he had just expressed. "I mean I could put up with it just as it was; it had a lot of good things, don't you think? I mean if everything was back at Poynton, if everything was all right." But the high flight of this idea showed somehow the broken wing. Fleda did n't understand his explanation unless it had reference to another and more wonderful exchange — the restoration to the great house not only of its tables and chairs but of its alienated mistress. This would imply the installation of his own life at Ricks, and obviously that of another person. Such another person could scarcely be Mona Brigstock. He put out his hand now; and once more she heard his unsounded words. "With everything patched up at the other place I could live here with *you*. Don't you see what I mean?"

She saw perfectly and, with a face in which she yet flattered herself that nothing of her vision appeared, simply gave him her hand. "Good-bye, good-bye."

He held her very firmly, keeping her even after the effort she made for release — an effort not repeated, as she felt it best not to show she was flurried. That solution — of her living with him at Ricks — disposed of him beautifully and disposed not less so of herself; it disposed admirably too of Mrs. Gereth. Fleda could only vainly wonder how it provided for poor Mona. While he looked at her, grasping her still, she felt that now indeed she was paying for his mother's extravagance at Poynton — the vividness of that lady's public plea that little Fleda Vetch was the person to ensure the general peace. It was to this vividness poor Owen had come back, and if Mrs. Gereth had had more discretion little Fleda Vetch would n't have been in a predicament. She saw that Owen had now his sharpest necessity of speech, and so long as he did n't let go her hand she could only submit to him. Her defence would be perhaps to look blank and hard; so she looked as blank and as hard as she could, with the reward of an immediate sense that this was not a bit what he wanted. It even made him flounder as for sudden compunction, some recall to duty and to honour. Yet he none the less brought out: "There's one thing I dare say I ought to tell you, if you're going so kindly to act for me; though of course you'll see for yourself it's a thing it won't do to tell *her*." What was it? He made her wait again, and while she waited, under firm coercion, she had the extraordinary impression that his simplicity was in eclipse. His natural honesty was like the scent of a flower, and she felt at this moment as if her nose had been brushed by the bloom without the odour. The allusion was undoubtedly to his mother; and was not what he meant about the matter in question the opposite of what he said — that it just *would* do to tell her? It would have been the first time he had intended the opposite of what he said, and there was certainly an interest in the example as well as a challenge to suspense in the ambiguity. "It's just that I understand from Mona, you know," he stammered; "it's just that she has made no bones about bringing home to me —!" He tried to laugh and in the effort faltered again.

"About bringing home to you?" — Fleda encouraged him.

He was sensible of it, he surmounted his difficulty. "Why, that if I don't get the things back — every blessed one of them except a few *she*'ll pick out — she won't have anything more to say to me."

Fleda after an instant encouraged him again. "To say to you?"

"Why she simply won't have me, don't you see?"

Owen's legs, not to mention his voice, had wavered while he spoke, and she felt his possession of her hand loosen so that she was free again. Her stare of perception broke into a lively laugh. "Oh you're all right, for you *will* get them. You will; you're quite safe; don't worry!" She fell back into the house with her hand on the door. "Good-bye, good-bye." She repeated it several times, laughing bravely, quite waving him away and, as he did n't move and save that he was on the other side of it, closing the door in his face quite as he had closed that of the drawing-room in hers. Never had a face, never at least had such a handsome one, been presented so straight to that offence. She even held the door a minute lest he should try to come in again. At last as she heard nothing she made a dash for the stairs and ran up.

IX

In knowing a while before all she needed she had
been far from knowing as much as that; so that once
above, where, in her room, with her sense of danger
and trouble, the age of Louis Seize suddenly struck
her as wanting in taste and point, she felt she now
for the first time knew her temptation. Owen had
put it before her with an art beyond his own dream.
Mona would cast him off if he did n't proceed to
extremities — if his negotiation with his mother
should fail he would be completely free. That negotiation depended on a young lady to whom he had
pressingly suggested the condition of his freedom;
and as if to aggravate the young lady's predicament
designing fate had sent Mrs. Gereth, as the parlour-
maid said, "up the back road." This would give the
young lady the more time to make up her mind that
nothing should come of the negotiation. There
would be different ways of putting the question to
Mrs. Gereth, and Fleda might profitably devote the
moments before her return to a selection of the way
that would most surely be tantamount to failure.
This selection indeed required no great adroitness;
it was so conspicuous that failure would be the reward
of an effective introduction of Mona. If that ab-
horred name should be properly invoked Mrs. Gereth
would resist to the death, and before envenomed
resistance Owen would certainly retire. His retire-

ment would be into single life, and Fleda reflected
that he had now gone away conscious of having practically told her so. She could only say as she waited
for the back road to disgorge that she hoped it was
a consciousness he enjoyed. There was something *she*
enjoyed, but that was a very different matter. To
know she had become to him an object of desire
gave her wings that she felt herself flutter in the air:
it was like the rush of a flood into her own accumu-
lations. These stored depths had been fathomless
and still, but now, for half an hour, in the empty
house, they spread till they overflowed. He seemed
to have made it right for her to confess to herself her
secret. Strange then there should be for him in return
nothing that such a confession could make right!
How could it make right his giving up Mona for
another woman? His position was a sorry appeal to
Fleda to legitimate that. But he did n't believe it
himself, he had none of the courage of his perversity.
She could easily see how wrong everything must be
when a man so made to be manly was wanting in
courage. She had upset him, yes, and he had spoken
out from the force of the jar of finding her there.
He had upset her too, goodness knew, but she was
one of those who could pick themselves up. She had
the real advantage, she considered, of having kept
him from seeing she had been overthrown.

She had moreover at present completely recovered
her feet, though there was in the intensity of the
effort required for this a vibration that throbbed
away into an immense allowance for the young man.
How could she after all know what, in the disturb-

ance wrought by his mother, Mona's relations with
him might have become ? If he had been able to keep
his wits, such as they were, more about him he would
probably have felt — as sharply as she felt on his
behalf — that so long as those relations were not
ended he had no right to say even the little he had
said. He had no right to appear to wish to draw in
another girl to help him to run away. If he was in a
plight he must get out of the plight himself, he must
get out of it first, and anything he should have to say
to any one else must be deferred and detached. She
herself at any rate — it was her own case that emerged
— could n't dream of assisting him save in the sense
of their common honour. She could never be the girl
to be drawn in; she could never lift her finger against
Mona. There was something in her that would make
it a shame to her for ever to have owed her happiness
to an interference. It would seem intolerably vulgar
to her to have "ousted" the daughter of the Brigstocks; and merely to have abstained even would n't
sufficiently assure her she had been straight. Nothing
was really straight but to justify her little pensioned
presence by her use; and now, won over as she was
to heroism, she could see her use only as some high
and delicate deed. She could n't in short do anything at all unless she could do it with a degree of
pride, and there would be nothing to be proud of in
having arranged for poor Owen to get off easily.
Nobody had a right to get off easily from pledges so
deep and sacred. How could Fleda doubt they had
been tremendous when she knew so well what any
pledge of her own would be ? If Mona was so formed

that she could hold such vows light this was Mona's particular affair. To have loved Owen apparently, and yet to have loved him only so much, only to the extent of a few tables and chairs, was not a thing she could so much as try to grasp. Of a different manner of loving she was herself ready to give an instance, an instance of which the beauty indeed would not be generally known. It would not perhaps if revealed be generally understood, inasmuch as the effect of the special pressure she proposed to exercise would be, should success attend it, to keep him tied to an affection that had died a sudden and violent death. Even in the ardour of her meditation Fleda remained in sight of the truth that it would be an odd result of her magnanimity to prevent her friend's shaking off a woman he disliked. If he did n't dislike Mona what was the matter with him? And if he did, Fleda asked, what was the matter with her own silly self?

Our young lady met this branch of the temptation it pleased her frankly to recognise by declaring that to encourage any such cruelty would be tortuous and base. She had nothing to do with his dislikes; she had only to do with his good nature and his good name. She had joy of him just as he was, but it was of these things she had the greatest. The worst aversion and the liveliest reaction would n't alter the fact — since one was facing facts — that but the other day his strong arms must have clasped a remarkably handsome girl as close as she had permitted. Fleda's emotion at this time was a wondrous mixture, in which Mona's permissions and Mona's beauty figured powerfully as aids to reflexion. She herself had no beauty, and *her* permissions were the stony stares she had just practised in the drawing-room — a consciousness of a kind appreciably to add to the strange sense of triumph that made her generous. We may not perhaps too much diminish the merit of that generosity if we mention that it could take the flight we are considering just because really, with the telescope of her long thought, Fleda saw what might bring her out of the wood. Mona herself would bring her out; at the least Mona possibly might. Deep down plunged the idea that even should she achieve what she had promised Owen there was still the contingency of Mona's independent action. She might by that time, under stress of temper or of whatever it was that was now moving her, have said or done the things there is no patching up. If the rupture should come from Waterbath they might all be happy yet. This was a calculation that Fleda would n't have committed to paper, but it affected the total of her sentiments. She was meanwhile so remarkably constituted that while she refused to profit by Owen's mistake, even while she judged it and hastened to cover it up, she could drink a sweetness from it that consorted little with her wishing it might n't have been made. There was no harm done, because he had instinctively known, poor dear, with whom to make it, and it was a compensation for seeing him worried that he had n't made it with some horrid mean girl who would immediately have dished him by making a still bigger one. Their protected error (for she indulged a fancy that it was hers too) was like some dangerous lovely living thing that she had caught and could keep — keep vivid and helpless in the cage of her own passion and look at and talk to all day long. She had got it well locked up there by the time that from an upper window she saw Mrs. Gereth again in the garden. At this she went down to meet her.

X

FLEDA's line had been taken, her word was quite ready: on the terrace of the painted pots she broke out before her benefactress could put a question. "His errand was perfectly simple: he came to demand that you shall pack everything straight up again and send it back as fast as the railway will carry it."

The back road had apparently been fatiguing to Mrs. Gereth; she rose there rather white and wan with her walk. A certain sharp thinness was in her ejaculation of "Oh!"—after which she glanced about her for a place to sit down. The movement was a criticism of the order of events that offered such a piece of news to a lady coming in tired; but Fleda could see that in turning over the possibilities this particular peril was the one that during the last hour her friend had turned up oftenest. At the end of the short grey day, which had been moist and mild, the sun was out; the terrace looked to the south, and a bench, formed as to legs and arms of iron representing knotted boughs, stood against the warmest wall of the house. The mistress of Ricks sank upon it and presented to her companion the handsome face she had composed to hear everything. Strangely enough it was just this fine vessel of her attention that made the girl most nervous about what she must drop in.

"Quite a 'demand,' dear, is it?" asked Mrs. Gereth, drawing in her cloak.

"Oh that's what I should call it!"— Fleda laughed to her own surprise.

"I mean with the threat of enforcement and that sort of thing."

"Distinctly with the threat of enforcement — of what would be called, I suppose, coercion."

"What sort of coercion?" said Mrs. Gereth.

"Why legal, don't you know? — what he calls setting the lawyers at you."

"Is that what he calls it?" She seemed to speak with disinterested curiosity.

"That's what he calls it," said Fleda.

Mrs. Gereth considered an instant. "Oh the lawyers!" she exclaimed lightly. Seated there almost cosily in the reddening winter sunset, only with her shoulders raised a little and her mantle tightened as if from a slight chill, she had never yet looked to Fleda so much in possession nor so far from meeting unsuspectedness halfway. "Is he going to send them down here?"

"I dare say he thinks it may come to that."

"The lawyers can scarcely do the packing," Mrs. Gereth playfully remarked.

"I suppose he means them — in the first place at least — to try to talk you over."

"In the first place, eh? And what does he mean in the second?"

Fleda debated; she had n't foreseen that so simple an enquiry could disconcert her. "I'm afraid I don't know."

"Did n't you ask?" Mrs. Gereth spoke as if she might have said "What then were you doing all the while?"

"I did n't ask very much," said her companion. "He has been gone some time. The great thing seemed to be to understand clearly that he would n't be content with anything less than what he mentioned."

"My just giving everything back?"

"Your just giving everything back."

"Well, darling, what did you tell him?" Mrs. Gereth blandly proceeded.

Fleda faltered again, wincing at the term of endearment, at what the words took for granted, charged with the confidence she had now committed herself to betray. "I told him I'd tell you!" She smiled, but felt her smile too poor a thing and even that Mrs. Gereth had begun to look at her with some fixedness.

"Did he seem very angry?"

"He seemed very sad. He takes it very hard," Fleda added.

"And how does *she* take it?"

"Ah that — that I felt a delicacy about asking."

"So you did n't get it out of him?" The words had the note of surprise.

Fleda was embarrassed; she had not made up her mind definitely to lie. "I did n't think you'd care." That small untruth she would risk.

"Well — I don't!" Mrs. Gereth declared; and Fleda felt less guilty to hear her, for the words were as far from the purpose as her own. "Did n't you say anything in return?" the elder woman continued.

"Do you mean in the way of justifying you?"

"I did n't mean to trouble you to do that. My justification," said Mrs. Gereth, sitting there warmly and, in the lucidity of her thought, which nevertheless hung back a little, dropping her eyes on the gravel — "my justification was all the past. My justification was the cruelty —!" But at this, with a short sharp gesture, she checked herself. "It's too good of me to talk — now." She produced these sentences with a cold patience, as if addressing Fleda in the girl's virtual and actual character of Owen's representative. Our young lady crept to and fro before the bench, combating the sense that it was occupied by a judge, looking at her boot-toes, reminding herself in doing so of Mona, and lightly crunching the pebbles as she walked. She moved about because she was afraid, putting off from moment to moment the exercise of the courage she had been sure she possessed. That courage would all come to her if she could only be equally sure that what she should be called upon to do for Owen would be to suffer. She had wondered, while Mrs. Gereth spoke, how that lady would describe her justification. She had described it as if to be irreproachably fair, give her adversary the benefit of every doubt and then dismiss the question for ever. "Of course," Mrs. Gereth went on, "if we did n't succeed in showing him at Poynton the ground we took it's simply that he shuts his eyes. What I supposed was that you would have given him your opinion that if I was the woman so signally to assert myself I'm also the woman to rest on it unshakeably enough."

Fleda stopped in front of her hostess. "I gave him my opinion that you're very logical, very obstinate and very proud."

"Quite right, my dear: I'm a rank bigot — about that sort of thing!" Mrs. Gereth jerked her head at the contents of the house. "I've never denied it. I'd kidnap — to save them, to convert them — the children of heretics. When I know I'm right I go to the stake. Oh he may burn me alive!" she cried with a happy face. "Did he abuse me?" she then demanded.

Fleda had remained there, gathering in her purpose. "How little you know him!"

Mrs. Gereth stared, then broke into a laugh that her companion had not expected. "Ah my dear, certainly not so well as you!" The girl, at this, turned away again — she felt she looked too conscious; and she was aware that during a pause Mrs. Gereth's eyes watched her as she went. She faced about afresh to meet them, but what she met was a question that re-enforced them. "Why had you a 'delicacy' as to speaking of Mona?"

She stopped again before the bench, and an inspiration came to her. "I should think *you* would know," she said with proper dignity.

Blankness was for a moment on Mrs. Gereth's brow; then light broke — she visibly remembered the scene in the breakfast-room after Mona's night at Poynton. "Because I contrasted you — told him *you* were the one?" Her eyes looked deep. "You were — you are still!"

Fleda gave a bold dramatic laugh. "Thank you, my love — with all the best things at Ricks!"

Mrs. Gereth considered, trying to penetrate, as it seemed; but at last she brought out roundly: "For you, you know, I'd send them back!"

The girl's heart gave a tremendous bound; the right way dawned upon her in a flash. Obscurity indeed the next moment engulfed this course, but for a few thrilled seconds she had understood. To send the things back "for her" meant of course to send them back if there were even a dim chance that she might become mistress of them. Fleda's palpitation was not allayed as she asked herself what portent Mrs. Gereth had suddenly descried of such a chance: the light could be there but by a sudden suspicion of her secret. This suspicion in turn was a tolerably straight consequence of that implied view of the propriety of surrender from which she was well aware she could say nothing to dissociate herself. What she first felt was that if she wished to rescue the spoils she wished also to rescue her secret. So she looked as innocent as she could and said as quickly as she might: "For me? Why in the world for me?"

"Because you're so awfully keen."

"Am I? Do I strike you so? You know I hate him," Fleda went on.

She had the sense for a while of Mrs. Gereth's regarding her with the detachment of some stern clever stranger. "Then what's the matter with you? Why do you want me to give in?"

Fleda hesitated; she felt herself reddening. "I've only said your son wants it. I have n't said *I* do."

"Then say it and have done with it!"

This was more peremptory than any word her friend, though often speaking in her presence with much point, had ever yet deliberately addressed her. It affected her like the crack of a whip, but she confined herself with an effort to taking it as a reminder that she must keep her head. "I know he has his engagement to carry out."

"His engagement to marry? Why, it's just that engagement we loathe!"

"Why should *I* loathe it?" Fleda asked with a strained smile. Then before Mrs. Gereth could reply she pursued: "I'm thinking of his general undertaking — to give her the house as she originally saw it."

"To give her the house!" — Mrs. Gereth brought up the words from the depth of the unspeakable. The effect was like the moan of an autumn wind, and she turned as pale as if she had heard of the landing, there on her coast, of a foreign army.

"I'm thinking," Fleda continued, "of the simple question of his keeping faith on an important clause of his contract: it does n't matter whether with a stupid person or with a monster of cleverness. I'm thinking of his honour and his good name."

"The honour and good name of a man you hate?"

"Certainly," the girl resolutely answered. "I don't see why you should talk as if one had a petty mind. You don't think so. It's not on that assumption you've ever dealt with me. I can do your son justice — as he put his case to me."

"Ah then he did put his case to you!" Mrs. Gereth

cried with an accent of triumph. "You seemed to speak just now as if really nothing of any consequence had passed between you."

"Something always passes when one has a little imagination," our young lady declared.

"I take it you don't mean that Owen has any!" Mrs. Gereth answered with her large laugh.

Fleda had a pause. "No, I don't mean that Owen has any," she returned at last.

"Why is it you hate him so?" her hostess abruptly put to her.

"Should I love him for all he has made you suffer?"

Mrs. Gereth slowly rose at this and, coming over the walk, took her young friend to her breast and kissed her. She then passed into one of Fleda's an arm perversely and imperiously sociable. "Let us move a little," she said, holding her close and giving a slight shiver. They strolled along the terrace and she brought out another question. "He *was* eloquent then, poor dear — he poured forth the story of his wrongs?"

Fleda smiled down at her companion, who, cloaked and perceptibly bowed, leaned on her heavily and gave her an odd unwonted sense of age and cunning. She took refuge in an evasion. "He could n't tell me anything I did n't know pretty well already."

"It's very true you know everything. No, dear, you have n't a petty mind; you 've a lovely imagination and you're the nicest creature in the world. If you were inane, like most girls — like every one in fact — I'd have insulted you, I'd have outraged you, and then you'd have fled from me in terror. No,

117

now that I think of it," Mrs. Gereth went on, "you would n't have fled from me: nothing, on the contrary, would have made you budge. You'd have cuddled into your warm corner, but you'd have been wounded and weeping and martyrised, and have taken every opportunity to tell people I'm a brute — as indeed I should have been!" They went to and fro, and she would n't allow Fleda, who laughed and protested, to attenuate with any light civility this spirited picture. She praised her cleverness and her patience; then she said it was getting cold and dark and they must go in to tea. She delayed quitting the place, however, and reverted instead to Owen's ultimatum, about which she asked another question or two; in particular whether it had struck Fleda that he really believed she'd give way.

"I think he really believes that if I try hard enough I can make you." After uttering which words our young woman stopped short and emulated the embrace she had received a few moments before.

"And you've promised to try: I see. You did n't tell me that either," Mrs. Gereth added as they moved. "But you're rascal enough for anything!" While Fleda was occupied in thinking in what terms she could explain why she had indeed been rascal enough for the reticence thus denounced, her companion broke out with a question somewhat irrelevant and even in form somewhat profane. "Why the devil, at any rate, does n't it come off?"

Fleda hesitated. "You mean their marriage?"

"Of course I mean their marriage!"

She thought again. "I have n't the least idea."

"You did n't ask him ?"

"Oh how in the world can **you** fancy ?" She spoke in a shocked tone.

"Fancy your putting a question so indelicate ? *I* should have put it — I mean in your place; but I'm quite coarse, thank God!" Fleda felt privately that she herself was coarse, or at any rate would presently have to be; and Mrs. Gereth, with a purpose that struck her as increasing, continued: "What then *was* the day to be ? Was n't it just one of these ?"

"I'm sure I don't remember."

It was part of the great rupture and an effect of Mrs. Gereth's character that up to this moment she had been completely and haughtily indifferent to that detail. Now, however, she had a visible reason for being sure. She bethought herself and she broke out: "Is n't the day past ?" Then stopping short she added: "Upon my word they must have put it off!" As Fleda made no answer to this she became insistent. "*Have* they put it off ?"

"I have n't the least idea," said the girl.

Her hostess was again looking at her hard. "Did n't he tell you — did n't he say anything about it ?"

Fleda meanwhile had had time to make her reflexions, which were moreover the continued throb of those that had occupied the interval between Owen's departure and his mother's return. If she should now repeat his words this would n't at all play the game of her definite vow; it would only play the game of her little gagged and blinded desire. She could calculate well enough the result of telling Mrs. Gereth, how she had had it from Owen's troubled lips that

Mona was only waiting for the restitution and would do nothing without it. The thing was to obtain the restitution without imparting that knowledge. The only way also not to impart it was not to tell any truth at all about it; and the only way to meet this last condition was to reply to her companion as she presently did. "He told me nothing whatever. He did n't touch on the subject."

"Not in any way?"

"Not in any way."

Mrs. Gereth watched her and considered. "You have n't the notion they're waiting for the things?"

"How should I have? I'm not in their counsels."

"I dare say they are — or that Mona is." Mrs. Gereth weighed it again; she had a bright idea. "If I don't give in I'll be hanged if she'll not break off."

"She'll never, never break off," said Fleda.

"Are you sure?"

"I can't be sure, but it's my belief."

"Derived from *him?*"

The girl hung fire a few seconds. "Derived from him."

Mrs. Gereth gave her a long last look, then turned abruptly away. "It's an awful bore you did n't really get it out of him! Well, come to tea," she added rather dryly, passing straight into the house.

XI

THE sense of her dryness, which was ominous of a complication, made Fleda, before complying, linger a little on the terrace: she felt the need moreover of taking breath after such a flight into the cold air of denial. When at last she rejoined Mrs. Gereth she found her erect before the drawing-room fire. Their tea had been set out in the same quarter, and the mistress of the house, for whom the preparation of it was generally a high and undelegated function, preserved a posture to which the hissing urn made no appeal. This omission was such a further sign of something to come that to disguise her apprehension Fleda straightway and without apology took the duty in hand; only however to be promptly reminded that she was performing it confusedly and not counting the journeys of the little silver shovel she emptied into the pot. "Not *five*, my dear — the usual three," said her hostess with the same irony; watching her then in silence while she clumsily corrected her mistake. The tea took some minutes to draw, and Mrs. Gereth availed herself of them suddenly to exclaim: "You have n't yet told me, you know, how it is you propose to 'make' me!"

"Give everything back?" Fleda looked into the pot again and uttered her question with a briskness that she felt to be a trifle overdone. "Why, by putting

the question well before you; by being so eloquent
that I shall persuade you, shall act on you; by making
you sorry for having gone so far," she said boldly.
"By simply and earnestly asking it of you, in short;
and by reminding you at the same time that it's the
first thing I ever have so asked. Oh you've done
things for me — endless and beautiful things," she
exclaimed; "but you've done them all from your own
generous impulse — I've never so much as hinted to
you to lend me a postage-stamp."

"Give me a cup of tea," said Mrs. Gereth. A moment later, taking the cup, she replied: "No, you've
never asked me for a postage-stamp."

"That gives me a pull!" Fleda returned with
briskness.

"Puts you in the situation of expecting I shall do
this thing just simply to oblige you?"

Well, the girl took it so. "You said a while ago that
for me you *would* do it."

"For you, but not for your eloquence. Do you
understand what I mean by the difference?" Mrs.
Gereth asked as she stood stirring her tea.

Fleda, to postpone answering, looked round, while
she drank it, at the beautiful room. "I don't in the
least like, you know, your having brought away so
much. It was a great shock to me, on my arrival
here, to find how you had plunged."

"Give me some more tea," said Mrs. Gereth; and
there was a moment's silence as Fleda poured out
another cup. "If you were shocked, my dear, I'm
bound to say you concealed your shock."

"I know I did. I was afraid to show it."

Mrs. Gereth drank off her second cup. "And you're not afraid now?"

"No, I'm not afraid now."

"What has made the difference?"

"I've pulled myself together." Fleda paused; then she added: "And I've seen Mr. Owen."

"You've seen Mr. Owen"— Mrs. Gereth concurred. She put down her cup and sank into a chair in which she leaned back, resting her head and gazing at her young friend. "Yes, I did tell you a while ago that for you I'd do it. But you have n't told me yet what you'll do in return."

Fleda cast about. "Anything in the wide world you may require."

"Oh 'anything' is nothing at all! That's too easily said." Mrs. Gereth, reclining more completely, closed her eyes with an air of disgust, an air indeed of yielding to drowsiness.

Fleda looked at her quiet face, which the appearance of oblivious sleep always made particularly handsome; she noted how much the ordeal of the last few weeks had added to its indications of age. "Well then, try me with something. What is it you demand?"

At this, opening her eyes, Mrs. Gereth sprang straight up. "Get him away from her!"

Fleda marvelled: her companion had in an instant become young again. "Away from Mona? How in the world —?"

"By not looking like a fool!" cried Mrs. Gereth very sharply. She kissed her, however, on the spot, to make up for this roughness, and with an officious hand took off the hat which, on coming into the house, our young lady had not removed. She applied a friendly touch to the girl's hair and gave a business-like pull to her jacket. "I say don't look like an idiot, because you happen not to be one — not the least bit. *I*'m idiotic; I've been so, I've just discovered, ever since our first days together. I've been a precious donkey. But that's another affair."

Fleda, as if she humbly assented, went through no form of controverting this; she simply stood passive to her friend's sudden invocation of her personal charms. "How can I get him away from her?" she presently demanded.

"By letting yourself go."

"By letting myself go?" She spoke mechanically, still more like an idiot, and felt as if her face flamed out the insincerity of her question. It was vividly back again, the vision of the real way to act on Mrs. Gereth. This lady's movements were now rapid; she turned off from her as quickly as she had seized her, and Fleda sat down to steady herself for full responsibility.

Her hostess, without taking up her appeal, gave a violent poke at the fire and again dealt with her. "You've done two things then to-day — have n't you? — that you've never done before. One has been asking me the service or favour or concession — whatever you call it — that you just mentioned; the other has been telling me (certainly too for the first time!) an immense little fib."

"An immense little fib?" Fleda felt weak; she was glad of the support of her seat.

"An immense big one then!" Mrs. Gereth said sharply. "You don't in the least 'hate' Owen, my darling. You care for him very much. In fact, my own, you're in love with him — there! Don't tell me any more lies!" she cried with a voice and a face under which Fleda recognised that there was nothing but to hold one's self and bear up. When once the truth was out it was out, and she could see more and more every instant that it offered the only way. She accepted therefore what had to come; she leaned back her head and closed her eyes as her companion had done just before. She would have covered her face with her hands but for the still greater shame. "Oh you're a wonder, a wonder," said Mrs. Gereth; "you're magnificent, and I was right, as soon as I saw you, to pick you out and trust you!" Fleda closed her eyes tighter at this last word, but her friend kept it up. "I never dreamed of it till a while ago — when, after he had come and gone, we were face to face. Then something stuck out of you; it strongly impressed me, and I did n't know at first quite what to make of it. It was that you had just been with him and that you were not natural. Not natural to *me*," she added with a smile. "I sat forward, I promise you, and all that this might mean was to dawn upon me when you said you had asked nothing about Mona. It put me on the scent, but I did n't show you, did I? I felt it was *in* you, deep down, and that I must draw it out. Well, I *have* drawn it, and it's a blessing. Yesterday, when you shed tears at breakfast, I was awfully puzzled. What has been the matter with you all the while? Why Fleda, it is n't a crime, don't you know that?" cried the delighted amazing woman. "When I was a girl I was always in love, and not always with such nice people as Owen. I did n't behave so well as you; compared with you I think I must have been odious. But if you're proud and reserved it's your own affair; I'm proud too, though I'm not reserved — that's what spoils it. I'm stupid above all — that's what I am; so dense I really blush for it. However, no one but you could have deceived me. If I trusted you more-over it was exactly to be cleverer than myself. You must be so now more than ever!" Suddenly Fleda felt her hands grasped: Mrs. Gereth had plumped down at her feet and was leaning on her knees. "Save him — save him: you *can!*" she passionately pleaded. "How could you not like him when he's such a dear? He *is* a dear, darling; there's no harm in my own boy! You can do what you will with him — you know you can! What else does he give us all this time for? Get him away from her: it's as if he entreated you, poor wretch! Don't abandon him to such a fate, and I'll never abandon *you*. Think of him with that creature, that family, that future! If you'll take him I'll give up everything. There, it's a solemn promise, the most sacred of my life. Get the better of her and he shall have every stick I grabbed. Give me your word and I'll accept it. I'll write for the packers to-night!"

Fleda, before this, had fallen forward on her com-panion's neck, and the two women, clinging together, had got up while the younger wailed on the other's bosom. "You smooth it down because you see more in it than there can ever be; but after my hideous double game how will you be able to believe in me again?"

"I see in it simply what *must* be, if you've a single spark of pity. Where on earth was the double game when you've behaved like such a saint? You've been beautiful, you've been exquisite, and all our trouble's over."

Fleda, drying her eyes, shook her head ever so sadly. "No, Mrs. Gereth, it is n't over. I can't do what you ask — I can't meet your condition."

Mrs. Gereth stared; the cloud again darkened her face. "Why, in the name of goodness, when you adore him? I know what you see in him," she declared in another tone. "You're quite right!"

Fleda gave a faint stubborn smile. "He cares for her too much."

"Then why does n't he marry her? He's giving you an extraordinary chance."

"He does n't dream I've ever thought of him," said Fleda. "Why should he if you did n't?"

"It was n't with me you were in love, my duck." Then Mrs. Gereth added: "I'll go and tell him."

"If you do any such thing you shall never see me again — absolutely, literally never!"

Mrs. Gereth looked hard at her young friend, betraying how she saw she must believe her. "Then you're perverse, you're wicked. Will you swear he does n't know?"

"Of course he does n't know!" cried Fleda indignantly.

Her benefactress was silent a little. "And that he has no feeling on *his* side?"

"For me?" Fleda stared. "Before he has even married her?"

Mrs. Gereth gave a sharp laugh at this. "He ought at least to appreciate your wit. Oh my dear, you *are* a treasure! Does n't he appreciate anything? Has he given you absolutely no symptom — not looked a look, not breathed a sigh?"

"The case," said Fleda coldly, "is as I 've had the honour to state it."

"Then he 's as big a donkey as his mother! But you know you 've got to account for their delay," Mrs. Gereth remarked.

"Why have I got to?" Fleda asked after a moment.

"Because you were closeted with him here so long. You can't pretend at present, you know, not to have any art."

The girl debated; she was conscious that she must choose between two risks. She had had a secret and the secret was spoiled. Owen had one, ripe but from yesterday, still unbruised, and the greater risk now was that his mother should lay her formidable hand upon it. All Fleda's tenderness for him moved her to protect it; so she faced the smaller peril. "Their delay," she brought herself to reply, "may perhaps be Mona's doing. I mean because he has lost her the things."

Mrs. Gereth jumped at this. "So that she 'll break altogether if I keep them?"

Fleda winced. "I 've told you what I believe about that. She 'll make scenes and conditions; she 'll worry him. But she 'll hold him fast; she 'll never let him go."

Mrs. Gereth turned it over. "Well, I'll keep them to try her," she finally pronounced; at which Fleda felt quite sick, as for having given everything and got nothing.

XII

"I MUST in common decency let him know I've talked of the matter with you," she said to her hostess that evening. "What answer do you wish me to write him?"

"Write him that you must see him again," said Mrs. Gereth.

Fleda looked very blank. "What on earth am I to see him for?"

"For anything you like!"

The girl would have been struck with the levity of this had she not already, in an hour, felt the extent of the change suddenly wrought in her commerce with her friend — wrought above all, to that friend's view, in her relation to the great issue. The effect of all that had followed Owen's visit was to make this relation the very key of the crisis. Pressed upon her, goodness knew, the crisis had been, but it now put forth big encircling arms — arms that squeezed till they hurt and she must cry out. It was as if everything at Ricks had been poured into a common receptacle, a public ferment of emotion and zeal, out of which it was ladled up, with a splash, to be tasted and talked about; everything at least but the one little treasure of knowledge that she kept back. She ought to have liked this, she reflected, because it meant sympathy, meant a closer union with the source of so much in her life that had been beautiful and renovating; but there were fine instincts in her that stood off. She had had — and it was not merely at this time — to recognise that there were things for which Mrs. Gereth's famous *flair* was not so happy as for bargains and "marks." It would n't be happy now as to the best action on the knowledge she had just gained; yet as from this moment they were still more intimately together, so a person deeply in her debt would simply have to stand and meet what was to come. There were ways in which she could sharply incommode such a person, and not only with the best conscience in the world but with a high brutality of good intentions. One of the straightest of these strokes, Fleda saw, would be the dance of delight over the mystery she, terrible woman, had profaned; the loud lawful tactless joy of the explorer leaping upon the strand. Like any other lucky discoverer she would take possession of the fortunate island. She was nothing if not practical: almost the only thing she took account of in her young friend's soft secret was the excellent use she could make of it — a use so much to her taste that she refused to feel a hindrance in the quality of the material. Fleda put into Mrs. Gereth's answer to her question a good deal more meaning than it would have occurred to her a few hours before that she was prepared to put, but she had on the spot a foreboding that even so broad a hint would live to be bettered.

"Do you suggest I shall propose to him to come down here again?" she soon proceeded.

"Dear no. Say you'll go up to town and meet him." It *was* bettered, the broad hint; and Fleda

felt this to be still more the case when, returning to
the subject before they went to bed, her companion
said: "I make him over to you wholly, you know —
to do what you like with. Deal with him in your own
clever way — I ask no questions. All I ask is that
you put it through."

"That's charming," Fleda replied, "but it does n't
tell me a bit, you'll be so good as to consider, in
what terms to write to him. It's not an answer from
you to the message I was to give you."

"The answer to his message is perfectly distinct.
He shall have everything in the place the minute
he'll say he'll marry you."

"You really pretend," Fleda asked, "to think me
capable of transmitting him that news?"

"What else can I really pretend — when you
threaten so to cast me off if I speak the word myself?"

"Oh if *you* speak the word —!" the girl murmured
very gravely; yet happy at least to know that in this
direction Mrs. Gereth confessed herself warned and
helpless. Then she added: "How can I go on living
with you on a footing of which I so deeply disap-
prove? Thinking as I do that you've despoiled him
far more than is just or merciful — for if I expected
you to take something I did n't in the least expect
you to take everything — how can I stay here without
a sense that I'm backing you up in your cruelty and
participating in your ill-gotten gains?" Fleda was
determined that if she had the chill of her exposed
and investigated state she should also have the convenience of it, and that if Mrs. Gereth popped in
and out of the chamber of her soul she would at least

return the freedom. "I shall quite hate, you know, in a day or two, every object that surrounds you — become blind to all the beauty and rarity that I formerly delighted in. Don't think me harsh; there's no use in my not being frank now. If I leave you everything's at an end."

Mrs. Gereth, however, was imperturbable: Fleda had to recognise that her advantage had become too real. "It's too beautiful, the way you care for him; it's music in my ears. Nothing else but such a passion could make you say such things; that's the way I should have been too, my dear. Why did n't you tell me sooner? I'd have gone right in for you; I never would have moved a candlestick. Don't stay with me if it torments you: don't, if it costs you so much, be where you see all the plunder. Go up to town — go back for a little to your father's. It need be only for a little; two or three weeks will make us all right. Your father will take you and be glad, if you'll only make him understand what it's a question of — of your getting yourself off his hands for ever. I'll make him understand, you know, if you feel shy. I'd take you up myself, I'd go with you to spare your being bored: we'd put up at an hotel and we might amuse ourselves a bit. We have n't had much innocent pleasure since we met, have we? But of course that would n't suit our book. I should be a bugaboo to Owen — I should be fatally in the way. Your chance is there — your chance is to be alone. For God's sake use it to the right end. If you're in want of money I've a little I can give you. But I ask no questions — not a question as small as your shoe!"

She asked no questions, but she took the most extraordinary things for granted: Fleda felt this still more at the end of a couple of days. On the second of these our young lady wrote to Owen: her emotion had to a certain degree cleared itself — there was something she could briefly say. If she had given everything to Mrs. Gereth and as yet got nothing, so she had on the other hand quickly reacted — it took but a night — against the discouragement of her first check. Her desire to serve him was too passionate, the sense that he counted upon her too sweet: these things caught her up again and gave her a new patience and a new subtlety. It should n't really be for nothing she had given so much; deep within her burned again the resolve to get something back. So what she wrote to Owen was simply that she had had a great scene with his mother, but that he must be patient and give her time. It was difficult, as they both had expected, but she was working her hardest for him. She had made an impression — she would do everything to follow it up. Meanwhile he must keep intensely quiet and take no other steps; he must only trust her and pray for her and believe in her perfect loyalty. She made no allusion whatever to Mona's attitude, nor to his not being, as regarded that young lady, master of the situation; but she said in a postscript, referring to his mother, "Of course she wonders a good deal why your marriage does n't take place." After the letter had gone she regretted having used the word "loyalty"; there were two or three vaguer terms she might as well have employed. The answer she immediately received from Owen was a little note the deficiencies of which she met by describing it to herself as pathetically simple, but which, to prove that Mrs. Gereth might ask as many questions as she liked, she at once made his mother read. He had no art with his pen, he had not even a good hand, and his letter, a short profession of friendly confidence, was couched but in a few familiar and colourless words of acknowledgement and assent. The gist of it was that he would certainly, since Miss Vetch recommended it, not hurry mamma too much. He would n't for the present cause her to be approached by any one else, but would nevertheless continue to hope she'd see she must really come round. "Of course, you know," he added, "she can't keep me waiting indefinitely. Please give her my love and tell her that. If it can be done peaceably I know you're just the one to do it."

Fleda had awaited his rejoinder in deep suspense; such was her imagination of the possibility of his having, as she tacitly phrased it, let himself go on paper that when it arrived she was at first almost afraid to open it. There was indeed a distinct danger, for if he should take it into his head to write her love-letters the whole chance of aiding him would drop: she should have to return them, she should have to decline all further communication with him; it would be the end alike of dreams and of realities. This imagination of Fleda's was a faculty that easily embraced all the heights and depths and extremities of things; that made a single mouthful in particular of any tragic or desperate necessity. She was perhaps at first just a trifle disappointed not to find in the risky note some syllable that strayed from the text; but the next moment she had risen to a point of view from which it presented itself as a production almost inspired in its simplicity. It was simple even for Owen, and she wondered what had given him the cue to be more so than usual. Then she admirably saw how natures that are right just do the things that are right. He was n't clever — his manner of writing showed it; but the cleverest man in England could n't have had more the instinct that in the conditions was the supremely happy one, the instinct of giving her something that would do beautifully to be shown to Mrs. Gereth. This was deep divination, for naturally he could n't know the line Mrs. Gereth was taking. It was furthermore explained — and that was the most touching part of all — by his wish that she herself should notice how awfully well he was behaving. His very bareness called her attention to his virtue, and these were the exact fruits of her beautiful and terrible admonition. He was cleaving to Mona; he was doing his duty; he was making tremendously sure he should be without reproach.

If Fleda handed her friend the letter as a triumphant gage of the innocence of the young man's heart her elation lived but a moment after Mrs. Gereth had pounced on the telltale spot in it. "Why in the world then does he still not breathe a breath about the day, the *day*, the DAY?" She repeated the word with a crescendo of superior acuteness; she proclaimed that nothing could be more marked than its absence — an absence that simply spoke volumes. What did it prove in fine but that she was producing

the effect she had toiled for — that she had settled or
was rapidly settling Mona?

Such a challenge Fleda was obliged in some manner to take up. "You may be settling Mona," she
returned with a smile, "but I can hardly regard it as
sufficient evidence that you're settling Mona's lover."

"Why not, with such a studied omission on his
part to gloss over in any manner the painful tension
existing between them — the painful tension that,
under Providence, I've been the means of bringing
about? He gives you by his silence clear notice that
his marriage is practically off."

"He speaks to me of the only thing that concerns
me. He gives me clear notice that he abates not one
jot of his demand."

"Well then let him take the only way to get it satisfied!"

Fleda had no need to ask again what such a way
might be, nor was the ground supplied her cut away
by the almost irritating confidence with which Mrs.
Gereth could make her own arguments wait on her
own wishes. These days, which dragged their length
into a strange uncomfortable fortnight, had already
borne more testimony to that element than all the
other time the conspirators had lived through. Our
young woman had been at first far from measuring
the extent of an element that Owen himself would
probably have described as her companion's "cheek."
She lived now in a kind of bath of boldness, felt as
if a fierce light poured in upon her from windows
opened wide; and the singular part of the ordeal was
that she could n't protest against it fully without

incurring even to her own mind some reproach of ingratitude, some charge of smallness. If Mrs. Gereth's apparent determination to hustle her into Owen's arms was accompanied with an air of holding her dignity rather cheap, this was after all only as a consequence of her being held in respect to some other attributes rather dear. It was a new version of the old story of being kicked upstairs. The wonderful woman was the same woman who, in the summer, at Poynton, had been so puzzled to conceive why a good-natured girl should n't have contributed more to the personal rout of the Brigstocks — should n't have been grateful even for the handsome published puff of Fleda Vetch. Only her passion was keener now and her scruple more absent; the prolonged contest made a demand on her, and her pugnacity had become one with her constant habit of using such weapons as she could pick up. She had no imagination about anybody's life save on the side she bumped against. Fleda was quite aware that she would have otherwise been a rare creature, but a rare creature was originally just what she had struck her as being. Mrs. Gereth had really no perception of anybody's nature — had only one question about persons: were they clever or stupid? To be clever meant to know the "marks." Fleda knew them by direct inspiration, and a warm recognition of this had been her friend's tribute to her character. The girl now had hours of sombre hope she might never see anything "good" again: that kind of experience was clearly so broken a reed, so fallible a source of peace. One would be more at peace in some vulgar little place that should owe its *cachet* to a Universal Provider. There were nice strong simplifying horrors in West Kensington; it was as if they beckoned her and wooed her back to them. She had a relaxed recollection of Waterbath; and of her reasons for staying on at Ricks the force was rapidly ebbing. One of these was her pledge to Owen — her vow to press his mother close; the other was the fact that of the two discomforts, that of being prodded by Mrs. Gereth and that of appearing to run after somebody else, the former remained for a while the more endurable.

As the days passed, however, it became plainer that her only chance of success would be in lending herself to this low appearance. Then moreover, at last, her nerves settling the question, the choice was simply imposed by the violence done her taste — done whatever was left of that high principle, at least, after the free and reckless satisfaction, for months, of great drafts and appeals. It was all very well to try to evade discussion: Owen Gereth was looking to her for a struggle, and it was n't a bit of a struggle to be disgusted and dumb. She was on too strange a footing — that of having presented an ultimatum and having had it torn up in her face. In such a case as that the envoy always departed; he never sat gaping and dawdling before the city. Mrs. Gereth every morning looked publicly into *The Morning Post*, the only newspaper she received; and every morning she treated the blankness of that journal as fresh evidence that everything was "off." What did the *Post* exist for but to tell you your children were wretchedly married? — so that if such a fount of misery was dry what could you do but infer that for once you had miraculously escaped? She almost taunted Fleda with supineness in not getting something out of somebody — in the same breath indeed in which she drenched her with a kind of appreciation more onerous to the girl than blame. Mrs. Gereth herself had of course washed her hands of the matter; but Fleda knew people who knew Mona and would be sure to be in her confidence — inconceivable people who admired her and had the "entrée" of Waterbath. What was the use therefore of being the most natural and the easiest of letter-writers, if no sort of side-light — in some pretext for correspondence — was, by a brilliant creature, to be got out of such barbarians? Fleda was not only a brilliant creature, but she heard herself commended in these days for attractions new and strange: she figured suddenly in the queer conversations of Ricks as a distinguished, almost as a dangerous, beauty. That retouching of her hair and dress in which her friend had impulsively indulged on a first glimpse of her secret was by implication very frequently repeated. She had the impression not only of being advertised and offered, but of being counselled, enlightened, initiated in ways she scarcely understood — arts obscure even to a poor girl who had had, in good society and motherless poverty, to look straight at realities and fill out blanks.

These arts, when Mrs. Gereth's spirits were high, were handled with a brave and cynical humour with which Fleda's fancy could keep no step: they left our young lady wondering what on earth her companion wanted her to do. "I want you to cut in!" — that was Mrs. Gereth's familiar and comprehensive phrase for the course she prescribed. She challenged again and again Fleda's picture, as she called it (though the sketch was too slight to deserve the name), of the indifference to which a prior attachment had committed the proprietor of Poynton. "Do you mean to say that, Mona or no Mona, he could see you that way, day after day, and not have the ordinary feelings of a man? Don't you know a little more, you absurd affected thing, what men *are*, the brutes?" This was the sort of interrogation to which Fleda was fitfully and irrelevantly treated. She had grown almost used to the refrain. "Do you mean to say that when, the other day, one had quite made you over to him, the great gawk, and he was, on this very spot, utterly alone with you — ?" The poor girl at this point never left any doubt of what she meant to say; but Mrs. Gereth could be trusted to break out in another place and at another time. At last Fleda wrote to her father that he must take her in a little, take her in while she looked about; and when, to her companion's delight, she returned to London that lady went with her to the station and wafted her on her way. *The Morning Post* had been delivered as they left the house, and Mrs. Gereth had brought it with her for the traveller, who never spent a penny on a newspaper. On the platform, however, when this young person was ticketed, labelled and seated, she opened it at the window of the carriage, exclaiming as usual, after looking into it a moment, "Nothing, nothing, nothing: don't tell *me!*" Every day that there was nothing was a nail in the coffin of the marriage. An instant later the train was off, but, moving quickly beside it, while Fleda leaned inscrutably forth, Mrs. Gereth grasped her friend's hand and looked up with wonderful eyes. "Only let yourself go, darling — only let yourself go!"

XIII

THAT she desired to ask no prudish questions Mrs.
Gereth conscientiously proved by closing her lips
tight after Fleda had gone to London. No letter
from Ricks arrived at West Kensington, and Fleda,
with nothing to communicate that could be to the
taste of either party, forbore to open a correspondence.
If her heart had been less heavy she might have been
amused to feel how much free rope this reticence of
Ricks seemed to signify to her she could take. She
had at all events no good news for her friend save in
the sense that her silence was not bad news. She was
not yet in a position to write that she had "cut in";
but neither, on the other hand, had she gathered
material for announcing that Mona was undissever-
able from her prey. She had made no use of the pen
so glorified by Mrs. Gereth to wake up the echoes of
Waterbath; she had sedulously abstained from enquiring what in any quarter, far or near, was said or
suggested or supposed. She only spent a matutinal
penny on *The Morning Post;* she only saw on each
occasion that that inspired sheet had as little to say
about the imminence as about the collapse of certain
nuptials. It was at the same time obvious that Mrs.
Gereth triumphed on these occasions much more
than she trembled, and that with a few such triumphs
repeated she should cease to tremble at all. What
came out most, however, was that she had had a rare

143

preconception of the circumstances that would have
ministered, had Fleda been disposed, to the girl's
cutting in. It was brought home to Fleda that these
circumstances would have particularly favoured
intervention; she was promptly forced to do them a
secret justice. One of the effects of her intimacy with
Mrs. Gereth was that she had quite lost all sense of
intimacy with any one else. The lady of Ricks had
made a desert round her, possessing and absorbing
her so utterly that other partakers had fallen away.
Had n't she been admonished, months before, that
people considered they had lost her and were recon-
ciled on the whole to the privation? Her present
position in the great unconscious town showed distinctly for obscure: she regarded it at any rate with
eyes suspicious of that lesson. She neither wrote notes
nor received them; she indulged in no reminders nor
knocked at any doors; she wandered vaguely in the
western wilderness or cultivated shy forms of that
"household art" for which she had had a respect
before tasting the bitter tree of knowledge. Her only
plan was to be as quiet as a mouse, and when she
failed in the attempt to lose herself in the flat surburb
she resembled — or thought she did — a lonely fly
crawling over a dusty chart.

How had Mrs. Gereth known in advance that if
she had chosen to be "vile" (that was what Fleda
called it) everything would happen to help her? —
especially the way her poor father doddered after
breakfast off to his club, giving the impression of
seventy when he was really fifty-seven and leaving
her richly alone for the day. He came back about

midnight, looking at her very hard and not risking long words — only making her feel by inimitable touches that the presence of his family compelled him to alter all his hours. She had in their common sitting-room the company of the objects he was fond of saying he had collected — objects, shabby and battered, of a sort that appealed little to his daughter: old brandy-flasks and match-boxes, old calendars and hand-books, intermixed with an assortment of penwipers and ash-trays, a harvest gathered in from penny bazaars. He was blandly unconscious of that side of Fleda's nature which had endeared her to Mrs. Gereth, and she had often heard him wish to goodness there was something intelligible she cared for. Why did n't she try collecting something? — it did n't matter what. She would find it gave an interest to life — there was no end to the little curiosities one could easily pick up. He was conscious of having a taste for fine things which his children had unfortunately not inherited. This indicated the limits of their acquaintance with him — limits which, as Fleda was now sharply aware, could only leave him to wonder what the mischief she was there for. As she herself echoed this question to the letter she was not in a position to clear up the mystery. She could n't have given a name to her business nor have explained it save by saying that she had had to get away from Ricks. It was intensely provisional, but what was to come next? Nothing could come next but a deeper anxiety. She had neither a home nor an outlook — nothing in all the wide world but a feeling of suspense. It was, morally speaking like figuring in society with a wardrobe of one garment.

Of course she had her duty — her duty to Owen — a definite undertaking, re-affirmed, after his visit to Ricks, under her hand and seal; but no sense of possession was attached to that, only a horrible sense of privation. She had quite moved from under Mrs. Gereth's wide wing; and now that she was really among the penwipers and ash-trays she was swept, at the thought of all the beauty she had forsworn, by short wild gusts of despair. If her friend should really keep the spoils she would never return to her. If that friend should on the other hand part with them what on earth would there be to return to? The chill struck deep as Fleda thought of the mistress of Ricks also reduced, in vulgar parlance, to what she had on her back: there was nothing to which she could compare such an image but her idea of Marie Antoinette in the Conciergerie, or perhaps the vision of some tropical bird, the creature of hot dense forests, dropped on a frozen moor to pick up a living. The mind's eye could indeed see Mrs. Gereth only in her thick, coloured air; it took all the light of her treasures to make her concrete and distinct. She loomed for a moment, in any mere house of compartments and angles, gaunt and unnatural; then she vanished as if she had suddenly sunk into a quicksand. Fleda lost herself in the rich fancy of how, if *she* were mistress of Poynton, a whole province, as an abode, should be assigned there to the great queen-mother. She would have returned from her campaign with her baggage-train and her loot, and the palace would unbar its shutters and the morning flash back from its halls. In the event of a surrender the poor woman would never again be able to begin to collect: she was now too old and too moneyless, and times were altered and good things impossibly dear. A surrender, furthermore, to any daughter-in-law save an oddity like Mona need n't at all be an abdication in fact; any other fairly nice girl whom Owen should have taken it into his head to marry would have been positively glad to have, for the museum, a custodian equal to a walking catalogue, a custodian versed beyond any one anywhere in the mysteries of ministration to rare pieces. A fairly nice girl would somehow be away a good deal and would at such times count it a blessing to feel Mrs. Gereth at her post.

Fleda had from the first days fully recognised that, quite apart from any question of letting Owen know where she was, it would be a charity to give him some sign: it would be weak, it would be ugly to be diverted from this kindness by the fact that Mrs. Gereth had attached a tinkling bell to it. A frank relation with him was only superficially discredited: she ought for his own sake to send him a word of cheer. So she repeatedly reasoned, but as repeatedly delaying performance: if her general plan had been to be as still as a mouse an interview like the interview at Ricks would be an odd contribution to that ideal. Therefore with a confused preference of practice to theory she let the days go by; she judged nothing so imperative as the gain of precious time. She should n't be able to stay with her father for ever, but she might now reap the benefit of having married her sister — Maggie's union had been built up round a small spare room. Concealed in this retreat she might try to paint again, and abetted by the grateful Maggie — for Maggie at least was grateful — she might try to dispose of her work. She had not indeed struggled with a brush since her visit to Waterbath, where the sight of the family splotches had put her immensely on her guard. Poynton, moreover, had been an impossible place for producing; no art more active than a Buddhistic contemplation could lift its head there. It had stripped its mistress clean of all feeble accomplishments; she sometimes unrolled, her needles and silks, her gold and silver folded in it, a big brave flowery square of ancient unfinished "work"; but her hand had sooner been imbrued with blood than with ink or with water-colour. Close to Fleda's present abode was the little shop of a man who mounted and framed pictures and desolately dealt in artists' materials. She sometimes paused before it to look at a couple of shy experiments for which its dull window constituted publicity; small studies placed there on sale and full of warning to a young lady without fortune and without talent. Some such young lady had brought them forth in sorrow; some such young lady, to see if they had been snapped up, had passed and re-passed as helplessly as she herself was doing. They never had been, they never would be snapped up; yet they were quite above the actual attainment of some other young ladies. It was a matter of discipline with Fleda to take an occasional lesson from them; besides which when she now quitted the house she had to look for reasons after she was out. The only place to find them was in the shop-windows. They likened her to a servant-girl taking her "afternoon," but that did n't signify: perhaps some day she would resemble such a person still more closely. This continued a fortnight, at the end of which the feeling was suddenly dissipated. She had stopped as usual in the presence of the little pictures and then, as she turned away, had found herself face to face with Owen Gereth.

At the sight of him two fresh waves passed quickly across her heart, one at the heels of the other. The first was an instant perception that their meeting was not an accident; the second a consciousness as prompt that the best place for it was the street. She knew before he told her that he had been to see her, and the next thing she knew was that he had had information from his mother. Her mind grasped these things while he said with a smile: "I saw only your back, but I knew like a shot. I was over the way. I 've been at your house."

"How came you to know my house?" Fleda asked.

"I like that!" he laughed. "How came you not to let me know you were there?"

Fleda, at this, thought it best also to laugh. "Since I did n't let you know why did you come?"

"Oh I say!" cried Owen. "Don't add insult to injury. Why in the world did n't you let me know? I came because I want awfully to see you." He rather floundered, then added: "I got the tip from mother. She has written to me — fancy!"

They still stood where they had met. Fleda's instinct was to keep him there; the more that she could already see him take for granted they would immediately proceed together to her door. He rose before her with a different air: he looked less ruffled and bruised than he had done at Ricks; he showed a recovered freshness. Perhaps, however, this was only because she had scarcely seen him at all till now in London form, as he would have called it — "turned out" as he was turned out in town. In the country, heated with the chase and splashed with the mire, he had always much reminded her of a picturesque peasant in national costume. This costume, as Owen wore it, varied from day to day; it was as copious as the wardrobe of an actor; but it never failed of suggestions of the earth and the weather, the hedges and ditches, the beasts and birds. There had been days when he struck her as all potent nature in one pair of boots. It did n't make him now another person that he was delicately dressed, shining and splendid, that he had a higher hat and light gloves with black seams and an umbrella as fine as a lance; but it made him, she soon decided, really handsomer, and this in turn gave him — for she never could think of him, or indeed of some other things, without the aid of his vocabulary — a tremendous pull. Yes, that was for the moment, as he looked at her, the great fact of their situation — his pull was tremendous. She tried to keep the acknowledgement of it from trembling in her voice as she said to him with more surprise than she really felt: "You 've then re-opened relations with her?"

"It 's she who has re-opened them with me. I got

her letter this morning. She told me you were here
and that she wished me to know it. She did n't say
much; she just gave me your address. I wrote her
back, you know, 'Thanks no end. Shall go to-day.'
So we *are* in correspondence again, are n't we? She
means of course that you've something to tell me from
her, hey? But if you have why have n't you let a
fellow know?" He waited for no answer to this, he
had so much to say. "At your house, just now, they
told me how long you've been here. Have n't you
known all the while that I'm counting the hours?
I left a word for you — that I would be back at six;
but I'm awfully glad to have caught you so much
sooner. You don't mean to say you're not going
home!" he exclaimed in dismay. "The young woman
there told me you went out early."

"I've been out a very short time," said Fleda,
who had hung back with the general purpose of
making things difficult for him. The street would
make them difficult; she could trust the street. She
reflected in time, however, that to betray she was
afraid to admit him would give him more a feeling of
facility than of anything else. She moved on with
him after a moment, letting him direct their course
to her door, which was only round a corner; she considered as they went that it might n't prove such
a stroke to have been in London so long and yet not
have called him. She desired he should feel she was
perfectly simple with him, and there was no simplicity in that. None the less, on the steps of the
house, though she had a key, she rang the bell; and
while they waited together and she averted her face

she looked straight into the depths of what Mrs. Gereth had meant by giving him the "tip." This had been perfidious, had been monstrous of Mrs. Gereth, and Fleda wondered if her letter had contained only what Owen repeated.

XIV

WHEN they had passed together into her father's little place and, among the brandy-flasks and pen-wipers, still more disconcerted and divided, the girl — to do something, though it would make him stay — had ordered tea, he put the letter before her quite as if he had guessed her thought. "She's still a bit nasty — fancy!" He handed her the scrap of a note he had pulled out of his pocket and from its envelope. "Fleda Vetch," it ran, "is at West Kensington — 10, Raphael Road. Go to see her and try, for God's sake, to cultivate a glimmer of intelligence." When, handing it back to him, she took in his face she saw how his heightened colour was the effect of watching her read such an allusion to his want of wit. Fleda knew what it was an allusion to, and his pathetic air of having received this buffet, tall and fine and kind as he stood there, made her conscious of not quite concealing her knowledge. For a minute she was kept mute by an angered sense of the trick thus played her. It was a trick because she considered there had been a covenant; and the trick consisted of Mrs. Gereth's having broken the spirit of their agreement while conforming in a fashion to the letter. Under the girl's menace of a complete rupture she had been afraid to make of her secret the use she itched to make; but in the course of these days of separation she had gathered pluck to hazard an indirect betrayal. Fleda measured her hesitations and the impulse she had finally obeyed, which the continued procrastination of Waterbath had encouraged, had at last made irresistible. If in her high-handed manner of playing their game she had not named the thing hidden she had named the hiding-place. It was over the sense of this wrong that Fleda's lips closed tight: she was afraid of aggravating her case by some sound that would quicken her visitor's attention. A strong effort, however, helped her to avoid the danger; with her constant idea of keeping cool and repressing a visible flutter she found herself able to choose her words. Meanwhile he had exclaimed with his uncomfortable laugh: "That's a good one for me, Miss Vetch, is n't it?"

"Of course you know by this time that your mother's very direct," said Fleda.

"I think I can understand well enough when I know what's to be understood," the young man returned. "But I hope you won't mind my saying that you've kept me pretty well in the dark about that. I've been waiting, waiting, waiting — so much has depended on your news. If you've been working for me I'm afraid it has been a thankless job. Can't she say what she'll do, one way or the other? I can't tell in the least where I am, you know. I have n't really learnt from you, since I saw you there, where *she* is. You wrote me to be patient, and I should like to know what else I've been. But I'm afraid you don't quite realise what I'm to be patient *with*. At Waterbath, don't you know? I've simply to account and answer, piece by piece, for my damned property. Mona glowers at me and waits, and I, hang it, I glower at *you* and do the same." Fleda had gathered fuller confidence as he continued; so plain was it that she had succeeded in not dropping into his mind the spark that might produce the glimmer his mother had tried to rub up. But even her small safety gave a start when after an appealing pause he went on: "I hope, you know, that all this time you're not keeping anything back from me."

In the full face of what she was keeping back such a hope could only make her wince; but she was prompt with her explanations in proportion as she felt they failed to meet him. The smutty maid came in with tea-things, and Fleda, moving several objects, eagerly accepted the diversion of arranging a place for them on one of the tables. "I've been trying to break your mother down because it has seemed there may be some chance of it. That's why I've let you go on expecting it. She's too proud to veer round all at once, but I think I speak correctly in saying I've made an impression."

In spite of ordering tea she had not invited him to sit down; she herself made a point of standing. He hovered by the window that looked into Raphael Road; she kept at the other side of the room; the stunted slavey, gazing wide-eyed at the beautiful gentleman and either stupidly or cunningly bringing but one thing at a time, came and went between the tea-tray and the open door.

"You pegged at her so hard?" Owen asked.

"I explained to her fully your position and put

before her much more strongly than she liked what seemed to me her absolute duty."

He waited a little. "And having done that you came away?"

She felt the full need of giving a reason for her movement, but at first only said with cheerful frankness: "I came away."

Her companion again seemed to search her. "I thought you had gone to her for several months."

"Well," Fleda replied, "I could n't stay. I did n't like it. I did n't like it at all—I could n't bear it," she went on. "In the midst of those trophies of Poynton, living with them, touching them, using them, I felt as if backing her up. As I was n't a bit of an accomplice, as I hate what she has done, I did n't want to be, even to the extent of the mere look of it — what is it you call such people? — an accessory after the fact." There was something she kept back so rigidly that the joy of uttering the rest was double. She yielded to the sharp need of giving him all the other truth. There was a matter as to which she had deceived him, and there was a matter as to which she had deceived Mrs. Gereth, but her lack of pleasure in deception as such came home to her now. She busied herself with the tea and, to extend the occupation, cleared the table still more, spreading out the coarse cups and saucers and the vulgar little plates. She was aware she produced more confusion than symmetry, but she was also aware she was violently nervous. Owen tried to help her with something: this made indeed for disorder. "My reason for not writing to you," she pursued, "was simply that I was hoping to hear more from Ricks. I've waited from day to day for that."

"But you've heard nothing?"

"Not a word."

"Then what I understand," said Owen, "is that practically you and Mummy have quarrelled. And you've done it — I mean you personally — for *me*."

"Oh no, we have n't quarrelled a bit!" Then with a smile: "We've only diverged."

"You've diverged uncommonly far!" — Owen laughed pleasantly back. Fleda, with her hideous crockery and her father's collections, could conceive that these objects, to her visitor's perception even more strongly than to her own, measured the length of the swing from Poynton and Ricks; she could n't forget either that her high standards must figure vividly enough even to Owen's simplicity to make him reflect that West Kensington was a tremendous fall. If she had fallen it was because she had acted for him. She was all the more content he should thus see she *had* acted, as the cost of it, in his eyes, was none of her own showing. "What seems to have happened," he said, "is that you've had a row with her and yet not moved her!"

She felt her way; she was full of the impression that, notwithstanding her scant help, he saw his course clearer than he had seen it at Ricks. He might mean many things, and what if the many should mean in their turn only one? "The difficulty is, you understand, that she does n't really see into your situation." She had a pause. "She does n't make out why your marriage has n't yet taken place."

157

Owen stared. "Why, for the reason I told you: that Mona won't take another step till mother has given full satisfaction. Everything must be there, every blessed 'stolen' thing. You see everything *was* there the day of that fatal visit."

"Yes, that's what I understood from you at Ricks," said Fleda; "but I have n't repeated it to your mother." She had hated at Ricks to talk with him about Mona, but now that scruple was swept away. If he could speak of Mona's visit as fatal she need at least not pretend not to notice it. It made all the difference that she had tried to assist him and had failed: to give him any faith in her service she must give him all her reasons but one. She must give him, in other words, with a corresponding omission, all Mrs. Gereth's. "You can easily see that, as she dislikes your marriage, anything that may seem to make it less certain works in her favour. Without my telling her, she has suspicions and views that are simply suggested by your delay. Therefore it did n't seem to me right to make them worse. By holding off long enough she thinks she may put an end to your engagement. If Mona's waiting she believes she may at last tire Mona out." This, in all conscience, Fleda felt to be lucid enough.

So the young man, following her attentively, appeared equally to feel. "So far as that goes," he promptly declared, "she *has* at last tired Mona out." He uttered the words with a strange approach to hilarity.

Fleda's surprise at this aberration left her a moment looking at him. "Do you mean your marriage is off?"

158

He answered with the oddest gay pessimism. "God knows, Miss Vetch, where or when or what my marriage is! If it is n't 'off' it certainly, at the point things have reached, is n't *on*. I have n't seen Mona for ten days, and for a week I have n't heard from her. She used to write me every week, don't you know? She won't budge from Waterbath and I have n't budged from town." Then he put it plain. "If she does break will mother come round?"

Fleda, at this, felt her heroism meet its real test — felt that in telling him the truth she should effectively raise a hand to push his impediment out of the way. Was the knowledge that such a motion would probably dispose for ever of Mona capable of yielding to the conception of still giving her every chance she was entitled to? That conception was heroic, but at the same moment it reminded our young woman of the place it had held in her plan she was also reminded of the not less urgent claim of the truth. Ah the truth — there was a limit to the impunity with which one could juggle with that value, which in itself never shifted. Was n't what she had most to remember the fact that Owen had a right to his property, and that he had also her vow to stand by him in the recovery of it? How did she stand by him if she hid from him the only process of recovery of which she was quite sure? For an instant that seemed to her the fullest of her life she debated. "Yes," she said at last, "if your marriage really drops she'll give up everything she has taken."

"That's just what makes Mona hesitate!" Owen

honestly stated. "I mean the idea that I shall get back the things only if she gives me up."

Fleda thought an instant. "You mean makes her hesitate to keep you — not hesitate to renounce you?"

He looked a trifle befogged. "She doesn't see the use of hanging on, as I haven't even yet put the matter into legal hands. She's awfully keen about that, and awfully disgusted that I don't. She says it's the only real way and she thinks I'm afraid to take it. She has given me time and then has given me again more. She says I give Mummy too much. She says I'm a muff to go pottering on. That's why she's drawing off so hard, don't you see?"

"I don't see very clearly. Of course you must give her what you offered her; of course you must keep your word. There must be no mistake about *that!*" the girl declared.

His bewilderment visibly increased. "You think then, as she does, that I *must* send down the police?"

The mixture of reluctance and dependence in this made her feel how much she was failing him: she had the sense of "breaking" too. "No no, not yet!" she said, though she had really no other and no better course to prescribe. "Doesn't it occur to you," she asked in a moment, "that if Mona is, as you say, drawing away, she may have in doing so a very high motive? She knows the immense value of all the objects detained by your mother, and to restore the spoils of Poynton she's ready — is that it? — to make a sacrifice. The sacrifice is that of an engagement she had entered upon with joy."

160

He had been blank a moment before, but he followed this argument with success — a success so immediate that it enabled him to produce with decision: "Ah she's not that sort! She wants them herself," he added; "she wants to feel they're hers; she does n't care whether I have them or not. And if she can't get them she does n't want *me*. If she can't get them she does n't want anything at all."

This was categoric: Fleda drank it in. "She takes such an interest in them?"

"So it appears."

"So much that they're *all*, in the whole business, and that she can let everything else absolutely depend upon them?"

Owen weighed it as if he felt the responsibility of his answer; but that answer nevertheless came, and, as Fleda could see, out of a wealth of memory. "She never wanted them particularly till they seemed to be in danger. Now she has an idea about them, and when she gets hold of an idea — oh dear me!" He broke off, pausing and looking away as with a sense of the futility of expression: it was the first time she had heard him explain a matter so pointedly or embark at all on a generalisation. It was striking, it was touching to her, as he faltered, that he appeared but half capable of floating his generalisation to the end. The girl, however, was so far competent to fill up his blank as that she had divined on the occasion of Mona's visit to Poynton what would happen in case of the accident at which he glanced. She had there with her own eyes seen

Owen's betrothed get hold of an idea. "I say, you know, *do* give me some tea!" he went on irrelevantly and familiarly.

Her profuse preparations had all this time had no sequel, and with a laugh that she felt to be awkward she hastily prepared his draught. "It's sure to be horrid," she said; "we don't have at all good things." She offered him also bread and butter, of which he partook, holding his cup and saucer in his other hand and moving slowly about the room. She poured herself a cup, but not to take it; after which, without wanting it, she began to eat a small stale biscuit. She was struck with the extinction of the unwillingness she had felt at Ricks to contribute to the bandying between them of poor Mona's name; and under this influence she presently resumed: "Am I to understand that she engaged herself to marry you without caring for you?"

He looked into Raphael Road. "She *did* care for me awfully. But she can't stand the strain."

"The strain of what?"

"Why of the whole wretched thing."

"The whole thing has indeed been wretched, and I can easily conceive its effect on her," Fleda sagaciously said.

Her visitor turned sharp round. "You *can*?" There was a light in his strong stare. "You can understand its spoiling her temper and making her come down on *me*? She behaves as if I were of no use to her at all!"

Fleda wondered even to extravagance. "She's rankling under the sense of her wrong."

"Well, was it I, pray, who perpetrated the wrong ?
Ain't I doing what I can to get the thing arranged ?"

The ring of his question made his anger at Mona
almost resemble for a minute an anger at Fleda; and
this resemblance in turn caused our young lady to
observe how it became him to speak, as he did for
the first time in her hearing, with that degree of heat,
and to use, for the first time too, such a term as "perpetrated." In addition his challenge rendered still
more vivid to her the mere flimsiness of her own aid.
"Yes, you've been perfect," she said. "You've had
a most difficult part. You've had to show tact and
patience as well as firmness with your mother, and
you've strikingly shown them. It's I who, quite
unintentionally, have deceived you. I haven't
helped you at all to your remedy."

"Well, you wouldn't at all events have ceased to
like me, would you ?" Owen demanded. It evidently
mattered to him to know if she really justified Mona.
"I mean of course if you *had* liked me — liked me
as *she* liked me," he explained.

Fleda looked this appeal in the face only long
enough to recognise that in her embarrassment she
must take instant refuge in a higher one. "I can
answer that better if I know how kind to her you've
been. *Have* you been kind to her ?" she asked as
simply as she could.

"Why rather, Miss Vetch! I've done every blessed
thing she has ever wished," he protested. "I rushed
down to Ricks, as you saw, with fire and sword, and
the day after that I went to see her at Waterbath."
At this point he checked himself, though it was just

163

the point at which her interest deepened. A different look had come into his face as he put down his empty teacup. "But why should I tell you such things for any good it does me? I gather you've no suggestion to make me now except that I shall request my solicitor to act. *Shall* I request him to act?"

Fleda scarce caught his words: something new had suddenly come into her mind. "When you went to Waterbath after seeing me," she asked, "did you tell her all about that?"

Owen looked conscious. "All about it?"

"That you had had a long talk with me without seeing your mother at all?"

"Oh yes, I told her exactly, and that you had been most awfully kind and that I had placed the whole thing in your hands."

Fleda gazed as at the scene he reported. "Perhaps that displeased her," she at last suggested.

"It displeased her fearfully." He brought it out with a rush.

"Fearfully?" broke from the girl. Somehow, at the word, she was startled.

"She wanted to know what right you had to meddle. She said you were n't honest."

"Oh!" Fleda cried with a long wail. Then she controlled herself. "I see."

"She abused you and I defended you. She denounced you —"

She checked him with a gesture. "Don't tell me what she did!" She had coloured up to her eyes, where, as with the effect of a blow in the face, she quickly felt the tears gathering. It was a sudden drop in her great flight, a shock to her attempt to watch over Mona's interests. While she had been straining her very soul in this attempt the subject of her magnanimity had been practically pronouncing her vile. She took it all in, however, and after an instant was able to speak with a smile. She would n't have been surprised to learn indeed that her smile was queer. "You spoke a while ago of your mother's and my quarrelling about you. It's much more true that you and Mona have quarrelled about *me*."

The proposition was fairly simple, but he seemed for an instant to have to walk round it. "What I mean to say is, don't you know, that Mona, if you don't mind my saying so, has taken into her head to be jealous."

"I see," said Fleda. "Well, I dare say our conferences have looked very odd."

"They 've looked very beautiful and they 've *been* very beautiful. Oh I 've told her the sort you are!" the young man pursued.

"That of course has n't made her love me better."

"No, nor love me," — he jumped at it now. "Of course, you know, she *says* — so far as that goes — that she loves me."

"And do you say you love her?"

"I say nothing else — I say it all the while. I said it the other day about ninety times." Fleda made no immediate rejoinder to this, and before she could choose one he repeated his question of a moment before. "*Am* I to tell my solicitor to act?"

She had at that moment turned away from this solution, precisely because she saw in it the great

chance for herself. If she should determine him
to adopt it she might put out her hand and take
him. It would shut in Mrs. Gereth's face the open
door of surrender: she would flare up and fight,
flying the flag of a passionate, an heroic defence.
The case would obviously go against her, but the
proceedings would last longer than Mona's patience
or Owen's propriety. With a formal rupture he would
be at large; and she had only to tighten her fingers
round the string that would raise the curtain on that
scene. "You tell me you 'say' you love her, but is
there nothing more in it than your saying so? You
would n't say so, would you, if it 's not true? What in
the world has become in so short a time of the affection
that led to your engagement?"

"The deuce knows what has become of it, Miss
Vetch!" Owen cried. "It seemed all to go to pot
as this horrid struggle came on." He was close to
her now and, with his face lighted again by the
relief of it, he looked all his helpless history into
her eyes. "As I saw you and noticed you more, as
I knew you better and better, I. felt less and less
— I could n't help it — about anything or any one
else. I wished I had known you sooner — I knew
I should have liked you better than any one in
the world. But it was n't you who made the difference," he eagerly continued, "and I was awfully
determined to stick to Mona to the death. It was she
herself who made it, upon my soul, by the state she
got into, the way she sulked, the way she took things
and the way she let me have it! She destroyed our
prospects and our happiness — upon my honour she

destroyed them. She made just the same smash of
them as if she had kicked over that tea-table. She
wanted to know all the while what was passing between us, between you and me; and she would n't
take my solemn assurance that nothing was passing
but what might have directly passed between me and
old Mummy. She said a pretty girl like you was
a nice old Mummy for me, and, if you 'll believe it,
she never called you anything else but that. I 'll be
hanged if I have n't been good, have n't I ? I have n't
breathed a breath of any sort to you, have I ? You 'd
have been down on me hard if I had, would n't you ?
You 're down on me pretty hard as it is, I think,
are n't you ? But I don't care what you say now, or
what Mona says either, or a single rap what any one
says : she has given me at last by her confounded
behaviour a right to speak out, to utter the way I feel
about it. The way I feel about it, don't you know ?
is that it had all better come to an end. You ask me
if I don't love her, and I suppose it 's natural enough
you should. But you ask it at the very moment I 'm
half-mad to say to you that there 's only one person on
the whole earth I *really* love, and that that person — "
Here he pulled up short, and Fleda wondered if it
were from the effect of his perceiving, through the
closed door, the sound of steps and voices on the
landing of the stairs. She had caught this sound herself with surprise and a vague uneasiness : it was not
an hour at which her father ever came in, and there
was no present reason why she should have a visitor.
She had a fear which after a few seconds deepened :
a visitor was at hand ; the visitor would be simply Mrs.

Gereth. That lady wished for a near view of the consequence of her note to Owen. Fleda straightened herself with the instant thought that if this was what Mrs. Gereth desired Mrs. Gereth should have it in a form not to be mistaken. Owen's pause was the matter of a moment, but during that moment our young couple stood with their eyes holding each other's eyes and their ears catching the suggestion, still through the door, of a murmured conference in the hall. Fleda had begun to move to cut it short when Owen stopped her with a grasp of her arm. "You're surely able to guess," he said with his voice down and her arm pressed as she had never known such a tone or such a pressure — "you're surely able to guess the one person on earth I love?"

The handle of the door turned and she had only time to jerk at him: "Your mother!"

But as the door opened the smutty maid, edging in, announced "Mrs. Brigstock!"

XV

Mrs. Brigstock, in the doorway, stood looking from one of the occupants of the room to the other; then they saw her eyes attach themselves to a small object that had lain hitherto unnoticed on the carpet. This was the biscuit of which, on giving Owen his tea, Fleda had taken a perfunctory nibble: she had immediately laid it on the table, and that subsequently, in some precipitate movement, she should have brushed it off was doubtless a sign of the agitation that possessed her. For Mrs. Brigstock there was apparently more in it than met the eye. Owen at any rate picked it up, and Fleda felt as if he were removing the traces of some scene that the newspapers would have characterised as lively. Mrs. Brigstock clearly took in also the sprawling tea-things and the marks as of a high tide in the full faces of her young friends. These elements made the little place a vivid picture of intimacy. A minute was filled by Fleda's relief at finding her visitor not to be Mrs. Gereth, and a longer space by the later sense of what was really more compromising in the case presented. It dimly occurred to her that the lady of Ricks had also written to Waterbath. Not only had Mrs. Brigstock never paid her a call, but Fleda would have been unable to figure her so employed. A year before the girl had spent a day under her roof, but never feeling that Mrs. Brigstock regarded this as constituting a bond. She

had never stayed in any house but Poynton in which
the imagination of a bond, on one side or the other,
prevailed. After the first astonishment she dashed
gaily at her guest, emphasising her welcome and
wondering how her whereabouts had become known
at Waterbath. Had n't Mrs. Brigstock quitted that
residence for the very purpose of laying her hand
on the associate of Mrs. Gereth's misconduct? The
spirit in which this hand was to be laid our young
woman was yet to ascertain; but she was a person
who could think ten thoughts at once — a circumstance which, even putting her present plight at its
worst, gave her a great advantage over a person who
required easy conditions for dealing even with one.
The very vibration of the air, however, told her that
whatever Mrs. Brigstock's sense might originally
have been it was now sharply affected by the sight
of Owen. He was essentially a surprise: she had
reckoned with everything that concerned him but
his personal presence. With that, in awkward silence,
she had begun to deal, as Fleda could see, while
she effected with friendly aid an embarrassed transit
to the sofa. Owen would be useless, would be deplorable: this aspect of the case Fleda had taken in as
well. Another aspect was that he would admire her,
adore her, exactly in proportion as she herself should
rise gracefully superior. Fleda felt for the first time
free to let herself "go," as Mrs. Gereth had said,
and she was full of the sense that to "go" meant
now to aim straight at the effect of moving Owen to
rapture at her simplicity and tact. It was her impression that he had no positive dislike of Mona's mother;

but she could n't entertain that notion without a glimpse of the implication that he had a positive dislike of Mrs. Brigstock's daughter. Mona's mother declined tea, declined a better seat, declined a cushion, declined to remove her boa : Fleda guessed that she had not come on purpose to be dry, but that the voice of the invaded room had itself given her the hint.

"I just came on the mere chance," she said. "Mona found yesterday somewhere the card of invitation to your sister's marriage that you sent us, or your father sent us, some time ago. We could n't be present — it was impossible; but as it had this address on it I said to myself that I might find you here."

"I 'm very glad to be at home," Fleda responded.

"Yes, that does n't happen very often, does it?" Mrs. Brigstock looked round afresh at Fleda's home.

"Oh I came back a while ago from Ricks. I shall be here now till I don't know when."

"We thought it very likely you 'd have come back. We knew of course of your having been at Ricks. If I did n't find you I thought I might perhaps find Mr. Vetch," Mrs. Brigstock went on.

"I 'm sorry he 's out. He 's always out — all day long."

Mrs. Brigstock's round eyes grew rounder. "All day long?"

"All day long," Fleda smiled.

"Leaving you quite to yourself?"

"A good deal to myself, but a little, to-day, as you see, to Mr. Gereth " — and the girl looked at Owen to draw him into their sociability. For Mrs. Brigstock he had immediately sat down; but the movement had not corrected the sombre stiffness possessing him at sight of her. Before he found a response to the appeal addressed to him Fleda turned again to her other visitor. "Is there any purpose for which you would like my father to call on you?"

Mrs. Brigstock received this question as if it were not to be unguardedly answered; upon which Owen intervened with pale irrelevance. "I wrote to Mona this morning of Miss Vetch's being in town; but of course the letter had n't arrived when you left home."

"No, it had n't arrived. I came up for the night — I 've several matters to attend to." Then looking with an intention of fixedness from one of her companions to the other, "I 'm afraid I 've interrupted your conversation," Mrs. Brigstock said. She spoke without effectual point, had the air of merely announcing the fact. Fleda had not yet been confronted with the question of the sort of person Mrs. Brigstock was; she had only been confronted with the question of the sort of person Mrs. Gereth scorned her for being. She was really somehow no sort of person at all, and it came home to Fleda that if Mrs. Gereth could see her at this moment she would scorn her more than ever. She had a face of which it was impossible to say anything but that it was pink, and a mind it would be possible to describe only had one been able to mark it in a similar fashion. As nature had made this organ neither green nor blue nor yellow there was nothing to know it by: it strayed and bleated like an unbranded sheep. Fleda felt for it at this moment much of the kindness of compassion, since Mrs. Brigstock had brought it with her to do something for her that she regarded as delicate. Fleda was quite prepared to assist its use might she only divine what it wanted to do. What she divined however, more and more, was that it wanted to do something different from what it had wanted to do in leaving Waterbath. There was still nothing to enlighten her more specifically in the way her visitor continued: "You must be very much taken up. I believe you quite espouse his dreadful quarrel."

Fleda gained time by a vague echo. "His dreadful quarrel?"

"About the contents of the house. Are n't you looking after them for him?"

"She knows how awfully kind you 've been to me," Owen explained to their young friend. He showed such discomfiture that he really gave away their situation; and Fleda found herself divided between the hope that he would take leave and the wish that he should see the whole of what the occasion might enable her to bring to pass for him.

She addressed herself to Mrs. Brigstock. "Mrs. Gereth, at Ricks the other day, asked me particularly to see him for her."

"And did she ask you also particularly to see him here in town?" Mrs. Brigstock's hideous bonnet seemed to argue for the unsophisticated truth; and it was on Fleda's lips to reply that such had indeed been Mrs. Gereth's request. But she checked herself, and before she could say anything else Owen had taken up the question.

"I made a point of letting Mona know that I should be here, don't you see? That's exactly what I wrote her this morning."

"She would have had little doubt you'd be here if you had a chance," Mrs. Brigstock returned. "If your letter had arrived it might have prepared me for finding you here at tea. In that case I certainly would n't have come."

"I'm glad then it did n't arrive. Should n't you like him to leave us?" Fleda asked.

Mrs. Brigstock looked at Owen and considered: nothing showed in her face but that it turned a deeper pink. "I should like him to come with *me*." There was no menace in her tone, but she evidently knew what she wanted. As Owen made no response to this Fleda glanced at him to invite him to assent; then for fear he would n't, and thus would make his case worse, she took upon herself to express for him all such readiness. She had no sooner spoken than she felt in the words a bad effect of intimacy: she had answered for him as if she had been his wife. Mrs. Brigstock continued to regard him without passion and spoke only to Fleda. "I've not seen him for a long time — I've particular things to say to him."

"So have I things to say to you, Mrs. Brigstock," Owen interjected. With this he took up his hat as for prompt departure.

The other visitor meanwhile kept at their hostess. "What's Mrs. Gereth going to do?"

"Is that what you came to ask me?" Fleda demanded.

"That and several other things."

174

"Then you had much better let Mr. Gereth go, and stay by yourself and make me a pleasant visit. You can talk with him when you like, but it's the first time you've been to see me."

This appeal had evidently a certain effect; Mrs. Brigstock visibly wavered. "I can't talk with him whenever I like," she returned; "he hasn't been near us since I don't know when. But there are things that have brought me here."

"They can't be things of any importance," Owen, to Fleda's surprise, suddenly asserted. He had not at first taken up Mrs. Brigstock's expression of a wish to carry him off: Fleda could see the instinct at the bottom of this to be that of standing by her, of seeming not to abandon her. But abruptly, all his soreness working within him, it had struck him he should abandon her still more if he should leave her to be dealt with by the messenger from Waterbath. "You must allow me to say, you know, Mrs. Brigstock, that I don't think you should come down on Miss Vetch about anything. It's very good of her to take the smallest interest in us and our horrid vulgar little squabble. If you want to talk about it talk about it with *me*." He was flushed with the idea of protecting Fleda, of exhibiting his consideration for her. "I don't like you cross-questioning her, don't you see? She's as straight as a die: *I*'ll tell you all about her!" he declared with a reckless laugh. "Please come off with me and let her alone."

Mrs. Brigstock, at this, became vivid at once; Fleda thought her look extraordinary. She stood straight up — a queer distinction in her whole person and in everything of her face but her mouth, which she gathered into a small tight orifice. The girl was painfully divided; her joy was deep within, but it was more relevant to the situation that she should n't appear to associate herself with the tone of familiarity in which Owen addressed a lady who had been, and was perhaps still, about to become his mother-in-law. She laid on Mrs. Brigstock's arm a repressive persuasive hand. Mrs. Brigstock, however, had already exclaimed on her having so wonderful a defender. "He speaks, upon my word, as if I had come here to be rude to you!"

At this, grasping her hard, Fleda laughed; then she achieved the exploit of delicately kissing her. "I'm not in the least afraid to be alone with you or of your tearing me to pieces. I'll answer any question that you can possibly dream of putting to me."

"I'm the proper person to answer Mrs. Brigstock's questions," Owen broke in again, "and I'm not a bit less ready to meet them than you are." He was firmer than she had ever seen him; it was as if she had n't dreamed he could be so firm.

"But she'll only have been here a few minutes. What sort of a visit is that?" Fleda cried.

"It has lasted long enough for my purpose," Mrs. Brigstock judiciously declared. "There was something I wanted to know, but I think I know it now."

"Anything you don't know I dare say I can tell you!" Owen observed as he impatiently smoothed his hat with the cuff of his coat.

Fleda by this time desired immensely to keep his companion, but she saw she could do so only at the cost of provoking on his part a further exhibition of the sheltering attitude which he exaggerated precisely because it was the first thing, since he had begun to "like" her, that he had been able frankly to do for her. It was not to her advantage that Mrs. Brigstock should be more struck than she already was with that benevolence. "There may be things you know that I don't," she presently said to her all reasonably and brightly. "But I've a sort of sense that you're labouring under some great mistake."

Mrs. Brigstock, at this, looked into her eyes more deeply and yearningly than she had supposed Mrs. Brigstock could look: it was the flicker of a mild muddled willingness to give her a chance. Owen, however, quickly spoiled everything. "Nothing's more probable than that Mrs. Brigstock is doing what you say; but there's no one in the world to whom you owe an explanation. I may owe somebody one — I dare say I do. But not you — no!"

"But what if there's one that it's no difficulty at all for me to give?" Fleda sweetly argued. "I'm sure that's the only one Mrs. Brigstock came to ask, if she came to ask any at all."

Again the good lady looked hard at her young friend. "I came, I believe, Fleda, just — you know — to plead with you."

Fleda, with her lighted face, hesitated a moment. "As if I were one of those bad women in a play?"

The remark was disastrous: Mrs. Brigstock, on whom the grace of it was lost, evidently thought it singularly free. She turned away as from a presence that had really defined itself as objectionable, and the girl had a vain sense that her good humour, in which there was an idea, was taken for impertinence, or at least for levity. Her allusion was improper even if she herself was n't. Mrs. Brigstock's emotion simplified: it came to the same thing. "I'm quite ready," that lady said to Owen rather grandly and woundedly. "I do want to speak to you very much."

"I'm completely at your service." Owen held out his hand to Fleda. "Good-bye, Miss Vetch. I hope to see you again to-morrow." He opened the door for Mrs. Brigstock, who passed before Miss Vetch with an oblique averted salutation. Owen and Fleda, while he stood at the door, then faced each other darkly and without speaking. Their eyes met once more for a long moment, and she was conscious there was something in hers that the darkness did n't quench, that he had never seen before and that he was perhaps never to see again. He stayed long enough to take it — to take it with a sombre stare that just showed the dawn of wonder; then he followed Mrs. Brigstock out of the house.

XVI

He had uttered the hope that he should see her the next day, but Fleda could easily reflect that he would n't see her if she were not there to be seen. If there was a thing in the world she desired at that moment it was that the next day should have no point of resemblance with the day that had just elapsed. She accordingly rose to the conception of an absence: she would go immediately down to Maggie. She ran out that evening and telegraphed to her sister, and in the morning she quitted London by an early train. She required for this step no reason but the sense of necessity. It was a strong personal need; she wished to interpose something, and there was nothing she could interpose but distance, but time. If Mrs. Brigstock had to deal with Owen she would allow Mrs. Brigstock the chance. To be there, to be in the midst of it, was the reverse of what she craved: she had already been more in the midst of it than had ever entered into her plan. At any rate she had renounced her plan; she had no plan now but the plan of separation. This was to abandon Owen, to give up the fine office of helping him back to his own; but when she had undertaken that office she had not foreseen that Mrs. Gereth would defeat it by a manœuvre so remarkably simple. The scene at her father's rooms had extinguished all offices, and the scene at her father's rooms was of Mrs. Gereth's producing.

179

Owen must at all events now act for himself: he had obligations to meet, he had satisfactions to give, and Fleda fairly ached with the wish he might be equal to them. She never knew the extent of her tenderness for him till she became conscious of the present force of her desire that he should be superior, be perhaps even sublime. She obscurely made out that superiority, that sublimity might n't after all be fatal. She closed her eyes and lived for a day or two in the mere beauty of confidence. It was with her on the short journey; it was with her at Maggie's; it glorified the mean little house in the stupid little town. Owen had grown larger to her: he would do, like a man, whatever he should have to do. He would n't be weak — not as she was: she herself was weak exceedingly.

Arranging her few possessions in Maggie's fewer receptacles she caught a glimpse of the bright side of the fact that her old things were not such a problem as Mrs. Gereth's. Picking her way with Maggie through the local puddles, diving with her into smelly cottages and supporting her, at smellier shops, in firmness over the weight of joints and the taste of cheese, it was still her own secret that was universally interwoven. In the puddles, the cottages, the shops she was comfortably alone with it; that comfort prevailed even while, at the evening meal, her brother-in-law invited her attention to a diagram, drawn with a fork on too soiled a tablecloth, of the scandalous drains of the Convalescent Home. To be alone with it she had come away from Ricks, and now she knew that to be alone with it she had come away from London. This advantage was of course menaced, though not immediately destroyed, by the arrival on the second day of the note she had been sure she should receive from Owen. He had gone to West Kensington and found her flown, but he had got her address from the little maid and then hurried to a club and written to her. "Why have you left me just when I want you most?" he demanded. The next words, it was true, were more reassuring on the question of his steadiness. "I don't know what your reason may be," they went on, "nor why you've not left a line for me; but I don't think you can feel that I did anything yesterday that it wasn't right for me to do. As regards Mrs. Brigstock certainly I just felt what was right and I did it. She had no business whatever to attack you that way, and I should have been ashamed if I had left her there to worry you. I won't have you worried by any one. No one shall be disagreeable to you but me. I didn't mean to be so yesterday, and I don't to-day; but I'm perfectly free now to want you, and I want you much more than you've allowed me to explain. You'll see how right I am if you'll let me come to you. Don't be afraid — I'll not hurt you nor trouble you. I give you my honour I'll not hurt any one. Only I *must* see you about what I had to say to Mrs. B. She was nastier than I thought she could be, but I'm behaving like an angel. I assure you I'm all right — that's exactly what I want you to see. You owe me something, you know, for what you said you would do and haven't done; what your departure without a word gives me to understand — doesn't it? — that you definitely can't do. Don't simply forsake me. See me if you only see me once.

I shan't wait for any leave, I shall come down to-morrow. I've been looking into trains and find there's something that will bring me just after lunch and something very good for getting me back. I won't stop long. For God's sake be there."

This communication arrived in the morning, but Fleda would still have time to wire a protest. She debated on that alternative; then she read the note over and found in one phrase an exact statement of her duty. Owen's simplicity had so expressed it that her subtlety had nothing to answer. She owed him something for her obvious failure — what she owed him was to receive him. If indeed she had known he would make this attempt she might have been held to have gained nothing by flight. Well, she had gained what she had gained — she had gained the interval. She had no compunction for the greater trouble she should give the young man; it was now doubtless right he should have as much trouble as possible. Maggie, who thought she was in her confidence, yet was immensely not, had reproached her for having quitted Mrs. Gereth, and Maggie was just in this proportion gratified to hear of the visitor with whom, early in the afternoon, Fleda would have to ask to be left alone. Maggie liked to see far, and now she could sit upstairs and rake the whole future. She had known that, as she familiarly said, there was something the matter with Fleda, and the value of that knowledge was augmented by the fact that there was apparently also something the matter with Mr. Gereth.

Fleda, downstairs, learned soon enough what this was. It was simply that, as he insisted afresh the moment he stood before her, he was now all right. When she asked him what he meant by that term he replied that he meant he could practically regard himself henceforth as a free man : he had had at West Kensington, as soon as they got into the street, such a beastly horrid scene with Mrs. Brigstock.

"I knew what she wanted to say to me : that's why I was determined to get her off. I knew I shouldn't like it, but I was perfectly prepared," said Owen. "She brought it out as soon as we got round the corner. She asked me point-blank if I was in love with you."

"And what did you say to that ?"

"That it was none of her business."

"Ah," said Fleda, "I'm not so sure!"

"Well, *I* am, and I'm the person most concerned. Of course I didn't use just those words : I was perfectly civil, quite as civil as she. But I told her I didn't consider she had a right to put me any such question. I said I wasn't sure that even Mona had, with the extraordinary line, you know — I mean that *she* knew — Mona had taken. At any rate the whole thing, the way *I* put it, was between Mona and me ; and between Mona and me, if she didn't mind, it would just have to remain."

Fleda waited for more. "All that didn't answer her question."

"Then you think I ought to have told her ?"

Again our young lady reflected. "I think I'm rather glad you didn't."

"I knew what I was about," said Owen. "It didn't strike me she had the least right to come down on us that way and try to overhaul us."

Fleda looked very grave, weighing the whole matter. "I dare say that when she started, when she arrived, she did n't mean to 'come down.'"

"What then did she mean to do?"

"What she said to me just before she went: she meant to plead with me."

"Oh I heard her — rather!" said Owen. "But plead with you for what?"

"For you, of course — to entreat me to give you up. She thinks me awfully designing — that I've taken some sort of possession of you."

Owen stared. "You have n't lifted a finger! It's I who have taken possession."

"Very true, you've done it all yourself." Fleda spoke gravely and gently, without a breath of coquetry. "But those are shades between which she's probably not obliged to distinguish It's enough for her that we're repulsively intimate."

"I am, but you're not!" Owen exclaimed.

Fleda gave a dim smile. "You make me at least feel that I'm learning to know you very well when I hear you say such a thing as that. Mrs. Brigstock came to get round me, to supplicate me," she went on; "but to find you there looking so much at home, paying me a friendly call and shoving the tea-things about — that was too much for her patience. She does n't know, you see, that I'm after all a decent girl. She simply made up her mind on the spot that I'm a very bad case."

"I could n't stand the way she treated you, and that was what I had to say to her," Owen returned.

"She's simple and slow, but she's not a fool: I

think she treated me on the whole very well." Fleda remembered how Mrs. Gereth had treated Mona when the Brigstocks came down to Poynton.

Owen evidently thought her painfully perverse. "It was you who carried it off; you behaved like a brick. And so did I, I consider. If you only knew the difficulty I had! I told her you were the noblest and straightest of women."

"That can hardly have removed her impression that there are things I put you up to."

"It did n't," Owen replied with candour. "She said our relation, yours and mine, is n't innocent."

"What did she mean by that?"

"As you may suppose, I put it to her straight. Do you know what she had the cheek to tell me?" Owen asked. "She did n't better it much. She said she meant that it's jolly unnatural."

Fleda considered afresh. "Well, it is!" she brought out at last.

"Then, upon my honour, it's only you who make it so!" Her perversity was distinctly too much for him. "I mean you make it so by the way you keep me off."

"Have I kept you off to-day?" Fleda sadly shook her head, raising her arms a little and dropping them.

Her gesture of resignation gave him a pretext for catching at her hand, but before he could take it she had put it behind her. They had been seated to-gether on Maggie's single sofa, and her movement brought her to her feet while Owen, looking at her reproachfully, leaned back in discouragement. "What good does it do me to be here when I find you only a stone?"

She met his eyes with all the tenderness she had not yet uttered, and she had not known till this moment how great was the accumulation. "Perhaps, after all," she risked, "there may be even in a stone still some little help for you."

He sat there a minute staring at her. "Ah you're beautiful, more beautiful than any one," he broke out, "but I'll be hanged if I can ever understand you! On Tuesday, at your father's, you were beautiful — as beautiful, just before I left, as you are at this instant. But the next day, when I went back, I found it had apparently meant nothing; and now again that you let me come here and you shine at me like an angel, it does n't bring you an inch nearer to saying what I want you to say." He remained a moment longer in the same position, then jerked himself up. "What I want you to say is that you like me — what I want you to say is that you pity me." He sprang up and came to her. "What I want you to say is that you'll *save* me!"

Fleda cast about. "Why do you need saving when you announced to me just now that you're a free man?"

He too hesitated, but he was not checked. "It's just for the reason that I'm free. Don't you know what I mean, Miss Vetch? I want you to marry me."

Miss Vetch, at this, put out her hand in charity; she held his own, which quickly grasped it a moment, and if he had described her as shining at him it may be assumed that she shone all the more in her deep still smile. "Let me know what you mean by your 'freedom' first," she said. "I gather that Mrs. Brigstock was not wholly satisfied with the way you disposed of her question."

"I dare say she was n't. But the less she 's satisfied the more I 'm free."

"What bearing have *her* feelings, pray?" Fleda asked.

"Why, Mona 's much worse than her mother, you know. She wants much more to give me up."

"Then why does n't she do it?"

"She will, as soon as her mother gets home and tells her."

"Tells her what?" Fleda went on.

"Why, that I 'm in love with *you!*"

Fleda debated. "Are you so very sure she will?"

"Certainly I 'm sure, with all the evidence I already have. That will finish her!" Owen declared.

This made his companion thoughtful again. "Can you take such pleasure in her being 'finished' — a poor girl you 've once loved?"

He waited long enough to take in the question; then with a serenity startling even to her knowledge of his nature, "I don't think I can have *really* loved her, you know," he pronounced.

She broke into a laugh that gave him a surprise as visible as the emotion it represented. "Then how am I to know you 'really' love — anybody else?"

"Oh I 'll show you that!" said Owen.

"I must take it on trust," the girl pursued. "And what if Mona does n't give you up?" she added.

He was baffled but a few seconds; he had thought of everything. "Why, that's just where you come in."

"To save you? I see. You mean I must get rid of her for you." His blankness showed for a little that he felt the chill of her cold logic, but as she waited for his rejoinder she knew to which of them it cost most. He gasped a minute, and that gave her time to say: "You see, Mr. Owen, how impossible it is to talk of such things yet!"

Like lightning he had grasped her arm. "You mean you *will* talk of them?" Then as he began to take the flood of assent from her eyes: "You *will* listen to me? Oh you dear, you dear—when, when?"

"Ah when it is n't mere misery!" The words had broken from her in a sudden loud cry, and what next happened was that the very sound of her pain upset her. She heard her own true note; she turned short away from him; in a moment she had burst into sobs; in another his arms were round her; the next she had let herself go so far that even Mrs. Gereth might have seen it. He clasped her, and she gave herself — she poured out her tears on his breast. Something prisoned and pent throbbed and gushed; something deep and sweet surged up — something that came from far within and far off, that had begun with the sight of him in his indifference and had never had rest since then. The surrender was short, but the relief was long: she felt his warm lips on her face and his arms tighten with his full divination. What she did, what she *had* done, she scarcely knew: she only was aware, as she broke from him again, of what had taken place on his own amazed part.

What had taken place was that, with the click of a spring, he saw. He had cleared the high wall at a bound; they were together without a veil. She had not a shred of a secret left; it was as if a whirlwind had come and gone, laying low the great false front she had built up stone by stone. The strangest thing of all was the momentary sense of desolation.

"Ah all the while you *cared?*" Owen read the truth with a wonder so great that it was visibly almost a sadness, a terror caused by his sudden perception of where the impossibility was not. That treacherously placed it perhaps elsewhere.

"I cared, I cared, I cared!" — she wailed it as to confess a misdeed. "How could n't I care? But you must n't, you must never never, ask! It is n't for us to talk about," she protested. "Don't speak of it, don't speak!"

It was easy indeed not to speak when the difficulty was to find words. He clasped his hands before her as he might have clasped them at an altar; his pressed palms shook together while he held his breath and while she stilled herself in the effort to come round again to the real and the thinkable. He assisted this effort, soothing her into a seat with a touch as anxious as if she had been truly something sacred. She sank into a chair and he dropped before her on his knees; she fell back with closed eyes and he buried his face in her lap. There was no way to thank her but this act of prostration, which lasted, in silence, till she laid consenting hands on him, touched his head and stroked it, let her close possession of it teach him his long blindness. He made the whole fall, as she yet felt it, seem only his — made her, when she rose again, raise him at last, softly, as if from the abasement of it. If in each other's eyes now, however, they saw the truth, this truth, to Fleda, looked harder even than before — all the harder that when, at the very moment she recognised it, he murmured to her ecstatically, in fresh possession of her hands, which he drew up to his breast, holding them tight there with both his own: "I'm saved, I'm saved — I *am!* I'm ready for anything. I have your word. Come!" he cried, as if from the sight of a response slower than he needed and in the tone he so often had of a great boy at a great game.

She had once more disengaged herself with the private vow that he should n't yet touch her again. It was all too horribly soon — her sense of this had come straight back. "We must n't talk, we must n't talk; we must wait!" — she had to make that clear. "I don't know what you mean by your freedom; I don't see it, I don't feel it. Where is it yet, where, your freedom? If it's real there's plenty of time, and if it is n't there's more than enough. I hate myself," she insisted, "for having anything to say about her: it's like waiting for dead men's shoes! What business is it of mine what she does? She has her own trouble and her own plan. It's too hideous to watch her so and count on her!"

Owen's face, at this, showed a reviving dread, the fear of some darksome process of her mind. "If you speak for yourself I can understand. But why is it hideous for me?"

"Oh I mean for myself!" Fleda quickly cried.

"*I* watch her, *I* count on her: how can I do anything else? If I count on her to let me definitely know how we stand I do nothing in life but what she herself has led straight up to. I never thought of asking you to 'get rid of her' for me, and I never would have spoken to you if I had n't held that I *am* rid of her, that she has backed out of the whole thing. Did n't she do so from the moment she began to put it off? I had already applied for the licence; the very invitations were half-addressed. Who but she, all of a sudden, required an unnatural wait? It was none of *my* doing; I had never dreamed of anything but coming up to the scratch." Owen grew more and more lucid and more confident of the effect of his lucidity. "She called it 'taking a stand' — taking it to see what mother would do. I told her mother would do what I'd make her do; and to that she replied that she'd like to see me make her first. I said I'd arrange that everything should be all right, and she said she really preferred to arrange it herself. It was a flat refusal to trust me in the smallest degree. Why then had she pretended so tremendously to care for me? And of course at present," said Owen, "she trusts me, if possible, still less."

Fleda paid this statement the homage of a minute's muteness. "As to that, naturally, she has reason."

"Why on earth has she reason?" Then as his companion, moving away, simply threw up her hands, "I never looked at you — not to call looking — till she had regularly driven me to it," he went on. "I know what I'm about. I do assure you I'm all right!"

"You're not all right — you're all wrong!" Fleda
cried in sudden despair. "You must n't stay here,
you must n't!" she repeated in still greater anxiety.
"You make me say dreadful things, and I feel as if I
made *you* say them." But before he could reply she
took it up in another tone. "Why in the world, if
everything had changed, did n't you break off?"

"I — ?" The words moved him to visible stupefaction. "Can you ask me that when I only wanted
to please you? Did n't you seem to show me, in your
wonderful way, that that was exactly how? If I
did n't break off it was just on purpose to leave it to
Mona. If I did n't break off it was just so that there
should n't be a thing to be said against me."

The instant after her challenge she had faced
him again in self-reproof. "There *is* n't a thing to
be said against you, and I don't know what folly
you make me talk! You *have* pleased me, and you 've
been right and good, and it 's the only comfort, and
you must go. Everything must come from Mona,
and if it does n't come we 've said entirely too much.
You must leave me alone — for ever."

"For ever?" Owen gasped.

"I mean unless everything 's different."

"Everything *is* different when I know you!"

Fleda winced at his knowledge; she made a wild
gesture which seemed to whirl it out of the room.
The mere allusion was like another attack from him.
"You don't know me — you don't — and you must
go and wait! You must n't break down at this
point."

He looked about him and took up his hat: it was
192

as if in spite of frustration he had got the essence of what he wanted and could afford to agree with her to the extent of keeping up the forms. He covered her with his fine simple smile, but made no other approach. "Oh I'm so awfully happy!" he cried.

She hung back now; she would only be impeccable even though she should have to be sententious. "You'll be happy if you're perfect!" she risked.

He laughed out at this, and she wondered if, with a new-born acuteness, he saw the absurdity of her speech and that no one was happy just because no one could be what she so easily prescribed. "I don't pretend to be perfect, but I shall find a letter to-night!"

"So much the better, if it's the kind of one you desire." That was the most she could say, and having made it sound as dry as possible she lapsed into a silence so pointed as to deprive him of all pretext for not leaving her. Still, nevertheless, he stood there, playing with his hat and filling the long pause with a strained and unsatisfied smile. He wished to obey her thoroughly, to appear not to presume on any advantage he had won from her; but there was clearly something he longed for besides. While he showed this by hanging on she thought of two other things. One of these was that the look of him after all failed to bear out his description of his bliss. As for the other, it had no sooner come into her head than she found it seated, in spite of her resolution, on her lips. It took the form of an inconsequent question. "When did you say Mrs. Brigstock was to have gone back?"

Owen stared. "To Waterbath? She was to have spent the night in town, don't you know? But when she left me after our talk I said to myself that she'd take an evening train. I know I made her want to get home."

"Where did you separate?" Fleda asked.

"At the West Kensington Station — she was going to Victoria. I had walked with her there, and our talk was all on the way."

Fleda turned it over. "If she did go back that night you'd have heard from Waterbath by this time."

"I don't know," said Owen. "I thought I might hear this morning."

"She can't have gone back," Fleda declared. "Mona would have written on the spot."

"Oh yes, she *will* have written bang off!" he cheerfully conceded.

She thought again. "So that even in the event of her mother's not having got home till the morning you'd have had your letter at the latest to-day. You see she has had plenty of time."

Owen took it in; then "Oh she's all right!" he laughed. "I go by Mrs. Brigstock's certain effect on her — the effect of the temper the old lady showed when we parted. Do you know what she asked me?" he sociably continued. "She asked me in a kind of nasty manner if I supposed you 'really' cared anything about me. Of course I told her I supposed you did n't — not a solitary rap. How could I ever suppose you did — with your extraordinary ways? It does n't matter. I could see she thought I lied."

194

"You should have told her, you know, that I had seen you in town only that one time," Fleda said.

"By Jove, I did — for *you*! It was only for you."

Something in this touched the girl so that for a moment she could n't trust herself to speak. "You 're an honest man," she said at last. She had gone to the door and opened it. "Good-bye."

Even yet, however, he hung back. "But say there 's no letter —" he anxiously began. He began, but there he left it.

"You mean even if she does n't let you off? Ah you ask me too much!" Fleda spoke from the tiny hall, where she had taken refuge between the old barometer and the old mackintosh. "There are things too utterly for yourselves alone. How can I tell? What do I know? Good-bye, good-bye! If she does n't let you off it will be because she *is* attached to you."

"She 's not, she 's not: there 's nothing in it! Does n't a fellow know? — except with *you*!" Owen ruefully added. With this he came out of the room, lowering his voice to secret supplication, pleading with her really to meet him on the ground of the negation of Mona. It was this betrayal of his need of support and sanction that made her retreat, harden herself in the effort to save what might remain of all she had given, given probably for nothing. The very vision of him as he thus morally clung to her was the vision of a weakness somewhere at the core of his bloom, a blessed manly weakness which, had she only the valid right, it would be all easy and sweet to take care of. She faintly sickened, however, with the sense that there was as yet no valid right poor Owen could give. "You can take it from my honour, you know," he painfully brought out, "that she quite loathes me."

Fleda had stood clutching the knob of Maggie's little painted stair-rail; she took, on the stairs, a step backward. "Why then does n't she prove it in the only clear way?"

"She *has* proved it. Will you believe it if you see the letter?"

"I don't want to see any letter," said Fleda. "You'll miss your train."

Facing him, waving him away, she had taken another upward step; but he sprang to the side of the stairs, and brought his hand, above the banister, down hard on her wrist. "Do you mean to tell me that I must marry a woman I hate?"

From her step she looked down into his raised face. "Ah you see it's not true that you're free!" She seemed almost to exult. "It's not true, it's not true!"

He only, at this, like a buffeting swimmer, gave a shake of his head and repeated his question: "Do you mean to tell me I must marry such a woman?"

Fleda gasped too; he held her fast. "No. Anything's better than that."

"Then in God's name what must I do?"

"You must settle that with Mona. You must n't break faith. Anything's better than that. You must at any rate be utterly sure. She must love you — how can she help it? *I* would n't give you up!" said Fleda. She spoke in broken bits, panting out her

196

words. "The great thing is to keep faith. Where's a man if he does n't? If he does n't he may be so cruel. So cruel, so cruel, so cruel!" Fleda repeated. "I could n't have a hand in that, you know: that's my position — that's mine. You offered her marriage. It's a tremendous thing for her." Then looking at him another moment, "*I* would n't give you up!" she said again. He still had hold of her arm; she took in his blank dread. With a quick dip of her face she reached his hand with her lips, pressing them to the back of it with a force that doubled the force of her words. "Never, never, never!" she cried; and before he could succeed in seizing her she had turned and, flashing up the stairs, got away from him even faster than she had got away at Ricks.

XVII

Ten days after his visit she received a communication from Mrs. Gereth — a telegram of eight words,
exclusive of signature and date. "Come up immediately and stay with me here" — it was characteristically sharp, as Maggie said; but, as Maggie added,
it was also characteristically kind. "Here" was an
hotel in London, and Maggie had embraced a condition of life which already began to produce in her
some yearning for hotels in London. She would have
responded on the spot and was surprised that her
sister seemed to wait. Fleda's demur, which lasted
but an hour, was expressed in that young lady's own
mind by the reflexion that in obeying her friend's
call she should n't know what she should be "in for."
Her friend's call, however, was but another name
for her friend's need, and Mrs. Gereth's bounty had
laid her under obligations more marked than any
hindrance. In the event — that is at the end of her
hour — she testified to her gratitude by taking the
train and to her mistrust by leaving her luggage.
She went as if going up for the day. In the train,
however, she had another thoughtful hour, during
which it was her mistrust that mainly deepened.
She felt as if for ten days she had sat in darkness
and looked to the east for a dawn that had not glimmered. Her mind had lately been less occupied with
Mrs. Gereth; it had been so exceptionally occupied

with Mona. If the sequel was to justify Owen's prevision of Mrs. Brigstock's action on her daughter this action was at the end of a week still thoroughly obscure. The stillness all round had been exactly what Fleda desired, but it gave her for a time a deep sense of failure, the sense of a sudden drop from a height at which she had had all things beneath her. She had nothing beneath her now; she herself was at the bottom of the heap. No sign had reached her from Owen — poor Owen who had clearly no news to give about his precious letter from Waterbath. If Mrs. Brigstock had hurried back to obtain that this letter should be written Mrs. Brigstock might then have spared herself so great an inconvenience. Owen had been silent for the best of all reasons — the reason that he had had nothing in life to say. If the letter had not been written he would simply have had to introduce some large qualification into his account of his freedom. He had left his young friend under her refusal to listen to him till he should be able, on the contrary, to extend that picture; and his present submission was all in keeping with the rigid honesty that his young friend had prescribed.

It was this that formed the element through which Mona loomed large; Fleda had enough imagination, a fine enough feeling for life, to be impressed with such an image of successful immobility. The massive maiden at Waterbath *was* successful from the moment she could entertain her resentments as if they had been poor relations who need n't put her to expense. She was a magnificent dead weight; there

was something positive and portentous in her quiet-
ude. "What game are they all playing?" poor Fleda
could only ask; for she had an intimate conviction
that Owen was now under the roof of his betrothed.
That was stupefying if he really hated his betrothed;
and if he did n't really hate her what had brought
him to Raphael Road and to Maggie's? Fleda had
no real light, but she felt that to account for the
absence of any sequel to their last meeting would
take a supposition of the full sacrifice to charity that
she had held up before him. If he had gone to Waterbath it had been simply because he had had to go.
She had as good as told him he would have to go;
that this was an inevitable incident of his keeping
perfect faith — faith so literal that the smallest sub-
terfuge would always be a reproach to him. When
she tried to remember that it was for herself he was
taking his risk she felt how weak a way that was of
expressing Mona's supremacy. There would be no
need of keeping him up if there was nothing to keep
him up to. Her eyes grew wan as she discerned in
the impenetrable air that Mona's thick outline never
wavered an inch. She wondered fitfully what Mrs.
Gereth had by this time made of it, and reflected with
a strange elation that the sand on which the mistress
of Ricks had built a momentary triumph was quaking
beneath the surface. As *The Morning Post* still held
its peace she would be of course more confident;
but the hour was at hand at which Owen would
have absolutely to do either one thing or the other.
To keep perfect faith was to inform against his
mother, and to hear the police at her door would be

Mrs. Gereth's awakening. How much she was beguiled Fleda could see from her having been for a
whole month quite as deep and dark as Mona. She
had left her young friend alone because of the certitude, cultivated at Ricks, that Owen had done the
opposite. He had done the opposite indeed, but much
good had that brought forth! To have sent for her
now, Fleda felt, was from this point of view wholly
natural: she had sent for her to show at last how
largely she had scored. If, however, Owen was really
at Waterbath the refutation of that boast would be
easy even to a primitive critic.

Fleda found Mrs. Gereth in modest apartments
and with an air of fatigue in her distinguished face,
a sign, as she privately remarked, of the strain of
that effort to be discreet of which she herself had
been having the benefit. It was a constant feature
of their relation that this lady could make Fleda
blench a little, and that the effect proceeded from
the intense pressure of her confidence. If the confidence had been heavy even when the girl, in the
early flush of devotion, had been able to feel herself
yield most, it drew her heart into her mouth now
that she had reserves and conditions, now that she
could n't simplify with the same bold hand as her
protectress. In the very brightening of the tired
look and at the moment of their embrace Fleda felt
on her shoulders the return of the load; whereupon
her spirit quailed as she asked herself what she had
brought up from her trusted seclusion to support it.
Mrs. Gereth's free manner always made a joke of
weakness, and there was in such a welcome a richness,

a kind of familiar nobleness, that suggested shame to a harried conscience. Something had happened, she could see, and she could also see, in the bravery that seemed to announce it had changed everything, a formidable assumption that what had happened was what a healthy young woman must like. The absence of luggage had made this young woman feel meagre even before her companion, taking in the bareness at a second glance, exclaimed upon it and roundly rebuked her. Of course she had expected her to stay.

Fleda thought best to show bravery too and to show it from the first. "What you expected, dear Mrs. Gereth, is exactly what I came up to ascertain. It struck me as right to do that first. Right, I mean, to ascertain without making preparations."

"Then you'll be so good as to make them on the spot!" Mrs. Gereth was most emphatic. "You're going abroad with me."

Fleda wondered, but she also smiled. "To-night — to-morrow?"

"In as few days as possible. That's all that's left for me now." Fleda's heart, at this, gave a bound; she wondered to what particular difference in Mrs. Gereth's situation as last known to her it referred. "I've made my plan," her friend continued: "I go at least for a year. We shall go straight to Florence; we can manage there. I of course don't look to you, however," she added, "to stay with me all that time. That will require to be settled. Owen will have to join us as soon as possible; he may not be quite ready to get off with us. But I'm convinced it's quite the right thing to go. It will make a good change. It will put in a decent interval."

Fleda listened; she was deeply mystified. "How kind you are to me!" she presently said. The picture suggested so many questions that she scarce knew which to ask first. She took one at a venture. "You really have it from Mr. Gereth that he'll give us his company?"

If Mr. Gereth's mother smiled in response to this Fleda knew that her smile was a tacit criticism of such a mode of dealing with her son. Fleda habitually spoke of him as Mr. Owen, and it was a part of her present system to appear to have relinquished that right. Mrs. Gereth's manner confirmed a certain betrayal of her pretending to more than she felt; her very first words had conveyed it, and it reminded Fleda of the conscious courage with which, weeks before, the lady had met her visitor's first startled stare at the clustered spoils of Poynton. It was her practice to take immensely for granted whatever she wished. "Oh if you'll answer for him it will do quite as well!" With this answer she put her hands on the girl's shoulders and held them at arm's length, as to shake them a little, while in the depths of her shining eyes Fleda saw something obscure and unquiet. "You bad false thing, why did n't you tell me?" Her tone softened her harshness, and her visitor had never had such a sense of her indulgence. Mrs. Gereth could show patience; it was a part of the general bribe, but it was also like the presentation of a heavy bill before which Fleda could only fumble in a penniless pocket. "You must perfectly have known at Ricks, and yet you practically denied it. That's why I call you bad and false!" It was apparently also why she again almost roughly kissed her.

"I think that before I satisfy you I had better know what you're talking about," Fleda said.

Mrs. Gereth looked at her with a slight increase of hardness. "You've done everything you need for modesty, my dear! If he's sick with love of you, you haven't had to wait for me to inform you."

Fleda knew herself turn pale. "Has he informed *you*, dear Mrs. Gereth?"

Dear Mrs. Gereth smiled sweetly. "How could he when our situation is such that he communicates with me only through you and that you're so tortuous you conceal everything?"

"Didn't he answer the note in which you let him know I was in town?" Fleda asked.

"He answered it sufficiently by rushing off on the spot to see you."

Mrs. Gereth met this allusion with a prompt firmness that made almost insolently light of any ground of complaint, and Fleda's own sense of responsibility was now so vivid that all resentments comparatively shrank. She had no heart to produce a grievance; she could only, left as she was with the little mystery on her hands, produce after a moment a question. "How then do you come to know that your son has ever thought —"

"That he would give his ears to get you?" Mrs. Gereth broke in. "I had a visit from Mrs. Brigstock."

Fleda opened her eyes. "She went down to Ricks?"

"The day after she had found Owen at your feet. She knows everything."

Fleda shook her head sadly: she was more startled than she cared to show. This odd journey of Mrs. Brigstock's, which, with a simplicity equal for once to Owen's, she had not divined, now struck her as at bottom of the hush of the last ten days. "There are things she does n't know!" she presently returned.

"She knows he 'd do anything to marry you."

"He has n't told her so," Fleda said.

"No, but he has told *you*. That's better still!" laughed Mrs. Gereth. "My dear child," she went on with an air that affected the girl as a blind profanity, "don't try to make yourself out better than you are. *I* know what you are — I have n't lived with you so much for nothing. You're not quite a saint in heaven yet. Lord, what a creature you 'd have thought me in my good time! But you do like it fortunately, you idiot. You're pale with your passion, you sweet thing. That's exactly what I wanted to see. I can't for the life of me think where the shame comes in." Then with a finer significance, a look that seemed to Fleda strange, she added: "It's all right."

"I 've seen him but twice," said Fleda.

"But twice?" Mrs. Gereth still smiled.

"On the occasion, at papa's, that Mrs. Brigstock told you of, and one day, since then, down at Maggie's."

"Well, those things are between yourselves, and

you seem to me both poor creatures at best." She spoke with a rich humour which made her attitude indeed a complacency. "I don't know what you've got in your veins. You absurdly exaggerate the difficulties. But enough's as good as a feast, and when once I get you abroad together —!" Mrs. Gereth checked herself as from excess of meaning; what might happen when she should get them abroad together was to be gathered only from the way she slowly rubbed her hands.

The gesture, however, made the promise so definite that for a moment her companion was almost beguiled. Yet there was still nothing to account for the wealth of her certitude: the visit of the lady of Waterbath appeared but half to explain it. "Is it permitted to be surprised," Fleda deferentially asked, "at Mrs. Brigstock's thinking it would help her to see you?"

"It's never permitted to be surprised at the aberrations of born fools," said Mrs. Gereth. "If a cow should try to calculate, that's the kind of happy thought she'd have. Mrs. Brigstock came down to plead with me."

Fleda mused a moment. "That's what she came to do with *me*," she then honestly returned. "But what did she expect to get of you — with your opposition so marked from the first?"

"She didn't know I want *you*, my dear. It's a wonder, with all my violence — the gross publicity I've given my desires. But she's as stupid as an owl — she doesn't feel your charm."

Fleda felt herself flush slightly, and her amusement

at this was ineffective. "Did you tell her all about my charm? Did you make her understand you want me?"

"For what do you take me? I was n't such a booby."

"So as not to aggravate Mona?" Fleda suggested.

"So as not to aggravate Mona, naturally. We 've had a narrow course to steer, but thank God we 're at last in the open!"

"What do you call the open, Mrs. Gereth?" Fleda demanded. Then as that lady faltered: "Do you know where Mr. Owen is to-day?"

His mother stared. "Do you mean he 's at Waterbath? Well, that 's your own affair. I can bear it if *you* can."

"Wherever he is I can bear it," Fleda said. "But I have n't the least idea where he is."

"Then you ought to be ashamed of yourself!" her friend broke out with a change of note that showed how deep a passion underlay everything she had said. The poor woman, catching her hand, however, the next moment, as if to retract something of this harshness, spoke more patiently. "Don't you understand, Fleda, how immensely, how devotedly I 've trusted you!" Her tone was indeed a supplication.

Fleda was infinitely shaken; she could n't immediately speak. "Yes, I understand. Did she go to you to complain of me?"

"She came to see what she could do. She had been tremendously upset the day before by what had taken place at your father's, and she had posted down to Ricks on the inspiration of the moment. She had n't meant it on leaving home; it was the sight of you closeted there with Owen that had suddenly determined her. The whole story, she said, was written in your two faces: she spoke as if she had never seen such an exhibition. Owen was on the brink, but there might still be time to save him, and it was with this idea she had bearded me in my den. 'What won't a mother do, you know?' — that was one of the things she said. What would n't a mother do indeed? I thought I had sufficiently shown her what! She tried to break me down by an appeal to my good nature, as she called it, and from the moment she opened on *you*, from the moment she denounced Owen's falsity, I was as good-natured as she could wish. I understood it as a plea for mere mercy — because you and he between you were killing her child. Of course I was delighted that Mona should be killed, but I was studiously kind to Mrs. Brigstock. At the same time I was honest, I did n't pretend to anything I could n't feel. I asked her why the marriage had n't taken place months ago, when Owen was perfectly ready; and I showed her how completely that fatuous mistake on Mona's part cleared his responsibility. It was she who had killed *him* — it was she who had destroyed his affection, his illusions. Did she want him now when he was estranged, when he was disgusted, when he had a sore grievance? She reminded me that Mona had a sore grievance too, but admitted she had n't come to me to speak of that. What she had come for was not to get the old things back, but simply to get

Owen. What she wanted was that I would, in simple pity, see fair play. Owen had been awfully bedevilled — she did n't call it that, she called it 'misled'; but it was simply you who had bedevilled him. He would be all right still if I would only see you well out of the way. She asked me point-blank if it was possible I could want him to marry you."

Fleda had listened in unbearable pain and growing terror, as if her companion, stone by stone, were piling some fatal mass upon her breast. She had the sense of being buried alive, smothered in the mere expansion of another will; and now there was but one gap left to the air. A single word, she felt, might close it, and with the question that came to her lips as Mrs. Gereth paused she seemed to herself to ask, in cold dread, for her doom. "What did you say to that?" she gasped.

"I was embarrassed, for I saw my danger — the danger of her going home and saying to Mona that I was backing you up. It had been a bliss to learn that Owen had really turned to you, but my joy did n't put me off my guard. I reflected intensely a few seconds; then I saw my issue."

"Your issue?" Fleda echoed.

"I remembered how you had tied my hands about saying a word to Owen."

Fleda wondered. "And did you remember the little letter that, with your hands tied, you still succeeded in writing him?"

"Perfectly; my little letter was a model of reticence. What I remembered was all that in those few words I forbade myself to say. I had been an angel of delicacy — I had effaced myself like a saint. It was n't for me to have done all that and then figure to such a woman as having done the opposite. Besides, it was none of her business."

"Is that what you said to her?" the girl asked.

"I said to her that her question revealed a total misconception of the nature of my present relations with my son. I said to her that I had no relations with him at all and that nothing had passed between us for months. I said to her that my hands were spotlessly clean of any attempt to make up to you. I said to her that I had taken from Poynton what I had a right to take, but had done nothing else in the world. I was determined that since I had bitten my tongue off to oblige you I would at least have the righteousness that my sacrifice gave me."

"And was Mrs. Brigstock satisfied with your answer?"

"She was visibly relieved."

"It was fortunate for you," said Fleda, "that she's apparently not aware of the manner in which, almost under her nose, you advertised me to him at Poynton."

Mrs. Gereth appeared to recall that scene; she smiled with a serenity remarkably effective as showing how cheerfully used she had grown to invidious allusions to it. "How should she be aware of it?"

"She would if Owen had described your outbreak to Mona."

"Yes, but he did n't describe it. All his instinct was to conceal it from Mona. He was n't conscious, but he was already in love with you!" Mrs. Gereth declared.

Fleda shook her head wearily. "No — I was only in love with *him!*"

Here was a faint illumination with which Mrs. Gereth instantly mingled her fire. "You dear old wretch!" she exclaimed; and she again, with ferocity, embraced her young friend.

Fleda submitted like a sick animal: she would submit to everything now. "Then what further passed?"

"Only that she left me thinking she had got something."

"And what had she got?"

"Nothing but her luncheon. But *I* got everything!"

"Everything?" Fleda quavered.

Mrs. Gereth, struck apparently by something in her tone, looked at her from a tremendous height. "Don't fail me now!"

It sounded so like a menace that, with a full divination at last, the poor girl fell weakly into a chair. "What on earth have you done?"

Mrs. Gereth stood there in all the glory of a great stroke. "I've settled you." She filled the room, to Fleda's scared vision, with the glare of her magnificence. "I've sent everything back."

"Everything?" Fleda wailed.

"To the smallest snuff-box. The last load went yesterday. The same people did it. Poor little Ricks is empty." Then as if, for a crowning splendour, to check all deprecation, "They're yours, you goose!" the wonderful woman concluded, holding up her handsome head and rubbing her white hands. But there were tears none the less in her deep eyes.

XVIII

FLEDA was slow to take in the announcement, but when she had done so she felt it to be more than her cup of bitterness would hold. Her bitterness was her anxiety, the taste of which suddenly sickened her. What had she on the spot become but a dire traitress to her friend? The treachery increased with the view of the friend's motive, a motive splendid as a tribute to her value. Mrs. Gereth had wished to make sure of her and had reasoned that there would be no such way as by a large appeal to her honour. If it be true, as men have declared, that the sense of honour is weak in women, some of the bearings of this stroke might have thrown a light on the question. What was now at all events put before Fleda was that she had been made sure of, since the greatness of the surrender imposed an obligation as great. There was an expression she had heard used by young men with whom she danced: the only word to fit Mrs. Gereth's intention was that Mrs. Gereth had designed to "fetch" her. It was a calculated, it was a crushing bribe; it looked her in the eyes and said awfully: "That's what I do for you!" What Fleda was to do in return required no pointing out. The sense at present of how little she had done it made her almost cry out with pain; but her first endeavour in face of the fact was to keep such a cry from reaching her companion. How little she had

212

done it Mrs. Gereth did n't yet know, and possibly there would be still some way of turning round before the discovery. On her own side too Fleda had almost made one: she had known she was wanted, but she had not after all conceived how magnificently much. She had been treated by her friend's act as a conscious prize, but her value consisted all in the power the act itself imputed to her. As high bold diplomacy it dazzled and carried her off her feet. She admired the noble risk of it, a risk Mrs. Gereth had faced for the utterly poor creature the girl now felt herself. The change it instantly wrought in her was moreover extraordinary: it transformed at a touch her feeling on the subject of concessions. A few weeks earlier she had jumped at the duty of pleading for them, practically quarrelling with the lady of Ricks for her refusal to restore what she had taken. She had been sore with the wrong to Owen, she had bled with the wounds of Poynton; now, however, as she heard of the replenishment of the void that had so haunted her she came as near sounding an alarm as if from the deck of a ship she had seen a person she loved jump into the sea. Mrs. Gereth had become in a flash the victim; poor little Ricks had yielded up its treasure in a night. If Fleda's present view of the "spoils" had taken precipitate form the form would have been a frantic command. It was indeed for mere want of breath she did n't shout "Oh stop them — it's no use; bring them back — it's too late!" And what most kept her breathless was her companion's very grandeur. Fleda distinguished as never before the purity of the passion concerned; it made Mrs. Gereth august and almost sublime. It was absolutely unselfish — she cared nothing for mere possession. She thought solely and incorruptibly of what was best for the objects themselves; she had surrendered them to the presumptive care of the one person of her acquaintance who felt about them as she felt herself and whose long lease of the future would be the nearest approach that could be compassed to committing them to a museum. Now it was indeed that Fleda knew what rested on her; now it was also that she measured as for the first time her friend's notion of the natural influence of a grand "haul." Mrs. Gereth had risen to the idea of blowing away the last doubt of what her young charge would gain, of making good still more than she was obliged to make it the promise of weeks before. It was one thing for the girl to have learnt that in a certain event restitution would be made; it was another for her to see the condition, with a noble trust, treated in advance as performed, and to know she should have only to open a door to find every old piece in every old corner. To have played such a card would be thus, for so grand a gambler, practically to have won the game. Fleda had certainly to recognise that, so far as the theory of the matter went, the game had been won. Oh she had been made sure of!

She could n't, however, succeed for so very many minutes in putting off her exposure. "Why did n't you wait, dearest? Ah why did n't you wait?" — if that inconsequent appeal kept rising to her lips to be cut short before it was spoken, this was only because at first the humility of gratitude helped her to gain time, enabled her to present herself very honestly as too overcome to be clear. She kissed her companion's hands, she did homage at her feet, she murmured soft snatches of praise, and yet in the midst of it all was conscious that what she really showed most was the dark despair at her heart. She saw the poor woman's glimpse of this strange reserve suddenly widen, heard the quick chill of her voice pierce through the false courage of endearments. "Do you mean to tell me at such an hour as this that you've really lost him?"

The tone of the question made the idea a possibility for which Fleda had nothing from this moment but terror. "I don't know, Mrs. Gereth; how can I say?" she asked. "I've not seen him for so long; as I told you just now, I don't even know where he is. That's by no fault of his," she hurried on: "he would have been with me every day if I had consented. But I made him understand, the last time, that I'll receive him again only when he's able to show me his release as quite signed and sealed. Oh he can't yet, don't you see? — and that's why he has n't been back. It's far better than his coming only that we should both be miserable. When he does come he'll be in a better position. He'll be tremendously moved by the wonderful thing you've done. I know you wish me to feel you've done it as much for me as for Owen, but your having done it for me is just what will delight him most! When he hears of it," said Fleda in panting optimism, "when he hears of it —!" There indeed, regretting her advance

215

and failing of every confidence, she quite broke
down. She was wholly powerless to say what Owen
would do when he heard of it. "I don't know what
he won't make of you and how he won't hug you!"
she had to content herself with meanly declaring.
She had drawn her terrible dupe and judge to a sofa
with a vague instinct of pacifying her and still, after
all, gaining time; but it was a position in which that
extraordinary character, portentously patient again
during this demonstration, looked far from inviting
a "hug." Fleda found herself tricking out the situation with artificial flowers, trying to talk even herself into the fancy that Owen, whose name she now
made simple and sweet, might come in upon them
at any moment. She felt an immense need to be
understood and justified; she abjectly averted her face
from all she might have to be forgiven. She pressed
on her hostess's arm as if to keep her quiet till she
should really know, and then, after a minute, she
poured out the clear essence of what in happier days
had been her "secret." "You must n't think I don't
adore him when I've told him so to his face. I love
him so that I'd die for him — I love him so that it's
horrible. Don't look at me therefore as if I had n't
been kind, as if I had n't been as tender as if he
were dying and my tenderness were what would save
him. Look at me as if you believe me, as if you feel
what I've been through. Darling Mrs. Gereth, I
could kiss the ground he walks on. I have n't a rag
of pride; I used to have, but it's gone. I used to
have a secret, but every one knows it now, and any
one who looks at me can say, I think, what's the

matter with me. It's not so very fine, my secret, and
the less one really says about it the better; but I want
you to have it from me because I was stiff before.
I want you to see for yourself that I've been brought
as low as a girl can very well be. It serves me right,"
Fleda laughed, "if I was ever proud and horrid to
you! I don't know what you wanted me, in those
days at Ricks, to do, but I don't think you can have
wanted much more than what I've done. The other
day at Maggie's I did things that made me afterwards
think of you! I don't know what girls may do; but
if he does n't know that there is n't an inch of me
that is n't his —!" Fleda sighed as if she could n't
express it; she piled it up, as she would have said;
holding Mrs. Gereth with dilated eyes she seemed to
sound her for the effect of these professions. "It's
idiotic," she wearily smiled; "it's so strange that
I'm almost angry for it, and the strangest part of
all is that it is n't even happiness. It's anguish — it
was from the first; from the first there was a bitterness
and a dread. But I owe you every word of the truth.
You don't do him justice either; he's a dear, I assure
you he's a dear: I'd trust him to the last breath. I
don't think you really know him. He's ever so much
cleverer than he makes any show of; he's remarkable in his own shy way. You told me at Ricks that
you wanted me to let myself go, and I've 'gone'
quite far enough to discover as much as that, as well
as all sorts of other delightful things about him.
You'll tell me I make myself out worse than I am,"
said the girl, feeling more and more in her companion's attitude a quality that treated her speech

as a desperate rigmarole and even perhaps as a piece of cold immodesty. She wanted to make herself out "bad" — it was a part of her justification; but it suddenly occurred to her that such a picture of her extravagance imputed a want of gallantry to the young man. "I don't care for anything you think," she declared, "because Owen, don't you know? sees me as I am. He's so kind that it makes up for everything!"

This attempt at gaiety was futile; the silence with which for a minute her great swindled benefactress greeted her troubled plea brought home to her afresh that she was on the bare defensive. "Is it a part of his kindness never to come near you?" Mrs. Gereth enquired at last. "Is it a part of his kindness to leave you without an inkling of where he is?" She rose again from where Fleda had kept her down; she seemed to tower there in the majesty of her gathered wrong. "Is it a part of his kindness that after I've toiled as I've done for six days, and with my own weak hands, which I haven't spared, to denude myself, in your interest, to that point that I've nothing left, as I may say, but what I have on my back — is it a part of his kindness that you're not even able to produce him for me?"

There was a high contempt in this which was for Owen quite as much, and in the light of which Fleda felt that her effort at plausibility had been mere grovelling. She rose from the sofa with an humiliated sense of rising from ineffectual knees. That discomfort, however, lived but an instant: it was swept away in a rush of loyalty to the absent. She herself could bear his mother's scorn, but to avert it from all *his* decency she broke out with a quickness that was like the raising of an arm. "Don't blame him — don't blame him: he'd do anything on earth for me! It was I," said Fleda eagerly, "who sent him back to her. I made him go, I pushed him out of the house. I declined to have anything to say to him except on another footing."

Mrs. Gereth stared as at some gross material ravage. "Another footing? What other footing?"

"The one I've already made so clear to you: my having it from her in black and white, as you may say, that she freely gives him up."

"Then you think he lies when he tells you he has recovered his liberty?"

Fleda failed of presence of mind a moment; after which she exclaimed with a certain hard pride: "He's enough in love with me for anything!"

"For anything apparently save to act like a man and impose his reason and his will on your incredible folly. For anything save to put an end, as any man worthy of the name would have put it, to your systematic, to your idiotic perversity. What are you, after all, my dear, I should like to know, that a gentleman who offers you what Owen offers should have to meet such wonderful exactions, to take such extraordinary precautions about your sweet little scruples?" Her resentment rose to a high insolence which Fleda took full in the face and which, for the moment at least, had the horrible force to present to her vengefully a showy side of the truth. It gave her a blinding glimpse of lost alternatives. "I don't know what to think of him," Mrs. Gereth went on; "I don't know what to call him: I'm so ashamed of him that I can scarcely speak of him even to *you*. But indeed I'm so ashamed of you both together that I scarcely know in common decency where to look." She paused to give Fleda the full benefit of this harsh statement; then she exclaimed with the very best of her coarseness: "Any one but a jackass would have tucked you under his arm and marched you off to the Registrar!"

Fleda wondered; with her free imagination she could wonder even while her cheek stung from a slap. "To the Registrar?"

"That would have been the sane sound immediate course to adopt. With a grain of gumption you'd both instantly have felt it. *I* should have found a way to take you, you know, if I had been what Owen's supposed to be. *I* should have got the business over first — then the rest could come when you liked! Good God, girl, your place was to stand before me as a woman honestly married. One does n't know what one has hold of in touching you, and you must excuse my saying that you're literally unpleasant to me to meet as you are. Then at least we could have talked, and Owen, if he had the ghost of a sense of humour, could have snapped his fingers at your refinements."

This stirring speech affected our young lady as if it had been the shake of a tambourine borne toward her from a gipsy dance: her head seemed to go round and she felt a sudden passion in her feet. The thrill, however, was but meagrely expressed in the flatness

with which she heard herself presently say: "I'll go
to the Registrar now."

"Now?" Magnificent was the sound Mrs. Gereth
threw into this monosyllable. "And pray who's to
take you?" Fleda gave a colourless smile, and her
companion continued: "Do you literally mean that
you can't put your hand upon him?" Fleda's sick
grimace appeared to irritate her; she made a short
imperious gesture. "Find him for me, you fool —
find him for me!"

"What do you want of him," Fleda dismally asked
— "feeling as you do to both of us?"

"Never mind how I feel, and never mind what
I say when I'm furious!" Mrs. Gereth still more
incisively added. "Of course I cling to you, you
wretches, or I should n't suffer as I do. What I want
of him is to see that he takes you; what I want of him
is to go with you myself to the place." She looked
round the room as if, in feverish haste, for a mantle
to catch up; she bustled to the window as if to spy
out a cab: she would allow half an hour for the job.
Already in her bonnet, she had snatched from the
sofa a garment for the street: she jerked it on as she
came back. "Find him, find him," she repeated;
"come straight out with me to try at least and get *at*
him!"

"How can I get *at* him? He'll come when he's
ready," our young woman quavered.

Mrs. Gereth turned on her sharply. "Ready for
what? Ready to see me ruined without a reason or
a reward?"

Fleda could at first say nothing; the worst of it all

was the something still unspoken between them. Neither of them dared utter it, but the influence of it was in the girl's tone when she returned at last with great gentleness: "Don't be cruel to me — I'm very unhappy." The words produced a visible impression on Mrs. Gereth, who held her face averted and sent off through the window a gaze that kept pace with the long caravan of her treasures. Fleda knew she was watching it wind up the avenue of Poynton — Fleda participated indeed fully in the vision; so that after a little the most consoling thing seemed to her to add: "I don't see why in the world you take so for granted that he's, as you say, 'lost.'"

Mrs. Gereth continued to stare out of the window, and her stillness denoted some success in controlling herself. "If he's not lost why are you unhappy?"

"I'm unhappy because I torment you and you don't understand me."

"No, Fleda, I don't understand you," said Mrs. Gereth, finally facing her again. "I don't understand you at all, and it's as if you and Owen were of quite another race and another flesh. You make me feel very old-fashioned and simple and bad. But you must take me as I am, since you take so much else *with* me!" She spoke now with the drop of her resentment, with a dry and weary calm. "It would have been better for me if I had never known you," she pursued, "and certainly better if I had n't taken such an extraordinary fancy to you. But that too was inevitable: everything, I suppose, is inevitable. It was all my own doing — you did n't run after me: I pounced on you and caught you up. You're a stiff little beggar, in spite of your pretty manners: yes, you're hideously misleading. I hope you feel how handsome it is of me to recognise the independence of your character. It was your clever sympathy that did it — your beautiful feeling for those accursed vanities. You were sharper about them than any one I had ever known, and that was a thing I simply could n't resist. Well," the poor lady concluded after a pause, "you see where it has landed us!"

"If you'll go for him yourself I'll wait here," said Fleda.

Mrs. Gereth, holding her mantle together, appeared for a while to consider. "To his club, do you mean?"

"Is n't it there, when he's in town, that he has a room? He has at present no other London address," Fleda said. "It's there one writes to him."

"How do *I* know, with my wretched relations with him?" Mrs. Gereth cried.

"Mine have not been quite so bad as that," Fleda desperately smiled. Then she added: "His silence, *her* silence, our hearing nothing at all — what are these but the very things on which, at Poynton and at Ricks, you rested your assurance that everything is at an end between them?"

Mrs. Gereth looked dark and void. "Yes, but I had n't heard from you then that you could invent nothing better than, as you call it, to send him back to her."

"Ah but on the other hand" — the girl sprung to this — "you've learned from them what you did n't know, you've learned by Mrs. Brigstock's visit that

223

he cares for me." She found herself in the position of availing herself of optimistic arguments that she formerly had repudiated; her refutation of her companion had completely changed its ground. A fever of ingenuity had started to burn in her, though she was painfully conscious, on behalf of her success, that it was visible as fever. She could herself see the reflexion of it gleam in her critic's sombre eyes.

"You plunge me in stupefaction," that personage answered, "and at the same time you terrify me. Your account of Owen's inconceivable, and yet I don't know what to hold on by. He cares for you, it does appear, and yet in the same breath you tell me that nothing is more possible than that he's spending these days at Waterbath. Pardon me if I'm so dull as not to see my way in such darkness. If he's at Waterbath he does n't care for you. If he cares for you he's not at Waterbath."

"Then where is he?" poor Fleda helplessly wailed. She caught herself up, however; she would do her best to be brave and clear. Before Mrs. Gereth could reply, with due obviousness, that this was a question for her not to ask but to answer, she found an air of assurance to say: "You simplify far too much. You always did and you always will. The tangle of life is much more intricate than you've ever, I think, felt it to be. You slash into it," cried Fleda finely, "with a great pair of shears; you nip at it as if you were one of the Fates! If Owen's at Waterbath he's there to wind everything up."

His mother shook her head with slow austerity. "You don't believe a word you're saying. I've frightened you, as you've frightened me: you're whistling in the dark to keep up our courage. I do simplify, doubtless, if to simplify is to fail to comprehend the inanity of a passion that bewilders a young blockhead with bugaboo barriers, with hideous and monstrous sacrifices. I can only repeat that you're beyond me. Your perversity's a thing to howl over. However," the poor woman continued with a break in her voice, a long hesitation and then the dry triumph of her will, "I'll never mention it to you again! Owen I can just make out; for Owen *is* a blockhead. Owen's a blockhead," she repeated with a quiet tragic finality, looking straight into Fleda's eyes. "I don't know why you dress up so the fact that he's disgustingly weak."

Fleda at last, before her companion's, lowered her look. "Because I love him. It's because he's weak that he needs me," she added.

"That was why his father, whom he exactly resembles, needed *me*. And I did n't fail his father," said Mrs. Gereth. She gave her visitor a moment to appreciate the remark; after which she pursued: "Mona Brigstock is n't weak. She's stronger than you!"

"I never thought she was weak," Fleda answered. She looked vaguely round the room with a new purpose: she had lost sight of her umbrella.

"I did tell you to let yourself go, but it's clear enough that you really have n't," Mrs. Gereth declared. "If Mona has got him —"

Fleda had accomplished her search; her hostess paused. "If Mona has got him?" the girl panted, tightening the umbrella.

"Well," said Mrs. Gereth profoundly, "it will be clear enough that Mona *has*."

"Has let herself go?"

"Has let herself go." Mrs. Gereth spoke as if she meant it to the fullest extent of her cynicism and saw it in every detail.

Fleda felt the tone and finished her preparation; then she went and opened the door. "We'll look for him together," she said to her friend, who stood a moment taking in her face. "They may know something about him at the Colonel's."

"We'll go there." Mrs. Gereth had picked up her gloves and her purse. "But the first thing," she went on, "will be to wire to Poynton."

"Why not to Waterbath at once?" Fleda asked.

Her companion wondered. "In *your* name?"

"In my name. I noticed a place at the corner."

While Fleda held the door open Mrs. Gereth drew on her gloves. "Forgive me," she presently said. "Kiss me," she added.

Fleda, on the threshold, kissed her. Then they both went out.

XIX

In the place at the corner, on the chance of its saving time, Fleda wrote her telegram — wrote it in silence under Mrs. Gereth's eye and then in silence handed it to her. "I send this to Waterbath, on the possibility of your being there, to ask you to come to me." Mrs. Gereth held it a moment, read it more than once; then keeping it, and with her eyes on her companion, seemed to consider. There was the dawn of a kindness in her look; Fleda measured in it, as the reward of complete submission, a slight relaxation of her rigour.

"Would n't it perhaps after all be better," she asked, "before doing this, to see if we can make his whereabouts certain?"

"Why so? It will be always so much done," said Fleda. "Though I'm poor," she added with a smile, "I don't mind the shilling."

"The shilling's *my* shilling," said Mrs. Gereth.

Fleda stayed her hand. "No, no — I'm superstitious. To succeed it must be all me!"

"Well, if that will make it succeed!" Mrs. Gereth took back her shilling, but she still kept the telegram. "As he's most probably not there —"

"If he should n't be there," Fleda interrupted, "there will be no harm done."

"If he 'should n't be' there!" Mrs. Gereth ejaculated. "Heaven help us, how you assume it!"

227

"I'm only prepared for the worst. The Brigstocks will simply send any telegram on."

"Where will they send it?"

"Presumably to Poynton."

"They'll read it first," said Mrs. Gereth. "Yes, Mona will. She'll open it under the pretext of having it repeated, and then will probably do nothing. She'll keep it as a proof of your immodesty."

"What of that?" asked Fleda.

"You don't mind her seeing it?"

Rather musingly and absently she shook her head. "I don't mind anything."

"Well then, that's all right," said Mrs. Gereth as wanting only to feel she had been irreproachably considerate. After this she was gentler still, yet had another point to clear up. "Why have you given, for a reply, your sister's address?"

"Because if he does come to me he must come to me there. If that telegram goes," said Fleda, "I return to Maggie's to-night."

Her friend seemed to wonder at this. "You won't receive him here with me?"

"No, I won't receive him here with you. Only where I received him last — only there again." As to this Fleda was firm.

But Mrs. Gereth had obviously now had some practice in following queer movements prompted by queer feelings. She resigned herself, though she fingered the paper a moment longer. She appeared to hesitate, then brought out: "You couldn't then, if I release you, make your message a little stronger?"

Fleda gave her a faint smile. "He'll come if he can."

She met fully what this conveyed; with decision she pushed in the telegram. But she laid her hand quickly on another form and with still greater decision wrote another message. "This from *me*," she said to Fleda when she had finished: "to catch him possibly at Poynton. Will you read it?"

Fleda turned away. "Thank you."

"It's stronger than yours."

"I don't care"—and the girl moved to the door. Mrs. Gereth, having paid for the second missive, rejoined her, and they drove together to Owen's club, where the elder lady alone got out. Fleda, from the hansom, watched through the glass doors her brief conversation with the hall-porter and then met in silence her return with the news that he had not seen Owen for a fortnight and was keeping his letters till called for. These had been the last orders; there were a dozen letters lying there. He had no more information to give, but they would see what they could find at Colonel Gereth's. To any connexion with this enquiry, however, Fleda now roused herself to object, and her friend had indeed to recognise that on second thoughts it could n't be quite to the taste of either of them to advertise in the remoter reaches of the family that they had forfeited the confidence of the master of Poynton. The letters lying at the club proved effectively that he was not in London, and this was the question that immediately concerned them. Nothing could concern them further till the answers to their telegrams should have had time to arrive. Mrs. Gereth had got back into the cab, and, still at the door of the club, they sat staring at their need of patience. Fleda's eyes rested, in the great hard street, on passing figures that struck her as puppets pulled by strings. After a little the driver challenged them through the hole in the top. "Any-where in particular, ladies?"

Fleda decided. "Drive to Euston, please."

"You won't wait for what we may hear?" Mrs. Gereth asked.

"Whatever we hear I must go." As the cab went on she added: "But I need n't drag *you* to the station."

Mrs. Gereth had a pause; then "Nonsense!" she sharply replied.

In spite of this sharpness they were now almost equally and almost tremulously mild; though their mildness took mainly the form of an inevitable sense of nothing left to say. It was the unsaid that occupied them — the thing that for more than an hour they had been going round and round without naming it. Much too early for Fleda's train, they encountered at the station a long half-hour to wait. Fleda made no further allusion to Mrs. Gereth's leaving her; their dumbness, with the elapsing min-utes, grew to be in itself a reconstituted bond. They slowly paced the great grey platform, and presently Mrs. Gereth took the girl's arm and leaned on it with a hard demand for support. It seemed to Fleda not difficult for each to know of what the other was think-ing — to know indeed that they had in common two alternating visions, one of which at moments brought them as by a common impulse to a pause. This was the one that was fixed; the other filled at times the whole space and then was shouldered away. Owen and Mona glared together out of the gloom and disappeared, but the replenishment of Poynton made a shining steady light. The old splendour was there again, the old things were in their places. Our friends looked at them with an equal yearning; face to face on the platform, they counted them in each other's eyes. Fleda had come back to them by a road as strange as the road they themselves had followed. The wonder of their great journeys, the prodigy of this second one, was the question that made her occasionally stop. Several times she uttered it, asked how this and that difficulty had been met. Mrs. Gereth replied with pale lucidity — was naturally the person most familiar with the truth that what she undertook was always somehow achieved. To do it was to do it—she had more than one kind of magnificence. She confessed there, audaciously enough, to a sort of arrogance of energy, and Fleda, going on again, her appeal more than answered and her arm rendering service, flushed in her diminished identity with the sense that such a woman was great.

"You do mean literally everything, to the last little miniature on the last little screen?"

"I mean literally everything. Go over them with the catalogue!"

Fleda went over them while they walked again; she had no need of the catalogue. At last she spoke once more. "Even the Maltese cross?"

"Even the Maltese cross. Why not that as well as everything else? — especially as I remembered how you like it."

Finally, after an interval, the girl exclaimed: "But the mere fatigue of it, the exhaustion of such a feat! I drag you to and fro here while you must be ready to drop."

"I'm very, very tired." Mrs. Gereth's slow head-shake was tragic. "I could n't do it again."

"I doubt if they'd bear it again!"

"That's another matter: they'd bear it if *I* could. There won't have been, this time either, a shake or a scratch. But I'm too tired — I very nearly don't care."

"You must sit down then till I go," said Fleda. "We must find a bench."

"No. I'm tired of *them :* I'm not tired of you. This is the way for you to feel most how much I rest on you." Fleda had a compunction, wondering as they continued to stroll whether it was right after all to leave her. She believed however that if the flame might for the moment burn low it was far from dying out; an impression presently confirmed by the way Mrs. Gereth went on: "But one's fatigue's nothing. The idea under which one worked kept one up. For you I *could* — I can still. Nothing will have mattered if *she*'s not there."

There was a question that this imposed, but Fleda at first found no voice to utter it: it was the thing that between them, since her arrival, had been so consciously and vividly unsaid. Finally she was able to breathe: "And if she *is* there — if she's there already?"

Mrs. Gereth's rejoinder too hung back; then when it came — from sad eyes as well as from lips barely moved — it was unexpectedly merciful. "It will be very hard." That was all now, and it was poignantly simple. The train Fleda was to take had drawn up; the girl kissed her as if in farewell. Mrs. Gereth submitted, then after a little brought out: "If we *have* lost —!"

"If we have lost?" Fleda repeated as she paused again.

"You'll all the same come abroad with me?"

"It will seem very strange to me if you want me. But whatever you ask, whatever you need, that I will now always do."

"I shall need your company," said Mrs. Gereth. Fleda wondered an instant if this were not practically a demand for penal submission — for a surrender that, in its complete humility, would be a long expiation. But there was none of the latent chill of the vindictive in the sequel. "We can always, as time goes on, talk of them together."

"Of the spoils —?" Fleda had selected a third-class compartment: she stood a moment looking into it and at a fat woman with a basket who had already taken possession. "Always?" she said, turning again to her friend. "Never!" she exclaimed. She got into the carriage and two men with bags and boxes immediately followed, blocking up door and window so long that when she was able to look out again Mrs. Gereth had gone.

XX

THERE came to her at her sister's no telegram in
answer to her own: the rest of that day and the whole
of the next elapsed without a word either from Owen
or from his mother. She was free, however, to her
infinite relief, from any direct dealing with suspense,
and conscious, to her surprise, of nothing that could
show her, or could show Maggie and her brother-in-
law, that she was excited. Her excitement was composed of pulses as swift and fine as the revolutions
of a spinning top: she supposed she was going round,
but went round so fast that she could n't even feel
herself move. Her trouble occupied some quarter
of her soul that had closed its doors for the day and
shut out even her own sense of it; she might perhaps
have heard something if she had pressed her ear to
a partition. Instead of that she sat with her patience
in a cold still chamber from which she could look
out in quite another direction. This was to have
achieved an equilibrium to which she could n't have
given a name: indifference, resignation, despair were
the terms of a forgotten tongue. The time even
seemed not long, for what were the stages of the
journey but the very items of Mrs. Gereth's surrender? The detail of that performance, which filled
the scene, was what Fleda had now before her eyes.
The part of her loss that she could think of was the
reconstituted splendour of Poynton. It was the beauty

234

she was most touched by that, in tons, she had lost
— the beauty that, charged upon big wagons, had
safely crept back to its home. But the loss was a gain
to memory and love; it was to her too at last that,
in condonation of her treachery, the spoils had crept
back. She greeted them with open arms; she thought
of them hour after hour; they made a company with
which solitude was warm and a picture that, at this
crisis, overlaid poor Maggie's scant mahogany. It
was really her obliterated passion that had revived,
and with it an immense assent to Mrs. Gereth's early
judgement of her. She equally, she felt, was of the
religion, and like any other of the passionately pious
she could worship now even in the desert. Yes, it
was all for *her;* far round as she had gone she had
been strong enough: her love had gathered them in.
She wanted indeed no catalogue to count them over;
the array of them, miles away, was complete; each
piece, in its turn, was perfect to her; she could have
drawn up a catalogue from memory. Thus again
she lived with them, and she thought of them without a question of any personal right. That they might
have been, that they might still be hers, that they
were perhaps already another's, were ideas that had
too little to say to her. They were nobody's at all —
too proud, unlike base animals and humans, to be
reducible to anything so narrow. It was Poynton
that was theirs; they had simply recovered their own.
The joy of that for them was the source of the strange
peace that had descended like a charm.

It was broken on the third day by a telegram from
Mrs. Gereth. "Shall be with you at 11.30 — don't

meet me at station." Fleda turned this over; she
was sufficiently expert not to disobey the injunction.
She had only an hour to take in its meaning, but that
hour was longer than all the previous time. If Maggie had studied her convenience the day Owen came,
Maggie was also at the present juncture a miracle
of refinement. Increasingly and resentfully mystified,
in spite of all reassurance, by the impression that
Fleda suffered much more than she gained from the
grandeur of the Gereths, she had it at heart to ex-
emplify the perhaps truer distinction of nature that
characterised the house of Vetch. She was not, like
poor Fleda, at every one's beck, and the announced
visitor was to see no more of her than what the arrangement of luncheon might tantalisingly show.
Maggie described herself to her sister as intending
for a just provocation even the agreement she had
had with her husband that he also should keep away.
Fleda accordingly awaited alone the subject of so
many manœuvres — a period that was slightly prolonged even after the drawing-room door, at 11.30,
was thrown open. Mrs. Gereth stood there with a
face that spoke plain, but no sound fell from her till
the withdrawal of the maid, whose attention had
immediately attached itself to the rearrangement of
a window-blind and who seemed, while she bustled
at it, to contribute to the pregnant silence; before
the duration of which, however, she retreated with
a sudden stare.

"He has done it," said Mrs. Gereth, turning her
eyes avoidingly but not unperceivingly about her
and in spite of herself dropping an opinion upon the

few objects in the room. Fleda, on her side, in her silence observed how characteristically she looked at Maggie's possessions before looking at Maggie's sister. The girl understood and at first had nothing to say; she was still dumb while their guest selected, after dryly balancing, a seat less distasteful than the one that happened to be nearest. On the sofa near the window the poor woman finally showed what the two last days had done for the age of her face. Her eyes at last met Fleda's. "It's the end."

"They're married?"

"They're married."

Fleda came to the sofa in obedience to the impulse to sit down by her; then paused before her while Mrs. Gereth turned up a dead grey mask. A tired old woman sat there with empty hands in her lap. "I've heard nothing," said Fleda. "No answer came."

"That's the only answer. It's the answer to everything." So Fleda saw; for a minute she looked over her companion's head and far away. "He was n't at Waterbath. Mrs. Brigstock must have read your telegram and kept it. But mine, the one to Poynton, brought something. 'We are here — what do you want?'" Mrs. Gereth stopped as if with a failure of voice; on which Fleda sank upon the sofa and made a movement to take her hand. It met no response; there could be no attenuation. Fleda waited; they sat facing each other like strangers. "I wanted to go down," Mrs. Gereth presently continued. "Well, I went."

All the girl's effort tended for the time to a single

aim — that of taking the thing with outward detachment, speaking of it as having happened to Owen and to his mother and not in any degree to herself. Something at least of this was in the encouraging way she said: "Yesterday morning?"

"Yesterday morning. I saw him."

Fleda hesitated. "Did you see *her?*"

"Thank God, no!"

Fleda laid on her arm a hand of vague comfort, of which Mrs. Gereth took no notice. "You've been capable, just to tell me, of this wretched journey — of this consideration that I don't deserve?"

"We're together, we're together," said Mrs. Gereth. She looked helpless as she sat there, her eyes, unseeingly enough now, on a tall Dutch clock, old but rather poor, that Maggie had had as a wedding-gift and that eked out the bareness of the room.

To Fleda, in the face of the event, it appeared that this was exactly what they were not: the last inch of common ground, the ground of their past intercourse, had fallen from under them. Yet what was still there was the grand style of her companion's treatment of her. Mrs. Gereth could n't stand upon small questions, could n't in conduct make small differences. "You're magnificent!" her young friend exclaimed. "There's an extraordinary greatness in your generosity."

"We're together, we're together," Mrs. Gereth lifelessly repeated. "That's all we *are* now; it's all we have." The words brought to Fleda a sudden vision of the empty little house at Ricks; such a vision might also have been what her companion found in the face of the stopped Dutch clock. Yet with this it was clear she would still show no bitterness: she had done with that, had given the last drop to those horrible hours in London. No passion even was left her, and her forbearance only added to the force with which she represented the final vanity of everything.

Fleda was so far from a wish to triumph that she was absolutely ashamed of having anything to say for herself; but there was one thing, all the same, that not to say was impossible. "That he has done it, that he could n't *not* do it, shows how right I was." It settled for ever her attitude, and she spoke as if for her own mind; then after a little she added very gently, for Mrs. Gereth's: "That's to say it shows he was bound to her by an obligation that, however much he may have wanted to, he could n't in any sort of honour break."

Blanched and bleak, Mrs. Gereth looked at her. "What sort of an obligation do you call that? No such obligation exists for an hour between any man and any woman who have hatred on one side. He had ended by hating her, and he hates her now more than ever."

"Did he tell you so?" Fleda asked.

"No. He told me nothing but the great gawk of a fact. I saw him but for three minutes." She was silent again, and Fleda, as before some lurid image of this interview, sat without speaking. "Do you wish to appear as if you don't care?" Mrs. Gereth presently demanded.

"I'm trying not to think of myself."

"Then if you're thinking of Owen how can you *bear* to think?"

Sadly and submissively Fleda shook her head; the slow tears had come into her eyes. "I can't. I don't understand — I don't understand!" she broke out.

"*I* do then." Mrs. Gereth looked hard at the floor. "There was no obligation at the time you saw him last — when you sent him, hating her as he did, back to her."

"If he went," Fleda asked, "does n't that exactly prove that he recognised one?"

"He recognised rot! You know what *I* think of him." Fleda knew; she had no wish to provoke a fresh statement. Mrs. Gereth made one — it was her sole faint flicker of passion — to the extent of declaring that he was too abjectly weak to deserve the name of a man. For all Fleda cared! — it was his weakness she loved in him. "He took strange ways of pleasing you!" her friend went on. "There was no obligation till suddenly, the other day, the situation changed."

Fleda wondered. "Suddenly —?"

"It came to Mona's knowledge — I can't tell you how, but it came — that the things I was sending back had begun to arrive at Poynton. I had sent them for you, but it was *her* I touched." Mrs. Gereth paused; Fleda was too absorbed in her explanation to do anything but take blankly the full cold breath of this. "They were there, and that determined her."

"Determined her to what?"

"To act, to take means."

240

"To take means?" Fleda repeated.

"I can't tell you what they were, but they were powerful. She knew how," said Mrs. Gereth.

Fleda received with the same stoicism the quiet immensity of this allusion to the person who had *not* known how. But it made her think a little, and the thought found utterance, with unconscious irony, in the simple interrogation: "Mona?"

"Why not? She's a brute."

"But if he knew that so well, what chance was there in it for her?"

"How can I tell you? How can I talk of such horrors? I can only give you, of the situation, what I see. He knew it, yes. But as she could n't make him forget it she tried to make him like it. She tried and she succeeded: that's what she did. She's after all so much less of a fool than he. And what *else* had he originally liked?" Mrs. Gereth shrugged her shoulders. "She did what you would n't!" Fleda's face had grown dark with her wonder at the sense of this, but her friend's empty hands offered no balm to the pain in it. "It was that if it was anything. Nothing else meets the misery of it. Then there was quick work. Before he could turn round he was married."

Fleda, as if she had been holding her breath, gave the sigh of a listening child. "At that place you spoke of in town?"

"At a Registry-office — like a pair of low atheists."

The girl considered. "What do people say of that? I mean the 'world.'"

"Nothing, because nobody knows. They're to be

married on the seventeenth at Waterbath church. If anything else comes out everybody's a little prepared. It will pass for some stroke of diplomacy, some move in the game, some outwitting of *me*. It's known there has been a great row with me."

Fleda was mystified. "People surely know at Poynton," she objected, "if, as you say, she's there."

"She was there, day before yesterday, only for a few hours. She met him in London and went down to see the things."

Fleda remembered that she had seen them only once. "Did *you* see them?" she then ventured to ask.

"Everything."

"Are they right?"

"Quite right. There's nothing like them," said Mrs. Gereth. At this her companion took up one of her hands again and kissed it as she had done in London. "Mona went back that night; she was not there yesterday. Owen stayed on," she added.

Fleda stared. "Then she's not to live there?"

"Rather! But not till after the public marriage." Mrs. Gereth seemed to muse; then she brought out: "She'll live there alone."

"Alone?"

"She'll have it to herself."

"He won't live with her?"

"Never! But she's none the less his wife, and you're not," said Mrs. Gereth, getting up. "Our only chance is the chance she may die."

Fleda appeared to measure it: she appreciated her visitor's magnanimous use of the plural. "Mona won't die," she replied.

"Well, *I* shall, thank God! Till then" — and with this, for the first time, Mrs. Gereth put out her hand — "don't desert me."

Fleda took her hand, clasping it for a renewal of engagements already taken. She said nothing, but her silence committed her as solemnly as the vow of a nun. The next moment something occurred to her. "I must n't put myself in your son's way, you know."

Mrs. Gereth gave a laugh of bitterness. "You're prodigious! But how shall you possibly be more out of it? Owen and I—" She did n't finish her sentence.

"That's your great feeling about him," Fleda said; "but how, after what has happened, can it be his about you?"

Mrs. Gereth waited. "How do you know what has happened? You don't know what I said to him."

"Yesterday?"

"Yesterday."

They looked at each other with a long deep gaze. Then, as Mrs. Gereth seemed again about to speak, the girl, closing her eyes, made a gesture of strong prohibition. "Don't tell me!"

"Merciful powers, how you worship him!" Mrs. Gereth wonderingly moaned. It was for Fleda the shake that made the cup overflow. She had a pause, that of the child who takes time to know that he responds to an accident with pain; then, dropping again on the sofa, she broke into tears. They were beyond control, they came in long sobs, which for a moment her friend, almost with an air of indifference, stood hearing and watching. At last Mrs. Gereth too sank down again. Mrs. Gereth soundlessly wearily wept.

XXI

"IT looks just like Waterbath; but, after all, we bore *that* together": these words formed part of a letter in which, before the seventeenth, Mrs. Gereth, writing from disfigured Ricks, named to Fleda the day on which she would be expected to arrive there on a second visit. "I shan't for a long time to come," the missive continued, "be able to receive any one who may *like* it, who would try to smooth it down, and me with it; but there are always things you and I can comfortably hate together, for you're the only person who comfortably understands. You don't understand quite everything, but of all my acquaintance you're far away the least stupid. For action you're no good at all; but action's over, for me, for ever, and you'll have the great merit of knowing when I'm brutally silent what I shall be thinking about. Without setting myself up for your equal I dare say I shall also know what are your own thoughts. Moreover, with nothing else but my four walls, you'll at any rate be a bit of furniture. For that, a little, you know, I've always taken you — quite one of my best finds. So come if possible on the fifteenth."

The position of a scrap of furniture was one that Fleda could conscientiously accept, and she by no means insisted on so high a place in the list. This communication made her easier, if only by its ac-

knowledgement that her friend had something left:
it still implied recognition of the principle of property.
Something to hate, and to hate "comfortably," was
at least not the utter destitution to which, after their
last interview, she had helplessly seemed to see the
ex-mistress of Poynton go forth. She remembered
indeed that in the state in which they first saw it she
herself had "liked" the blest refuge of Ricks; and
she now wondered if the tact for which she was commended had then operated to make her keep her
kindness out of sight. She was at present ashamed of
such obliquity and made up her mind that if this
happy impression, quenched in the translated spoils,
should revive on the spot, she would utter it to her
companion without reserve. Yes, she was capable
of as much "action" as that: all the more that the
spirit of her hostess seemed for the time at least
wholly to have failed. The mother's three minutes
with the son had been a blow to all talk of travel,
and after her woeful hour at Maggie's she had, like
some great moaning wounded bird, made her way
with wings of anguish back to the nest she knew
she should find empty. Fleda, on that dire day,
could neither keep her nor give her up; she had
pressingly offered to return with her, but Mrs.
Gereth, in spite of the theory that their common
grief was a bond, had even declined all escort to
the station, conscious apparently of something abject
in her collapse and almost fiercely eager, as with
a personal shame, to be unwatched. All she had
said to Fleda was that she would go back to Ricks
that night, and the girl had lived for days after with

a dreadful image of her position and her misery there. She had had a vision of her now lying prone on some unmade bed, now pacing a bare floor as a lioness deprived of her cubs. There had been moments when her mind's ear was strained to listen for some sound of grief wild enough to be wafted from afar. But the first sound, at the end of a week, had been a note announcing, without reflexions, that the plan of going abroad had been abandoned. "It has come to me indirectly, but with much appearance of truth, that *they* are going — for an indefinite time. That quite settles it; I shall stay where I am, and as soon as I've turned round again I shall look for you." The second letter had come a week later, and on the fifteenth Fleda was on her way to Ricks.

Her arrival took the form of a surprise very nearly as violent as that of the other time. The elements were different, but the effect, like the other, arrested her on the threshold: she stood there stupefied and delighted at the magic of a passion of which such a picture represented the low-water mark. Wound up but sincere, and passing quickly from room to room, Fleda broke out before she even sat down. "If you turn me out of the house for it, my dear, there is n't a woman in England for whom it would n't be a privilege to live here." Mrs. Gereth was as honestly bewildered as she had of old been falsely calm. She looked about at the few sticks that, as she afterwards phrased it, she had gathered in, and then hard at her guest, as to protect herself against a joke all too cruel. The girl's heart gave a leap, for this stare was the sign of an opportunity. Mrs. Gereth was all unwitting; she did n't in the least know what she had done. Therefore as Fleda could tell her, Fleda suddenly became the one who knew most. That counted for the moment as a splendid position; it almost made all the difference. Yet what contradicted it was the vivid presence of the artist's idea. "Where on earth did you put your hand on such beautiful things?"

"Beautiful things?" Mrs. Gereth turned again to the little worn bleached stuffs and the sweet spindle-legs. "They're the wretched things that were here — that stupid starved old woman's."

"The maiden-aunt's, the nicest, the dearest old woman that ever lived? I thought you had got rid of the maiden-aunt."

"She was stored in an empty barn — stuck away for a sale; a matter that, fortunately, I've had neither time nor freedom of mind to arrange. I've simply, in my extremity, fished her out again."

"You've simply, in your extremity, made a delight of her." Fleda took the highest line and the upper hand, and as Mrs. Gereth, challenging her cheerfulness, turned again a lustreless eye over the contents of the place, she broke into a rapture that was unforced, yet that she was conscious of an advantage in being able to feel. She moved, as she had done on the previous occasion, from one piece to another, with looks of recognition and hands that lightly lingered, but she was as feverishly jubilant now as she had of old been anxious and mute. "Ah the little melancholy tender tell-tale things: how can they *not* speak to you and find a way to your heart? It's not the great chorus of Poynton; but

248

you're not, I'm sure, either so proud or so broken as to be reached by nothing but that. This is a voice so gentle, so human, so feminine — a faint far-away voice with the little quaver of a heart-break. You've listened to it unawares; for the arrangement and effect of everything — when I compare them with what we found the first day we came down — shows, even if mechanically and disdainfully exercised, your admirable, your infallible hand. It's your extraordinary genius; you make things 'compose' in spite of yourself. You've only to be a day or two in a place with four sticks for something to come of it!"

"Then if anything has come of it here, it has come precisely of just four. That's literally, by the inventory, all there are!" said Mrs. Gereth.

"If there were more there would be too many to convey the impression in which half the beauty resides — the impression somehow of something dreamed and missed, something reduced, relinquished, resigned: the poetry, as it were, of something sensibly *gone*." Fleda ingeniously and triumphantly worked it out. "Ah there's something here that will never be in the inventory!"

"Does it happen to be in your power to give it a name?" Mrs. Gereth's face showed the dim dawn of an amusement at finding herself seated at the feet of her pupil.

"I can give it a dozen. It's a kind of fourth dimension. It's a presence, a perfume, a touch. It's a soul, a story, a life. There's ever so much more here than you and I. We're in fact just three!"

"Oh if you count the ghosts —!"

"Of course I count the ghosts, confound you! It seems to me ghosts count double — for what they were and for what they are. Somehow there were no ghosts at Poynton," Fleda went on. "That was the only fault."

Mrs. Gereth, considering, appeared to fall in with this fine humour. "Poynton was too splendidly happy."

"Poynton was too splendidly happy," Fleda promptly echoed.

"But it's cured of that now," her companion added.

"Yes, henceforth there'll be a ghost or two."

Mrs. Gereth thought again: she found her young friend suggestive. "Only *she* won't see them."

"No, 'she' won't see them." Then Fleda said: "What I mean is, for this dear one of ours, that if she had (as I *know* she did; it's in the very touch of the air!) a great accepted pain —"

She had paused an instant, and Mrs. Gereth took her up. "Well, if she had?"

Fleda still hung fire. "Why, it was worse than yours."

Mrs. Gereth debated. "Very likely." Then she too hesitated. "The question is if it was worse than yours."

"Mine?" Fleda looked vague.

"Precisely. Yours."

At this our young lady smiled. "Yes, because it was a disappointment. She had been so sure."

"I see. And you were never sure."

"Never. Besides, I'm happy," said Fleda.

Mrs. Gereth met her eyes a while. "Goose!" she quietly remarked as she turned away. There was a curtness in it; nevertheless it represented a considerable part of the basis of their new life.

On the eighteenth *The Morning Post* had at last its clear message, a brief account of the marriage, from the residence of the bride's mother, of Mr. Owen Gereth of Poynton Park to Miss Mona Brigstock of Waterbath. There were two ecclesiastics and six bridesmaids and, as Mrs. Gereth subsequently said, a hundred frumps, as well as a special train from town: the scale of the affair sufficiently showed that the preparations had been in hand for some time back. The happy pair were described as having taken their departure for Mr. Gereth's own seat, famous for its unique collection of artistic curiosities. The newspaper and letters, the fruits of the first London post, had been brought to the mistress of Ricks in the garden; and she lingered there alone a long time after receiving them. Fleda kept at a distance; she knew what must have happened, for from one of the windows she saw her rigid in a chair, her eyes strange and fixed, the newspaper open on the ground and the letters untouched in her lap. Before the morning's end she had disappeared and the rest of that day remained in her room: it recalled to Fleda, who had picked up the newspaper, the day, months before, on which Owen had come down to Poynton to make his engagement known. The hush of the house at least was the same, and the girl's own waiting, her soft wandering, through the hours: there

251

was a difference indeed sufficiently great and of which her companion's absence might in some degree have represented a considerate recognition. That was at any rate the meaning Fleda, devoutly glad to be alone, attached to her opportunity. Mrs. Gereth's sole allusion the next day to the subject of their thoughts has already been mentioned: it was a dazzled glance at the fact that Mona's quiet pace had really never slackened.

Fleda fully assented. "I said of our disembodied friend here that she had suffered in proportion as she had been sure. But that's not always a source of suffering. It's Mona who must have been sure!"

"She was sure of *you!*" Mrs. Gereth returned. But this did n't diminish the satisfaction taken by Fleda in showing how serenely and lucidly she herself could talk.

XXII

HER relation with her wonderful friend had however in becoming a new one begun to shape itself
almost wholly on breaches and omissions. Something had dropped out altogether, and the question
between them, which time would answer, was whether
the change had made them strangers or yokefellows.
It was as if at last, for better or worse, they were, in
a clearer cruder air, really to know each other. Fleda
wondered how Mrs. Gereth had escaped hating her:
there were hours when it seemed that such a feat
might leave after all a scant margin for future acci-
dents. The thing indeed that now came out in its
simplicity was that even in her shrunken state the
lady of Ricks was larger than her wrongs. As for
the girl herself, she had made up her mind that her
feelings had no connexion with the case. It was her
claim that they had never yet emerged from the seclusion into which, after her friend's visit to her at
her sister's, we saw them precipitately retire: if she
should suddenly meet them in straggling procession
on the road it would be time enough to deal with
them. They were all bundled there together, likes
with dislikes and memories with fears; and she had
for not thinking of them the excellent reason that
she was too occupied with the actual. The actual
was not that Owen Gereth had seen his necessity
where she had pointed it out; it was that his mother's

bare spaces demanded all the tapestry the recipient of her bounty could furnish. There were moments during the month that followed when Mrs. Gereth struck her as still older and feebler and as likely to become quite easily amused.

At the end of it, one day, the London paper had another piece of news: "Mr. and Mrs. Owen Gereth, who arrived in town last week, proceed this morning to Paris." They exchanged no word about it till the evening, and none indeed would then have been uttered had not the mistress of Ricks irrelevantly broken out: "I dare say you wonder why I declared the other day with such assurance that he would n't live with her. He apparently *is* living with her."

"Surely it's the only proper thing for him to do."

"They're beyond me — I give it up," said Mrs. Gereth.

"I don't give it up — I never did," Fleda returned.

"Then what do you make of his aversion to her?"

"Oh she has dispelled it."

Mrs. Gereth said nothing for a minute. "You're prodigious in your choice of terms!" she then simply ejaculated.

But Fleda went luminously on; she once more enjoyed her great command of her subject. "I think that when you came to see me at Maggie's you saw too many things, you had too many ideas."

"You had none at all," said Mrs. Gereth. "You were completely bewildered."

"Yes, I did n't quite understand — but I think I understand now. The case is simple and logical enough. She's a person who's upset by failure and who blooms and expands with success. There was something she had set her heart upon, set her teeth about — the house exactly as she had seen it."

"She never saw it at all, she never looked at it!" cried Mrs. Gereth.

"She does n't look with her eyes; she looks with her ears. In her own way she had taken it in; she knew, she felt when it had been touched. That probably made her take an attitude that was extremely disagreeable. But the attitude lasted only while the reason for it lasted."

"Go on — I can bear it now," said Mrs. Gereth. Her companion had just perceptibly paused.

"I know you can, or I should n't dream of speaking. When the pressure was removed she came up again. From the moment the house was once more what it had to be her natural charm reasserted itself."

"Her natural charm!" — Mrs. Gereth could barely articulate.

"It's very great; everybody thinks so; there must be something in it. It operated as it had operated before. There's no need of imagining anything very monstrous. Her restored good humour, her splendid beauty and Mr. Owen's impressibility and generosity sufficiently cover the ground. His great bright sun came out!"

"And his great bright passion for another person went in. Your explanation would doubtless be perfect if he did n't love you."

Fleda was silent a little. "What do you know about his 'loving' me?"

255

"I know what Mrs. Brigstock herself told me."

"You never in your life took her word for any other matter."

"Then won't yours do?" Mrs. Gereth demanded. "Haven't I had it from your own mouth that he cares for you?"

Fleda turned pale, but she faced her companion and smiled. "You confound, Mrs. Gereth. You mix things up. You've only had it from my own mouth that I care for *him!*"

It was doubtless in contradictious allusion to this (which at the time had made her simply drop her head as in a strange vain reverie) that Mrs. Gereth said, a day or two later to her inmate: "Don't think I shall be a bit affected if I'm here to see it when he comes again to make up to you."

"He won't do that," the girl replied. Then she added, smiling: "But if he should be guilty of such bad taste it wouldn't be nice of you not to be disgusted."

"I'm not talking of disgust; I'm talking of its opposite," said Mrs. Gereth: "of any reviving pleasure one might feel in such an exhibition. I shall feel none at all. You may personally take it as you like; but what conceivable good will it do?"

Fleda wondered. "To me, do you mean?"

"Deuce take you, no! To what we don't, you know, by your wish, ever talk about."

"The spoils?" Fleda considered again. "It will do no good of any sort to anything or any one. That's another question I'd rather we shouldn't discuss, please," she gently added.

Mrs. Gereth shrugged her shoulders. "It certainly is n't worth it!"

Something in her manner prompted her companion, with a certain inconsequence, to speak again. "That was partly why I came back to you, you know — that there should be the less possibility of anything painful."

"Painful?" Mrs. Gereth stared. "What pain can I ever feel again?"

"I meant painful to myself," Fleda, with a slight impatience, explained.

"Oh I see." Her friend was silent a minute. "You use sometimes such odd expressions. Well, I shall last a little, but I shan't last for ever."

"You'll last quite as long —" But she suddenly dropped.

Mrs. Gereth took her up with a cold smile that seemed the warning of experience against hyperbole. "As long as what, please?"

The girl thought an instant; then met the difficulty by adopting, as an amendment, the same tone. "As any danger of the ridiculous."

That did for the time, and she had moreover, as the months went on, the protection of suspended allusions. This protection was marked when, in the following November, she received a letter directed in a hand a quick glance at which sufficed to make her hesitate to open it. She said nothing then or afterwards; but she opened it, for reasons that had come to her, on the morrow. It consisted of a page and a half from Owen Gereth, dated from Florence, but with no other preliminary. She knew that during the summer he had returned to England with his wife and that after a couple of months they had again gone abroad. She also knew, without communication, that Mrs. Gereth, round whom Ricks had grown submissively and indescribably sweet, had her own view of her daughter-in-law's share in this second migration. It was a piece of calculated insolence — a stroke odiously directed at showing whom it might concern that now she had Poynton fast she was perfectly indifferent to living there. *The Morning Post*, at Ricks, had again been a resource: it was stated in that journal that Mr. and Mrs. Owen Gereth proposed spending the winter in India. There was a person to whom it was clear she led her wretched husband by the nose. Such was the light in which the contemporary scene was offered to Fleda until, in her own room, late at night, she broke the seal of her letter.

"I want you inexpressibly to have as a remembrance something of mine — something of real value. Something from Poynton is what I mean and what I should prefer. You know everything there, and far better than I what's best and what is n't. There are a lot of differences, but are n't some of the smaller things the most remarkable? I mean for judges, and for what they'd bring. What I want you to take from me, and to choose for yourself, is the thing in the whole house that's most beautiful and precious. I mean the 'gem of the collection,' don't you know? If it happens to be of such a sort that you can take immediate possession of it — carry it right away with you — so much the better. You're to have it on the spot, whatever it is. I humbly entreat of you to go down there and see. The people have complete instructions: they'll act for you in every possible way and put the whole place at your service. There's a thing mamma used to call the Maltese cross and that I think I've heard her say is very wonderful. Is *that* the gem of the collection? Perhaps you'd take it or anything equally convenient. Only I do want you awfully to let it be the very pick of the place. Let me feel that I can trust you for this. You won't refuse if you'll simply think a little what it must be that makes me ask."

Fleda read that last sentence over more times even than the rest: she was baffled — she couldn't think at all of what in particular made him ask. This was indeed because it might be one of so many things. She returned for the present no answer; she merely, little by little, fashioned for herself the form that her answer should eventually wear. There was only one form that was possible — the form of doing, at her time, what he wished. She would go down to Poynton as a pilgrim might go to a shrine, and as to this she must look out for her chance. She lived with her letter, before any chance came, a month, and even after a month it had mysteries for her that she couldn't meet. What did it mean, what did it represent, to what did it correspond in his imagination or his soul? What was behind it, what was before it, what was, in the deepest depth, within it? She said to herself that with these questions she was under no obligation to deal. There was an answer to them that, for practical purposes, would do as well as another: he had found in his marriage a happiness so much greater than, in the distress of his dilemma, he had been able to take heart to believe, that he now felt he owed her a token of gratitude for having kept him in the straight path. That explanation, I say, she could throw off; but no explanation in the least mattered: what determined her was the simple strength of her impulse to respond. The passion for which what had happened had made no difference, the passion that had taken this into account before as well as after, found here an issue that there was nothing whatever to choke. It found even a relief to which her imagination immensely contributed. Would she act upon his offer? She would act with secret rapture. To have as her own something splendid that he had given her, of which the gift had been his signed desire, would be a greater joy than the greatest she had believed to be left her, and she felt that till the sense of this came home she had even herself not known what burned in her successful stillness. It was an hour to dream of and watch for; to be patient was to draw out the sweetness. She was capable of feeling it as an hour of triumph, the triumph of everything in her recent life that had not held up its head. She moved there in thought — in the great rooms she knew; she should be able to say to herself that, for once at least, her possession was as complete as that of either of the others whom it had filled only with bitterness. And a thousand times yes — her choice should know no scruple: the thing she should go down to take would be up to the height of her privilege. The whole place was in her eyes, and she spent for weeks her private hours in a luxury of comparison and debate. It should be one of the smallest things because it should be one she could have close to her; and it should be one of the finest because it was in the finest he saw his symbol. She said to herself that of what it would symbolise she was content to know nothing more than just what her having it would tell her. At bottom she inclined to the Maltese cross — with the added reason that he had named it. But she would look again and judge afresh; she would on the spot so handle and ponder that there should n't be the shade of a mistake.

Before Christmas she had a natural opportunity to go to London: there was her periodical call on her father to pay as well as a promise to Maggie to redeem. She spent her first night in West Kensington, with the idea of carrying out on the morrow the purpose that had most of a motive. Her father's affection was not inquisitive, but when she mentioned to him that she had business in the country that would oblige her to catch an early train he deprecated her excursion in view of the menace of the weather. It was spoiling for a storm: all the signs of a winter gale were in the air. She replied that she would see what the morning might bring; and it brought in fact what seemed in London an amendment. She was to go to Maggie the next day, and now that she started her eagerness had become suddenly a pain. She pictured her return that evening with her trophy under her cloak; so that after looking, from the doorstep, up and down the dark street, she decided with a new nervousness and sallied forth to the nearest place of access to the "Underground." The December dawn was dolorous, but there was neither rain nor snow; it was not even cold, and the atmosphere of West Kensington, purified by the wind, was like a dirty old coat that had been bettered by a dirty old brush. At the end of almost an hour, in the larger station, she had taken her place in a third-class compartment; the prospect before her was the run of eighty minutes to Poynton. The train was a fast one, and she was familiar with the moderate measure of the walk to the park from the spot at which it would drop her.

Once in the country indeed she saw that her father was right: the breath of December was abroad with a force from which the London labyrinth had protected her. The green fields were black, the sky was all alive with the wind; she had, in her anxious sense of the elements, her wonder at what might happen, a reminder of the surmises, in the old days of going to the Continent, that used to worry her on the way, at night, to the horrid cheap crossings by long sea. Something, in a dire degree at this last hour, had begun to press on her heart: it was the sudden imagination of a disaster, or at least of a check, before her errand was achieved. When she said to herself that something might happen she wanted to go faster than the train. But nothing could happen save a dismayed discovery that, by some altogether unlikely chance, the master and mistress of the house had already come back. In that case she must have had a warning, and the fear was but the excess of her hope. It was every one's being exactly where every one was that lent the quality to her visit. Beyond lands and seas and alienated for ever, they in their different ways gave her the impression to take as she had never taken it. At last it was already there, though the darkness of the day had deepened; they had whizzed past Chater — Chater which was the station before the right one. Off in that quarter was an air of wild rain, but there shimmered straight across it a brightness that was the colour of the great interior she had been haunting. That vision settled before her — in the house the house was all; and as the train drew up she rose, in her mean compartment, quite proudly erect with the thought that all for Fleda Vetch then the house was standing there.

But with the opening of the door she encountered a shock, though for an instant she could n't have named it: the next moment she saw it was given her by the face of the man advancing to let her out, an old lame porter of the station who had been there in Mrs. Gereth's time and who now recognised her. He looked up at her so hard that she took an alarm and before alighting broke out to him: "They've come back?" She had a confused absurd sense that even he would know that in this case she must n't be there. He hesitated, and in a few seconds her alarm had completely changed its ground: it seemed to leap, with her quick jump from the carriage, to the ground that was that of his stare at her. "Smoke?" She was on the platform with her frightened sniff; it had taken her a minute to become aware of an extraordinary smell. The air was full of it, and there were already heads at the windows of the train, looking out at something she could n't see. Some one, the only other passenger, had got out of another carriage, and the old porter hobbled off to close his door. The smoke was in her eyes, but she saw the station-master, from the end of the platform, identify her too and come straight at her. He brought her a finer shade of surprise than the porter, and while he was coming she heard a voice at a window of the train say that something was "a good bit off — a mile from the town." That was just what Poynton was. Then her heart stood still at the white wonder in the station-master's face.

"You 've come down to it, miss, already ?"

At this she knew. "Poynton 's on fire ?"

"Gone, miss — with this awful gale. You were n't wired ? Look out!" he cried in the next breath, seizing her; the train was going on, and she had given a lurch that almost made it catch her as it passed. When it had drawn away she became more conscious of the pervading smoke, which the wind seemed to hurl in her face.

"*Gone?*" She was in the man's hands; she clung to him.

"Burning still, miss. Ain't it quite too dreadful ? Took early this morning — the whole place is up there."

In her bewildered horror she tried to think. "Have they come back ?"

"Back ? They 'll be there all day!"

"Not Mr. Gereth, I mean — nor his wife ?"

"Nor his mother, miss — not a soul of *them* back. A pack o' servants in charge — not the old lady's lot, eh? A nice job for caretakers! Some rotten chimley or one of them portable lamps set down in the wrong place. What has done it is this cruel cruel night." Then as a great wave of smoke half-choked them he drew her with force to the little waiting-room. "Awkward for you, miss — I see!"

She felt sick; she sank upon a seat, staring up at him. "Do you mean that great house is *lost?*"

"It was near it, I was told, an hour ago — the fury of the flames had got such a start. I was there myself at six, the very first I heard of it. They were fighting it then, but you could n't quite say they had got it down."

Fleda jerked herself up. "Were they saving the things?"

"That's just where it was, miss — to get *at* the blessed things. And the want of right help — it maddened me to stand and see 'em muff it. This ain't a place, like, for anything organised. They don't come up to a *reel* emergency."

She passed out of the door that opened toward the village, and met a great acrid gust. She heard a far-off windy roar which, in her dismay, she took for that of flames a mile away, and which, the first instant, acted upon her as a wild solicitation. "I must go there." She had scarcely spoken before the same omen had changed into an appalling check.

Her vivid friend moreover had got before her; he clearly suffered from the nature of the control he had to exercise. "Don't do that, miss — you won't

265

care for it at all." Then as she waveringly stood her ground: "It's not a place for a young lady, nor, if you'll believe me, a sight for them as are in any way affected."

Fleda by this time knew in what way she was affected: she became limp and weak again; she felt herself give everything up. Mixed with the horror, with the kindness of the station-master, with the smell of cinders and the riot of sound was the raw bitterness of a hope that she might never again in life have to give up so much at such short notice. She heard herself repeat mechanically, yet as if asking it for the first time: "Poynton's *gone?*"

The man faltered. "What can you call it, miss, if it ain't really saved?"

A minute later she had returned with him to the waiting-room, where, in the thick swim of things, she saw something like the disc of a clock. "Is there an up-train?"

"In seven minutes."

She came out on the platform: everywhere she met the smoke. She covered her face with her hands. "I'll go back."

A LONDON LIFE

A LONDON LIFE

I

IT seemed to be raining, but she did n't mind —
she would put on stout shoes and walk over to Plash.
She was so restless and nervous that it was a pain;
there were strange voices that frightened her — they
threw out the ugliest intimations — in the empty
rooms at home. She would see old Mrs. Berrington,
whom she liked because of her simplicity, and old
Lady Davenant, who was staying with Mrs. Berrington and who was interesting for reasons with
which that charm had nothing to do. Then she would
come back to the children's tea: she liked even
better the last half-hour in the schoolroom, with the
bread and butter, the candles and the red fire, the
little spasms of confidence of Miss Steet the nursery-
governess, and the society of Scratch and Parson —
their nicknames would have made you suppose them
dogs — her small magnificent nephews, whose flesh
was so firm yet so soft and their eyes so delightful
when they listened to stories. Plash was the dower-
house and about a mile and a half, through the park,
from Mellows. The rain was nothing after all; there
was only a greyness in the air, covering all the strong
rich green, and a pleasant damp earthy smell, and
the walks were smooth and hard, so that the expedition was not arduous.

The girl had been in England more than a year,

but there were satisfactions she had not yet got used
to nor ceased to enjoy, and one of these was the accessibility, the convenience of the country. Within
the lodge-gates or without them it seemed all alike
a park — it was all so intensely and immutably
"property." The very name of Plash, which was
quaint and old, had n't lost its effect on her, nor had
it become indifferent that the place was a dower-
house — the little red-walled, ivied, lawned and gar-
dened and kept-up asylum to which old Mrs. Berrington had retired when, on his father's death, her
son came into the estates. Laura Wing thought
thoroughly ill of the custom of the expropriation of
the widow in the evening of her days, when honour
and abundance should attend her more than ever;
but her condemnation of this wrong forgot itself
when so many of the consequences looked right —
barring a little dampness: which was the fate sooner
or later of most of her unfavourable judgements of
English institutions. Iniquities in such a country
somehow always made pictures; and there had been
dower-houses in the novels, mainly of fashionable
life, on which her later childhood was fed. The in-
iquity did n't as a general thing prevent the occupation of these retreats by old ladies with wonderful
reminiscences and rare voices, whose reverses had
not deprived them of a great deal of becoming her-
editary lace. In the park, halfway, suddenly, our
young woman stopped with a pain — a moral pang
— that almost took away her breath; she looked
at the misty glades and the grand old beeches, so
familiar they were now and loved quite as if she

owned them; they seemed in their unlighted December bareness conscious of all the trouble and they bristled for her with all the facts of the present difference. A year ago she knew nothing, and now she knew pretty well everything; and the worst of her knowledge — or at least the worst of the fears she had raised upon it — had come to her in that beautiful place, where everything spoke of peace and decency, of happy submission to immemorial law. The place was the same, but her eyes were other: they had seen such sad bad things in so short a time. Yes, the time was short and everything was strange. Laura Wing was too uneasy even to sigh, and as she walked on she lightened her tread almost as going on tiptoe.

At Plash the house seemed to shine in the wet air — the tone of the mottled red walls and the limited but perfect lawn to be the work of an artist's brush. Lady Davenant was in the drawing-room, in a low chair by one of the windows, reading the second volume of a novel. There was the same look of crisp chintz, of fresh flowers wherever flowers could be put, of a wall-paper in the bad taste of years before, that had yet been kept so that no more money should be spent and was almost covered over with amateurish drawings and superior engravings, all framed in narrow gilt and wide margins. The room had its bright durable sociable air, the air Laura liked in so many English things — that of being meant for daily life, for long periods, for uses of high decorum. But more than ever to-day was it discordant that such an habitation, with its chintzes and its British poets,

271

its well-worn carpets and domestic art — the whole effect so native and sincere — should have to do with lives that were n't really right. Of course however it had to do but indirectly, and the wrong life was not old Mrs. Berrington's nor yet keen Lady Davenant's. If Selina and Selina's doings were not an implication of such an interior, any more than it was for such reactions themselves a demonstration of grounds, this was because she had come from so far off and was a foreign element altogether. Yet it was there she had found her occasion, all the influences that had so transformed her — her sister had this theory of her whole change and that when young she had seemed born for innocence; found it if not at Plash at least at Mellows, since the two places had after all so much in common and there were rooms at the great house remarkably like Mrs. Berrington's parlour.

Lady Davenant always had a head-dress of a peculiar style, original and appropriate — a white veil or cape that came in a point to the place on her forehead where her smooth hair began to show and then covered her shoulders. It was always exquisitely fresh and was partly the reason why she struck the girl rather as a fine portrait than as a living person. And yet she was full of life, old as she was, and had been made finer, sharper and more delicate, by nearly eighty years of it. It was the hand of a master that Laura seemed to see in her face, the witty expression of which shone like a lamp through the ground-glass of her good-breeding; nature was always an artist, but not so much of an artist as that.

Infinite knowledge this admirer imputed to her, and that was why she had to be liked a little fearfully. Lady Davenant was not as a general thing fond of the young or of invalids; but she made an exception, as regards youth, for a marked specimen of American freshness, the sister of the daughter-in-law of her dearest friend. She took an interest in Laura partly perhaps to make up for the tepidity with which she viewed Selina. At all events she had assumed the general responsibility of providing the nice creature with a husband. She professed an equal indifference to persons suffering from other forms of misfortune, but was capable of finding excuses for them if once they had been sufficiently to blame. She expected a great deal of attention, always wore gloves in the house and never had anything in her hand but a book. She neither embroidered nor wrote — only read — with a dainty apparatus of markers, pencils, paper-knives — read and remembered and talked. She had no particular twaddle for girls, but generally addressed them in the same manner that she found effective with her contemporaries. Laura Wing felt this as an honour, but very often did n't know what she meant and was ashamed to ask. Once in a while Lady Davenant was ashamed to tell. Mrs. Berrington had gone to a cottage to see an old woman who was ill — an old woman who had anciently been in her service for years. Unlike her guest she was fond of young people and invalids, but she was less interesting to Laura, except for the spell of wondering how she could have such depths of placidity. She had long cheeks, like the wide blank margins of old folios, and kind eyes and sedate satin streamers, and was devoted to birds: somehow she always made Laura think secretly of a tablet of fine white soap — nothing else was so smooth and clean.

"And what's going on *chez vous* — who is there and what are they doing?" Lady Davenant asked after the first greetings.

"There is n't any one but me and the children and the governess."

"What, no party — no private theatricals? How do your *vingt ans* live?"

"Oh it does n't take so much to keep me going," said Laura. "I believe there were some people coming on Saturday, but they've been put off or can't come. Selina has gone to London."

"And what has she gone to London for?"

"Oh I don't know — she has so many things to do."

"And where's Mr. Berrington?"

"He has been away somewhere; but I believe he comes back to-morrow — or next day."

"Or day after!" said Lady Davenant. "And do they never go away together?" she presently went on.

"Yes, sometimes — but they don't come back together."

"Do you mean they quarrel on the way?"

"I don't know what they do, Lady Davenant — I don't understand," the girl quavered all unguardedly. "I don't think they're very happy."

"Then they ought to be ashamed of themselves. They've everything so comfortable — what more do they want?"

"Yes, and the children are such dears!"

"Certainly — charming. And is she a good person, the present governess? Does she look after them properly?"

"Yes — she seems very good; it's a blessing. But I think she's unhappy too."

"Bless us, what a house! Does she want some one to make love to her?"

"No, but she wants Selina to see — to appreciate," Laura explained.

"And does n't she appreciate when she leaves them that way quite to the young woman?"

"Miss Steet thinks she does n't notice how they come on — she's never there."

"And has she wept and told you so? You know they're always crying, governesses — whatever line you take. You should n't draw them out too much — they're always looking for a chance. She ought to be thankful to be let alone. You must n't be too sympathetic — it's mostly wasted," the old lady went on.

"Oh I'm not; I assure you I'm not" — Laura was quite eager about it. "On the contrary, I see so much all round that I don't sympathise with."

"Well, you must n't be an impertinent little American either!" her good friend cried. Laura sat with her half an hour, while the conversation took a turn through the affairs of Plash and through Lady Davenant's own, which were visits in prospect and ideas suggested more or less directly by them as well as by the books she had been reading, a heterogeneous pile, on a table near her, all of them new and clean and from a great circulating library. The old woman had ideas and Laura liked them — though they often struck her as very sharp and hard — because at Mellows she had no diet of that sort. There had never been an idea in the house, no more than a pin in a pudding — since she came at least; and there was wonderfully little reading. Lady Davenant still went from country-house to country-house all winter, as she had done all her life, and when Laura civilly asked it of her she enumerated the places and mentioned some of the people she probably should find at each. Such an array was much less imposing to the girl than it would have been a year before: she herself had now seen a great many places and people and the freshness of her curiosity was gone. But she still cared for Lady Davenant's descriptions and judgements, because they were the thing in her life which — when she met the old woman from time to time — most represented talk, the rare sort of talk that was not the mere bandying of chaff. That was what she had dreamed of before she came to England, but in Selina's set the dream had not come true. In Selina's set people only harried each other from morning till night with extravagant accusations — it was all a kind of horse-play of false criminal charges. When Lady Davenant was accusatory it was within the limits of perfect verisimilitude.

Laura waited for the return of Mrs. Berrington, who failed to appear, so that she gathered her waterproof in with the design of going. But she was secretly unwilling — she had walked over to Plash with a vague hope that some soothing hand would be laid upon her pain. If there was no comfort at the dower-house she could n't think where to look for it, since there was certainly none at home — not even with Miss Steet and the children. It was not Lady Davenant's main characteristic that she was comforting, and Laura had not aspired to be coaxed or coddled into forgetfulness: she wanted rather to be taught a certain fortitude — how to live and hold up her head even while knowing what things horribly meant. A cynical indifference, it was n't exactly this she wished to acquire; but were n't there some sorts of indifference that might be philosophic and noble? Could n't Lady Davenant teach them if she should take the trouble? The girl remembered to have heard that there had been years before some disagreeable occurrences in *her* family; it was n't a race in which the ladies inveterately turned out well. Yet who to-day had the stamp of honour and credit — of a past that was either no one's business or was part and parcel of a fair public record — and carried it so much as a matter of course? She herself had been a good woman, and that was the only thing that told in the long run. It was Laura's own idea to be a good woman and that this would make it an advantage for Lady Davenant to show her how not to feel too much. As regards feeling enough, that was a branch in which she had no need to take lessons.

The old woman positively liked cutting new books when they had n't been so dealt with before coming to her hand; it was a task she never remitted to her maid, and while her young visitor sat there she went through the greater part of a volume with the paper-knife. She did n't proceed very fast — there was a kind of patient awkward fumbling of her aged hands; but as she passed her blade into the last leaf she said abruptly: "And how's your sister going on? She's very light!" This was added before Laura had time to reply.

"Oh Lady Davenant!" she exclaimed vaguely, slowly, vexed with herself as soon as she had spoken for having uttered the words as a protest, whereas she wished to draw her companion out. To correct this impression she again threw back her waterproof.

"Have you ever spoken to her?" Lady Davenant asked.

"Spoken to her?"

"About her behaviour. I dare say you have n't — you Americans have such abysses of false delicacy. I dare say Selina would n't speak to you if you were in her place (pardon the supposition!) and yet she's capable —" But the speaker paused, preferring not to say of what young Mrs. Berrington was capable. "It's a bad house for a girl."

"It only gives me a horror," said Laura, pausing in turn.

"A horror of your sister? That's not what one should aim at. You ought to get married — and the sooner the better. My dear child, I 've neglected you dreadfully."

"I 'm much obliged to you, but if you think marriage looks to me happy —!" the girl returned, laughing without hilarity.

"Make it happy for some one else and you'll be happy enough yourself. You ought to get out of your situation."

Laura Wing considered deferentially, though this was not a new reflexion to her. "Do you mean I should leave Selina altogether? I feel as if I should abandon her — as if I should be a coward."

"Oh my dear, it isn't the business of little girls to serve as parachutes to fly-away wives! That's why if you haven't spoken to her you need n't take the trouble at this time of day. Let her go — let her go!"

"Let her go?" — Laura wondered at the recommendation.

Her companion gave her a sharper glance. "Let her stay then! Only get out of the house. You can come to me, you know, whenever you like. I don't know another girl I'd say that to."

"Oh Lady Davenant," she began again, but only getting as far as this; in a moment she had covered her face with her hands — she had burst into tears.

"Ah my dear, don't cry or I shall take back my invitation! It would never do for me if you were to *larmoyer*. If I've offended you by the way I've spoken of Selina I think you're too sensitive. We should n't feel more for people than they feel for themselves. She has no tears, I'm very sure."

"Oh she has, she has!" cried the girl, sobbing with an odd effect as she put forth this pretension for her sister.

"Then she's worse than I thought. I don't mind

them so much when they're merry, but I hate 'em when they're sentimental."

"She's so changed — so changed!" Laura went on.

"Never, never, my dear: *c'est de naissance*."

"You never knew my mother," Laura quavered; "when I think of mother —!" The words failed her while she sobbed.

"I dare say mother was very nice," said Lady Davenant less cruelly. "It would take that to account for *you*: such women as Selina are always easily enough accounted for. I did n't mean it was inherited — for that sort of thing skips about. I dare say there was some improper ancestress — except that you Americans don't seem to have foremothers."

Laura gave no sign of having heard this observation; she was occupied in brushing away her tears. "Everything's so changed — you don't know," she proceeded in a moment. "Nothing could have been happier — nothing could have been sweeter. And now to be so dependent — so helpless — so poor!"

"Have you nothing at all?" asked Lady Davenant with simplicity.

"Only enough to pay for my clothes."

"That's a good deal, for a girl. You're uncommonly dressy, you know."

"I'm sorry I seem so. That's just the way I don't want to look."

"You Americans can't help it. I don't care for the way you dress; it is n't interesting and it's timid

—as if you were afraid of your milliners; but you 'wear' your very features and your eyes look as if they had just been sent home. I confess, however, you're not so smart as Selina."

"Yes, is n't she splendid?" Laura said with proud inconsequence. "And the worse she is the better she looks."

"Oh my child, if the bad women looked as bad as they are—! It's only the good ones who can afford that," the old lady murmured.

"It was the last thing I ever thought of — that I should be ashamed," the girl declared.

"Oh keep your shame till you have more to do with it. It's like lending your umbrella — when you've only one."

"If anything were to happen — publicly — I should die, I should die!" And Laura had a motion that carried her to her feet. This time she settled herself for departure. Her friend's admonition rather frightened than sustained her.

Lady Davenant leaned back in her chair with a kind firm look. "It would be very bad, I dare say. But it would n't prevent my taking you in."

Laura acknowledged this assurance with distended musing eyes. "Think of having to come to that!"

She seemed to amuse her hostess. "Yes, yes, you must come; you're so original!"

"I don't mean I don't feel your kindness," the girl returned, blushing. "But to be only protected — always protected and offered a refuge: is that a life?"

"Most women are only too thankful, and I'm bound

to say I think you're *difficile*." Lady Davenant used a good many French words, in the old-fashioned manner and with a pronunciation not absolutely pure: when she did so she reminded her visitor of the works of Mrs. Gore. "But you shall be better protected than even by me. *Nous verrons bien cela.* Only you must stop crying — this is n't a crying country."

"No, one must have courage here. It takes courage to marry for such an awfully second-rate reason."

"Any reason 's good enough that keeps a woman from being an old maid. Besides, you 'll like him."

"He must like me first," said the girl with a sad smile.

"There 's the uppish little American again! It is n't necessary. You 're far too proud. You expect too much."

"I 'm proud for what I am — that 's very certain. But I don't expect anything," Laura Wing protested. "That 's the only form my pride takes. Please give my love to Mrs. Berrington. I 'm so sorry — so sorry," she went on, to change the talk from the subject of her marrying. She wanted to marry but wanted also not to want it and above all not to appear to. She lingered in the room, mildly moving about: the place when this occasional inmate was there, was so safe and sound, always so pleasant to her, that to go away — to return to her own barren precarious home —had the effect of her forfeiting a privilege of sanctuary. The afternoon had faded but the lamps been brought in, the smell of flowers was in the air and the old house of Plash seemed to recog-

nise the hour that suited it best. The quiet old lady
in the firelight, encompassed with the symbolic security of chintz and water-colour, gave her a sudden
vision of how blest it would be to jump all the middle
dangers of life and have arrived at the end safely,
sensibly, with a cap and gloves and formulas and
phrases, above all with consideration and memories.
"And, Lady Davenant, what does *she* think?" she
asked abruptly, stopping short and referring to Mrs.
Berrington.

"Think? Bless your soul, she does n't do that!
If she did the things she says would be unpardon-
able."

"The things she says — ?"

"That's what makes them so beautiful — that they
ain't spoiled by preparation. You could never think
of them *for* her." The girl smiled at this description
of the dearest friend of the describer, but wondered a
little what this judge would say to visitors about *her*,
Laura Wing's, accepting asylum under her roof. The
speech was after all a flattering proof of confidence.
"She wishes it had been you — I happen to know
that," said the old woman. And then as Laura
seemed not to understand: "That Lionel had taken
a fancy to."

"I would n't have married him," Lionel's sister-
in-law promptly enough declared.

"Don't say that or you 'll make me think it won't
be easy to help you. I shall depend on your not refusing anything so good."

"I don't call him good. If he were good his wife
would be better."

"Very likely; and if you had married him *he* would be better, and that's more to the purpose. Lionel's as *bête* as a comic song, but you 've cleverness for two."

"And you have it for fifty, dear Lady Davenant. Never, never — I shall never marry a man I can't respect!" Laura said.

She had come a little nearer her old friend and taken her hand; this critic held her a moment and with the other hand pushed aside one of the flaps of the waterproof. "And what is it your clothing costs you ?" — with a look at the dress underneath and no heed to her declaration.

"I don't exactly know: it takes almost everything that's sent me from America. But that's dreadfully little — only a few pounds. I'm a wonderful manager. Besides," the girl added, "Selina wants one to be dressed."

"And does n't she pay any of your bills ?"

"Why she gives me everything — food, shelter, carriages."

"Does she never give you money ?"

"I would n't take it," Laura said. "They need everything they have — their life's tremendously expensive."

"That I'll warrant!" cried the old woman. "It was a most beautiful property, but I don't know what has become of it now. *Ce n'est pas pour vous blesser*, but the hole you Americans *can* make —!"

Laura interrupted immediately, holding up her head; Lady Davenant had dropped her hand and she herself had receded a step. "Selina brought

Lionel a very considerable fortune and every dollar of it was paid."

"Yes, I know it was; Mrs. Berrington told me it was most satisfactory. That's not always the case with the fortunes you young ladies are supposed to bring!" the old lady made no scruple of mocking.

Her companion looked over her head a moment. "Why do your men marry for money?"

"Why indeed, my dear? And before your troubles what used your father to give you for your personal expenses?"

"He gave us everything we asked — we had no particular allowance."

"And I dare say you asked for everything?" said Lady Davenant.

"No doubt we were very dressy, as you say."

"No wonder he went bankrupt — for he did, did n't he?"

"He had dreadful reverses but he only sacrificed himself — he protected others."

"Well, I know nothing about these things and I only ask *pour me renseigner*," Mrs. Berrington's guest went on. "And after their reverses your father and mother lived I think only a short time?"

Laura had covered herself again with her mantle; her eyes were now bent upon the ground, and, standing there before her friend with her umbrella and her air of momentary submission and self-control, she might very well have been a young person in reduced circumstances applying for a place. "It was short enough, but it seemed — some parts of it — terribly long and painful. My poor father — my dear father," the girl went on. But her voice trembled and she checked herself.

"I feel as if I were cross-questioning you, which God forbid!" said the old woman. "But there's one thing I should really like to know. Did Lionel and his wife, when you were poor, come freely to your assistance?"

"They sent us money repeatedly — it was *her* money of course. It was almost all we had."

"And if you've been poor and know what poverty is, tell me this: has it made you afraid to marry a poor man?"

It might have seemed to Laura's hostess that in answer to this she became uneasy, and then Lady Davenant heard her speak not quite with the ideal heroic ring. "I'm afraid of so many things to-day that I don't know where my fears end."

"I've no patience with the highstrung way you take things!" her adviser cried. "But I have to know, you know."

"Oh don't try to know any more shames, any more horrors!" the girl wailed with sudden passion, turning away.

The old woman got up, drew her round again and kissed her. "I think after all you'd fidget me," she remarked, releasing her. Then as if this were too cheerless a leave-taking she added with more sympathy, as Laura had a hand on the door: "Mind what I tell you, my dear: let her go!" It was to this Laura's lesson in philosophy reduced itself, she reflected, as she walked back to Mellows in the rain, which had now come on, and through the grey blurred park.

II

THE children were still at tea and poor Miss Steet
sat between them, consoling herself with strong cups,
crunching melancholy morsels of toast and dropping
an absent gaze on her little charges as they exchanged
small, loud remarks. She always when Laura came
in fetched a sigh from inward depths — it was her
way of expressing appreciation of the visit — and
she was the one person the girl frequently saw who
struck her as more unhappy than herself. But Laura
none the less envied her — thought her position had
more dignity than that of her employer's dependent
sister. Miss Steet had related her life to the children's
pretty young aunt, and this personage judged that
though it had had painful elements nothing so disagreeable had ever occurred in it, or was likely to
occur, as the odious possibility of her sister's making
a scandal. She had two sisters — Laura knew all
about them — and one of them was married to a
clergyman in Staffordshire (a very ugly part) and
had seven children and four hundred a year; while
the other, the elder, was unbecomingly fat and filled
(it was rather a tight fit for her) a position as matron
in an orphanage at Liverpool. Neither seemed destined to go into the English divorce-court, and such
a circumstance on the part of one's near relations
struck Laura as in itself almost sufficient to constitute happiness. Miss Steet never lived in a state of

nervous anxiety — everything about her was respectable. She made our young woman almost angry sometimes by her drooping martyr-like air. Laura was near breaking out at her with "Mercy on us, what have *you* got to complain of? Don't you earn your living as an honest girl and are you obliged to see things going on about you that you hate?"

But she could n't so express herself, because she had promised Selina, who made a great point of this, that she would never be too familiar with such people. Selina was not without her ideas of decorum — very far from it indeed; she only set them up in such queer places. She was not familiar with her children's governess; she was not even familiar with her children themselves. That was why it was after all impossible to address much of a remonstrance to Miss Steet when she sat as if she were tied to the stake and the faggots being lighted. If martyrs in this situation had tea and cold meat served them they would strikingly have resembled the morbid representative of education at Mellows. Laura could n't have denied it to be natural she should have liked Mrs. Berrington *sometimes* just to look in and give a sign she was pleased with her system; but poor Miss Steet only knew by the servants or by Laura whether Mrs. Berrington were ever at home: she was as nearly as possible never, and the governess had a way of silently intimating (it was her trick of putting her head on one side when she looked at Scratch and Parson — of course *she* called them Geordie and Ferdy) that she was immensely handicapped and even that they, small hopeless unfortunates, were.

Perhaps this was so, though they certainly showed
it little in their appearance and manner, and Laura
was at least sure that if Selina had been perpetually
dropping in Miss Steet would have taken that discomfort even more tragically. The sight of this young
woman's either real or fancied wrongs did n't diminish her conviction that she herself would at the pinch
have found courage to become a governess. She
would have had to teach very young children, for
she knew she was too ignorant for higher flights.
But Selina would never have consented to that,
would have held it a disgrace or, even worse, have
branded it as an affectation — Selina was so fright-
fully "down" on affectation. Laura had proposed to
her six months before that she should dispense with
a paid governess and suffer *her*, a useless inmate, to
take charge of the little boys: in that way she should
not feel so completely dependent — she should be
doing something in return. "And pray what would
happen when you came to dinner? Who would look
after them then?" Mrs. Berrington had demanded
with a very shocked air. Laura had replied that perhaps it was n't absolutely necessary she should come
to dinner — she could dine early, with the children;
so that if her presence in the drawing-room should
be required the children had their nurse (and what
did they have their nurse *for?*). Selina had looked as
if she was deplorably superficial and answered that
they had their nurse to dress them and attend to their
clothes — did their Spartan aunt wish the poor little
ducks to go in rags? She had her own ideas of
thoroughness and, when Laura hinted that after all

at that hour the children were in bed, declared that even when they were asleep she desired the governess to be at hand — such was the way a mother felt who really took an interest. Selina was strenuous indeed — she had thought it all out; she described the evening hours in the quiet schoolroom, with high authority, as the proper time for the governess to "get up" the children's lessons for the next day. Laura was conscious of her own ignorance; nevertheless she presumed to believe she could have taught Geordie and Ferdy the alphabet without anticipatory nocturnal researches. She wondered what her sister supposed Miss Steet taught them — if she had a cheap theory that they were in Latin and algebra.

The governess's evening hours in the quiet schoolroom would have suited Laura well — so at least she believed; by touches of her own she would make the place even prettier than it was already, and in the winter nights near the bright fire would get through a grand course of reading. There was the question of a new piano (the old one was pretty bad: Miss Steet had a finger!) and perhaps she should have to ask Selina for that — but it would be all. The schoolroom at Mellows was not a charmless place, and the girl often wished she might have spent her own early years in so dear a scene. It was a panelled parlour in a wing, looking out on the great cushiony lawns and a part of the terrace where the peacocks used most to spread their tails. There were quaint old maps on a wall and "collections" — birds and shells — under glass cases and a wonderful pictured screen made by old Mrs. Berrington, when Lionel was young, out of primitive woodcuts illustrative of nursery-tales. The place was a setting for rosy childhood, and Laura believed her sister never knew how delightful Scratch and Parson looked there. Old Mrs. Berrington had known in the case of Lionel — it had all been arranged for him. That was the story told by ever so many other things in the house, which betrayed the full perception of a comfortable, liberal, deeply domestic effect, addressed to eternities of possession, residing thirty years before in the unquestioned and unquestioning old lady whose sofas and "corners" — she had perhaps been the first person in England to have corners — had most to say about her cleverness.

Laura Wing envied English children, the boys at least, and even her own chubby nephews in spite of the cloud that hung over them; but she had already felt the incongruity apparent to-day between Lionel Berrington at thirty-five and the elements massed about his younger years. She did n't dislike her brother-in-law, though she admired him scantly and much pitied him; but she marvelled at the waste involved in some human institutions — the English landed gentry for instance — when she noted how much it had taken to produce so little. The sweet old wainscoted parlour, the view of the garden that reminded her of scenes in Shakespeare's comedies, all that was exquisite in the home of his forefathers —what visible reference was there to these fine things in poor Lionel's stable-stamped composition? When she came in this evening and saw his small sons making competitive noises in their mugs — Miss Steet checked this impropriety on her entrance—she asked herself what *they* would have to show twenty years later for the frame that made them just then a picture. Would they be wonderfully ripe and noble, the perfection of human culture ? The contrast was before her again, the sense of the same curious duplicity (in the literal meaning of the word) that she took in at Plash — the way the genius of such an old house was all peace and decorum and yet the spirit that prevailed there, outside the schoolroom, contentious and impure. She had often before been struck with this—with that perfection of machinery that can still at certain times make English life go on of itself with a stately rhythm long after corruption is within it.

She had half a purpose of asking Miss Steet to dine with her that night downstairs, so absurd did it seem to her that two young women who had so much in common — enough at least for that — should sit feeding alone at opposite ends of the big empty house, melancholy at such a time. She would n't have cared just now if Selina did think such a course familiar : she indulged sometimes in a rage of humility, placing herself near to those who toiled and were sordid. But when she saw how much cold meat the governess had already consumed she felt it would be a vain form to propose to her another repast. She sat down with her, and presently, in the firelight, the two children had placed themselves in position for a story. They were dressed as the mariners of England and smelt of the ablutions to which they had been condemned before tea and the odour of which was but partly overlaid by that of bread and butter. Scratch wanted an old story and Parson a new, and they exchanged from side to side a good many powerful arguments. While they were so engaged Miss Steet described at her visitor's invitation the walk she had taken with them and laid bare that she had been thinking for a long time of asking Mrs. Berrington — if she only had an opportunity — whether she should approve of her giving them a few elementary notions of botany. But no chance had come — she had had the idea for a long time. She was rather fond of the study herself; she had gone into it a little — she seemed to intimate that there had been times when she extracted a blest support from it. Laura suggested that botany might be a little dry for such young children in winter and from text-books — that the better way would be perhaps to wait till the spring and show them out of doors, in the garden, some of the peculiarities of plants. To this Miss Steet rejoined that her idea had been to teach some of the general facts slowly — it would take a long time — and then they would be all ready for the spring. She spoke of the spring as if it would n't arrive till some very remote future. She had hoped to lay the question before Mrs. Berrington that week — but was it not already Thursday? Laura said "Oh yes, you had better do anything with the children that will keep them profitably occupied"; she came near saying anything that would people a little the vacuity of the young woman herself.

She had rather a dread of new stories — it took the little boys so long to get initiated and the first steps were so terribly bestrewn with questions. Receptive silence broken only by an occasional rectification

on the part of the listener never descended until
after the tale had been told a dozen times. The matter was settled for "Riquet with the Tuft," but on
this occasion the girl's heart was n't much in the adventure. The children stood on either side, leaning
against her, and she had an arm round each; their
little bodies were thick and strong and their voices
had the quality of silver bells. Their mother had certainly gone too far; but there was nevertheless a limit
to the tenderness one could feel for the neglected
and compromised bairns. It was difficult to take a
sentimental view of them — they would never take
such a view of themselves. Geordie would grow up
a master-hand at polo and care more for that pas-
time than for anything in life, and Ferdy perhaps
would develop into "the best shot in England."
Laura felt these possibilities stir within them; they
were in the things they said to her, in the things they
said to each other. At any rate they would never
in the world make a reflexion, be capable of a reaction, on anything with which their arms and legs, and
perhaps their "tummies," were n't primarily concerned. They contradicted each other on a question
of ancestral history to which their attention apparently had been drawn by their nurse, whose people
had been tenants for generations. Their grandfather
had had the hounds for fifteen years — Ferdy maintained that he had *always* had them. Geordie ridi-
culed this idea, like a man of the world; he had had
them till he went into volunteering — then he had
got up a splendid regiment, had spent thousands of
pounds on it. Ferdy was of the opinion that this was

wasted money — he himself intended to have a real regiment, to be a colonel in the Guards. Geordie looked as if he thought that a superficial ambition and could see beyond it; his own most definite view was that he would have back the hounds. He did n't see why papa did n't have them — unless it was because he would n't take the trouble.

"I know — it 's because mamma 's a Yankee!" Ferdy announced with confidence.

"And what has that to do with it?" asked Laura.

"Mamma spends so much money — there is n't any more for anything!"

This startling speech drew a gasp from Miss Steet; she blushed and assured Laura that she could n't imagine where the child had picked up such an extraordinary idea. "I 'll look into it — you may be sure I 'll look into it," she said; while Laura impressed on Ferdy that he must never, never, never, under any circumstances, either utter or listen to a word that should be wanting in respect to his mother.

"If any one should say anything against any of my people I 'd give him a good one!" Geordie shouted, his hands in his little blue pockets.

"I 'd hit him in the eye!" cried Ferdy with cheerful inconsequence.

"Perhaps you don't care to come to dinner at half-past seven," the girl said to Miss Steet; "but I should be very glad — I 'm all alone."

"Thank you so much. All alone, really?" murmured the governess.

"Why don't you get married? then you would n't be alone," Geordie interposed with ingenuity.

"Children, you're really too dreadful this evening!" Miss Steet woefully returned.

"I shan't get married — I want to have the hounds," proclaimed Geordie, who had apparently been much struck with his brother's explanation.

"I'll come down afterwards, about half-past eight, if you'll allow me," said Miss Steet, looking conscious and responsible.

"Very well — perhaps we can have some music; we'll try something together."

"Oh music — *we* don't go in for music!" said Geordie with clear superiority; and while he spoke Laura saw Miss Steet get up suddenly, looking even less alleviated than usual. The door of the room had been pushed open and Lionel Berrington stood there. He had his hat on and a cigar in his mouth and his face was red, which was its usual state. He took off his hat as he came into the room, but did n't stop smoking and turned a little redder than before. There were several ways in which his sister-in-law often wished he might have been other, but she had never disliked him for a certain boyish shyness that was in him, which came out in his dealings with almost all women. He was abashed at the very housemaids, the governess of his children made him uncomfortable, and Laura had already noticed that he had the same effect upon Miss Steet. He was fond of his children, but saw them hardly oftener than their mother, and they never knew if he was at home or away. Indeed his goings and comings were so frequent that Laura herself scarce knew: it was an accident that on this occasion his absence had been marked for her. Selina had had her reasons for wishing not to go up to town while her husband was on the spot, and she believed, resentfully, that he stayed there to watch her, to keep her from moving. It was her theory that she herself was perpetually at home — that few women were more domestic, more glued to the fireside and absorbed in the duties belonging to it; and, unreasonable as she was, she recognised the fact that for her to establish this theory she must sometimes put her domesticity on record. It was not enough for her to maintain that her husband would see her by his hearthstone if he were sometimes near it himself. Therefore she disliked to be caught in the crude fact of absence — to go away under his nose; what she preferred was to take the next train after his own and return an hour or two before him. She managed this often with great spirit, in spite of her not being able to be sure when he *would* return. Of late, however, she had ceased to take so much trouble, and Laura, by no desire of the girl's own, was enough in the confidence of her impatiences and perversities to know that for her to have wished (four days before the moment I write of) to put him on a wrong scent — or to keep him at least off the right one — she must have had in her head something exceptionally dreadful. This was why the girl had been so worried and why the sense of an impending catastrophe, which had lately gathered strength against her, was at present almost intolerably pressing: she knew how little Selina could afford to surpass herself.

Lionel startled her by turning up in that unex-

pected way, though she could n't have expressed
when it would have been natural to look for him.
This attitude, at Mellows, was left to the servants,
most of them inscrutable and incommunicative,
erect in a wisdom that was founded on telegrams —
Laura could n't speak to the butler but he pulled one
out of his pocket. It was a house of telegrams; they
crossed each other a dozen times an hour, coming
and going, and Selina in particular lived in a cloud
of them. Her sister had but vague ideas as to what
they were all about; once in a while, when they fell
under her eyes, she either failed to understand them
or judged them to be about horses. There were
an immense number of horses, in one way and another, in Mrs. Lionel's life. Then she had so many
friends who were always rushing about like herself
and making appointments and putting them off
and wanting to know if she were going to certain
places or would go if they did, or else would come
up to town and dine and "do a theatre." There were
also a good many theatres in the existence of this
active lady. Laura remembered how fond their poor
father had been of telegraphing, but it was never
about the theatre: at all events she tried to give her
sister the benefit or the excuse of heredity. Selina
had her own opinions, which were superior to this:
she once remarked to Laura that it was idiotic of a
woman to write — to telegraph was the only way not
to get into trouble. If doing so sufficed to keep a lady
out of it Mrs. Lionel's career should have flowed
like the rivers of Eden.

III

LAURA, as soon as her brother-in-law had been in the room a moment, knew a particular fear; she had seen him twice noticeably under the influence of liquor; she had not liked it at all and now recognised some of the signs. She was afraid the children would discover them, or at any rate Miss Steet, and felt the importance of not letting him stay in the room. She thought it almost a sign he should have come in at all — he was so rare a deliberate apparition. He looked at her very hard, smiling as if to say "No, no, I'm not — not if you think it!" She saw with relief in a moment that he was not very bad, and liquor disposed him apparently to tenderness, for he indulged in an interminable kissing of Geordie and Ferdy, during which Miss Steet turned away delicately, looking out of the window. The little boys asked him no questions to celebrate his return — they only announced they were going to learn botany, to which he replied "Are you really? Why I never did," and looked askance at the governess, fairly blushing as from the hope that she would let him off from carrying that subject further. To Laura and to Miss Steet he was only too explanatory, though his explanations were not quite coherent. He had come back an hour before — he was going to spend the night — he had driven over from Churton — he was thinking of taking the last train "up." Was

Laura dining at home? Was any one coming? He should enjoy a quiet dinner awfully.

"Certainly I'm alone," said the girl. "I suppose you know Selina's away."

"Oh yes — I know where Selina is!" And Lionel Berrington looked round, smiling at every one present, taking in Scratch and Parson. He stopped while he continued to smile and Laura wondered what he was so much pleased at. She preferred not to ask — she was sure it was something that wouldn't give *her* pleasure; but after waiting a moment he went on: "Selina's in Paris, my dear: that's where Selina is!"

"In Paris?" Laura repeated.

"Yes, in Paris, my dear — God bless her! Where else do you suppose? Geordie my boy, where should *you* think your mummy would naturally be?"

"Oh I don't know," said Geordie, who had no reply prepared that would express affectingly the desolation of the nursery. "If I were mummy I'd be jolly."

"Well now, that's just your mummy's idea — she wants to be jolly," returned his father. "Were you ever in Paris, Miss Steet?"

Miss Steet gave a nervous laugh and said No but she had been to Boulogne; while to her added confusion Ferdy announced that he knew where Paris was — it was in America. "No, it ain't — it's in Scotland!" cried Geordie; and Laura asked Lionel how he knew — whether his wife had written to him.

"Written to me? when did she ever write to me? No, I saw a fellow in town this morning who saw her there — at breakfast yesterday. He came over last night. That's how I know my wife's in Paris. You can't have better proof than that!"

"I suppose it's a very pleasant season there," the governess murmured as from a desperate sense of duty.

"I dare say it's very pleasant indeed — I dare say it's awfully amusing!" laughed Mr. Berrington. "Shouldn't you like to run over with me for a few days, Laura — just to have a go at the theatres? I don't see why we should always be moping at home. We'll take Miss Steet and the children and give mummy a pleasant surprise. Now who do you suppose she was *with* in Paris — who do you suppose she was seen *with?*"

Laura had turned pale, she looked at him hard, beseechingly, in the eyes: there was a name she was terribly afraid he would mention. "Oh sir, in that case we had better go and get ready!" Miss Steet quavered betwixt a laugh and a groan and in a spasm of discretion; and before Laura knew it had gathered Geordie and Ferdy together and swept them out of the room. The door closed behind her with a very quick softness and Lionel remained a moment staring at it.

"I say, what does she mean? — ain't that damned impertinent?" he stammered. "What did she think I was going to say? Does she suppose I'd say any harm before — before *her?* Dash it, does she suppose I'd give away my wife to the servants?" Then he added: "And I wouldn't say any harm before you, Laura. You're too good and too nice and I like you too much!"

"Won't you come downstairs? won't you have some tea?" the girl asked uneasily.

"No, no, I want to stay here — I like this place," he replied very gently and reasoningly. "It's a deuced nice place, an awfully jolly room. It used to be this way — always — when I was a little chap. I was a rough un', my dear; I was n't a pretty little lamb like that pair. I think it's because you look after them — that's what makes 'em so sweet. The one in my time — what was her name? I think it was Bald or Bold — I rather think she found me a handful. I used to kick her shins — I was shockingly vicious. And do *you* see it's kept so well, Laura?" — he looked about him. "'Pon my soul, it's the prettiest room in the house. What does she want to go to Paris for when she has got such a charming house? Now can you answer me that, Laura?"

"I suppose she has gone to get clothes: her dress-maker lives in Paris, you know."

"Dressmaker? Clothes? Why she has got whole rooms full of clothes. Has n't she got whole rooms full — ?"

"Speaking of clothes I must go and change mine," Laura said. "I've been out in the rain — I've been to Plash — I'm decidedly damp."

"Oh you've been to Plash? You've seen my mother? I hope she's in very good health." But before the girl could say he went on: "Now I want you to guess who she's in Paris with. Motcomb saw them together — at that place, what's-his-name? close to the Madeleine." And as Laura kept still, not wishing at all to guess, he continued: "It's the ruin of any woman, you know; I can't think what she has got in her head." Laura made no answer, and as he had hold of her arm, she having turned away, she led him this time out of the room. She had a horror of the name, the name in her mind and apparently on his lips, though his tone was so strange, so almost detached. "My dear girl, she's with Lady Ringrose — what do you say to that?" he broke out as they passed along the corridor to the staircase.

"With Lady Ringrose?"

"They went over on Tuesday — they're knocking about there alone."

"I don't know Lady Ringrose," Laura said, infinitely relieved that the name was n't the one she had feared. Lionel learned on her arm as they went downstairs.

"I rather hope not — I promise you she has never put her foot in this house! If Selina expects to bring her here I should like half an hour's notice; yes, half an hour would do. She might as well be seen with —" And Lionel Berrington checked himself. "She has had at least fifty —!" Again he stopped short. "You must pull me up, you know, if I say anything you don't like!"

"I don't understand you — let me alone, please!" the girl cried, disengaging herself with an effort from his arm. She hurried down the rest of the steps and left him there looking after her, and as she went heard him give a laugh without sense.

IV

SHE determined not to go to dinner, she wished for
that day not to meet him again. He would drink
more, he would be worse, she did n't know what he
might say. Besides she was too angry — not with
him but with Selina, and in addition to being angry
she was sick. She knew who Lady Ringrose was;
she knew so many things to-day that when she was
younger — and only a little — she had n't expected
ever to know. Her eyes had been opened very wide
in England and certainly they had been opened to
Lady Ringrose. She had heard what Lady Ringrose had done and perhaps a good deal more, and it
was n't very different from what she had heard of
other women. She knew Selina had been to her
house; she had an impression her ladyship had been
to Selina's, in London, though she herself had not
seen her there. But she had n't known they were
so intimate as this — that Selina would rush over
to Paris with her. What they had gone to Paris for
was not necessarily criminal; there were a hundred
reasons, familiar to ladies who were fond of change,
of movement, of the theatres and of new bonnets;
but nevertheless it was the fact of the free adventure
quite as much as the companion in it that excited
Laura's disgust.

She was n't ready to pronounce the companion
so much worse, though Lionel appeared to be, than

twenty other women who were her sister's intimates
and whom she herself had seen in London, at Grosvenor Place, and even under the motherly old beeches
at Mellows. But she thought it vulgar and low in
Selina to go abroad that way, like a commercial
traveller, capriciously, clandestinely, without giving
notice, when she had signified that she was simply
spending three or four days in town. It was in the
worst possible taste and had in its *cabotinage* the
mark of Selina's complete irremediable frivolity —
the worst accusation (Laura tried to cling to that
judgement) she really laid herself open to. Of course
frivolity that was never ashamed was like a neglected
cold — you could die of it morally as well as of anything else. Laura knew this and it was why she was
inexpressibly vexed with her sister. She hoped she
should get a letter from Selina the next morning
(Mrs. Lionel might make at least that sacrifice
to propriety) giving her a chance to dispatch an answer that had already taken form in her brain. It
scarcely diminished Laura's eagerness for such an
opportunity that she had a vision of Selina's profanely
showing her letter across the table, at the place near
the Madeleine, to Lady Ringrose (who would be
far too much painted — Selina herself, to do her
justice, was n't yet) while the French waiters, in
white aprons, revolved about *ces dames*. It was new
work for our young woman to estimate these shades,
the gradations, the probabilities of horridness, and
of the side of the line on which, or rather how far
on the wrong side, Lady Ringrose was situated.

A quarter of an hour before dinner Lionel sent

word to her room that she was to sit down without
him — he had a headache and would n't appear.
This was an unexpected grace and it simplified the
position for Laura; so that, smoothing her ruffles,
she betook herself to the table. Before doing this
however she went back to the schoolroom and told
Miss Steet she must contribute her company. The
little boys were in bed and she took the governess
downstairs with her and made her sit opposite, thinking she would be a safeguard if Lionel were to change
his mind. Miss Steet, a very shrinking bulwark, was
more frightened than herself. The dinner was dull
and the conversation rare; the governess ate three
olives and looked at the figures on the spoons. Laura
had more than ever her sense of impending calamity;
a draught of misfortune seemed to blow through
the house; it chilled her feet under her chair. The
letter she had had in her head went out like a flame
in the wind and her only thought now was to wire
to Selina the first thing in the morning and in quite
different words. She scarce spoke to Miss Steet at
all and there was very little the governess could say,
having already detailed again and again every fact
of her history. After dinner she dragged her companion to the drawing-room, where they sat down
to the piano together. They played duets for an
hour, mechanically, violently; Laura had no sense
of what compositions; she only knew their playing
was execrable. In spite of this, "That's a very nice
thing, that last," she heard a vague voice say behind
her at the end; and she became aware her brother-
in-law had rejoined them.

Miss Steet was pusillanimous — she retreated on the spot, though Lionel had already forgotten his anger at her rude way of sweeping his children from under his nose. Laura would have gone too if Lionel had n't insisted he had something very particular to say to her. That made her want to go more, but she had to listen to him when he expressed the hope that she had n't taken offence at anything he had said before. He did n't strike her as tipsy now; he had slept it off or got rid of it, and she saw no traces of his headache. He was still conspicuously merry, as if he had got some good news and were very much encouraged. She knew the news he had got, and she might have thought, in view of his manner, that it could n't really have seemed to him so bad as he had pretended to think it. It was, however, not the first time she had seen him pleased at having a case against his wife, and she was to learn on this occasion how extreme a satisfaction he could take in his wrongs. She would n't sit down again; she only lingered by the fire, pretending to warm her feet, and he walked to and fro in the long room, where the lamp-light to-night was limited, stepping on certain figures of the carpet as if his triumph were alloyed with hesitation.

"I never know how to talk to you — you 're so beastly clever," said Lionel. "I can't treat you like a little girl in a pinafore — and yet of course you 're only a young lady. You 're so deuced good — that makes it worse," he went on, stopping in front of her with his hands in his pockets and the air he himself had of being a good-natured but dissipated boy;

with his small stature, his smooth fat suffused face, his round watery light-coloured eyes and his hair growing in curious infantile rings. He had lost one of his front teeth and always wore a stiff white scarf, with a pin representing some symbol of the turf or the chase. "I don't see why *she* could n't have been a little more like you. If I could have had a shot at you first!"

"I don't care for any compliments at my sister's expense," the girl returned with some majesty.

"Oh I say, Laura, don't put on so many frills, as Selina says. You know what your sister is as well as I!" They stood looking at each other and he appeared to see something in her face which led him to add: "You know at any rate how little we hit it off."

"I know you don't love each other — it's too dreadful."

"Love each other? she hates me as she'd hate a hump on her back. She'd do me any devilish turn she could. There is n't a sentiment of loathing that she does n't have for me! She'd like to stamp on me and hear me crack like a black beetle, and she never opens her mouth but she insults me." Lionel Berrington delivered himself of these assertions without violence, without passion or the sting of a new discovery; there was a familiar gaiety in his trivial little tone and he had the air of being so sure of what he said that he did n't need to exaggerate in order to prove enough.

"Oh Lionel!" — Laura had turned pale. "Is that the particular thing you wished to say to me?"

"And you can't say it's my fault — you won't pretend to do that, will you?" he went on. "Ain't I quiet, ain't I kind, don't I go steady? Haven't I given her every blessed thing she has ever asked for?"

"You haven't given her an example!" — his companion spoke with spirit. "You don't care for anything in the wide world but to amuse yourself from the beginning of the year to the end. No more does she — and perhaps it's even worse in a woman. You're both as selfish as you can live, with nothing in your head or your heart but your vulgar pleasure, incapable of a perception, incapable of a concession, incapable of a sacrifice!" She at least spoke with passion; something pent up in her soul broke out and gave her relief, almost a momentary joy.

It made Lionel stare; he coloured, but after a moment he threw back his head in derision. "Don't you call me kind when I stand here and take all that? If I'm so keen for my pleasure what pleasure do *you* give me? Look at the way I take it, Laura. You ought to do me justice. Haven't I sacrificed my home? and what more can a man do?"

"I don't think you care any more for your home than Selina does. And it's so sacred and so beautiful, your home, God forgive you! You're all blind and senseless and heartless, and I don't know what poison's in your veins. There's a curse on you and there'll be a judgement!" — the girl glowed like a young prophetess.

"What do you want me to do? Do you want me to stay at home and read the Bible?" her relative asked in a tone that her deep seriousness caused to sound hopelessly foolish.

"It would n't do you any harm, once in a while."

"There 'll be a judgement on *her* — that's very sure, and I know where it will be delivered," said Lionel Berrington, indulging in a visible approach to a wink. "Have I done the half to her she has done to me? I won't say the half, but the hundredth part? Answer me truly, dear!"

"I don't know what she has done to you," Laura threw off with impatience.

"That's exactly what I want to tell you. But it's difficult. I 'll bet you five pounds she's doing it now!"

"You 're too unable to make yourself respected," the girl remarked, not shrinking now from the enjoyment of an advantage — that of feeling herself superior and taking her opportunity.

Her brother-in-law seemed to feel for the moment the prick of this observation. "What has such a piece of nasty boldness as that to do with respect? She's the first that ever defied me!" exclaimed the young man, whose aspect somehow scarcely confirmed this pretension. "You know all about her — don't make believe you don't," he continued in another tone. "You see everything — you 're one of the sharp ones. There's no use beating about the bush, Laura — you 've lived in this precious house and you 're not so green as that comes to. Besides, you 're so good yourself that you need n't give a shriek if one's obliged to say what one means. Why did n't you grow up as you are a little sooner? Then — over there in New York — it would certainly have been you I'd have made up to. *You*'d have respected me — eh? Now don't say you would n't." He rambled on, turning about the room again, partly like a person whose sequences were naturally slow, but also a little as if, though he knew what he had in mind, there were still a scruple attached to it that he was trying to work off.

"I take it this is n't what I must sit up to listen to, Lionel, is it?" Laura said wearily.

"Why you don't want to go to bed at nine o'clock, do you? That's all rot of course. But I want you to help me."

"To help you how?"

"I'll tell you — but you must give me my head. I don't know what I said to you before dinner — I had had too many brandys-and-sodas. Perhaps I was too free — if I was I beg your pardon. I made the governess bolt — very proper in the superintendent of one's children. Do you suppose they saw anything? I should n't care for that. I did take half a dozen or so; I was thirsty and I was awfully gratified."

"You've little enough to gratify you."

"Now that's just where you're wrong, my dear," Lionel declared. "I don't know when I've warmed to anything so much as to what I told you."

"What you told me?"

"About her being in Paris. I hope she'll stay a month!"

"I don't understand you," Laura said.

"Are you very sure, Laura? My dear, it suits my

book! If I had 'fixed' it as you say, myself, I could n't have fixed it better. You know yourself he's not the first."

Laura was silent; his round eyes were fixed on her face and she saw something she had not seen before — a little shining point which on Lionel's part might represent an idea, but which made his expression awkward as well as eager. "He?" she presently asked. "Whom are you speaking of?"

"Why of Charley Crispin, God damn him!"

She had paled at the imprecation. "What has he to do —?"

"He has everything to do. Is n't he with her there?"

"How should I know? You said Lady Ringrose is with her."

"Lady Ringrose is a mere blind — and a devilish poor one at that. I'm sorry to have to say it to you, but Charley Crispin's in plain English her lover. I mean Selina's. And he ain't the first."

There was another short silence while they stood opposed, and then Laura asked — and the question was unexpected — "Why do you call him Charley?"

"Does n't he call me Lion, like all the rest?" said her brother-in-law with a stare.

"You're the most extraordinary people. I suppose you've a certain amount of proof before you say such things to me?"

"Proof? — I've oceans of proof! And not only about Crispin, but about Bamborough."

"And pray who's Bamborough?"

"Did you never hear of Lord Bamborough? He

has gone to India. That was before you came. I don't say all this for my pleasure, Laura," Mr. Berrington added.

"Don't you indeed?" the girl ambiguously quavered. "I thought you were so glad."

"I'm glad to know it, but I'm not glad to tell it. When I say I'm glad to know it I mean I'm glad to be fixed at last. Oh I've got the tip! It's all open country now and I know just how to go. I've gone into it most extensively; there's nothing you can't find out to-day — if you go to the right place. I've — I've —" He hung fire, but went on: "Well, it's no matter what I've done. I know where I am and it's a great comfort. She's up a tree if ever a woman was. Now we'll see who's a beetle and who's a toad!" Lionel concluded gaily, though with some mixture of metaphor.

"It's not true — it's not true — it's not true," Laura said slowly.

"That's just what she'll say — though that's not the way she'll say it. Oh if she could get off by your saying it *for* her! — for you, my dear, would be believed."

"Get off — what do you mean?" the girl asked with a coldness she failed to feel, for she was tingling all over with shame and rage.

"Why what do you suppose I'm talking about? I'm going to haul her up and to have it out."

"You're going to make a scandal?"

"*Make* it? Bless my soul, it isn't me! And I should think it was 'made' enough. I'm going to appeal to the laws of my country — that's what I'm going to do. She pretends I'm stopped, whatever she does. But that's all gammon — I ain't!"

"I understand — but you won't do anything so horrible," said Laura very gently.

"Horrible as you please, but less so than going on in this way. I have n't told you the fiftieth part; you'll easily understand I *can't*. They're not nice things to say to a girl like you — especially about Bamborough, if you did n't know it. But when they happen you've got to look at them, have n't you? That's the way I see it."

"It's not true — it's not true — it's not true," Laura Wing repeated in the same way, slowly shaking her head.

"Of course you stand up for your sister — but that's just what I wanted to say to you, that you ought to have some pity for *me* and some sense of justice. Have n't I always been nice to you?" Lionel asked. "Have you ever had so much as a nasty word from me?"

This appeal touched the girl; she had eaten her brother-in-law's bread for months, she had had the use of all the luxuries with which he was surrounded, and to herself personally she had never known him anything but kind. She made no direct response however; she only said: "Be quiet, be quiet and leave her to me. I'll answer for her."

"Answer for her — what do you mean?"

"She shall be better. She shall be reasonable. There shall be no more talk of these horrors. Leave her to me. Let me go away with her somewhere."

314

"Go away with her? I would n't let you come within a mile of her if you were *my* sister!"

"Oh shame, shame!" she cried, turning away from him.

She hurried to the door of the room, but he stopped her before she reached it. He got his back to it, he barred her way and she had to stand there and hear him. "I have n't said what I wanted — for I told you I wanted you to help me. I ain't cruel — I ain't insulting — you can't make out that against me: I 'm sure you know in your heart that I 've swallowed what would sicken most men. Therefore I tell you you ought to be fair with me, you ought to be just *for* me. You 're too clever not to be; *you* can't pretend to swallow —" He paused a moment and went on, and she saw it was his idea — an idea very simple and bold. He wanted her to side with him — to watch for him — to help him to get his divorce. He forbore to say she owed him as much for the hospitality and protection she had in her poverty enjoyed, but she was sure this was in his heart. "Of course she 's your sister, but when one's sister 's a perfect bad 'un there 's no law to force one to jump into the mud to save her. It *is* mud, my dear, and mud up to your neck. You had much better think of her children — you had much better stop in *my* boat."

"Do you ask me to help you with evidence against her?" — she herself put it straight. She had stood there passive, waiting while he talked, covering her face with her hands, which she parted a little, looking at him.

3¹5

He just faltered. "I ask you not to deny what you've seen — what you feel to be true."

"Then of the abominations of which you say you've proof you have n't proof."

"Why have n't I proof?"

"If you want *me* to come forward!"

"I shall go into court with a strong case. You may do what you like. But I give you notice and I expect you not to forget I 've given it. Don't forget — because you 'll be asked — that I 've told you to-night where she is and with whom she is and what measures I intend to take."

"Be asked — be asked?" the girl repeated.

"Why of course you 'll be cross-examined."

"Oh mother, mother!" poor Laura broke out. Her hands were over her face again and as her companion, opening the door, let her pass, she burst into tears. He looked after her, distressed, compunctious, half-ashamed, and he exclaimed to himself: "The bloody brute, the bloody brute!" But the words had reference to his wife.

V

"AND are you telling me the perfect truth when you say Captain Crispin was n't there?"

"The perfect truth?" Mrs. Lionel straightened herself to her height, threw back her head and measured her critic up and down; it is to be surmised that this was one of the many ways in which she knew she looked very handsome indeed. Her critic was her own tiresome little sister, and even in a discussion with a person long since initiated she was not incapable of feeling that her beauty was a new advantage. At this juncture she had at first the air of depending upon it mainly to produce an effect upon Laura; then, after an instant's reflexion, she determined to arrive at her result in another way. She exchanged her expression of scorn, of resentment at the challenge to her veracity, for a look of refined amusement; she smiled patiently, as remembering that of course Laura could n't understand of what impertinence she had been guilty. There was a quickness of perception and lightness of hand which, to her sense, this near American relative had in spite of nearness never acquired: the girl's earnest, almost barbarous probity blinded her to the importance of certain pleasant little forms. "My poor child, the things you do say! One does n't put a question about the perfect truth in a manner that implies that a person's telling a perfect lie. However, as it's only

317

you I don't mind satisfying your really too tactless curiosity. I have n't the least idea whether Captain Crispin was there or not. I know nothing of his movements and he does n't keep me informed — why should he, poor man? — of his whereabouts. He was not there for *me* — is n't that all that need interest you? As far as I was concerned he might have been at the North Pole. I neither saw him nor heard of him. I did n't see the end of his nose!" Selina continued, still with her wiser, her tolerant brightness, looking straight into her sister's eyes. Her own were clear and lovely, and she was but little less handsome than if she had been proud and freezing. Laura wondered at her more and more; stupefied suspense was now almost the girl's constant state of mind.

Mrs. Lionel had come back from Paris the day before, but had not appeared at Mellows the same night, though there was more than one train she might have taken. Neither had she gone to the house in Grosvenor Place — she had spent the night at an hotel. Her husband was absent again; he was supposed to be in Grosvenor Place, so that they had not yet met. Little as she was a woman to admit she had been in the wrong, she was yet known to have recognised later the gravity of her mistake in not at this moment going straight to her own house. It had given Lionel a degree of advantage, made it appear perhaps a little that she had a bad conscience and was afraid to face him. But she had had her reasons for putting up at an hotel, and she thought it needless to express them pedantically. She came home by a morning train, the second day, and arrived before luncheon, of which meal she partook in the company of her sister and in that of Miss Steet and the children, sent for in honour of the occasion. After luncheon she let the governess go, but kept Scratch and Parson — kept them on ever so long in the morning-room, where she remained; longer than she had ever kept them before. Laura was conscious she herself ought to have been pleased at this, but there was a perversity even in Selina's manner of doing right: Laura wanted so immensely now to see her alone — had something so serious to say to her. Selina hugged her children repeatedly, encouraging their sallies; she laughed extravagantly at the innocence of their remarks, so that at table Miss Steet was quite abashed by her unusual high spirits. Laura was unable to question her about Captain Crispin and Lady Ring-rose while Geordie and Ferdy were there: they would n't understand of course, but names were always reflected in their limpid little minds and they gave forth the image later — often in the most extraordinary connexions. It was as if Selina knew what she was waiting for and were determined to make her wait. The girl wished her to go to her room, to which she might follow her. But Selina showed no thought of moving, and one could never entertain the idea for her, on any occasion, that it would be suitable she should change her dress. The dress she wore — whatever it was — was too becoming to her, and to the moment, for that. Laura noticed how the very folds of her garment published that she had been to Paris; she had spent only a week there, but the mark of her *couturière* was all over her: it was simply to confer with this great artist that, from her own account, she had crossed the Channel. The signs of the conference were so conspicuous that it was as if she had said "Don't you see the proof that it was for nothing but *chiffons?*" She walked up and down the room with Geordie at her neck, in an access of maternal tenderness; he was much too big to nestle gracefully in her bosom, but that only made her seem younger, more flexible, fairer in her tall strong slimness. Her distinguished figure bent itself hither and thither, but always in perfect freedom, as she romped with her children; and there was another moment, when she came slowly down the room, holding one of them in each hand and singing to them while they looked up at her beauty, charmed and listening and a little surprised at such new ways — a moment when she might have passed for some grave antique statue of a young matron, or even for a picture of Saint Cecilia. This morning, more than ever, Laura was struck with her air of youth, the inextinguishable freshness that would have made any one exclaim at her being the mother of such bouncing little boys. Her sister had always admired her, thought her the prettiest woman in London, the beauty with the finest points; and now these points were so vivid (especially her finished slenderness and the grace, the natural elegance of every turn — the fall of her shoulders had never looked so perfect) that the girl almost detested them: they affected her as an advertisement of danger and even of shame.

Miss Steet at last came back for the children, and as soon as she had taken them away Selina observed that she would go over to Plash — just as she was: she rang for her hat and jacket and for the carriage. Laura could see she would n't give her just yet the advantage of a retreat to her room. The hat and jacket were quickly brought, but after they were put on Selina kept her maid in the drawing-room, talking to her a long time, telling her elaborately what she wished done with the things she had brought from Paris. Before the maid departed the carriage was announced, and the footman, leaving the door of the room open, hovered within earshot. Laura then, losing patience, turned out the maid and closed the door; she stood before her sister, who was prepared for the drive. She asked her abruptly, fiercely, but colouring with her question, whether Captain Crispin had been in Paris. We have heard Mrs. Lionel's answer — quite vain to her companion; the perception of which it doubtless was that led Selina to break out with a greater show of indignation: "I never heard of such extraordinary ideas for a girl to have and such extraordinary things for a girl to talk about! My dear, you 've acquired a freedom — you 've emancipated yourself from conventionality — and I suppose I must congratulate you." Laura only stood there with fixed eyes and no retort to the sally, and her sister went on with another change of tone: "And pray if he *was* there what is there so monstrous? Has n't it happened he has been in London when I have? Why is it then so awful he should be in Paris?"

"Awful, awful, too awful!" Laura wailed, still facing her — facing her all the more intensely that she knew how little Selina liked it.

"My dear, you do indulge in a style of innuendo, for a respectable young woman!" Mrs. Lionel cried with an angry laugh. "You've ideas of a lowness that when I was a girl —!" She paused; her sister saw she hadn't the assurance to finish her sentence on that particular note.

"Don't talk about my innuendoes and my ideas — you might remember those in which I've heard *you* indulge! Ideas? what ideas did I ever have before I came here?" Laura Wing asked with a trembling voice. "Don't pretend to be shocked, Selina; that's too cheap a defence. You've said things to me — if you choose to talk of freedom! What's the talk of your house and what does one hear if one lives with you? I don't care what I hear now — it's all odious and there's little choice and my sweet sensibility has gone God knows where! — so that I'm very glad if you understand I don't care what I say. If one talks about your affairs, my dear, one mustn't be too particular!" the girl continued with a flash of passion.

Mrs. Lionel buried her face in her hands. "Merciful powers, to be insulted, to be covered with outrage, by one's wretched little sister!"

"I think you should be thankful there's one human being — however wretched — who cares enough for you to care about the truth in what concerns you," Laura said. "Selina, Selina, are you hideously deceiving us?"

"Us?" Selina repeated with her ready decision. "Whom do you mean by us?"

Laura cast about; she had asked herself if it would be best to be explicit about the dreadful scene she had had with Lionel; but she had not, in her mind, settled that point. However, it was settled now in an instant. "I don't mean your friends — those of them I've seen. I don't think *they* care a straw — I had never imagined such people. But last week Lionel spoke to me — he told me he knew it as a certainty."

"Lionel spoke to you?" said Lionel's wife, holding up her head with a stare. "And what is it he knows?"

"That Captain Crispin was in Paris and that you were absolutely with him. He believes you went there to meet him."

"He said this to *you?*"

"Yes, and much more — I don't know why I should make a secret of it."

"The disgusting beast!"—Selina uttered it slowly and solemnly. "He enjoys the right — the legal right — to pour forth his vileness upon *me;* but when he's so lost to every feeling as to begin to talk to you in such a way —!" And she paused in the extremity of her reprobation.

"Oh it wasn't his talk that shocked me — it was his believing it," Laura said. "That, I confess, made an impression on me."

"Did it indeed? I'm infinitely obliged to you! You're a tender, loving little sister."

"Yes, I am, if it's tender to have cried about

323

you — all these days — till I'm blind and sick!"
the girl declared. "I hope you're prepared to meet
him. His mind is quite made up to apply for a divorce."

Her voice almost failed her as she said this —
it was the first time that in talking with Selina she
had pronounced the horrible word. She had heard
it, however, often enough on the lips of others; it
had been bandied lightly enough in her presence
under those somewhat austere ceilings of Mellows,
of which the admired decorations and mouldings,
in the taste of the middle of the last century, all in
delicate plaster and reminding her of Wedgewood
pottery, consisted of slim festoons, urns and trophies and knotted ribbons, so many symbols of domestic affection and irrevocable union. Selina herself had flashed it at her with light superiority, as
if it were some precious jewel kept in reserve, which
she could convert at any moment into property,
so that it would constitute a happy provision for
her future. The idea — associated with her own
point of view — was apparently too familiar to Mrs.
Berrington to be the cause of her changing colour;
it struck her indeed, as presented by Laura, in a
ludicrous light, for her pretty eyes expanded a moment and she smiled pityingly. "Well, you're a poor
dear innocent after all. Lionel would be about
as able to divorce me — even if I were the most
abandoned of my sex — as he would be to write
a leader in the *Times*."

"I know nothing about that," said Laura.

"So I perceive — as I also perceive that you must

have shut your eyes very tight. Should you like to know a few of the reasons — heaven forbid I should attempt to go over them all; there are millions! — why his hands are tied?"

"Not in the least."

"Should you like to know that his own life is too base for words, and that his impudence in talking about me would be sickening if it were n't grotesque?" Selina went on with increasing passion. "Should you like me to tell you to what he has stooped — to the very gutter; and the charming history of his relations with —"

"No, I don't want you to tell me anything of the sort," Laura interrupted. "Especially as you were just now so pained by the licence of my own allusions."

"You listen to him then — but it suits your purpose not to listen to me!"

"Oh Selina, Selina!" the girl almost shrieked as she turned away.

"Where have your eyes been, or your senses, or your powers of observation? You can be clever enough when it suits you!" Mrs. Lionel continued, breathing another blast of irony. "And now perhaps, as the carriage is waiting, you 'll let me go about my duties."

Laura turned again and stopped her, holding her arm as she passed toward the door. "Will you swear — will you swear by everything that 's most sacred?"

"Will I swear what?" And now she thought Selina visibly blanched.

"That you did n't lay eyes on Captain Crispin in Paris."

Her companion waited, but only an instant. "You're really too odious, but as you're pinching me to death I'll swear to get away from you. I never laid eyes on him."

The organs of vision Selina was prepared to take oath she had not misapplied were, as her sister looked into them, an abyss of indefinite prettiness. The girl had sounded them before without discovering a conscience at the bottom of them, and they had never helped any one to find out anything about their possessor except that she was one of the beauties of London. Even while Selina spoke Laura had a cold horrible sense of not believing her, and at the same time a desire, colder still, to extract a reiteration of the pledge. Was it the asseveration of her innocence she wished her to repeat, or only the attestation of her falsity? One way or the other it seemed to her that this would settle something, and she went on inexorably: "By our dear mother's memory — by our poor father's?"

"By my mother's, by my father's," said Mrs. Berrington, "and by that of any other member of the family you like!" Laura let her go; she had not been pinching her, as Selina described the pressure, but had clung to her with insistent hands. As she opened the door Selina said in a changed voice: "I suppose it's no use to ask you if you care to drive to Plash."

"No, thank you, I don't care — I shall take a walk."

"I suppose therefore your friend Lady Davenant has gone."

"No, I think she's still there."

"That's a treat!" Selina groaned as she went off.

VI

Laura Wing hastened to her room to prepare herself for her walk; but when she reached it she simply fell on her knees, shuddering, beside her bed. She buried her face in the soft counterpane of wadded silk; she remained there a long time, with a kind of aversion to lifting it again to the day. It burned with horror and there was coolness in the smooth glaze of the silk. It seemed to her she had been concerned in a hideous bargain, and her uppermost feeling was, strangely enough, that she was ashamed — not of her sister but of herself. She did n't believe her — that was at the bottom of everything, and she had made her lie, she had brought out her perjury, she had associated it with the sacred images of the dead. She took no walk, she remained in her room, and quite late, towards six o'clock, she heard on the gravel outside her windows the wheels of the carriage bringing back the mistress of the house. She had evidently been elsewhere as well as to Plash; no doubt she had been to the vicarage — she was capable even of that. She could pay "duty-visits" in such a fashion —she called at the vicarage about three times a year — and could equally go and be nice to her mother-in-law with her fresh lips still fresher for the lie she had just told. For it was as plain as an aching nerve to Laura that she did n't believe her, and if she did n't believe her the words she had spoken

were a lie. It was the lie, the lie to *her* and which
she had dragged out of her that seemed to the girl
the ugliest thing. If she had admitted her folly, if
she had explained, attenuated, sophisticated, there
would have been a difference in her favour; but now
she was bad because she was hard. She had a surface of polished metal. And she could make plans
and calculate, she could act and do things for a particular effect. She could go straight to old Mrs.
Berringon and to the parson's wife and his many
daughters — just as she had kept the children after
luncheon on purpose so long — because that looked
innocent and domestic and denoted a mind void of
guile.

A servant came to Laura's door to tell her tea was
ready; and on her asking who else was below —
for she had heard the wheels of a second vehicle just
after Selina's return — she learned that Lionel had
come back. At this news she requested that her tea
should be brought to her room — she resolved not to
go to dinner. When the dinner-hour came she sent
down word she had a headache and was going to bed.
She wondered if Selina would come to her — that
lady could forget disagreeable scenes amazingly;
but her fervent hope of being left alone was gratified.
Indeed Selina would have another call on her attention if her meeting with her husband proved half the
shock of battle that might be expected. Laura had
found herself listening hard after knowing her brother-
in-law in the house: she half expected to hear indications of violence — loud cries or the sound of a
scuffle. It was a matter of course to her that some

dreadful scene had n't been slow to take place, something discretion should keep her out of even if she had n't been too sick. She did n't go to bed — partly for not knowing what might happen in the house. But she was restless also for herself: things had reached a point when it seemed to her she must make up her mind. She left her candles unlighted — she sat up till the small hours in the glow of the fire. What had been settled by her scene with Selina was that worse things were to come — looking into her fire as the night went on she had a rare prevision of the catastrophe that hung over them all — and she considered, or tried to consider, what it would be best for her, in anticipation, to do. The first thing was to take flight.

It may be related without delay that Laura took no flight and that though the fact takes from the interest properly to be felt in her character she did n't even make up her mind. That was not so easy when action had to ensue. At the same time she had n't the excuse of a conviction that by not acting — that is by not withdrawing from her brother-in-law's roof — she should be able to hold Selina up to her duty, to drag her back into the straight path. The hopes connected with that project were now a phase she had left behind her; she had n't to-day an illusion about her sister large enough to cover a sixpence. She had passed through the period of superstition, which had lasted longest — the time when it had seemed to her, as at first, a profanation to question the integrity of so near a relative and so brilliant a figure, to judge and condemn the earlier born whose beauty and success she had ever been proud of and who carried herself, though without undue rigour, as one native to an upper air. She had called herself at hours of prompt penitence for premature suspicion a little presumptuous prig: so strange she had originally felt the impulse of criticism in regard to her bright protectress. But the revolution was complete and she had a desolate lonely freedom that struck her as not the ugliest thing in the world only because Selina's behaviour was uglier. She supposed she should learn, though she was afraid of the knowledge, what had passed between that lady and her husband while her vigil ached itself away; yet it appeared the next day to her surprise that nothing was changed in the situation save Selina's knowing at present how much more she was tracked. As this had not a chastening effect nothing had been gained by her own appeal. Whatever Lionel had said to his wife he said nothing to Laura; he left her at perfect liberty to forget the subject he had opened up to her so luminously. This was quite in the note of his instinctive good nature: it had come over him that after all she would n't much like it, so that if the free use of the grey ponies could make up to her for the shock she might order them every day in the week and banish the bad moment from her mind.

Laura ordered the grey ponies very often and drove herself all over the country. She visited not only the neighbouring but the distant poor, and never went out without stopping for one of the vicar's fresh daughters. The house was now half the time full of visitors and when it was not its master and mistress were staying with their friends either together or singly. Sometimes — almost always when she was asked — Laura Wing accompanied her sister, and on two or three occasions she paid an independent visit. Selina had often told her she wanted her to have her own friends, so that the girl now equally desired to make a show of these recruits. She had arrived at no decision whatever, had embraced in intention no particular course. She drifted on, shutting her eyes, averting her head and, as it seemed to herself, hardening her heart. This admission will doubtless suggest to the reader that she was a weak inconsequent spasmodic young person, with a standard not really, or at any rate not continuously, high; and it is not to be wished she shall sail under false colours. It must even be related of her that since she could n't escape and live in lodgings and paint fans — there were reasons why this combination was impossible — she determined to try and be happy in the given circumstances, to float in shallow and turbid water. She gave up the attempt to sound the rather base compact her companions seemed to have made; she knew it was n't final but served them sufficiently for the time; and if it served them why should n't it serve her, the dependent impecunious tolerated small sister, representative of the class whom it behooved above all to mind their own business? The time was coming round when the whole house would move up to town, and there, in the crowd, with still more complications but also more diversions, the strain would be less and indifference easier.

Whatever Lionel had said to his wife that evening

she had found something to say to *him:* this Laura could see, though not so much from any change in the simple cast of his little round red countenance, animated only by its fixed blue glare, and in the vain bustle of his existence, as from the grand manner in which Selina now carried herself. She was "smarter" than ever and her waist was smaller and her back straighter and the fall of her shoulders finer; her long eyes were more oddly charming and the extreme detachment of her elbows from her sides conduced still more to the exhibition of her beautiful arms. So she floated, with a serenity not disturbed by the general state of being extremely waited for, through the interminable succession of her engagements. Her photographs were not to be purchased in the Burlington Arcade — she had kept out of that; but she looked more than ever as they would have represented her had they been on exhibition. There were times when Laura thought her brother-in-law's formless desistence too frivolous for nature : it even gave her a sense of deeper dangers. It was as if he had been digging away in the dark and they would all tumble into the hole. It befell her to ask herself if the things he had said to her the afternoon he fell upon her in the schoolroom had not all been a clumsy practical joke, a crude desire to startle, that of a schoolboy playing with a sheet in the dark; or else mere brandy-and-soda, which came to the same thing. However this might be, she was forced to admit that the impression of brandy-and-soda had not again been given her. More striking still meanwhile was Selina's capacity to recover from shocks and condone imputations; she kissed again — kissed Laura — without tears, and proposed problems connected with the re-arrangement of trimmings and of the flowers at dinner, proposed them as candidly and earnestly as if there had never been a sharper debate between them. Captain Crispin was not mentioned; much less of course, so far as Laura was concerned, was he seen. But Lady Ringrose appeared; she came down for two days, during an absence of Lionel's. Laura found her with surprise no such great Jezebel, but a clever little woman with a single eye-glass and short hair who had read Lecky and could give useful hints about water-colours: a reconciliation that encouraged the girl, since this was the direction in which it now seemed to her best she herself should grow.

VII

In Grosvenor Place, on the Sunday afternoons of the first weeks of the animated season, Mrs. Lionel was usually at home: this indeed was the only time a visitor who had not made an appointment could hope to be admitted to her presence. Very few hours in the twenty-four did she spend in her own house. Gentlemen calling on these occasions rarely found her sister — Selina had the field to herself. It was understood between the pair that Laura should take such parts of the day for going to see her old women: it was in this manner Selina qualified the girl's independent social resources. The old women however were not a dozen in number; they consisted mainly of Lady Davenant and the elder Mrs. Berrington, who had rather a dull house in Portman Street. Lady Davenant lived, with a brighter modern economy, at Queen's Gate and also was usually at home of a Sunday afternoon: her visitors were not all men, like Selina Berrington's, and Laura's maidenly bonnet was not a false note in her drawing-room. Selina liked her sister, naturally enough, to make herself useful, but of late, somehow, the occasions depending in any degree on her aid had grown rarer and she had been scantly appealed to — though it would have seemed she might be liberally — on behalf of the weekly chorus of gentlemen. It came to be recognised on Selina's part that nature had dedicated poor Laura more to the relief of old women than to that of young men. Laura had a distinct sense of interfering with the free interchange of anecdote and pleasantry that went on at the home fireside: the anecdotes were mostly such an immense secret that they could n't be told fairly if she were there, and she had their due distinctness on her conscience. There was an exception however; when Selina expected Americans she invariably appealed to her to "stick it out": not apparently so much because her conversation would be good for these pilgrims as because theirs would be good for her.

One Sunday about the middle of May she prepared herself to pay her respects to Lady Davenant, who had made a long absence from town at Easter but would now have returned. The weather was charming; she had from the first established her right to tread the London streets alone — if she was a poor girl she could have the detachment as well as the helplessness of it — and she promised herself the pleasure of a walk through the Park, where the new grass was bright. A moment before she quitted the house her sister sent for her to the drawing-room; the servant gave her a note scrawled in pencil: "That man from New York is here — Mr. Wendover, who brought me the introduction the other day from the Schoolings. He's rather a dose — you must positively come down and talk to him. Take him out with you if you can." The description was not alluring, but Selina had never made a request to which she had n't instantly responded: it seemed to her she was there for that. She joined the circle in the drawing-room and found it to consist of five persons, one of whom was Lady Ringrose. Lady Ringrose was at all times and in all places a fitful apparition; she had described herself to Laura during her visit at Mellows as "a bird on the branch." She had no fixed habit of receiving on Sunday, but was in and out as she liked, and she was one of the few specimens of her sex who, in Grosvenor Place, ever turned up, as she said, at the consecrated hours. Of the three gentlemen two were known or knowable to Laura; she made sure the big one with the red hair was in the Guards and the other in the Rifles; the latter looked like a rosy child and as if he ought to be sent up to play with Geordie and Ferdy: his social nickname indeed was the Babe. Selina's admirers were of all ages — they ranged from infants to octogenarians.

She introduced the third gentleman to her sister; a tall fair slender young man who was open to the charge of a mistake in the shade of his tight perpendicular coat, ordering it of too clear a blue. This added however to the candour of his appearance, and if he was a dose, as Selina had described him, he could only operate beneficially. There were moments when our young woman's heart quite opened to the compatriot, and now, though preoccupied and a little disappointed at having been detained, she tried to like Mr. Wendover, whom her sister had compared invidiously, as it seemed to her, with the other conversers. It struck her that his surface at least was as glossy as theirs. The Babe, whom she remembered to have heard spoken of as a dangerous

337

flirt, was in conversation with Lady Ringrose and the guardsman with their hostess; so she did her best to entertain the American visitor, as to whom any one could easily see (she thought) that he had brought a letter of introduction — he wished so to maintain the credit of those who had given it him. Laura scarcely knew these people, American friends of Selina's who had spent a period of festivity in London and gone back across the sea before her own advent; but Mr. Wendover gave her all possible information about them. He lingered upon them, returned to them, qualified and corrected statements he had made at first, discoursed upon them *à perte de vue*. He seemed to fear to leave them lest he should find nothing again so good, and he indulged in a parallel that was almost elaborate between Miss Fanny and Miss Katie. Selina told her sister afterwards she had wretchedly overheard him — that he talked of the What-do-you-call-'ems as if he had been a nursemaid: on which Laura defended the poor youth even to extravagance. She reminded her relative that people in London were always saying Lady Mary and Lady Susan: why then should n't Americans use the Christian name with the humbler prefix to which they had to resign themselves? There had been a time when Mrs. Lionel had been content enough to be Miss Lina, even though she was the elder sister: and the girl liked to think there were still old far-away friends, friends of the family, for whom, even should she live to sixty years of spinsterhood, she would never be anything but Miss Laura. This was as good as Donna Anna or Donna Elvira:

English people could never call people as other people did for fear of resembling the servants.

Mr. Wendover appealed not less than he abounded: however his letter might be regarded in Grosvenor Place he evidently took it all seriously himself, but his eyes wandered, ever so yearningly, to the other side of the room, and our young woman felt that though he had often seen persons like Miss Laura before — not that he betrayed this too crudely — he had never seen any one like Lady Ringrose. His glance lingered also on Mrs. Lionel, who, to do her justice, abstained from showing, by the way she returned it, that she wished her sister to get him safely off. Her smile was particularly pretty on Sunday afternoons and he was welcome to enjoy it as part of the decoration of the place. Whether or no the young man should prove absorbing, he was at any rate absorbed; indeed she afterwards learned that what Selina deprecated in him was the fact that he would certainly participate with all his powers. He would be one of the sort that notice all kinds of little things — things one never saw nor heard of — in the newspapers or in society, and would call on one (a dreadful prospect) to explain and even defend them. One had n't come there to explain England to the Americans; the more particularly as one's life had been a burden to one during the first years of one's marriage through one's having to explain America to the English. As for defending England to one's original countrymen one had much rather defend it *from* them: there were too many — too many for those who were already there. This was the class

339

Selina wished to spare — she did n't care about the
English. They could obtain an eye for an eye and a
cutlet for a cutlet by going over to the States; which
she had no desire to do — not for all the cutlets or
even for all the eyes in Christendom.

When Mr. Wendover and his young benefactress
had at last cut loose from the Schoolings he let her
know confidentially that he had come over really to
see London: he had time that year; he did n't know
when he should have it again — if ever, as he said —
and he had made up his mind that this was about
the best use he could make of four months and thirteen days. He had heard so much of it; it was talked
of so much to-day; a man felt as if he ought to know
something about it. Laura wished the others could
hear this — that England was coming up, was making her way at last to a place among the topics of
societies more in the swim. She thought Mr. Wendover after all remarkably like an Englishman, in spite
of his remarking that he believed she had resided in
London quite a time. He talked a great deal about
things being characteristic, and wanted to know,
lowering his voice to make the enquiry, if Lady Ringrose were not strikingly so. He had heard of her very
often, he said; and he observed that it was very interesting to see her: he could n't have used a different tone if he had been speaking of the prime minister or the laureate. Laura was blank as to what he
had heard of Lady Ringrose; she doubted its being
what she had heard from her brother-in-law: if this
had been the case he never would have mentioned
it. She foresaw how much his friends in London

would have to do in the way of teaching him the characteristic: he would go about in much the same way
English travellers did in America, fixing his attention
mainly on society — he let Laura know this to be
especially what he wished to go into — and neglecting the antiquities, the "objects of interest," quite
as if he failed to believe in their importance. He
would ask questions it was impossible to answer;
as to whether for instance, gracious heaven, society
were very different in the two countries. If you said
yes you gave a wrong impression and if you said no
you did n't give a right one: that was the kind of
thing that, as Selina said, wore one to a thread. Laura
found her new acquaintance, on the present occasion
and later, more philosophically analytic of his impressions than those of her countrymen she had
hitherto encountered in her new home: the latter, in
regard to such impressions, usually exhibited either
a profane levity or a tendency to mawkish idealism.

Selina called out at last that Laura need n't stay
if she had prepared herself to go out: whereupon the
girl, having nodded and smiled good-bye at the other
members of the circle, took a more formal leave of
Mr. Wendover — expressed the hope, as an American girl might in such a case, that they should see
him again. Selina asked him to come and dine four
days later; which was as much as to say that relations
must be suspended till then. Mr. Wendover took it
so and, having accepted the invitation, departed at
the same time as Laura. He passed out of the house
with her and she asked him in the street which way
he was going. He was too awfully tense, but she

liked him; he appeared not to deal in chaff, and this was a change that relieved her — she had so often had to pay out that coin when no fumbling in her poor pockets seemed to produce it. She hoped he would ask her leave to go with her the way she was going — and this not on particular but on general grounds. It would be American, it would remind her of old times; she should like him to be as American as that. There was no reason for her taking so quick an interest in his nature, inasmuch as she had not fallen under his spell; but there were moments when to be reminded of the way people felt and acted overseas affected her as really romantic. Mr. Wendover did n't disappoint her, and the bright chocolate-coloured vista of the Fifth Avenue seemed to surge before her as he said "May I have the pleasure of making my direction the same as yours?" and moved round, systematically, to take his place between her and the curbstone. She had never walked much with young men in America — she had been brought up in the new school, the school of attendant maids and the avoidance of certain streets — and had very often done so in English lanes; yet, as at the top of Grosvenor Place she crossed over to the Park, proposing they should take that way, the breath of her native land was in her nostrils. It was certainly only another native who could have that tension; Mr. Wendover's almost made her laugh, just as her eyes grew dull when people "slanged" each other hilariously in her sister's house; but at the same time he gave her a feeling of high respectability. It would be respectable still if she were to go on with him indefinitely —

if she never were to come home at all. He asked her after a while, as they went, if he had violated the custom of the country in offering her his "escort"; whether by the law of the land a gentleman might walk with a young lady — the first time he saw her — not because their roads lay together but for the sake of the walk.

"Why should I care if it's the law of the land? I'm not English, you know," said Laura Wing. Then her companion explained that he only wanted a general hint, that with so kind a guide he might n't appear to have taken a liberty. The point was simply — and rather comprehensively and strenuously he began to set forth the point. Laura stopped him short, telling him she did n't care about it, and he almost irritated her by calling her kind. She was intensely so, but was n't pleased it should be recognised so soon; and he still gave on her nerves when he asked if she continued to go by American usage and did n't find that if one lived there one had to "do as the Romans did." His very phrases made her wince, and she was weary of the perpetual opposition of the countries, was weary of the perpetual comparison; she having not only heard it from others but heard it a great deal from herself. She held there were certain differences you felt if you belonged to one or the other nation, and that this was the end of it: there was no use trying to express them. Those you *could* express were not real or not important, were in short not worth talking of. Mr. Wendover asked her if she liked English society and if it were superior to American; also if the social tone were

very high in London. She thought his questions
"academic" — the term she used to see applied in
the *Times* to certain speeches in Parliament. Bend-
ing his long leanness over her — he had no more
physical personality than a consulted thermometer
— and walking almost sidewise to give her a proper
attention, he struck her as innocent, as incapable
of guessing that she had had a certain observation of
life. They were talking of totally different things:
English society, as he asked her judgement on it and
she had happened to see it and should be able to
"speak up" about it, was an affair he did n't suspect.
If she *were* to speak up it would be more than he
doubtless bargained for; but she 'd do so not to make
him open his eyes — only to relieve herself. She had
thought of that before in regard to two or three persons she had met — of the satisfaction of breaking
out with some of her "views." It would make little
difference that the person would perhaps fail to understand her; the one understanding best would be
far from understanding all. "I want to get out of it,
please — out of the set I live in, the one I 've tumbled
into through my sister, the people you saw just now.
There are thousands of people in London different
from that and ever so much nicer; but I don't see
them, I don't know how to get at them; and after all,
poor dear man, what power have you to help me?"
That was in the last analysis what she would have
had to say.

Mr. Wendover asked about Selina in the tone of
a person who took that lady for a very leading fact,
and this by itself was again a trial to Laura. A lead-

ing fact—Selina? Gracious goodness, no: whatever a leading fact might be! One might have to live with her, to hold one's tongue about her; but at least one was n't bound to exaggerate her position. The young man forbore decorously to make use of the expression, but Laura could see he imagined her sister a "professional beauty," and she guessed that as this product had n't yet been taught to grow in the Western world the desire really to get *at* it, after having read so much about it, had been one of the motives of Mr. Wendover's pilgrimage. Mrs. Schooling, who must have been a weariness, had described Mrs. Lionel as, though transplanted, the very finest flower of a rich ripe society, and pronounced her as clever and virtuous as she was beautiful. Meanwhile Laura knew what Selina thought of Fanny Schooling and her incurable provinciality. "Now was that a good example of London talk, what I heard — I only heard a little of it, but the conversation was more general before you appeared — in your sister's drawing-room? I don't mean literary, intellectual talk — I suppose there are special places to hear that; I mean — I mean —" Mr. Wendover meant heaven knew what, but they had arrived at Lady Davenant's door and his companion cut him short. A fancy had taken her on the spot, and the fact that it was perverse seemed — since the benefits of perversity were so numerous all round her — only to recommend it.

"If you want to hear London talk there will be some very good going on in here," she said. "If you would like to come in with me —?"

"Oh you're very kind; I should be delighted"

— she inspired him clearly with the effort not to think too slowly. They stepped into the porch and the young man, forestalling her hint, lifted the knocker and gave a postman's rap. She laughed at him for this and he looked bewildered; the idea of taking him in with her had cleared her mind of heavier things. Their acquaintance achieved in that moment a long, long jump. She explained to him who Lady Davenant was and that if he was in search of the characteristic it would be a pity he should n't know her; and then she added before he could put the question:

"And what I'm doing's *not* in the least usual. No, it's not the custom for decent girls here to take strange gentlemen, the first time they see them, off to call on their friends."

"So that Lady Davenant will think it rather extraordinary?" Mr. Wendover eagerly asked; not as if that idea frightened him, but so that his observation on this point should also be well founded. He had entered into Laura's proposal with complete serenity.

"Oh most extraordinary!" said Laura, as they went in. The old lady however concealed such surprise as she may have felt, and greeted her friend's friend as if she must often have seen him. She took him altogether for granted and asked him no questions about his arrival, his departure, his hotel or his business in England. He noticed, as he afterwards confided to Laura, her omission of these forms; but he was not wounded by it — he only made a mark against it as a proof of the difference between English and American manners: in New York people always

346

asked the arriving stranger the first thing about the
steamer and the hotel. He seemed greatly impressed
with Lady Davenant's antiquity, though he confessed
to his companion on a subsequent occasion that he
thought her a little flippant, a little frivolous even for
her years. "Oh yes," said the girl on that occasion, "I've no doubt you considered she talked too
much for one so old. In America old ladies sit silent
and listen to the young." Mr. Wendover stared a
little and replied to this that with her — with Laura
Wing — it was impossible to tell which side she was
on, the American or the English: sometimes she
seemed to take one, sometimes the other. At any
rate, he added, smiling, with regard to the other
great division it was easy to see — she was on the
side of the old. "Of course I am," she said; "when
one *is* old!" And then he wanted to know, according
to his wont, if she were thought so in England; to
which she answered that it was England that had
made her so.

Lady Davenant's bright drawing-room was filled
with mementoes and especially with a collection of
portraits of distinguished people, mainly fine old
prints with signatures, an array of precious auto-
graphs. "Oh it's a cemetery," she said when the
young man asked her some question about one of
the pictures; "they're my contemporaries, they're
all dead and those things are the tombstones with the
inscriptions. I'm the grave-digger — I look after the
place and try to keep it a little tidy. I've dug my
own little hole," she went on to Laura, "and when
you're sent for you must come and put me in." This

evocation of mortality led Mr. Wendover to ask her if she had known Charles Lamb; at which she stared an instant, replying: "Dear me, no — one did n't meet him."

"Oh I meant to say Lord Byron," Mr. Wendover gently pleaded.

"Bless me, yes; I was in love with him. But he did n't notice me, fortunately — we were so many poor things. He was very nice-looking but very vulgar." Lady Davenant then addressed Laura as if her odd satellite had not been there, or rather perhaps as if their interests and knowledge were identical. Before they went away the young man asked her if she had known Garrick and she replied: "Oh dear no, we did n't have them in our houses in those days."

"He must have been dead long before you were born!" Laura exclaimed.

"I dare say; but one used to hear of him."

"I think I meant Edmund Kean," said Mr. Wendover.

"You make little mistakes of a century or two," the girl laughed. She felt now as if she had known Mr. Wendover a long time.

"Oh he was very clever," said Lady Davenant.

"Very magnetic, I suppose," Mr. Wendover went on.

"What's that? I believe he used to get tipsy."

"Perhaps you don't use that expression in England?" Laura's companion enquired.

"Oh I dare say we do if it's American; we talk American now. You seem very good-natured people, but such a jargon as you *do* speak!"

348

"I like *your* way, Lady Davenant," Mr. Wendover benevolently smiled.

"Thank you for nothing! But you might do worse," the old woman cried, adding afterwards sharply: "Please go out!" They were taking leave of her, but she kept Laura's hand and, for the young man, nodded with decision at the open door. "Now, would n't *he* do?" she asked when he had passed into the hall.

"Do for what?"

"For a husband of course."

"For a husband — for whom?"

"Why — for me," said Lady Davenant.

"I don't know — I think he might tire you."

"Oh if he's tiresome!" — yet the old lady looked as if there were worse things.

"I think he's very good," said Laura.

"Well then he'll do."

"Ah perhaps *you* won't!" Laura laughed, smiling back at her and turning away.

VIII

SHE was of a serious turn by nature and, unlike many serious persons, made no particular study of the art of being gay. Had her circumstances been different she might have invoked that relief, but she lived in a merry house (heaven save the mark! as she used to say) and therefore was n't forced to amuse herself in order to see what amusement was like. The diversions she sought were of a serious cast, and she preferred such as showed most the note of difference from Selina's interests and Lionel's. She felt she was most divergent when she attempted to cultivate her mind, and it was a branch of such cultivation to visit the curiosities, the antiquities, the monuments of London. She was fond of the Abbey and the British Museum — she had extended her researches as far as the Tower. She read the works of Mr. John Timbs and made notes of the old corners of history that had n't yet been abolished — the houses in which great men had lived and died. She planned a general tour of inspection of the ancient churches of the City and a pilgrimage to the queer places commemorated by Dickens. It must be added that though her designs were great her adventures had as yet been small. She had lacked opportunity and independence; people had other things to do than to go with her, so that it was not till she had been some time in the land, and till a good while after she had begun to go out alone, that she entered upon the privilege of visiting public institutions by herself. There were some aspects of London that frightened her, but there were certain spots, the Poets' Corner in the Abbey and the room of the Elgin Marbles, where she liked better to be alone than not to have the right companion. At the time Mr. Wendover presented himself in Grosvenor Place she had begun to put in, as they said, a museum or something of that sort whenever she had a chance. In addition to her idea that such places were sources of knowledge — it is to be feared the poor girl's notions of knowledge were at once conventional and crude — they were occasions for detachment, an escape from worrying thoughts. She forgot Selina and she "qualified" herself a little — though for what she hardly knew.

The day Mr. Wendover dined in Grosvenor Place they talked of Saint Paul's, which he expressed a desire to see, wishing to get some idea of the great past, as he said, in England as well as of the bewildering present. Laura mentioned that she had spent half an hour the summer before in the big black temple on Ludgate Hill; whereupon he asked her if he might entertain the hope that — should it consort with her patience to go again — she would serve as his guide there. She had taken him to see Lady Davenant, who was so remarkable and worth a long journey, and now he should like to pay her back, to show *her* something. The difficulty would be that there was probably nothing she had n't seen; but if she could think of an unexplored corner he was completely at her service. They sat together at dinner and she told him she would think of something before the repast was over. A little while later she let him know that a charming place had occurred to her — a place to which she was afraid to go alone and where she should be grateful for a protector: she would tell him more about it afterwards. It was then settled between them that on a certain afternoon of the same week they would investigate Saint Paul's, extending their ramble as much further as they had time. Laura lowered her voice for this discussion as if the range of allusion had had some impropriety. She was now still more of the mind that Mr. Wendover was very decent — his eyes, though so steady, were somehow such a denial of experience. An acquaintance with that light had come to strike the girl as scarce compatible with decency. His principal defect was that he treated all subjects as equally important; but that was perhaps better than treating them with uniform levity. If one took an interest in him one might n't despair of infecting him with the poison of perception.

She said nothing at first to her sister about her appointment with him: the feelings with which she regarded Selina were not such as to make it easy to talk over matters of conduct, as it were, with this votary of pleasure at any price, or at any rate make that report of her arrangements which she would have made to a person of fine judgement. None the less, as she had a horror of positively hiding anything (Selina herself did that enough for two) it was her purpose to mention at luncheon on the day of the event that she had agreed to accompany Mr. Wendover to the City. It so happened, however, that Mrs. Lionel made no appearance at this repast; Laura partook of it in the company of Miss Steet and her young charges. It very often happened now that the sisters failed to meet in the morning, for Selina remained very late in her room and there had been a considerable intermission of the girl's earlier custom of going to her there. It was Selina's habit to send forth from this fragrant sanctuary little hieroglyphic notes in which she expressed her wishes or gave her directions for the day. On the morning I speak of her maid put into Laura's hand one of these communications, which contained the words: "Please be sure and replace me with the children at lunch — I meant to give them that hour to-day. But I've a frantic appeal from Lady Watermouth; she's *much* worse and entreats me to come to her, so I rush for the 12.30 train." These lines required no answer and Laura had no questions to ask about Lady Watermouth. She knew her for endlessly ill, in exile, condemned to forego the diversions of the age and calling out to her friends from a house she had taken at Weybridge for a special soothing air and where Selina had already been to her. Selina's devotion to this stricken comrade seemed laudable — she had her so much on her mind. Laura had noted on her sister's part in relation to other persons and objects these sudden intensities of charity, and had said to herself, watching them: "Is it because she's bad? — does she want to make up for it somehow and to buy herself off from the penalties?"

Mr. Wendover called for his charming guide and

they agreed to go in a romantic Bohemian manner
— the young man was very docile and appreciative
about this — walking the short distance to the Victoria Station and taking the mysterious underground
railway. In the carriage she forestalled the question
she knew he would presently put: "No, no, this
is very exceptional; if we were both English — and
both what we are otherwise — we would n't go so
far."

"And if only one of us were English?"

"It would depend on which one."

"Well, say me."

"Oh in that case I certainly — on so short an acquaintance — would n't go sight-seeing with you."

"Well, I 'm glad I 'm American," said Mr. Wendover, sitting opposite to her.

"Yes, you may thank your fate. It 's much simpler," Laura added.

"Oh you spoil it!" the young man exclaimed —
a speech of which she took no notice, but which made
her think him brighter, as they used to say at home.
He was brighter still after they had descended from
the train at the Temple Station — they had meant
to go on to Blackfriars, but jumped out on seeing the
sign of the Temple, fired with the thought of visiting
that institution too — to become free of that old
garden of the Benchers which lies beside the foggy
crowded river, and look at the tombs of the crusaders
in the low Romanesque church where the cross-legged
figures sleep so close to the endless uproar. They
lingered in the flagged homely courts of brick, with
their much-lettered door-posts, their dull old win-

dows and atmosphere of consultation, lingered to
talk of Johnson and Goldsmith and to remark how
London opened one's eyes to Dickens; and Mr.
Wendover was brightest of all when they stood later
on, in the high bare cathedral, which diffused an
influence they scarce knew whether to call a soiled
clearness or an impaired gloom, saying the effect
was fine but wondering why it was n't finer and letting
a glance as cold as the dusty colourless glass fall
upon epitaphs that made most of the defunct bores
even in death. Mr. Wendover was decorous, yet he
was increasingly gay, and these qualities appeared
in him even through the rigour of Laura's discipline
— she was beginning to teach him wickedly to criti-
cise. Saint Paul's, somehow, had n't proved queer
enough, and they felt the advantage of having the
other place — the one Laura had had in mind at
dinner — to fall back upon: that perhaps would have
the right intensity. They entered a hansom now —
they had come to that, though they had walked also
from the Temple to Ludgate Hill — and drove to
Lincoln's Inn Fields, Laura making the reflexion
as they went that it was really a charm to thread the
London labyrinth under valid protection and that
perhaps she had thereby been unjust to her sister.
The charity of a doubt came into her mind — a doubt
Selina might have the benefit of. What she liked in
her present undertaking was the spice of the unfore-
seen, and it might have been the same mere happy
sense of getting the heavy British order itself off
her back that had led that lady to go over to Paris
and ramble with Captain Crispin. Possibly they had

done nothing worse than visit together the Invalides and Notre Dame; and if any one were to meet *her* driving that way, so far from home, with Mr. Wendover — Laura did n't finish this tacit sentence, overtaken as she was by the thought of falling again into her old assumption, which she had been in and out of a hundred times, that Mrs. Lionel *had* met Captain Crispin, the very charge she so passionately repudiated. She herself at least would never deny that she had spent the afternoon with Mr. Wendover: she would simply say that he was an American and had brought a letter of introduction.

The cab stopped at the Soane Museum, which our young woman had always wanted to see, a compatriot having once named it to her as one of the most curious things in London and one of the least known. While her friend was paying the cabman she looked over the important old-fashioned square — which led her to wonder how London could be so endlessly big and if one might ever know a tenth of the items in the sum — and saw a great bank of cloud hanging above it, the definite portent of a summer storm. "We're going to have thunder; you had better keep the cab," she said; upon which her companion told the man to wait, so that they should not afterwards, in the wet, have to walk for another conveyance. The heterogeneous objects collected by the late Sir John Soane are arranged in a fine old dwelling-house, and the place has the effect of some Saturday afternoon of one's youth — a long, rummaging visit, under indulgent care, to some eccentric and rather alarming old travelled person. Our young friends

wandered from room to room and thought everything
queer and some few objects interesting. Mr. Wendover said it would be a very good place to find a thing
you could n't find anywhere else — it illustrated the
prudent virtue of keeping. They took note of the
sarcophagi, the mummies, the idols, pagodas, the artless old maps and medals. They admired the fine
Hogarths and there were uncanny unexpected objects
Laura edged away from and would have preferred
not to be in the room with. They had been there half
an hour — it had grown much darker — when they
heard a tremendous peal of thunder and became
aware the storm had broken. They watched it a
while from the upper windows — a violent June
shower with quick sheets of lightning and a rainfall
that danced on the pavements. They took it sociably,
they lingered at the window, inhaling the odour of
the fresh wet that drenched the sultry town. They
would have to wait till it had passed, and they resigned themselves easily to this idea, repeating very
often that it would pass very soon. One of the keepers
told them of other rooms to see, of objects of high
interest in the basement. They made their way down
— it grew much darker and they heard a great deal
of thunder — and entered a part of the house which
presented itself to Laura as a series of dim irregular
vaults, passages and little narrow avenues, encumbered with strange vague things, obscured for the time
but some of which had an ambiguous sinister look,
so that she wondered the keepers could quite bear it.
"It's very fearful — it looks like a cave of idols!"
she said to her companion; and then she added "Just

look there: is that a person or a thing?" As she spoke they drew nearer the object of her reference — a figure half blocking a small vista of curiosities, a figure that answered her question by uttering a short shriek as they approached. The immediate cause of this cry was apparently a vivid flash of lightning, which penetrated into the room and cleared up both Laura's face and that of the equivocal person. The girl recognised her sister, as Mrs. Lionel had unguardedly recognised hers. "Why Selina!" broke from her lips before she had time to check the sound. At the same moment the figure turned quickly away, and then Laura saw it accompanied by another, a tall gentleman with a tawny beard that shone in the dusk. These wanderers retreated together — melted away as it were, disappearing in the gloom or in the labyrinth of wonders. The whole encounter had been but the business of an instant.

"Was it Mrs. Berrington?" Mr. Wendover asked with interest while Laura still stared.

"Oh no, I only thought so at first," she managed very quickly to answer. She had made sure of the gentleman — his beard was Captain Crispin's most noted feature — and her heart, while she gasped, seemed to her to jump up and down. She was glad her companion could n't see her face, yet she wanted to get out, to rush up the stairs, where he *would* see it, to escape from the place. She wanted not to be there with *them* — she was overwhelmed with a sudden horror. "She has lied, she has lied again, lied again!" — that was the rhythm to which her thought began to dance. She took a few steps one way and then another: she was afraid of another view of the dreadful deceivers. She impressed on her companion that it was time they should go off, and then when he showed her the way back to the staircase pleaded she had n't half seen the place. She pretended suddenly to a deep interest in it and lingered there roaming and prying. She was flurried still more by the thought of his noting her flurry, and she wondered whether he believed the scared woman who had rushed away was *not* Selina. If she was n't Selina why had she scrambled off like a frightened cat, and if she was nothing less what would Mr. Wendover think of her behaviour and of her own, and of the strange accident of their meeting? What must she herself think of that? so astonishing was it that in the immensity of London so infinitesimally small a chance should have become so unmistakeable. What a queer place to come to — for people like them! They would get away as soon as possible, of that she could be sure; and she would wait a little to give them time.

Mr. Wendover did n't dwell on the incident — that was a relief, though his silence itself seemed to prove him mystified. They went upstairs again and on reaching the door found to their surprise that their cab had disappeared — a circumstance the more singular as the man, though her friend had had his shillings ready, was still unpaid. The rain fell straight, though with less violence, and the square had been cleared of vehicles by the deluge. The doorkeeper, in tribute to the dismay of his visitors, explained that the cab had been seized by another couple who had gone out a few minutes before; the gentleman had assured the driver they would make any loss by the people he was waiting for up to him and give him good money for the new job. This observer risked the candid surmise that cabby would make ten shillings by the stroke. But there were plenty more cabs; there would be one up in a minute and the rain moreover was going to stop. "Well, that *is* sharp practice!" said Mr. Wendover. He made no further allusion to the identity of the lady.

IX

THE rain did stop while they stood there, and a brace of hansoms was not slow to appear. Laura told her companion he must put her straight into one; she could go home alone — she had taken up enough of his time. He deprecated this course very respectfully; urged that he had it on his conscience to deliver her at her own door; but she sprang into the cab and closed the apron with a movement that settled the matter. She wanted to get away from him — it would be too awkward, the long, pottering drive back. Her hansom started off while Mr. Wendover, smiling sadly, lifted his hat. Her case was far from easy even without him; especially as before she had gone a quarter of a mile she felt her action had been too marked and wished she had let him come. His puzzled innocent air of wondering what was the matter annoyed her, and she was in the absurd situation of half-disliking a desistence which she would have disliked still more his being guiltless of. That would have flattered her by its seeming to share her burden, and yet would have covered her with shame by showing he had guessed that what she had seen was wrong. It would n't occur to him that there was a scandal so near her; he thought with no nimbleness of such things, of which every one else about her *did* seem to think with nimbleness; and yet since there was — but since there was, after all, she scarcely knew what

361

manner would sit on him most gracefully. As to what he might be prepared to suspect by having London lights, or at least gleams, on Selina's reputation, of this she was unable to judge, not knowing what was said, because of course it was n't said to Selina's sister. Lionel would undertake to give her the benefit of this any moment she would allow him, but how in the world could *he* know either, for how should things be said to him? Then, in the rattle of the hansom, passing through streets for which the girl had no eyes, "She has lied, she has lied, she has lied!" kept repeating itself. Why had she written and signed that flat falsehood about her going down to Lady Watermouth? How could she have been at Lady Watermouth's when she was making so very different and so extraordinary a use of the hours she had announced her intention of spending there? What had been the need of that misrepresentation and why did she lie before she was driven to it?

It was because she was false altogether and deception came out of her with her breath; she was so depraved that it was easier for her to fabricate than to let it alone. Laura would n't have asked her to give an account of her day, but she would ask her now. She shuddered at one moment, as she found herself saying — even in silence — such things of her sister, and the next sat staring out of the front of the cab at the stiff problem presented by that lady's turning up with the partner of her guilt at such a serious place, of all the places in London. She shifted this fact about in various ways to account for it — not unconscious as she did so that it was a fine ex-

ercise of ingenuity for an honest girl. Plainly it was
a rare accident: if it had been their plan, that of the
pair, to spend the day together, the Soane Museum
would yet certainly not have been intended. They
had been near it on some other business, they had
been near it on foot and they had rushed in to take
refuge from the rain. But on what other business,
how had they come to be near it and above all to be
on foot? How could Selina do anything so reckless
from her own point of view as roam the very streets
— even in out-of-the-way quarters — with her suspected lover? Laura felt the want of proper knowledge to answer such questions. It was too little clear
to her where ladies went, and how they proceeded,
when consorting with gentlemen in regard to their
meetings with whom they had to lie. She knew nothing of where Captain Crispin lived; most probably
— for she vaguely remembered having heard Selina
say of him that he was very poor — he had chambers in that part of the town, and they were either
going to the place he occupied or coming from it. If
Selina had neglected to take her way in a four-
wheeler with the glasses up this was through some
chance that would n't seem natural till it was explained, like that of their having darted into a public institution. Then no doubt it would hang together
with the rest only too well. The explanation most
exact would probably be that the couple had snatched
a walk together — in the course of a day of many
edifying episodes — for the "lark" of it, and for the
sake of the walk had taken the risk, which in that part
of London, so little haunted by their "set," had ap-

peared to them small. The last thing Selina could
have expected was to meet her sister in such a
strange corner — her sister with a young man of her
own!

Laura was dining out that night with both her relatives, a combination now rather rare. She was by no
means always invited with them, and Selina constantly went without Lionel. Appearances, however,
sometimes got a sop thrown them; three or four
times a month Lionel and she entered the brougham
together like people who still had forms, who still
said "my dear." This was to be one of those occasions, and Mrs. Lionel's harmless unmarried sister
had also been asked. When Laura reached home she
learned, on enquiry, that Selina had not yet come in,
and she went straight to her own room. If her sister
had been there she would have gone to hers instead,
would have cried out to her as soon as she had closed
the door: "Oh stop, stop, in God's name — stop before you go any further, before exposure and ruin
and shame come down and bury us!" That was
what was in the air — the vulgarest disgrace, and the
girl, harder now than ever about her sister, was conscious of a more passionate desire to save herself.
But Selina's absence made the difference to this impulse that during the next hour some chill settled on
it from other feelings: she found herself suddenly
late and began to dress. They were to go together
after dinner to a couple of balls; a diversion that struck
her as ghastly for people who carried such horrors in
their breasts. Ugly would be the drive of husband,
wife and sister in pursuit of pleasure, all with falsity

and detection and hate between them. Selina's maid came to her door to tell her Mrs. Berrington was in the carriage — an extraordinary piece of punctuality, which made her wonder, as Selina was always dreadfully late for everything. Laura went down as quickly as she could, passed through the open door, where the servants were grouped in the foolish majesty of their superfluous attendance, and through the file of dingy gazers who had paused at the sight of the carpet across the pavement and the waiting carriage, in which Selina sat in pure white splendour, a tiara on her head and a proud patience in her face, as if she herself were really a sore trial. As soon as the girl had taken her place she said to the footman: "Is Mr. Berrington there?" — to which the man replied: "No ma'am, not yet." It was not new to Laura that if there was any one later as a general thing than Selina it was Selina's husband. "Then he must take a hansom. Go on." The footman mounted and they rolled away.

Several different things had been during the last couple of hours present to Laura's mind as destined to mark — one or the other — this inevitable encounter with her companion; but the words Selina spoke the moment the brougham began to move were of course exactly those she had not foreseen. It was possible she might take this tone or that tone or even no tone at all; one was quite prepared for her presenting a face of blankness to any form of interrogation and saying "What on earth are you talking about?" It was in short conceivable she would utterly deny that she had been at that preposterous

place, that they had stood face to face there and that
she had fled in confusion. She was capable of explaining the incident by an idiotic error on Laura's
part, by her having seized on another person, by her
seeing Captain Crispin in every bush; though doubtless she would be taxed — of course she would say
that was the woman's own affair — to supply a reason
for the embarrassment of the other lady. But she
was not prepared for Selina's breaking out with:
"Will you be so good as to inform me if you're engaged to be married to Mr. Wendover?"

"Engaged to him? I've seen him but three times."

"And is that what you usually do with gentlemen
you've seen but three times?"

"Are you talking about my having gone with him
to see some sights? I see nothing wrong in that. To
begin with you see what he is. One might go with
him anywhere. Then he brought us an introduction
— we have to do something for him. Moreover you
threw him upon me the moment he came — you
asked me to take charge of him."

"I did n't ask you to be disgusting! If Lionel were
to know it he would n't tolerate it, so long as you live
with us."

Laura for a little held her breath. "I shall not live
with you long." The sisters, side by side, with their
heads turned, looked at each other, a deep crimson
leaping into the face of the younger. "I would n't
have believed it — that you're so bad," she said.
"You're horrible!" She saw Selina had not taken
up the idea of denying — she judged that would be
hopeless: the recognition on either side had been too

sharp. She looked radiantly handsome, especially with the strange new expression this last word had brought into her eyes. This expression had the effect of showing more of her morally than had ever yet looked out — something of the full extent and the miserable limit.

"It's different for a married woman, especially when she's married to a cad. It's in a girl that such things are odious — scouring London with strange men. I'm not bound to explain to you — there would be too many things to say. I have my reasons — I have my conscience. It was the oddest of all things, our meeting in that place — I know that as well as you," Selina went on with her wonderful affected clearness; "but it was not your finding me that was out of the way; it was my finding you — with your remarkable escort! That was incredible. I pretended not to recognise you, so that the gentleman who was with me should n't see you, should n't know you. He questioned me and — if you want to know — I simply disowned you. You may thank me for saving you! You had better wear a veil next time — one never knows what may happen. I met an acquaintance at Lady Watermouth's and he came up to town with me. He happened to talk about old prints; I told him how I've collected them and we spoke of the bother one has about the frames. He insisted on my going with him to that place — from Waterloo — to see such an excellent model."

Laura had turned her face to the window of the carriage again; they were spinning along Park Lane, passing in the quick flash of other vehicles an end-

less succession of ladies with "dressed" heads, of
gentlemen in white neckties. "Why I thought the
frames you have all so pretty!" she phrased in a
trembling voice. Then she added: "I suppose it
was your eagerness to save your companion the shock
of seeing me — in my dishonour — that led you to
steal our cab."

"Your cab?"

"Your delicacy was expensive for you!"

"You don't mean you were knocking about in
cabs with him!" Selina cried.

"Of course I know you don't really think a word
of what you say about me," Laura went on; "though
I don't know that it makes your speaking so a bit
less unspeakably base."

The brougham pulled up in Park Lane and Mrs.
Lionel bent herself to have a view through the front
glass. "We're there, but there are two other carriages," she pronounced for all answer. "Ah there
are the Collingwoods."

"Where are you going — where are you going —
where are you going?" Laura broke out.

The carriage moved on to set them down, and
while the footman was getting off the box Selina
said: "I don't pretend to be better than other women,
but you do!" And being on the side of the house
she quickly stepped out and carried her crowned
brilliancy through the long-lingering daylight and
into the open entrance.

X

"WHAT do you intend to do? You'll grant that
I've a right to ask you that."

"To do? I shall do as I've always done — not so
badly, as it seems to me."

This scene found its opportunity in Mrs. Lionel's
room in the early morning hours, after her return
from the entertainment to which reference was last
made. Laura had come home before her — had
found herself incapable of "going on" when Selina
quitted the house in Park Lane at which they had
dined. That lady, with the night still before her,
stepped into her carriage with her usual air of graceful resignation to a brilliant lot. She had taken the
precaution, however, to provide herself with a defence
against a little sister bristling with righteousness in
the person of Mrs. Collingwood, to whom she offered
a lift; they being bent upon the same business and
Mr. Collingwood having a use of his own for his
brougham. The Collingwoods were a happy pair
who could discuss such a divergence before their
friends candidly, amicably, with a great many "My
loves" and "Don't mention it's" and "Not for the
world's." Lionel Berrington disappeared after dinner, without holding any communication with his
wife, and Laura expected to find he had taken the
carriage in order to repay her in kind for her having driven off from Grosvenor Place without him.

369

But it was not new to our young woman that he really spared his wife more than she spared him; not so much perhaps because he would n't do the "nastiest" thing as because he could n't. Selina could always be nastier. There was ever a perversity as for perversity's sake in her actions: if two or three hours before it had been her fancy to keep a third person out of the carriage she had now her reasons for bringing such a person in. Laura knew she would n't only pretend, but would really believe, that her vindication of her conduct on their way to dinner had been powerful and that she had "come off best." What need therefore to thresh out further a subject she had once for all chopped into atoms? Laura, however, had needs of her own, and her remaining in the carriage when the footman next opened the door was intimately connected with them.

"I don't care to go in. If you'll allow me to be driven home and send back the carriage for you, that's what I shall like best."

Selina stared and the girl knew what she would have said if she could have spoken her thought. "Oh you're furious that I have n't given you a chance to fly at me again, and you must take it out in sulks!" These were the ideas — ideas of rage and rancour — into which Selina could translate feelings too fine and too sad, positively too tender in their woe, for her to imagine. Mrs. Collingwood protested, said it was a shame Laura should n't go in and enjoy herself when she looked so lovely. "Does n't she look lovely?" She appealed to Mrs.

Lionel. "Bless us, what's the use of being so pretty? Now if she had *my* mug —!"

"I think she looks rather cross," said Selina, getting out with her friend and leaving their junior to her own inventions. Laura had a vision, as the carriage drove away again, of what her situation would have been, or her peace of mind, if Selina and Lionel had been good attached people like the Collingwoods, and at the same time of the oddity of a "refined" woman's — the poor girl had still these transatlantic flights! — being ready to accept favours from a person as to whose behaviour she had the lights that must have come to a member of their general circle in regard to Selina. She accepted favours herself and she only wanted to be refined — that was oppressively true; but if she had n't been Selina's sister she would never have driven in her carriage. This conviction was strong as the vehicle conveyed her to Grosvenor Place, but was not in its nature consoling. The prevision of disgrace was now so vivid that if it had not already overtaken them she felt she had only to thank the loose mysterious, the rather ignoble tolerance of people like Mrs. Collingwood. There were plenty of that species, even among the good; perhaps indeed exposure and dishonour would begin only when the bad had got hold of the facts. Would the bad be most horrified and do most to spread the scandal? There were in any event plenty of them too.

Laura sat up for her sister late and with that nice question to sharpen her torment — the question of whether if she was hard and merciless in judgement it would be with the bad too she should associate herself. Was she all wrong after all — was she cruel by being too rigid? Was Mrs. Collingwood's attitude the right one and ought she only to propose to herself to "allow" more and more, and to allow ever, and to smooth things down by gentleness, by sympathy, by not looking at them too hard? It was not the first time the just measure seemed to slip from her hands as she became conscious of possible, or rather of very actual, differences of standard and usage. On this occasion Geordie and Ferdy asserted themselves, by the mere force of lying asleep upstairs in their little cribs, as on the whole the just measure. Laura went into the nursery to look at them when she came home — it was her habit almost any night — and yearned over them as mothers and maids do alike over the pillow of rosy childhood. They were an antidote to all sophistry; for Selina to forget *them* — that was the beginning and the end of shame. She came back to the library, where she should best hear the sound of their mother's return; the hours passed as she sat there without bringing it round. Carriages came and went all night; the soft shock of swift hoofs was on the wooden roadway long after the summer dawn grew fair — till it was merged in the rumble of the waked-up day. Lionel had not come in when she returned, and he continued absent, to her satisfaction; for if she wanted not to miss Selina she had no desire at present to have to tell her brother-in-law why she was waiting there. She prayed Selina might arrive first: then she should have more time to think of something that harassed

her particularly — the question of whether she ought
to tell him whom she had seen in a far-away corner
of the town with Captain Crispin. Almost impossible
as she found it now to feel any tenderness for his wife,
she yet detested the idea of bearing witness against
her: notwithstanding which she might still make up
her mind to do so on the chance of its preventing the
last scandal — a catastrophe to which she saw Selina
rush straight. That this unfortunate was capable at a
given moment of going off with her lover, and capable
of it precisely because it was the greatest ineptitude
as well as the greatest wickedness — there was a voice
of prophecy, of warning, to that effect in the silent
empty house. If repeating to Lionel what she had
seen would contribute to prevent anything, or to
stave off the danger, was n't it her duty to denounce
his wife, flesh and blood of her own as she was, to
his further reprobation? This point was not intolerably difficult to determine, as she kept her vigil,
only because even what was righteous in that reprobation could n't present itself to her as fruitful or
efficient. What could Lionel either make or mar,
after all, and what intelligent or authoritative step
was he capable of taking? Mixed with all that now
haunted her was her consciousness of what his own
absence at such an hour represented in the way of the
"low." He might be at some sporting club or might
be anywhere else; in any case he was n't where he
ought to be at three o'clock in the morning. Such
the husband such the wife, she said to herself; and
she recognised for Selina a kind of advantage, which
one grudged her, should she arrive and say: "And

where's *he*, please — where's the beautiful soul and perfect gentleman on whose behalf you have undertaken to preach so much better than he himself practises?"

But still Selina did n't arrive — not even to take that advantage; despite which and just in proportion as her dragging it out was useless, did the girl find it impossible to go to bed. A new fear had seized her, the fear the mad creature would never come back at all — that they were already in presence of the dreaded catastrophe. This deprived her so of rest that she paced the lower rooms back and forth, listening to every sound, roaming till she was tired. She knew it for absurd, any image of such a flight in a ball-dress and tiara, but she reasoned that other clothes might very well have been sent away in advance somewhere — Laura had her own ripe views about Selina's maid; and at any rate, for herself, that was the fate she had to expect, if not to-night then some other night soon, and it all came to the same thing: to sit counting the hours till a hope definitely failed and a hideous certainty remained. She had fallen into such a state of apprehension that when at last she heard a carriage stop at the door she was almost happy in spite of her forecast of her sister's resentment at finding her and at this new form of meddling. They met in the hall — Laura had gone out at the opening of the house-door. Selina stopped short, seeing her, but said nothing — on account apparently of the presence of the sleepy footman. Then she moved straight to the stairs, where she paused again, asking the man if Mr. Berrington had come in.

"Not yet, ma'am."

"Ah!" said Mrs. Lionel portentously; with which she proceeded to the stairs.

"I've sat up on purpose — I want particularly to speak to you," Laura began, following her.

"Ah!" Selina repeated, more superior still. She went fast, almost as if she wished to get to her room before she could be overtaken. But her sister was close behind her and passed into the room with her. Laura closed the door, then told her she had found it impossible to go to bed without asking her what she intended to do.

"Your behaviour's too monstrous!" Selina flashed out. "What on earth do you wish to make the servants suppose?"

"Oh the servants — in *this* house; as if one could put any idea into their heads that's not there already!" Laura thought. But she said nothing of that, she only repeated her question; aware she was exasperating, but also aware she couldn't be anything else. Selina, whose maid, having outlived surprises, had gone to rest, began to divest herself of some of her attributes, and it was not till after a moment, during which she stood before the glass, that she made her answer about doing as she had always done. To this Laura returned that she ought to have wit to see how important it was to *her* to know what was likely to happen, so that she might take time by the forelock and think of her own situation. If anything should happen she would infinitely rather be out of — be as far away as possible. Therefore she must take her measures.

It was in the mirror that they looked at each other — in the strange candle-lighted duplication of the scene that their eyes met. Selina drew the diamonds out of her hair, and in this occupation for a minute she was silent. Presently she asked: "What are you talking about — what do you allude to as happening?"

"Why it seems to me there's nothing left for you but to go away with him. If there's a prospect of that insanity —!" But here Laura stopped; something so unexpected was taking place in her companion's face — the working that precedes a sudden gush of tears. Mrs. Lionel dashed down the glittering pins she had detached from her tresses, and the next moment had flung herself into an armchair and was crying and sobbing. Laura forbore to go to her; she made no motion to soothe or reassure her, she only stood and watched her tears and wondered what they signified. Somehow even the slight relief of having affected her in that particular and, as it had lately come to seem, impossible way was not all convincing as to the price of the symptoms. Since one had come so utterly to disbelieve her word there was nothing of great price about Selina any more. But she continued for some moments to cry passionately, and while this went on Laura waited with closed lips. At last from the midst of her sobs Selina broke out: "Go away, go away — leave me alone!"

"Of course I make you angry," said the girl; "but how can I see you rush to your ruin — to that of all of us — without holding on to you and dragging you back?"

"Oh you don't understand anything about anything!" Mrs. Lionel wailed, her beautiful hair tumbling all over her.

"I certainly don't understand how you can give such a tremendous handle to Lionel."

At the mention of her husband's name Selina always gave a bound, and she sprang up now, shaking back her wonderful mane. "I give him no handle and you don't know what you're talking about! I know what I'm doing and what becomes me, and I don't care what any one makes of it. He's welcome to all the handles in the world, for all he can do with them!"

"In the name of common pity think of your children!" Laura pleaded.

"Have I ever thought of anything else? Have you sat up all night for the pleasure of accusing me of cruelty? Are there sweeter or more delightful children in the world, and isn't that a little *my* merit, pray?" Selina went on, sweeping away her tears. "Who has made them what they are, hey? — is it their lovely father? Perhaps you'll say it's you! Certainly you've been nice to them, but you must remember that you only came here the other day. Isn't it only for *them* that I'm trying to keep myself alive?"

This formula struck Laura as grotesque, so that she replied with a laugh which betrayed too much that impression: "Die for them — that would be better!"

Her sister, on this, looked at her with an extraordinary cold gravity. "Don't interfere between me and my children. And for God's sake cease to harry me!"

Laura turned away: she said to herself that these were depths, even if but depths of inanity, and the poor woman affected her as already down and under everything. She felt sick and helpless, and practically had got the certitude she both wanted and dreaded. "I don't know what has become of your mind!" she cried while she went to the door. But before she reached it Selina had flung herself forward in a strange but really not encouraging revulsion. Her arms were about our young woman, they clung tight and the checked tears again became a flood. She besought Laura to save her, to stay with her, to help her against herself, against *him*, against Lionel, against everything — to forgive her also all the horrid things she had said to her. She melted, liquefied, spread like a tide, and the room was deluged with her repentance, her desolation, her confession, her vain vows and the articles of apparel detached from her and that might have been floating out to sea. Laura remained with her an hour, and before they separated the guilty woman had given a tremendous promise, kneeling with her head in her sister's lap, never again so long as she lived to consent to see Captain Crispin or address a word to him, spoken or written. The girl went terribly tired to bed.

A month later she lunched with Lady Davenant, whom she had not seen since the day she took Mr. Wendover to make his bow. The old woman had found herself committed to entertain a small company, and as she disliked set parties had sent Laura a request for support. She had disencumbered herself, at the end of so many years, of the burden of hospitality, yet now and again invited people for a sign she was n't too old. Her young friend suspected her of choosing stupid ones on purpose to prove this better — to show she could submit not only to the extraordinary but, what was much more difficult, to the usual. When they had been properly fed, however, she encouraged them to disperse; on this occasion Laura was, as the party broke up, the only person she asked to stay. She wished to be told in the first place why she had been so long neglected, and in the second how that young man had behaved — the one who had come that Sunday. Lady Davenant did n't remember the young man's name, though he had been so good-natured since then as to leave a card. If he had behaved well that was a very good reason for the girl's neglect and Laura need give no other. Laura herself would n't have behaved well if at such a time she had been running after old women. There was nothing the girl in general liked less than being spoken of off-hand as a marriageable article, being planned and arranged for in this particular. It made too light of her independence, and though in general such inventions passed for a charity they had always betrayed for her at bottom an impertinence, as if people of any spirit could be moved about like a game of chequers. There was a liberty in the way Lady Davenant's imagination disposed of her — making so light of her preferences — but she forgave it because in point of fact this old friend was n't obliged to think of her at all.

"I knew you were almost always out of town now, on Sundays — and so have we been," Laura said.

"And then I 've been a great deal with my sister — more than before."

"More than before what?"

"Well, a great difference we had, frankly speaking, about a certain matter."

"And now you 've made it all up?"

"To the point of being able to talk of it — we could n't before without painful scenes — and that has cleared the air. We 've gone about together a good deal," Laura explained. " She has wanted me constantly with her."

"That 's very nice. And where has she taken you?" asked the old woman.

"Oh it 's I who have taken *her* rather." But Laura stopped.

"Where do you mean? — to say her prayers?"

"Well, to some concerts — and to the National Gallery."

Lady Davenant laughed profanely at this, and the girl watched her with a mournful face. "My dear child, you 're too delightful! You 're trying to reform her by Beethoven and Bach, by Rubens and Titian?"

"She 's very intelligent about music and pictures — she has excellent ideas," Laura said.

"And you 've been trying to draw them out? That 's most commendable."

"I think you 're laughing at me, but I don't care," the girl declared with a smile of no great bravery.

"Because you 've a consciousness of success? — in what do they call it? — the attempt to raise her

tone? You've been trying to wind her up and *have*
raised her tone?"

"Oh Lady Davenant, I don't know and I don't
understand!" Laura broke out. "I don't understand anything any more — I've given up trying."

"That's what I recommended you to do last winter.
Don't you remember that day at Plash?"

"You told me to let her go," Laura returned.

"And evidently you haven't taken my advice."

"How can I — how can I?"

"Of course, how can you? And meanwhile if
she doesn't go it's so much gained. But even if she
should won't that nice young man remain?" Lady
Davenant asked. "I hope very much Selina hasn't
taken you altogether away from him."

Her young visitor had a pause, but then went on:
"What nice young man would ever look at me if anything bad should happen?"

"I would never look at *him* if he should let that
prevent him!" the old woman cried. "It isn't for
your sister he loves you, I suppose; is it?"

"He doesn't love me at all."

"Ah then he talks about it?" Lady Davenant
demanded, with some eagerness, laying her hand on
the girl's arm. Laura sat near on her sofa and looked
at her, for all answer to this, with a tragic ambiguity.
"Doesn't he come to the house — doesn't he say
anything?" she continued with a voice of kindness.

"He comes to the house very often."

"And don't you like him?"

"Yes, very much — more than I did at first."

"Well, as you liked him at first well enough to
381

bring him straight to see me, I suppose that means that now you're immensely pleased with him."

"He's a perfect gentleman," said Laura.

"So much the better. But why then does n't he speak out?"

"Perhaps that's the very reason! Seriously," the girl added, "I don't know what he comes to the house for."

"Is he in love with your sister?"

"I sometimes think so."

"And does she encourage him?"

"She abhors him."

"Oh then I like him! I shall immediately write to him to come and see me: I shall appoint an hour and give him a piece of my mind."

"If I believed that, I should kill myself," Laura said.

"You may believe what you like, but I wish you did n't show your feelings so in your charming eyes. They might be those of a poor widow with fifteen children. When I was young I managed to flourish, whatever occurred; and I'm sure I looked smart."

"Oh yes, Lady Davenant — for you it was different. You were safe in so many ways," the girl explained. "And you were surrounded with consideration."

"I don't know; some of us were very wild and exceedingly ill thought of, and I did n't cry about it. However, there are natures and natures. If you'll come and stay with me to-morrow I'll take you in."

"You know how kind I think you," Laura made answer, "but I've promised Selina not to leave her."

"Well then if she keeps you she must at least go straight!" the old woman cried with some asperity. Laura made no answer to this and Lady Davenant asked after a moment: "And what's Lionel remarkably doing?"

Laura thought. "Well, he's keeping remarkably quiet."

"Does n't it please him, his wife's improvement?" The girl got up; apparently she was made uncomfortable by the ironic effect, if not by the ironic motive, of this question. Her hostess was kind but extremely penetrating; her very next words pierced further. "Of course if you 're really protecting her I can't count upon you:" words not adapted to enliven Laura, who would have liked immensely to transfer herself to Queen's Gate and had her very private ideas as to the efficacy of her protection. Lady Davenant kissed her and then suddenly said: "Oh by the way, his address. You must tell me that."

Laura stared. "Whose address?"

"The young man's whom you brought here. But it's no matter," her friend added; "my servant will have entered it — from his card."

"Lady Davenant, you won't do anything so loathsome!" our young woman cried, seizing her hand.

"Why is it loathsome if he comes so often? It's rubbish, his caring for Selina — somebody else's wife — when you 're there."

"Why is it rubbish — when so many people do care?"

"Oh well, he's different — I could see that; or if he is n't he ought to be!"

"He likes to observe — he came here to take notes," said Laura. "And he thinks Selina a very interesting London specimen."

"In spite of her dislike of him?"

"Oh he does n't know that!" she exclaimed.

"Why not? he is n't a fool."

"Well, I've made it seem —!" But here she stopped; her colour had risen.

Lady Davenant stared. "Made it seem that she has a mind to him? Mercy, to do that how fond of him you must be!" An observation which had the effect of driving the girl straight out of the house.

XI

ON one of the last days of June Mrs. Lionel put
before her sister a note she had received from "your
dear friend," as she called him, Mr. Wendover. This
was the manner in which she usually designated
that gentleman, but she had naturally, in the present
phase of her relations with Laura, never indulged in
any renewal of the eminently perverse insinuations
by means of which she had attempted, after the incident at the Soane Museum, to throw dust in her
eyes. Mr. Wendover proposed to Mrs. Berrington
that she and Miss Wing should honour with their
presence a box he had obtained for the opera three
nights later — an occasion of high curiosity, the first
appearance of a young American singer of whom
remarkable things were expected. Laura left it
to Selina to decide whether they should accept this
invitation, and Selina made a show of two or three
differing minds. First she said the thing would n't
fit in with other matters, and she wrote to the young
man to this effect. Then on second thoughts she
opined she might very well go, and telegraphed an
acceptance. Later she saw reason to regret her acceptance and made known the change again to her sister,
who remarked that it was still not too late to retract.
Selina left her in ignorance till the next day as to
whether she had taken this step, and then announced
that she had let the matter stand — they would

gratify Mr. Wendover. To which Laura replied that she was glad — *for* Mr. Wendover. "And for yourself," Selina said, leaving the girl to wonder why every one — this universality was represented by Mrs. Lionel Berrington and Lady Davenant — had taken up the idea that she entertained a passion for her compatriot. She was clearly conscious that such was not the case, though rejoiced that their good relations had n't yet suffered the wrong of her being forced to infer that Lady Davenant had put into practice the intervention terribly threatened. Laura was surprised to learn afterwards that Selina had, in London parlance, "thrown over" a dinner in order to make the evening at the opera possible. The dinner would have made her too late, and she did n't care for it: she wanted to hear the whole performance.

The sisters dined together alone, without any question of Lionel, and on alighting at Covent Garden found Mr. Wendover awaiting them in the portico. His box proved a place of ease, and Selina was gracious to him: she thanked him for his consideration in not stuffing it full of people. He assured her that he expected but one other inmate — a gentleman of a shrinking disposition, who would take up no room. The gentleman came in after the first act; he was introduced to the ladies as Mr. Booker of Baltimore. He knew all about the young lady they had come to listen to, and was not so chary of his knowledge but that he attempted more or less to impart it while she was singing. Before the second act was over Laura made out Lady Ringrose in a box

on the other side of the house and accompanied by
a lady unknown to her. There was apparently another
person in the box, behind the two ladies, whom they
turned round from time to time to talk with. Laura
made no observation about Lady Ringrose to her
sister, and noticed that Selina never resorted to the
glass to look at her. That Mrs. Lionel's circum-
spection had been effectively exercised, however, was
proved by the fact that at the end of the second act
(the opera was Meyerbeer's *Huguenots*) she suddenly
said, turning to Mr. Wendover: "I hope you won't
mind very much if I go for a short time to sit with a
friend I see opposite." She smiled with all her sweetness as she announced this intention, and had the
benefit of the fact that a plea for indulgence is highly
becoming to a pretty woman. But she abstained
from looking at her sister, and this critic, after a
wondering glance at her, looked at Mr. Wendover.
She felt him disappointed — even slightly wounded:
he had taken some trouble to get his box and it had
been no small pleasure to him to see it graced by the
presence of a celebrated beauty. His situation collapsed if the celebrated beauty was about to transfer
her light to another quarter. Laura wondered what
had come into their companion's head — to make her
so inconsiderate, so rude. Selina surrounded her
defection, all smilingly, with conciliatory graces, but
gave no particular reason for it, withheld the name
of the friends aimed at, and betrayed no consciousness
that ladies did n't usually roam the lobbies. Laura
asked her no question, but said to her after an hesitation: "You won't be long, surely. You know you

ought n't to leave me here." Selina took no notice of this — excused herself in no way to the girl. Mr. Wendover merely exclaimed, jocosely gallant in reference to Laura's last remark: "Oh so far as leaving you here goes —!" In spite of his great defect — and it was his only one that she could see — of having only an ascending scale of seriousness, she judged him interestedly enough to feel a real pleasure in noticing that though he was annoyed at Selina's going away and not saying she would come back soon, he conducted himself as a gentleman should, yielded respectfully, discreetly, to her wish. He suggested that her friends might perhaps instead be induced to come to his box, but when she had objected, "Oh you see there are too many," he put her shawl on her shoulders, opened the door, offered her his arm. While this was going on Laura saw Lady Ringrose study them hard with her glass. Selina declined Mr. Wendover's escort; she said "Oh no, you stay with *her* — I dare say *he*'ll take me," and gazed inspiringly at Mr. Booker. Selina never mentioned a name when the pronoun would do. Mr. Booker of course sprang to the service required and led her away with an injunction from his friend to bring her back promptly. As they went off Laura heard her say to her companion — and she knew Mr. Wendover could also hear it — "Nothing would have induced me to leave her alone with *you !*" She thought this a very extraordinary speech — she thought it even vulgar; especially in view of the fact that the speaker had never seen the young man till half an hour before and since then had not exchanged

twenty words with him. It came to their ears so
distinctly that Laura was moved to notice it by
exclaiming with a laugh: "Poor Mr. Booker, what
does she suppose I'd do to him?"

"Ah it's for you she's afraid," said Mr. Wendover.

Laura went on in a moment: "She ought n't to
have left me alone with you, either."

"Oh yes, she ought — after all!" the young man
returned.

The girl had uttered these words from no desire
to provoke a snicker or a "tribute," but because they
simply expressed a part of the judgement she privately
passed on Selina's behaviour. She had a sense of
wrong — of being made light of; for Mrs. Lionel
sufficiently knew that "real ladies" did n't (for the
appearance of the thing) arrange to leave their unmarried sisters sitting singly and publicly at the play-
house with a couple of young men — the couple
constituted as soon as Mr. Booker should come back.
It displeased her that the people in the opposite box,
the people Selina had joined, should see her exhibited
in this light. She drew her curtain a little, moved
rather more behind it and heard her companion utter
a vague appealing protecting sigh which seemed to
express his sense — her own corresponding with it —
that the glory of the occasion had somehow suddenly
departed. At the end of some minutes she noted
among Lady Ringrose and her companions a movement that must have signified Selina's coming in.
The two ladies in front turned round — something
went on at the back of the box. "She's there," Laura
said, indicating the place; but Mrs. Lionel did n't

show herself — she remained masked by the others. Neither was Mr. Booker visible; he had not, seemingly, been persuaded to remain, and indeed Laura could see there would n't have been room for him. Mr. Wendover observed ruefully that as Mrs. Berrington evidently could see nothing at all from where she had gone she had exchanged a very good place for a very bad one. "I can't imagine, I can't imagine —!" said the girl; but she paused, losing herself in reflexions and wonderments, in guesses that soon became anxieties. Suspicion of Selina was now so rooted in her heart that it could make her unhappy even when it pointed nowhere, and by the end of half an hour she felt how little her fears had really been lulled since that scene of dishevelment and contrition in the early dawn.

The opera resumed its course, but Mr. Booker did n't come back. The American singer trilled and warbled, executed remarkable flights, and there was much applause, every symptom of success; but Laura grew more and more deaf to the music — she had no eyes but for Lady Ringrose and her friend. She watched them earnestly, tried to sound with her glass the curtained dimness behind them. Their attention was all for the stage and they gave no present sign of having any fellow listeners. These others had either gone away or were leaving them very much to themselves. Laura failed to piece together a particular motive on her sister's part, but her conviction deepened that such an affront had not been put on Mr. Wendover for the mere sweet sake of a chat with Lady Ringrose. There was something else, there was some

one else, in the affair; and when once the girl's idea
had become as definite as that it took but little longer
to associate itself with the image of Captain Crispin.
This vision made her draw back further behind her
curtain, bringing the blood to her face; but if she
coloured for shame she coloured also for anger.
Captain Crispin was there, in the opposite box; those
horrible women concealed him — she forgot how
harmless and well-read Lady Ringrose had appeared
to her that time at Mellows: they had lent themselves
to this atrocious proceeding. Selina was nestling
there in safety with him by their favour, and she had
had the baseness to lay an honest girl, the most loyal,
the most unselfish of sisters, under contribution to the
same end. Laura burned with the sense that she had
been unsuspectingly part of a scheme, that she was
being used as the two women opposite were used, but
that she had been outraged into the bargain, inasmuch
as she was not, like them, a conscious accomplice,
and not a person to be given away in that manner
before hundreds of people. It came back to her how
bad Selina had been the day of the business in Lincoln's
Inn Fields, and how in spite of supervening comedies
the woman who had then found such words of injury
would be sure to break out in a new spot with a new
weapon. Accordingly, while the pure music filled
the place and the rich picture of the stage glowed
beneath it, she found herself face to face with the
strange inference that the evil of Selina's nature
made her wish — since she had given herself to it —
to bring her sister to her own colour by putting an
appearance of "fastness" on her. The girl said to

herself that she would have succeeded, in the cynical view of London; and to her troubled spirit the immense theatre had a myriad eyes, eyes that she knew, eyes that would know her, that would see her sitting there with a strange young man. She had recognised many faces already and her imagination quickly multiplied them.

However, after she had burned a while with this particular revolt she ceased to think of herself and of what, as regarded herself, Selina had intended: all her thought went to the mere calculation of the cruel creature's return. As she did n't return, and still did n't, Laura felt a sharp constriction of the heart. She scarce knew what she feared, scarce knew what she supposed. She was so nervous — as she had been the night she waited till morning for their absentee to re-enter the house in Grosvenor Place — that when Mr. Wendover occasionally made a remark she failed to understand him and was unable, as she would have called it, to bear up. Fortunately he said but little; he was preoccupied — either wondering also what Selina was "up to" or, more probably, quite absorbed in the music. What she *had* comprehended, however, was that when at three different moments she said restlessly "Why does n't Mr. Booker come back?" he replied "Oh there's plenty of time — we're very comfortable." These words she was conscious of; she intensely noted them and they interwove themselves with her restlessness. She also noted in her tension that after her third appeal Mr. Wendover said something about looking up his friend if she did n't mind being left alone a moment. He quitted the box and during this interval Laura tried more than ever to see with her glass what had become of her sister. But it was as if the ladies opposite had arranged themselves, had arranged their curtains, on purpose to frustrate such an attempt: it was impossible to her even to assure herself of what she had begun to suspect, that Selina was now not with them. If she was n't with them where in the world had she gone? As the moments multiplied before Mr. Wendover's return she went to the door of the box and stood watching the lobby for the chance that he would bring back the absentee. Presently she saw him advance alone, and something in the expression of his face made her step out into the lobby to meet him. He wore the simper of civility, but looked in spite of it embarrassed and strange, especially on seeing her stand there as if she wished to leave the place.

"I hope you don't want to go," he said as he held the door for her to pass back into the box.

"Where are they, where are they?" she demanded, remaining in the corridor.

"I saw our friend; he has found a place in the stalls, near the door by which you go into them — just here under us."

"And does he like that better?"

Mr. Wendover's smile seemed to strain down at her. "Mrs. Berrington has made such an amusing request of him."

"An amusing request?"

"She made him promise not to come back."

"Made him promise —?" Laura stared.

393

"She asked him — as a particular favour to her — not to join us again. And he said he would n't."

"Ah the monster!" Laura cried, all red again.

"Do you mean poor Mr. Booker?" Mr. Wendover asked. "Of course he had to assure her that the wish of so lovely a lady was law. But he does n't understand!" laughed the young man.

"No more do I. And where 's the lovely lady?" said Laura, trying to recover herself.

"He has n't the least idea."

"Is n't she with Lady Ringrose?"

"If you like I 'll go and see."

Laura hesitated, looking down the curved lobby, where nothing was in sight but the little numbered doors of the boxes. They were alone in the lamp-lit bareness; the climax of the act roared and trilled and boomed behind them. In a moment she said: "I 'm afraid I must trouble you to put me into a cab."

"Ah you won't see the rest? *Do* stay — what difference does it make?" And her companion still held open the door of the box. Her eyes met his, in which it seemed to her that as well as in his voice there was conscious sympathy, supplication, vindication, tenderness. Then she gazed at the vulgar vista again; something said to her that if she should return she would be taking the most important step of her life. She considered this, and while she did so a great burst of applause filled the place as the curtain fell. "See what we 're losing! And the last act is so fine," said Mr. Wendover. She returned to her seat and he closed the door of the box behind them.

Then, in this little upholstered receptacle which

was so public and yet so private, Laura passed the strangest moments she had known. A sign of their strangeness was that when she presently saw that while she was in the lobby Lady Ringrose and her companion had quite disappeared she remarked it without a comment, holding herself silent. Their box was empty, but Laura looked at it without in the least feeling this to portend that Selina would now come round. She would never come round again, nor would she have gone home from the opera. That was by this time absolutely definite to our young woman, who had first been hot and now was cold with the sense of what Selina's injunction to poor Mr. Booker exactly meant. It was worthy of her, for it was simply a vicious little kick as she took her flight. Grosvenor Place would n't shelter her that night and would never shelter her more: that was why she tried to splash her sister with the mud into which she herself had jumped. She would n't have dared treat her in such a fashion if they had had a prospect of meeting again. The strangest part of the crisis was that what ministered most to the girl's suppressed emotion was not the tremendous reflexion that this time Selina had really "bolted" and that on the morrow all London would know: this had taken the glare of certainty — and a very hideous hue it was — whereas the chill now diffused was that of a mystery waiting to be cleared. Laura's spirit was all suspense — suspense of which she returned the pressure, trying to twist it into faith. There was a chance in life that sat there beside her, but it would go for ever if it did n't move nearer that night;

whereby she listened, she watched for it to move. I need scarce mention that this chance presented itself in the person of Mr. Wendover, who more than any one concerned with her had it in his hand to redeem her detestable position. To-morrow he would know, and would think sufficiently little of a young person of *that* breed: therefore it could only be a question of his speaking on the spot. That was what she had come back into the box for — to give him his opportunity. It was open to her to feel he had asked for it — adding everything together.

The poor girl added, added, deep in her heart, all the while she said nothing. The music was not there now to keep them silent; yet he broke no silence any more than she did, and that for some minutes was a part of her sum. She felt as if she were running a race with dire dishonour; she would get in first if she should get in before the shame of the morrow. But this was n't far off and every minute brought it nearer. It would be there in fact virtually that night if Mr. Wendover should begin to measure the brutality of Selina's not turning up at all. The comfort had been hitherto that he did n't measure brutalities. There were violins that emitted tentative sounds in the orchestra; they shortened the time and made her uneasier, — made her sure that he could lift her out of her mire if he would. It did n't appear to promise for him, his also observing Lady Ringrose's empty box without a reassuring word about it. Laura waited for him to suggest that her sister would obviously now turn up; but no such sound of cheer fell from his lips. He must either like Selina's being

away or judge it damningly, and in either case why
did n't he speak? If he had nothing to say, why *had*
he said, why had he *done*, what did he mean —? But
the girl's inward challenge to him lost itself in a mist
of faintness; she was screwing herself up to a purpose of her own, and it hurt almost to anguish, while
the whole place about became a blur and a swim
through which she heard the tuning of fiddles. Before
she knew it she had said to him: "Why have you
come so often?"

"So often? To see you, do you mean?"

"To see *me* — it was for that? Why have you
come?" she went on. He was evidently surprised,
and his surprise gave her a point of anger, a desire
almost that her words should hurt him, lash him.
She spoke low, but she heard herself, and she thought
that if what she said sounded to *him* in the same
way —! "You 've come very often — too often, too
often!"

He coloured, looked frightened, was unmistakeably
discomposed. "Why you 've been so kind, so delightful," he stammered.

"Yes, of course, and so have you! Did you come
for Selina? She 's married, you know, and devoted
to her husband." A single minute had sufficed to
show the girl that her companion was quite unpre-
pared for her question, that he was distinctly not the
victim of a sentiment — by any spell of hers at least
— and was thus face to face with a situation entirely
new. The effect of this was to make her say wilder
things.

"Why what 's more natural, when one likes people,

than to come often? Perhaps I've bored you —with our American way," said Mr. Wendover.

"And is it because you like me that you've kept me here?" Laura asked. She got up, leaning against the side of the box; she had pulled the curtain far forward and was out of sight of the house.

He rose, but more slowly; he had got over his first confusion. He smiled at her, but his smile was dreadful. "Can you have any doubt as to what I've come for? It's a pleasure to me that you like me well enough to ask."

For an instant she thought he was coming nearer, but he didn't: he stood there twirling his gloves. Then an unspeakable shame, a great horror, horror of herself, of him, of everything, came over her, and she sank into a chair at the back of the box, with averted eyes, trying to get further into her corner. "Leave me, leave me, go away!" she said in the lowest tone he could hear. The whole house seemed to be listening to her, pressing into the box.

"Leave you alone — in this place — when I love you? I can't do that — indeed I can't," she heard him articulate.

"You don't love me — and you torture me by staying!" Laura went on in a convulsed voice. "For God's sake go away and don't speak to me, don't let me see you or hear of you again!"

Mr. Wendover still stood there, exceedingly agitated, as well he might be, by this inconceivable sally. Unaccustomed feelings possessed him and they moved him in different directions. Her command that he should take himself off was passionate, yet he attempted to resist, to speak. How would she get home? would she see him to-morrow? would she let him wait for her outside? To this Laura only replied "Oh dear, oh dear, if you would only go!" and at the same instant sprang up, gathering her cloak round her as to escape from him, to rush away herself. He checked any such movement, however, clapping on his hat and holding the door. One moment more he looked at her — her own eyes were closed; then he brought forth pitifully "Oh Miss Wing, oh Miss Wing!" and stepped out of the box.

When he had gone she collapsed into one of the chairs again and sat there with her face buried in a fold of her mantle. For many minutes she was perfectly still — she was ashamed even to move. The one thing that could have justified her, tempered the grotesqueness of her monstrous overture, would have been, on his side, the quick response of unmistakeable passion. It had n't come, and she had nothing left but to loathe herself. She did so, violently, for a long time, in the dark corner of the box, and she felt how he must loathe her too. "I love you!" — how pitifully the poor little make-believe words had quavered out and how much disgust they must have represented! "Poor man — poor dear man!" she suddenly heard herself wail: compassion filled her mind at the sense of the way she had used him. At the same moment a flare of music broke out; the last act of the opera had begun and she had sprung up and quitted the box.

The passages were empty and she made her way without trouble. She descended to the vestibule;

there was no one to stare at her, and her only fear was that Mr. Wendover would be there. But he was not, apparently, and she saw she should be able to get quickly away. Selina would have taken the carriage — she could be sure of that, or if she had n't it would n't have come back yet; besides, one could n't possibly wait there so long as while it was called. Laura was in the act of asking one of the attendants, in the portico, to get her a cab, when some one hurried up to her from behind, overtaking her — a gentleman in whom, turning round, she recognised Mr. Booker. He looked almost as bewildered as Mr. Wendover, and his attention disconcerted her scarce less than if his friend had reappeared. "Oh are you going away alone? What must you think of me?" this young man exclaimed; and he began to tell her something about her sister and to ask her at the same time if he might n't go with her, render her some help. He put no question about Mr. Wendover, and she afterwards judged that that distracted gentleman had sought him out and sent him to her assistance; also that he himself was at that moment watching them from behind some column. He would have been hateful if he had shown himself; yet — in this later consciousness — there was a voice in her heart that commended his delicacy. He effaced himself to look after her, he provided for her departure by proxy.

"A cab, a cab — that's all I want!" she said to Mr. Booker; and she almost pushed him out of the place with the wave of the hand with which she indicated her need. He rushed off to call one, and a minute afterwards the messenger she had already dispatched rattled up in a hansom. She quickly got into it and as she rolled away saw Mr. Booker returning in all haste with another. She gave a passionate moan — all this awkwardness so mocked at her tragedy.

XII

THE next day at five o'clock she drove to Queen's Gate, turning distractedly to Lady Davenant in order to turn somewhere. Her old friend was at home and by extreme good fortune alone; looking up from her book, in her place by the window, she gave the visitor's entrance a sharp glance over her glasses. This glance was acquisitive; she said nothing, but laying down her book stretched out her two gloved hands. Laura took them and she drew her down toward her, so that the girl sank on her knees and in a moment hid her face, sobbing, in the old woman's lap. There was nothing said for some time: Lady Davenant only pressed her tenderly — stroked her with wise old hands. "Is it very bad?" she asked at last. Then Laura got up, saying as she took a seat: "Have you heard of it and do people know?"

"I have n't heard anything. Is it very bad?" Lady Davenant repeated.

"We don't know where Selina is—and her maid's gone."

Lady Davenant took her time for judgement. "Lord, what a donkey!" she then ejaculated, putting the paper-knife into her book to keep her place. "And whom has she persuaded to take her — Charles Crispin?" she added.

"We suppose — we suppose —!" said Laura.

"And he's another," her friend interrupted. "And who supposes — Geordie and Ferdy?"

"I don't know; it's all black darkness!"

"My child, it's a blessing," the old woman declared, "and now you can live in peace."

"In peace!" cried Laura; "with my wretched sister leading such a life?"

"Oh my dear, I dare say it will be very comfortable; I'm sorry to say anything in favour of such doings, but it very often is. Don't worry; you take her too hard. Has she gone abroad?" Lady Davenant asked. "I dare say they'll find some pretty, amusing place."

"I don't know anything about it. I only know she's gone. I was with her last evening and she left me without a word."

"Well, that was better. I hate 'em when they make parting scenes: it's too mawkish!" Laura's hostess cried.

"Lionel has people watching them," said the girl; "agents, detectives, I don't know what. He has had them for a long time. I didn't know it."

"Do you mean you'd have told her if you had? What's the use of detectives now? Isn't he rid of her?"

"Oh I don't know, he's as bad as she! He talks too horribly — he wants every one to know it," Laura groaned.

"And has he told his mother?"

"I suppose so: he rushed off to see her at noon. She'll be overwhelmed."

"Overwhelmed? Not a bit of it!" Lady Davenant almost gaily returned. "When did anything in the world overwhelm her and what do you take her for? She'll only make some delightful odd speech. As for people knowing it," she added, "they'll know it whether he wants 'em or not. My poor child," she went on, "how long do you expect to make believe?"

"Lionel expects some news to-night," Laura said. "As soon as I know where she is I shall start."

"Start for where?"

"To go to her — to do something."

"Something preposterous, my dear. Do you expect to bring her back?"

"He won't take her in," said Laura with her dried dismal eyes. "He wants his divorce — it's too hideous!"

"Well, as she wants hers, *quoi de plus simple?*"

"Yes, she wants hers. Lionel swears by all the gods she can't get it."

"Bless me, won't one do?" Lady Davenant asked. "We shall have some pretty reading."

"It's awful, awful, awful!" Laura wailed.

"Yes, they ought n't to be allowed to publish 'em. I wonder if we could n't stop that. At any rate he had better be quiet: tell him to come and see me."

"You won't influence him; he's dreadful against her. Such a house as it is to-day!"

"*Bien entendu!*" Lady Davenant sighed.

"Yes, but it's terrible for me: it's all more sickening than I can bear."

"My dear child, come and stay with me," said the old woman gently.

"Oh I can't desert her; I can't abandon her!"

"Desert — abandon? What a way to put it! Has n't she abandoned you?"

"She has no heart — she's too base!" cried the girl. Her face was white and the tears now rose again to her eyes.

Her friend got up and came and sat on the sofa beside her; she put her arms round her and the two women embraced. "Your room's all ready," the elder remarked. And then she said: "When did she leave you? When did you see her last?"

"Oh in the strangest maddest cruelest way, the way most insulting to me. We went to the opera together and she left me there with a gentleman. We know nothing about her since."

"With a gentleman?"

"With Mr. Wendover — that American, and something too dreadful happened."

"Dear me, did he kiss you?" Lady Davenant asked.

Laura got up quickly, turning away. "Good-bye. I'm going, I'm going!" And in reply to an irritated protesting sound from her friend she went on: "Anywhere — anywhere to get away!"

"To get away from your American?"

"I asked him to marry me!" The girl turned back with her tragic face.

"He ought n't to have left you to it."

"I knew this horror was coming and it took possession of me there in the box from one moment to the other — the idea of making sure of some other life, some protection, some respectability. First I thought he liked me, he had behaved as if he did.

And I like him, he's a very good man," Laura explained. "So I asked him, I could n't help it, it was too hideous — I offered myself!" She spoke as if telling she had stabbed him, standing there with dilated eyes.

Lady Davenant got up again and went to her; drawing off a glove she felt the wet cheek with the back of her hand. "You're ill, you're in a fever. I'm sure that whatever you said it was very charming."

"Yes, I'm ill," said Laura.

"Upon my honour you shan't go home, you shall go straight to bed. And what did he say to you?"

"Oh it was too miserable!" cried the girl, pressing her face again into her companion's kerchief. "I was all horribly mistaken: he had never thought!"

"Why the deuce then did he run about that way after you? He was a brute to say it!"

"He did n't say it and he never ran about. He behaved like a perfect gentleman."

"I've no patience — I wish I had seen him that time!" Lady Davenant declared.

"Yes, that would have been nice! You'll never see him. If he *is* a gentleman he'll rush away."

"Bless me, what a rushing away!" the old woman frankly mocked. Then passing her arm round Laura she added: "You'll please to come upstairs with me."

Half an hour later she had with her butler some conversation which led to his consulting a little register into which it was his law to transcribe with great neatness, from their cards, the addresses of new visitors. This volume, kept in the drawer of the hall table, revealed the fact that Mr. Wendover was staying in George Street, Hanover Square. "Get into a cab immediately and tell him to come to see me this evening," Lady Davenant said. "Make him understand that it interests him very nearly, so that no matter what his engagements may be he must give them up. Go quickly and you'll just find him: he'll be sure to be at home to dress for dinner." She had calculated justly: at a few minutes before ten o'clock the door of her drawing-room was thrown open and Mr. Wendover was announced.

"Sit there," said the old woman; "no, not in that one, nearer to me. We must talk low. My dear sir, I won't bite you!"

"Oh this is very comfortable." Mr. Wendover replied vaguely, smiling through his visible anxiety. It was no more than natural he should wonder what Laura Wing's peremptory friend wanted of him at that hour of the night; but nothing could exceed the gallantry of his attempt to conceal the symptoms of alarm.

"You ought to have come before, you know," Lady Davenant went on. "I've wanted to see you more than once."

"I've been dining out — I hurried away. This was the first possible moment, I assure you."

"I too was dining out and I stopped at home on purpose to see you. But I did n't mean to-night, for you've done very well," his hostess explained. "I was quite intending to send for you — the other day. But something put it out of my head. Besides, I knew she would n't like it."

"Why Lady Davenant, I made a point of calling, ever so long ago — after that day!" the young man insisted, not reassured, or at any rate not enlightened.

"I dare say you did — but you must n't justify yourself: that's just what I don't want; it is n't what I sent for you for. I've something very particular to say to you, but it's very difficult. *Voyons un peu!*"

The old woman reflected a little, with her eyes on his face, which had grown more grave as she went on; its expression showed that he failed as yet to understand her and that he at least was not exactly trifling. Lady Davenant's musings apparently helped her little if she was seeking an artful approach, for they ended in her saying abruptly: "I wonder if you know what a capital girl it is."

"Do you mean — do you mean — ?" he stammered, pausing as if he had given her no right not to allow him to conceive alternatives.

"Yes, I do mean. She's upstairs in bed."

"Upstairs in bed!" Mr. Wendover stared.

"Don't be afraid — I'm not going to send for her!" laughed his hostess. "Her being here, after all, has nothing to do with it, except that she *did* come — yes, certainly, she did come. But my keeping her — that was my own doing. My maid has gone to Grosvenor Place to get her things and let them know she'll stay here for the present. Now am I clear?"

"Not in the least" — and the young man was almost stern.

Lady Davenant, however, was not of a composition to suspect him of sternness or to care very much if she did, and she ranged liberally on. "Well, we must be patient; we shall work it out together. I was afraid you'd go away; that's why I lost no time. Above all I want you to understand she has not the least idea I've sent for you, and that you must promise me never, never, never to let her know. She'd be much too disgusted. It's quite my own idea — I've taken it on my shoulders. I know very little about you of course, but she has spoken to me well of you. Besides, I'm very clever about people, and I liked you that day, though you seemed to think I was a hundred and eighty. You're very *comme il faut*."

"You do me great honour," Mr. Wendover brought forth in pain.

"I'm glad you're pleased! You *must* be if I tell you I like you now even better. I see what you are, except for the question of fortune. It does n't perhaps matter much, but have you any money? I mean have you a fine income?" Lady Davenant wound up.

"No indeed, I have n't!" And the young man laughed in his bewilderment. "I've very little money indeed."

"Well, I dare say you've as much as I. Besides, that would be a proof she's not mercenary."

"You have n't in the least made it plain whom you're talking about," said Mr. Wendover. "I've no right to assume anything."

"Are you afraid of betraying her? I'm more devoted to her even than I want you to be. She has told me what happened between you last night — what she said to you at the opera. That's what I want to talk to you about," the old woman explained.

"She was certainly very strange," her guest returned.

"I'm not so sure she was very strange. However, you're welcome to think it, for goodness knows she says so herself. She's overwhelmed with horror at her own words; she's really very much upset."

Mr. Wendover had a pause. "I assured her I admire her — beyond every one. I was most kind to her."

"Did you say it in that tone? You should have thrown yourself at her feet! From the moment you did n't — surely you understand women well enough to know!" Lady Davenant cried.

"You must remember where we were — in a public place, with very little room for throwing!" her visitor said.

"Ah so far from blaming you she says your behaviour was perfect. It's only I who want to have it out with you," she blandly continued. "She's so clever, so charming, so good and so unhappy."

"When I said just now she was strange I meant only in the way she turned against me."

Laura's protectress made what she would have called a *moue*. "She turned against you?"

"She told me she hoped she should never see me again."

"And you, should you like to see her?"

"Not now — not now!" Mr. Wendover eagerly declared.

"I don't mean now; I'm not such a fool as that. I mean some day or other when she has stopped accusing herself — if she ever does."

"Ah Lady Davenant, you must leave that to me," the young man returned after a moment's thought.

"Don't be afraid to tell me I'm meddling with what does n't concern me," said his hostess. "Of course I know I'm meddling; I sent for you here to meddle. Who would n't for that fine creature? She makes one melt."

"I'm exceedingly sorry for her. I don't know what she thinks she said," Mr. Wendover gasped.

"Well, that she asked you why you had come so often to Grosvenor Place. I don't see anything so awful in that — if you did go."

"Yes, I went very often. I *liked* to go." He confessed to the aggravation.

"Now, that's exactly where I wish to prevent a misconception," said Lady Davenant. "If you liked to go you had a reason for liking, and Laura Wing was the reason, was n't she?"

"I thought her charming, and I think her so now more than ever."

"Then you're a dear good man. *Vous lui faisiez votre cour*, in short."

Mr. Wendover made no immediate response: the two sat looking at each other. "It is n't easy for me to talk of these things," he said at last; "but if you mean I wished to ask her to be my wife I'm bound to tell you I had no such intention."

"Ah then I'm at sea. You thought her charming and went to see her every day. What then in the name of decency did you wish her to be?"

"I did n't go every day. Moreover I think you've a very different idea in this country of what constitutes — well, what constitutes making love. A man commits himself much sooner," Laura's friend rue-fully stated.

"Oh I don't know what *your* odd ways may be!" Lady Davenant exclaimed with some sharpness.

"Yes, but I was justified in supposing that those ladies did: they at least are American."

"'They,' my dear sir!" the old woman echoed. "For heaven's sake don't mix up that nasty Selina with it!"

"Why not, if I admired her too? I do extremely, and I thought the house most interesting."

"Mercy on us, if that's your idea of a pleasant place! But I don't know — I've always kept out of it," Lady Davenant added, checking herself. Then she went on: "If you're so fond of Mrs. Lionel I'm sorry to inform you that she's absolutely good-for-nothing."

"Good-for-nothing?" He candidly wondered.

"Nothing to speak of! I've been thinking whether I'd tell you, and have decided to do so because I judge your learning it for yourself would be a matter of a very short time. Selina has bolted, as they say."

"Bolted?" Mr. Wendover quavered.

"I don't know what you call it in America."

"In America we don't do it," he made bold to say.

"Ah well, if they stay, as they do usually abroad, that's better. I suppose you did n't think her capable of behaving herself, did you?" the old woman rather grimly asked.

"Do you mean she has left her husband — with some one else?"

"Neither more nor less, my dear; with a *mangeur de cœurs* called Crispin. It appears it all came off last evening, and she had her own reasons for doing it in the most offensive way — publicly, clumsily, with the vulgarest bravado. Laura has told me what took place, and you must let me say I think you might, as a man of the world, have been a little sharper about guessing it."

"I saw something was wrong, but I did n't understand. I 'm afraid I 'm not very quick at these things," Lady Davenant's guest could as a man of the world but candidly confess.

"Your state 's the more gracious; but assuredly you 're not sharp if you could call there so often and not see through Selina."

"Mr. Crispin, whoever he is, was never there," Mr. Wendover almost humbly pleaded.

"Oh she was a keen enough rascal!" his companion threw off.

"I knew she was fond of amusement, but that 's what I liked to see" — the young man understood himself. "I wanted to see a house of that sort."

"'Fond of amusement' is a very pretty phrase!" said Lady Davenant, laughing at his artless categories. "And did Laura Wing seem to you in her place in such a *repaire?*"

"Why it was natural she should be with her sister, and she always struck me as very gay," he explained.

"That was your enlivening effect! And did she," his hostess pressed, "strike you as very gay last night, with this scandal hanging over her?"

"She did n't talk much," he was bound to recognise.

"She knew it was coming — she felt it, she saw it, and that's what makes her sick now, that at *such* a time she should have challenged you, when she felt herself about to be associated — in people's minds, of course — with such a vile business. In people's minds and in yours — when you should know what had happened," Lady Davenant lucidly concluded.

"Ah Miss Wing is n't associated —" said Mr. Wendover. He spoke slowly, but rose to his feet with an air of trouble that was not lost on his companion: she noted it indeed with an inward sense of triumph. She was very deep, but she had never been so deep as when she made up her mind to mention the scandal of the house of Berrington to her visitor and breathed to him that Laura Wing regarded herself as near enough to it to have caught a personal stain. "I'm extremely sorry to hear of Mrs. Berrington's misconduct," he continued gravely, standing before her. "And I'm no less obliged to you for your interest."

"Don't mention it," she said, getting up too and smiling. "I mean my interest. As for the other matter it will all come out. Lionel will haul her up."

"Dear me, how dreadful!" And he looked indeed hot and sad.

"Yes, dreadful enough. But don't betray me."

"Betray you?" he repeated as if his thoughts had gone astray a moment.

"I mean to the girl. Think of her shame!"

"Her shame?" He took it up again with his flushed wonder.

414

"It seemed to her, with what was becoming so clear to her, that an honest man might save her from it, might give her his name and his faith and help her to pick her steps in the mud. She exaggerates the force of the splash, the stigma of her relationship. At that rate, don't you know, where would some of us be? But those are her ideas, they're absolutely sincere, and they had possession of her at the opera. She seemed to see she was lost—she stuck out a hand (seeing there a kind gentleman) to be saved." And Lady Davenant, with her fine old face lighted by her bright sagacity and her eyes on Mr. Wendover's, paused, lingering on this word. "Of course she must have taken it very hard indeed. One's really lost, thank goodness, but by one's *own* indecency!"

"I'm very sorry for her," said Mr. Wendover, who seemed to wince and who spoke with a gravity that committed him to nothing.

"So am I! And of course if you were n't in love with her you were n't, were you?"

"I must bid you good-bye, I'm leaving London." That was the only answer Lady Davenant got to her question.

"Good-bye then. She's the nicest girl I know. But, once more, mind you don't let her suspect!"

"How can I let her suspect anything when I shall never see her again?"

"Oh don't say that," said Lady Davenant very gently.

"She drove me away from her with a kind of rage."

"Oh gammon!" cried the old woman.

"I'm going home," he said, looking at her with his hand on the door.

"Well, it's the best place for you. And for her too!" she added as he went out. But she wasn't sure the last words reached him.

XIII

LAURA WING went to bed ill for three days, but
on the fourth made up her mind she was better,
though this was not the opinion of Lady Davenant,
who would n't hear of her being afoot. The remedy
she urged was lying still and yet lying still; but against
this specific our young woman rebelled — it might
be good for chills, but it brought on fever. She assured her friend that it killed her to do nothing; to
which her friend replied by asking what she proposed
to do. Laura had her idea and held it tight, but there
was no use in producing it before Lady Davenant,
who would have knocked it to pieces. On the afternoon of the first day Lionel Berrington came, and
though his intention was honest he brought no heal-
ing. Hearing she was ill he wanted to look after her —
take her back to Grosvenor Place and make her comfortable: he spoke as if he had all the appliances for
that state, though there happened to be a bar to
his own profit of them. This impediment was the
"cheeky" aspect of Miss Steet, who went sniffing
about as if she knew a lot should she only condescend
to tell it. He saw more of the children now; "I'm
going to have 'em in every day, poor little devils," he
said; and he spoke as if the discipline of suffering
had already begun for him and a kind of holy change
had taken place in his life. Nothing had been said
yet in the house, of course, as Laura knew, about

417

Selina's disappearance, in the way of treating it as irregular; but he described the servants, with some natural humour, as pretending so hard not to be aware of anything in particular that they were like pickpockets looking with unnatural interest the other way after they have cribbed a fellow's watch. To a certainty, in a day or two, the governess would give him warning: she would come and tell him she could n't stay in such a place, and he would in return pronounce her a donkey for not feeling the place more respectable now than it had ever been.

This information Selina's husband imparted to Lady Davenant, to whom he expressed himself with infinite confidence and candour, taking a highly philosophical view of his position and declaring that it suited him down to the ground. His wife could n't have pleased him better if she had done it on purpose; he knew where she had been every hour since she quitted Laura at the opera — knew where she was at that moment and was expecting to find another precious report on his return to Grosvenor Place. So if it suited *her* it was all right, was n't it? and the whole thing would go straight as a shot. Lady Davenant took him up to see Laura, though she viewed their meeting with extreme disfavour, the girl being in no state for free conversation. In general Laura had little enough mind for it, but she insisted on seeing Lionel: she declared that if this were not allowed her she would go after him, ill as she was — would dress herself and drive to his house. She dressed herself now, after a fashion; she got upon a sofa to receive her brother-in-law. Lady Davenant left him

418

alone with her for twenty minutes, at the end of which she came back to remove him. This visit was not fortifying to its subject, whose idea — the idea of which I have said that she was tenacious — was to pursue her sister, take possession of her, cling to her and bring her home. Lionel of course would n't hear of taking her back, nor would Selina presumably hear of coming; but this made no difference for Laura's design. She would work it, would compass it, would go down on her knees, would find the eloquence of angels, would achieve miracles. It made her meanwhile frantic not to begin, especially as even in fruitless action she should escape from herself — an object of which her horror was not yet extinguished.

As she lay there through inexorably conscious hours the picture of that hideous moment in the box alternated with the vision of her sister's guilty flight. She wanted to flee herself — to go off and keep going for ever. Lionel was fussily kind to her and did n't abuse Selina — he did n't tell her again how that lady's behaviour suited his book. He simply resisted with an exasperating dogged grin her pitiful appeal for knowledge of their false friend's whereabouts. He knew what she wanted it for and would n't help her in any such game. If she would promise, solemnly, to be quiet, he would tell her when she got better, but he would n't lend her a hand to make a fool of herself. Her work was cut out for her — she was to stay and mind the children : if she was so keen for her duty she need n't go further than that for it. He talked a great deal about the children and figured himself as pressing the little deserted darlings to his bosom. He was not a comedian, and she could see that he really believed he was going to be better and "purer" now. Laura said she was sure Selina would make an attempt to get them — or at least one of them; and he replied grimly "Yes, my dear, she had better try!" The girl was so angry with him, in her hot, tossing weakness, for refusing to tell her even whether the desperate pair had crossed the Channel, that she was guilty of the immorality of feeling the difference in badness between husband and wife too distinct (for it *was* distinct, she could see that) when he made his dry little remark about Selina's trying. He told her he had already seen his solicitor, the clever Mr. Smallshaw, and she replied that she did n't care.

On the fourth day of her absence from Grosvenor Place she got up at an hour of independence (in the afternoon rather late) and prepared herself to go out. Lady Davenant had recognised her in the morning as better, and she fortunately had n't the complication of exposure to medical sapience, having absolutely refused to see a doctor. Her old friend had been constrained to absence — she had scarcely quitted her before — and Laura had begged the hovering rustling lady's-maid to leave her alone, had assured her she was doing beautifully. She had no plan but to leave London that night; she had a moral certainty that Selina had gone to the Continent. She had always done so in any freedom, and what freedom, now, had ever been so great? The Continent was fearfully vague, but she would deal sharply with Lionel and would show him she had a right to knowledge. He would certainly be in town; he would be in a complacent bustle with his lawyers. She had pretended to him that she did n't believe he had yet gone to them, but in her heart she believed it perfectly. If he did n't satisfy her she would go to Lady Ringrose, odious as it would be to her to ask a favour of this depraved creature: unless indeed Lady Ringrose had joined the little party to France, as on the occasion of Selina's last wicked excursion. On her way downstairs she met one of the footmen, whom she easily induced to call her a cab as quickly as possible — she was obliged to go out for half an hour. He expressed the respectful hope that she was better and she replied that she was perfectly well — he would please tell her ladyship when she came in. To this the footman rejoined that her ladyship *had* come in — she had returned five minutes before and had gone to her room. "Miss Frothingham told her you were asleep, Miss," said the man, "and her ladyship said it was a blessing and you were not to be disturbed."

"Very good, I 'll see her," Laura remarked with dissimulation: "only please let me have my cab."

The man went downstairs and she stood there listening; presently she heard the house-door close — he had gone out on his errand. Then she descended very softly — she prayed he might not be long. The door of the drawing-room stood open as she passed it, and she paused before it, thinking she heard sounds in the lower hall. They appeared to subside and then she found herself faint — she was terribly impatient for her cab. Partly to sit down till it came (there was a seat on the landing, but another servant might come up or down and see her), and partly to look out at the front window for her means of release, she went for a moment into the drawing-room. She stood at the window, but the footman was slow; then she sank upon a chair — she felt very weak. Just after she had done so she became aware of steps on the stairs and got up quickly, supposing her messenger back, though she had not heard wheels. What she saw was not the footman she had sent out, but the expansive person of the butler, followed apparently by a visitor. This functionary ushered the visitor in with the remark that he would call her ladyship, and before she knew it she was face to face with Mr. Wendover. At the same moment she heard a cab drive up, while Mr. Wendover instantly closed the door.

"Don't turn me away; do see me — do see me!" he said. "I asked for Lady Davenant — they told me she was at home. But it was you I wanted, and I wanted her to help me. I was going away — but I could n't. You look very ill — do listen to me! You don't understand — I 'll explain everything. Ah how ill you look!" the young man cried, as the climax of this sudden soft distressed appeal. Laura, for all answer, tried to push past him, but the result of this movement was that she found herself caught in his arms. He stopped her, but she disengaged herself, she got her hand at the door. He was leaning against it, so she could n't open it, and as she stood there panting she shut her eyes so as not to see him.

"If you'd let me tell you what I think — I'd do anything in the world for you!" he went on.

"Let me go — you persecute me!" the girl cried, pulling at the door-handle.

"You don't do me justice — you're too cruel!" Mr. Wendover persisted.

"Let me go — let me go!" she only repeated, with her high quavering distracted note; and as he moved a little she got the door open. But he followed her out: would she see him that night? where was she going? might n't he go with her? would she see him to-morrow?

"Never, never, never!" she flung at him as she hurried away. The butler was on the stairs, descending from above; so he checked himself, letting her go. Laura passed out of the house and flew into her cab with extraordinary speed, for Mr. Wendover heard the wheels bear her away while the servant was reporting in measured accents that her ladyship would come down immediately.

Lionel was at home, in Grosvenor Place: she burst into the library and found him playing papa. Geordie and Ferdy were sporting round him, the presence of Miss Steet had been dispensed with, and he was holding his younger son by the stomach, horizontally, between his legs, while the child made little sprawling movements which were apparently intended to represent the act of swimming. Geordie stood impatient on the brink of the imaginary stream, protesting that it was his turn now, and as soon as he saw his aunt he rushed at her with the request that she would take him up in the same fashion.

She was struck with the superficiality of their childhood; they seemed to have no sense that she had
been away and no care that she had been ill. But
Lionel made up for this; he greeted her with affectionate jollity, said it was a good job she had come back
and remarked to the children that they would have
great larks now auntie was home again. Ferdy asked
if she had been with mummy, but did n't wait for
an answer, and she observed that they put no question about their mother and made no further allusion
to her while they remained in the room. She wondered whether their father had drilled them in this
discretion, and reflected that even if he had they
did n't generally mind his injunctions. It added to the
ugliness of Selina's flight that even her children
did n't miss her, and to the dreariness, somehow,
for poor Laura, of the whole situation, that one could
neither spend tears on the mother and wife, since
she was n't worth it, nor sentimentalise about the
little boys, since they did n't inspire it. "Well, you
do look seedy — I 'm bound to say that!" Lionel
exclaimed; and he recommended strongly a glass of
port, while Ferdy, not seizing this reference, suggested that daddy should take her by the waistband
and teach her to "strike out." He represented himself in the act of drowning, but Laura interrupted
this feat, when the servant answered the bell —
Lionel having rung for the port — by ordering the
children away to Miss Steet. "Tell her she must
never leave us again," Lionel said to Geordie as the
butler took him by the hand; but the only touching
consequence of this appeal was that the child piped

back to his father, over his shoulder, "Well, you
must n't either, you know!"

"You must tell me or I 'll kill myself — I give you
my word!" Laura said to her brother-in-law with
unnecessary violence as soon as they had left the
room.

"I say, I say," he rejoined, "you *have* got a temper and you *are* a wilful one! What do you want to
threaten me for? Don't you know me well enough
to know that ain't the way? That's the tone Selina
used to take. Surely you don't want to begin and
imitate her!" She only sat there looking at him
while he leaned against the chimney smoking a short
cigar. There was a silence during which she felt a
heat of irrational anger at the thought that a little
ignorant red-faced jockey should have the luck to
be in the right as against her flesh and blood. She
considered him helplessly, with something in her
eyes that had never been there before — something
that apparently after a minute affected him. Later
on, however, she saw very well that it was not her
threat that had acted, and even at the moment she
had a sense, from the way he returned the light of
her eyes, that this was in no manner the first time a
baffled woman had told him she would kill herself.
He had always accepted his kinship with her, but
even in her trouble it was part of her consciousness
that he now lumped her with a mixed group of female
figures, a little wavering and dim, who were associated
in his memory with scenes of violence, with impor-
tunities and ultimatums. It is apt to be the disadvantage of women, on occasions of measuring their

strength with men, that they may feel in the man a
larger experience, and feel their own precious sub-
stance, their general "side," alas, as part of that
resource. It is doubtless as a provision against such
emergencies that nature has opened to them operations of the mind quite independent of experience.
Laura felt the dishonour of her race the more that her
brother-in-law seemed so horribly at his ease about
it: he had an air of perverse prosperity, as if his misfortune had turned into that. It came to her that he
really liked the idea of the public letting-in of light —
the fresh occupation, the bustle and importance and
celebrity of it. That was sufficiently incredible, but
as she was of the wrong party it was also humiliating.
Moreover, higher spirits always really suggest, to the
further humiliation of the depressed, finer wisdom,
and such an attribute on Lionel's part could be but
supremely crushing. "I have n't the least objection
at present to telling you what you want to know. I
shall have made my little arrangements very soon
and you'll be subpœnaed."

"Subpœnaed?" the girl repeated, mechanically.

"You'll be called as a witness on my side."

"On your side?"

"Of course you're on my side, ain't you?"

"Can they force me to come?" asked Laura in
answer to this.

"No, they can't force you, if you leave the country."

"That's exactly what I want to do."

"That will be idiotic," said Lionel, "and very bad
for Selina. If you don't help me you ought at least
to help *her*."

She sat a moment with her eyes on the ground. " Where is she — where is she ? " she then asked.

"They're at Brussels, at the Hôtel de Flandres. They appear to like it very much."

"Are you telling me the truth ? "

"Lord, my dear child, *I* don't lie!" Lionel exclaimed. "You'll make a jolly mistake if you go to her," he added. "If you've seen her with him how shall you be able properly to lie for her ? "

"I won't see her with him."

"That's all very well, but he'll take care of that. Of course if you *are* ready for family perjury —!" Lionel subjoined.

"I'm ready for anything."

"Well, I've been kind to you, my dear," he continued, smoking, his chin in the air.

"Certainly you've been kind to me."

"If you want to defend her you had better keep away from her," said Lionel. "Besides, for yourself, you see, it won't be the best thing in the world — to be known to have been *in* it."

"I don't care for myself," Laura returned musingly.

"Don't you care for the children, that you're so ready to throw them over ? For you would, my dear, you know. If you go to Brussels you never come back here — you never cross this threshold — you never touch them again!"

She appeared to listen to this last declaration, but made no reply to it; she only observed after a moment with a certain impatience "Oh the children will do anyway!" Then she added passionately: "You *won't*, Lionel; in mercy's name tell me you won't!"

"I won't what?"

"Do the awful thing you say."

"Divorce her? The devil I won't!"

"Then why do you speak of the children — if you've no pity for them?"

Lionel stared an instant. "I thought you said yourself they'd do anyway!"

Laura bent her head, resting it on the back of her hand and over the leathern arm of the sofa. So she remained, while Lionel stood smoking; but at last, to leave the room, she got up with an effort that was a physical pain. He came to her, to detain her, with a little good intention that had no felicity for her, trying to take her hand persuasively. "Dear old girl, don't try and behave just as *she* did! If you'll stay quietly here I won't call you, I give you my honour I won't; there! You want to see the doctor — that's the sort of person *you* want to see. And what good will it do you, even if you bring her home in pink paper? Do you candidly suppose I'll ever look at her — except across the court-room?"

"I must, I must, I must!" Laura cried, jerking herself away from him and reaching the door.

"Well then, good-bye," he said in the sternest tone she had ever heard him use.

She made no answer, she only escaped. She locked herself in her room; she remained there an hour. At the end of this time she came out and went to the door of the schoolroom, where she asked Miss Steet to be so good as to come and speak to her. The governess followed her to her quarters, and there Laura took her partly into her confidence. There

were things she wanted to do before going, and she
was too weak to act without aid. She did n't want it
from the servants, if only Miss Steet would learn
from them if Mr. Berrington were dining at home.
Laura had it in presentable form that her sister was
ill and that she was hurrying to join her abroad. It
had to be mentioned, that way, that Mrs. Berrington
had left the country, though of course there was no
spoken recognition between the two young women
of the ground or nature of her absence. There was
only a tacit hypocritical assumption that she was on a
visit to friends and that her departure had taken
place on normal lines. Laura knew Miss Steet to
know the truth, and the governess knew *she* knew it.
This young woman lent a hand, very confusedly, to
her friend's preparations; she ventured not to be
sympathetic, as that would point too much to badness, but succeeded perfectly in being dismal. She
suggested that Laura was ill herself, but Laura replied that this was a trifle when one's near relative
was so much worse. She elicited the fact that Mr.
Berrington was dining out — the butler believed with
his mother — but was of no use when it came to
finding in "Bradshaw," brought up from the hall,
the hour of the night-boat to Ostend. Laura found it
herself; it was conveniently late, and it was a gain to
her that she was so near the Victoria Station, where
she would take the train for Dover. The governess
wanted to go to the station with her, but our heroine would n't listen to this — she would only allow
her to see she got a cab. Laura let her help her
still further; she sent her down to talk to Lady

Davenant's maid when that personage arrived in
Grosvenor Place to enquire, from her mistress, what
in the world had become of poor Miss Wing. The
maid intimated, Miss Steet said on her return, that
her ladyship would have come herself if she had n't
been too angry. She was very bad indeed; it was revealed that her wrath was terrible; and it was truly
rather a sign of this that she had sent back her young
friend's dressing-case and her clothes. Laura also
borrowed money from the governess — she had too
little in her pocket. The latter brightened up as the
preparations advanced; she had never before been
concerned in a flurried night-episode with a bold
unavowed side; the very imprudence of it (for a sick
girl alone) was romantic, and before Laura had
gone down to the cab she began to say that foreign
life must be fascinating and to make wistful reflexions. She saw the coast clear in the nursery — the
children asleep for their aunt to come in. She kissed
Ferdy while her companion pressed her lips upon
Geordie, and Geordie while Laura hung for a moment over Ferdy. At the door of the cab she tried to
make her take more money, and our heroine had an
odd sense that if the vehicle had not rolled away
she would have thrust into her hand a keepsake for
Captain Crispin.

A quarter of an hour later Laura sat in the corner
of a railway-carriage, muffled in her cloak — the July
evening was fresh, as so often in London, fresh enough
to add to her sombre thoughts the suggestion of the
wind in the Channel — waiting in vain impatience for
the train to get into motion. Her impatience itself

had brought her too early to the station, where it seemed to her she had already spent an age. A lady and a gentleman had taken places in the carriage — it was not yet the moment for the outward crowd of tourists — and had left their accessories there while they strolled up and down the platform. The long English twilight was still in the air, but there was dusk under the grimy arch of the station and Laura flattered herself that the off-corner of her compartment was in shadow. This, however, apparently did n't prevent her being recognised by a gentleman who stopped at the door, looking in, with the movement of a person who was going from carriage to carriage. As soon as he saw her he entered quickly, so that the next moment Mr. Wendover was seated on the edge of the place beside her, leaning toward her, speaking to her low and with clasped hands. She fell back in her seat, closing her eyes again. He barred the way out.

"I 've followed you here — I saw Miss Steet — I want to entreat you not to go! Don't, don't! I know what you 're doing. Don't go, I beseech you. I saw Lady Davenant, I wanted to ask her to help me, I could bear it no longer. I 've thought of you, night and day, these four days. Lady Davenant has told me things, and I entreat you not to go!"

Laura opened her eyes — there was something in his voice, in his pressing nearness — and looked at him a moment: it was the first time she had done so since the first of those detestable moments in the box at Covent Garden. She had never spoken to

him of Selina in any but an honourable sense. Now
she said "I'm going to my sister."

"I know it, and I wish so immensely you'd give
it up. It is n't good — it's a great mistake. Stay
here and let me talk to you."

The girl raised herself, she stood up in the carriage.
Mr. Wendover did the same; Laura saw that the
lady and gentleman outside were nearer the door,
but fortunately not looking in. "What have you to
say? It's my own business!" she returned under
her breath. "Go out, go out, go out!"

"Do you suppose I'd speak if I did n't care — do
you suppose I'd care if I did n't love you?" the
young man groaned close to her face.

"What is there to care about? Because people
will know it and talk? If it's bad it's the right thing
for me! If I don't go to her where else shall I go?"

"Come to me, dear, dear Miss Wing!" Mr. Wendover went on. "You're ill, you're mad! I love you
— I assure you I do!"

She pushed him away with her hands. "If you
follow me I'll jump off the boat!"

"Take your places, take your places!" cried the
guard from the platform. Mr. Wendover had to slip
out, the lady and gentleman were coming in. Laura
huddled herself into her corner again and presently
the train drew away.

Mr. Wendover did n't get into another compartment; he went back that evening to Queen's Gate.
He knew how interested his old friend there, as he
now appraised her, would be to hear what Laura
had undertaken — though, as he learned on entering

her drawing-room again, she had already had the
news from her maid — and he felt the need, felt it
sharply, to tell her once more how her words of four
days before had fructified in his heart, what a strange
ineffaceable impression she had made on him: to
tell her in short and to repeat it over and over, that
he was taking the most extraordinary interest —!
Lady Davenant was unappeasably vexed at the girl's
perversity, but she counselled him patience, an artful patience and a long and deep diplomacy. A week
later she heard from Laura Wing, at Antwerp, of her
sailing to America from that port — a letter containing no mention whatever of Selina or of the re-
ception Selina's sister had been treated to at Brussels.
To America Mr. Wendover followed his young compatriot — that at least she had no right to forbid —
and there, for the moment, he has had a chance to
practise the interested arts prescribed by Lady
Davenant. He knows she has no money and that she
is staying with distant relatives in Virginia; a situation that he — perhaps too superficially — figures as
unspeakably dreary. He knows further that Lady
Davenant has sent her fifty pounds, and he himself
has a project of transmitting funds, not directly to
Virginia, but by the roundabout road of Queen's
Gate. Now, however, that Lionel Berrington's deplorable suit is coming on he reflects with some satisfaction that the Court of Probate and Divorce is far
from the banks of the Rappahannock. "Berrington
versus Berrington and Others" is coming on — but
these are matters of the present hour.

THE CHAPERON

THE CHAPERON

I

AN old lady, in a high drawing-room, had had her chair moved close to the fire, where she sat knitting and warming her knees. She was dressed in deep mourning; her face had a faded nobleness, tempered however by the somewhat illiberal compression of her lips in obedience to something she had thought of. She was far from the lamp, but though her eyes were fixed on her active needles she was not looking at them. What she really saw was quite another train of affairs. The room was spacious and dim; the thick London fog had oozed into it even through its superior defences. It was full of dusky massive valuable things. The old lady sat motionless save for the regularity of her clicking needles, which seemed as personal to her and as expressive as prolonged fingers. If she was studying a question she was studying it thoroughly.

When she looked up, on the entrance of a girl of twenty, it might have been guessed that the appearance of this young lady was not an interruption but rather a contribution to her thought. The young lady, who was charming to behold, was also in deep mourning, which had a juvenility, if mourning can ever seem young, and an air of having been freshly put on. She went straight to the bell beside the chimney-

piece and pulled it, while in her other hand she held
a sealed and directed letter. Her companion glanced
in silence at the letter, then looked still harder at her
own business. The girl hovered near the fireplace
without speaking, and after a due and a dignified
interval the butler appeared in response to the bell.
The time had been sufficient to make the silence
between the ladies seem long. The younger one asked
the butler to see that her letter should be posted,
and after he had gone out moved vaguely about the
room as to give her grandmother — for such was the
elder personage — a chance to begin a colloquy of
which she herself preferred not to strike the first note.
Since equally with herself her companion was on the
face of it capable of holding out, the tension, though
it was already late in the evening, might have lasted
long. But the old lady after a little seemed to recognise, a trifle ungraciously, the girl's superior resources.

"Have you written to your mother?"

"Yes, but only a few lines, to tell her I shall come
and see her in the morning."

"Is that all you've got to say?" asked the grandmother.

"I don't quite know what you want me to say."

"I want you to say you've made up your mind."

"Yes, I've done that, granny."

"You intend to respect your father's wishes?"

"It depends on what you mean by respecting them.
I do justice to the feelings by which they were dic-
tated."

"What do you mean by justice?" the old lady re-
torted.

The girl had a pause and then said: "You'll see my idea of it."

"I see it already! You'll go and live with her."

"I shall talk the situation over with her to-morrow and tell her I think that will be best."

"Best for her, no doubt!"

"What's best for her's best for me."

"And for your brother and sister?" As the girl made no reply to this her grandmother went on: "What's best for them is that you should acknowledge some responsibility in regard to them and, considering how young they are, try to do something for them."

"They must do as I've done — they must act for themselves. They have their means now — and they're free."

"Free? They're mere children."

"Let me remind you that Eric's older than I."

"He doesn't like his mother," said the old lady as if that were an answer.

"I never said he did. And she adores him."

"Oh your mother's adorations —!"

"Don't abuse her now," the girl returned after a pause.

The old lady forbore to abuse her, but made up for it the next moment by saying: "It will be dreadful for Edith."

"What will be dreadful."

"Your desertion of her."

"The desertion's on her side."

"Her consideration for her father does her honour."

"Of course I'm a brute, *n'en parlons plus*," said the girl. "We must go our respective ways," she added in a tone of extreme wisdom and philosophy.

Her grandmother straightened out the work she had been busy with and began to roll it up. "Be so good as to ring for my maid," she said after a minute. The young lady rang, and there was another wait and another conscious hush. Before the maid came her mistress remarked: "Of course then you'll not come to *me*, you know."

"What do you mean by 'coming' to you?"

"I can't receive you on that footing."

"She'll not come *with* me — if you mean that."

"I don't mean that," said the old lady, who got up as her maid came in. This attendant took her work from her, gave her an arm and helped her out of the room, while Rose Tramore, standing before the fire and staring into it, faced the idea that her relative's door would now at every juncture be closed to her. She lost no time however in brooding over this anomaly: it only gave point to her resolve to act. All she could do to-night was to go to bed, for she was spent and done. She had been living by her imagination in a prospective struggle, and it had left her as exhausted as a real fight. Moreover this was the culmination of a crisis, of weeks of suspense, of a long hard strain. Her father had been laid in his grave five days before, and that morning his will had been read. In the afternoon she had got Edith off to Saint Leonard's with their Aunt Julia and then had had a wretched talk with Eric. Lastly she had made up her mind to act in opposition to the

THE CHAPERON

formidable will, to a clause which embodied if not
exactly a provision certainly a recommendation most
emphatic. She went to bed and slept the sleep of
the just.

II

"Oh my dear, how charming! I must take another house!" It was in these words her mother responded to the announcement Rose had just formally made and with which she had vaguely expected to produce a certain dignity of effect. In the way of emotion there was apparently no effect at all, and the girl was wise enough to know that this was not simply on account of the general line of non-allusion taken by the extremely pretty woman before her, who looked like her elder sister. Mrs. Tramore had never betrayed to her daughter the slightest consciousness that her position was peculiar; but the recollection of something more than that fine policy was required to explain such a failure to appreciate Rose's sacrifice. It was simply a fresh reminder that she had never appreciated anything, that she was nothing but a tinted and stippled surface. Her situation was peculiar indeed. She had been the heroine of a scandal which had grown dim only because, in the eyes of the London world, it paled in the lurid light of the more contemporaneous. That attention had been fixed on it for several days, fifteen years before; there had been a high relish of the vivid evidence as to his wife's misconduct with which, in the divorce-court, Charles Tramore had judged well to regale a cynical public. The case had been so awfully bad that he obtained his decree. The folly of the wife had been

442

inconceivable, in spite of other examples: she had heartlessly quitted her children, had followed the "other fellow" abroad. The other fellow had n't married her, not having had time: he had lost his life in the Mediterranean by the capsizing of a boat before the prohibitory term had expired.

Mrs. Tramore had striven to extract from this accident the austere advantage of widowhood; but her mourning had only made her deviation more public — she was a widow whose husband was awkwardly alive. She had not prowled about the Continent on the classic lines; she had come back to London to take her chance. But London would give her no chance, would have nothing to say to her; as many persons had remarked, you could never tell how London would behave. It would receive Mrs. Tramore again on no terms whatever, and when she was spoken of, which now was not often, it was inveterately said of her that she "went" nowhere. Apparently she had not the qualities for which London compounds, even though in the cases in which it does compound you may often wonder what these qualities are. She had not at any rate been successful: her lover was dead, her husband was liked and her children were pitied, since in payment for a topic London will parenthetically pity. It was thought interesting and magnanimous that Charles Tramore had n't married again. The disadvantage to his children of the miserable story was thus left uncorrected, and this, rather oddly, was counted as *his* sacrifice. His mother, whose arrangements were elaborate, looked after them a great deal, and they

443

enjoyed a mixture of laxity and discipline under the roof of their aunt, Miss Tramore, who was independent, having, for reasons the two ladies had exhaustively discussed, determined to lead her own life. She had set up a home at Saint Leonard's, and that contracted shore had played a considerable part in the upbringing of the little Tramores. They knew about their mother, as the phrase was, but they did n't know her; which was naturally deemed more pathetic for them than for her. She had a house in Chester Square and an income and a victoria — it served all purposes, as she never went out in the evening — and flowers on her window-sills, and a remarkable appearance of youth. The income was supposed to be in part the result of a bequest from the man for whose sake she had committed the error of her life, and in the appearance of youth there was a slightly impertinent hint that it was a sort of afterglow of the same connexion.

Each of her children, as they grew older, fortunately showed signs of a separate character or at least of the desire to take a line. Edith, the second girl, clung to her Aunt Julia; Eric, the son, clung frantically to polo; while Rose, the elder daughter, appeared to cling mainly to herself. Collectively of course they clung to their father, whose attitude in the family group, however, was casual and intermittent. He was charming and vague; he was like a clever actor who often did n't come to rehearsal. Fortune, which but for that one stroke had been generous to him, had provided him with deputies and trouble-takers, as well as with whimsical opinions, with a reputation for excellent taste, with whist at his club, with perpetual cigars on morocco sofas, and with a beautiful absence of purpose. Nature had thrown in a remarkably fine hand, which he sometimes passed over his children's heads when these were glossy from the nursery brush. On Rose's eighteenth birthday he said to her that she might go to see her mother on condition that her visits should be limited to an hour each time and to four in the year. She was to go alone; the other children were not included in the decree. This was the result of a visit that he himself had paid his repudiated wife at her urgent request, their only encounter during the fifteen years. The girl knew as much as this from her Aunt Julia, who was full of telltale secrecies. She availed herself eagerly of the licence, and in the course of the period that elapsed before her father's death spent with Mrs. Tramore exactly eight hours by the watch. Her father, who was somehow perverse and disconcerting without detriment to his amiability, spoke to her of her mother only once afterwards. This occasion had been the sequel of her first visit, and he had made no use of it to ask how she judged and liked the odd character in Chester Square. He had only said "Did she take you out?" and when Rose answered "Yes, she put me straight into a carriage and drove me up and down Bond Street," had rejoined sharply "See that that never occurs again." It never did, but once was enough, every one they knew having, as if eager for the effect of the thing, happened to be in Bond Street at that particular hour.

After this the periodical interview took place

445

privately and in Mrs. Tramore's charming little wasted drawing-room. Rose knew that, rare as these occasions were, her mother would n't have kept her "all to herself" had there been anybody she could have shown her to. But in the poor lady's social void there was no one; she had after all her own correctness and she consistently preferred isolation to inferior contacts. So her daughter was exposed in the way of communication only to the maternal; it was not necessary to be definite in qualifying that. The girl had by this time a collection of ideas, gathered by impenetrable processes; she had tasted, in the ostracism of her ambiguous parent, of the acrid fruit of the tree of knowledge. She not only had an approximate vision of what every one had done, but had a private judgement for each case. She had a particular vision of her father, which did n't interfere with his being dear to her, but which was directly concerned in her resolution, after his death, to do the special thing he had expressed the wish she should n't do. In the general estimate her grandmother and her grandmother's money had their place, and the strong probability that any enjoyment of this prize would now be withheld from her. It included Edith's marked inclination to receive the law, and doubtless eventually a more substantial memento, from Miss Tramore, and opened the question whether her own course might n't contribute to make her sister's appear heartless. The answer to this question would verily depend on the success that might attend her own, which would very possibly be small. Eric's attitude was eminently simple; he did n't care to

know people who did n't know *his* people. If his
mother should ever get back into society perhaps he
would take her up. Rose Tramore had decided to
do what she could to bring this consummation about;
and strangely enough — so mixed were her supersti-
tions and her heresies — a large part of her motive
lay in the value she attached to such a consecration.

Of her mother intrinsically she thought very little
now, and if her eyes were fixed on a special achieve-
ment it was much more for the sake of that achieve-
ment and to satisfy an inward energy than because her
heart was wrung by this sufferer. Her heart had not
been wrung at all, though she had quite held it out
for the experience. Her purpose was a pious game,
yet still essentially a game. Among the ideas I have
mentioned she had her idea of triumph. She had
caught the inevitable note, the pitch, on her very
first visit to Chester Square. She had arrived there in
intense excitement, and her excitement been left on
her hands in a manner that reminded her of a difficult
air she had once heard sung at the opera when no one
applauded the performer. That flatness had made
her sick, and so did this in another way. A part of
her agitation rose from her Aunt Julia's having told
her, in the manner of a burst of confidence, a quaint
truth she was not to repeat — that she was in appearance the very image of the lady in Chester
Square. The motive that prompted this declaration
was between Aunt Julia and her conscience; but it was
a great emotion to the girl to find her entertainer so
beautiful. She was tall and exquisitely slim; she had
hair more exactly to Rose Tramore's taste than any

other she had ever seen, even to every detail in the
way it was dressed, and a complexion and a figure of
the kind that are always spoken of as "lovely." Her
eyes were irresistible, and so were her clothes, though
the clothes were perhaps a little more precisely the
right thing than the eyes. Her appearance was
marked to her daughter's sense by the highest distinction; though it may be mentioned that this had
never been the opinion of all the world. It was a
revelation to Rose that she herself might look a little
like that. She knew however that Aunt Julia had n't
seen her deposed sister-in-law for a long time, and
she had a general impression that Mrs. Charles was
to-day a more complete production — for instance
as regarded her air of youth — than she had ever
been. There was no excitement on her side — that
was all on her visitor's; there was no emotion —
that was excluded by the plan, to say nothing of
conditions more primal. Rose had from the first a
glimpse of her mother's plan. It was to mention
nothing and imply nothing, neither to acknowledge,
to explain nor to extenuate. She would leave everything to her loved child; with her loved child she was
secure. She only wanted to get back into society;
she would leave even that to her loved child, whom
she treated not as a high-strung and heroic daughter,
a creature of exaltation, of devotion, but as a new
charming clever useful friend, a little younger than
herself. Already on that first day she had talked
about dressmakers. Of course, poor thing, it was to
be remembered that in her desert-life there were not
many things she *could* talk about. "She wants to go

out again; that's the only thing in the wide world she wants," Rose had promptly, compendiously said to herself. There had been a sequel to this observation, addressed, in intense engrossment, to the walls of her own room, half an hour before she had, on the important evening, made known her decision to her grandmother. "Then I'll *take* her out!"

"She'll drag you down, she'll drag you down!" Julia Tramore permitted herself to remark to her niece the next day in a tone of feverish prophecy.

As the girl's own theory was that all the dragging there might be would be upward, and moreover administered by herself, she could look at her aunt with a cold and inscrutable eye. "Very well then, I shall be out of your sight, from the pinnacle you occupy, and I shan't trouble you."

"Do you reproach me for my disinterested exertions, for the way I've toiled over you, the way I've lived for you?" Miss Tramore demanded.

"Don't reproach *me* for being kind to my mother and I won't reproach you for anything."

"She'll keep you out of everything — she'll make you miss everything," Miss Tramore continued.

"Then she'll make me miss a great deal that's odious," said the girl.

"You're too young for such extravagances," her aunt declared.

"And yet Edith, who's younger than I, seems to be too old for them: how do you arrange that? My mother's society will make me older," Rose replied.

"Don't speak to me of your mother; you *have* no mother."

"Then if I'm an orphan I must settle things for myself."

"Do you justify her, do you approve of her?" cried Miss Tramore, who was inferior to her niece in capacity for retort and whose limitations made the girl appear pert.

Rose looked at her a moment in silence and then said, turning away: "I think she's charming."

"And do you propose to become charming in the same manner?"

"Her manner's perfect; it would be an excellent model. But I can't discuss my mother with you."

"You'll have to discuss her with some other people!" Miss Tramore proclaimed, going out of the room.

III

Rose wondered if this were a general or a particular vaticination. There was something her aunt might have meant by it, but her aunt rarely meant the best thing she might have meant. Miss Tramore had come up from Saint Leonard's in response to a telegram from her own parent, an occasion like the present bringing with it for a few hours a certain lapse of differences. "Do what you can to stop her," the old lady had said; but her daughter saw the most she could do was not much. They both had a baffled sense that Rose had thought the question out a good deal further than they; and this was particularly irritating to Mrs. Tramore, as consciously the cleverer of the two. A question thought out as far as *she* could think it had always appeared to her to have performed its human uses: she had never encountered a ghost emerging from that extinction. Their great contention was that Rose would cut herself off, and certainly if she was n't afraid of that she was n't afraid of anything. Julia Tramore could only tell her mother how little the girl was afraid. She was already prepared to leave the house, taking with her the possessions, or her share of them, that had accumulated there during her father's illness. There had been a going and coming of her maid, a thumping about of boxes, an ordering of four-wheelers: it appeared to old Mrs. Tramore that something of the flagrancy, the indecency of her granddaughter's prospective connexion had already gathered about the place. It was a violation of that decorum of bereavement which was still fresh there, and from the indignant gloom of the mistress of the house you might have inferred not so much that the daughter was about to depart as that the mother was about to arrive. There had been no conversation on the dreadful subject at luncheon; for at luncheon at Mrs. Tramore's (her son never came to it) there were always, even after funerals and other miseries, stray guests of both sexes whose policy it was to be cheerful and superficial. Rose had sat down as if nothing had happened — nothing worse, that is, than her father's death; but no one had spoken of anything that any one else was thinking of.

Before she left the house a servant brought her a message from her grandmother — the old lady desired to see her in the drawing-room. She had on her bonnet and went down as if she were about to step into her cab. Mrs. Tramore sat there with her eternal knitting, from which she forbore even to raise her eyes as, after a silence that seemed to express the fulness of her reprobation while Rose stood motionless, she began: "I wonder if you really understand what you're doing."

"I think so. I'm not so stupid."

"I never thought you were, but I don't know what to make of you now. You're giving up everything."

The girl was tempted to ask if her grandmother called herself "everything"; but she checked this question, answering instead that she knew she was giving up much.

"You're taking a step of which you'll feel the effect to the end of your days," Mrs. Tramore went on.

"In a good conscience, I heartily hope," said Rose.

"Your father's conscience was good enough for his mother; it ought to be good enough for his daughter."

Rose sat down — she could afford to — as if she wished to be very attentive and were still accessible to argument. But this demonstration only ushered in after a moment the surprising words "I don't think papa had any conscience."

"What in the name of all that's unnatural do you mean?" Mrs. Tramore cried over her glasses. "The dearest and best creature that ever lived!"

"He was kind, he had charming impulses, he was delightful. But he never reflected."

Mrs. Tramore stared as if at a language she had never heard, a farrago, a *galimatias*. Her life was made up of items, but she had never had to deal intellectually with a fine shade. Then while her needles, which had paused an instant, began to fly again, she rejoined: "Do you know what you are, my dear? You're a dreadful little prig. Where do you pick up such talk?"

"Of course I don't mean to judge between them," Rose pursued. "I can only judge between my mother and myself. Papa couldn't judge *for* me." And with this she got up.

"One would think you were horrid. I never thought so before."

"Thank you for that."

"You're embarking on a struggle with society,"

continued Mrs. Tramore, indulging in an unusual flight of oratory. "Society will put you in your place."

"Has n't it too many other things to do?" asked the girl.

This question had an ingenuity that led her grandmother to meet it with a merely provisional and somewhat sketchy answer. "Your ignorance would be melancholy if your behaviour were n't so insane."

"Oh no, I know perfectly what she 'll do!" Rose replied almost gaily. "She 'll drag me down."

"She won't even do that," the old lady declared contradictiously. "She 'll keep you for ever in the same dull hole."

"I shall come and see *you*, Granny, when I want something more lively."

"You may come if you like, but you 'll come no further than the door. If you leave this house now you don't enter it again."

Rose had a pause. "Do you really mean that?"

"You may judge whether I choose such a time to joke."

"Good-bye then," said our young woman.

"Good-bye."

Rose quitted the room successfully enough, but the other side of the door, on the landing, she sank into a chair and buried her face in her hands. She had burst into tears and she sobbed there a minute, trying hard to recover herself, so as to go downstairs without showing traces, since she must pass before servants and again perhaps before Aunt Julia. Mrs. Tramore was too old to cry; she could only drop her knitting and, for a long time, sit with her head bowed and her eyes closed.

Rose had reckoned justly with her Aunt Julia; there were no footmen, but this vigilant virgin was posted at the foot of the stairs. She offered no challenge, however; she only said: "There's some one in the parlour who wants to see you." The girl demanded a name, but Miss Tramore only mouthed inaudibly and winked and waved. Rose instantly reflected that there was only one man in the world her aunt would look such deep things, make such wild gestures about. "Captain Jay?" her own eyes asked, while Miss Tramore's were those of a conspirator: they were for their moment the only embarrassed eyes Rose had encountered that day. They contributed to make Aunt Julia's further response evasive, after her niece had desired to know if she had communicated in advance with this visitor. Miss Tramore merely said that he had been upstairs with her mother — had n't Granny, in the drawing-room, mentioned it? — and had been waiting down there for herself. She thought herself acute in not putting the question of the girl's seeing him first as a favour to either party; she presented it as a duty and wound up with the proposition: "It's not fair to him, it's not kind, not to let him speak to you before you go."

"What does he want to say?" Rose returned.

"Go in and find out."

She really knew, for she had found out before; but after standing uncertain an instant she went in. "The parlour" was the name that had always been borne by a spacious sitting-room downstairs, an apart-

ment occupied by her father during his frequent
phases of residence in Hill Street — episodes increasingly frequent after his house in the country had, in
consequence, as Rose perfectly knew, of his spending
too much money, been disposed of at a sacrifice which
he always characterised as horrid. He had been left
with the place in Hertfordshire, and his mother with
the London house, on the general understanding that
they would change about; but during the last years
the community had grown more rigid, mainly at his
mother's expense. The parlour was full of his memory and his habits and his things — his books and
pictures and *bibelots*, objects that belonged now to
Eric. Rose had sat in it for hours since his death; it
was the spot on which she could still be nearest to
him. But she felt far from him as Captain Jay rose
erect on her opening the door. This was a very different presence. He had not liked Captain Jay. She
herself had, but not enough to make a great complication of her father's coldness. This afternoon, however, she foresaw complications. At the very outset
for instance she was not pleased with his having arranged such a surprise for her with her grandmother
and her aunt. It was probably Aunt Julia who had
sent for him; her grandmother would n't have done
it. It placed him immediately on their side, and Rose
was almost as disappointed at this as if she had n't
known it was quite where he would naturally be. He
had never paid her a special visit, but if that was what
he wished why should n't he have waited till she
should be under her mother's roof? She knew the
reason, but had an angry prospect of enjoyment in

making him express it. She liked him enough, after all, if it were measured by the idea of what she could make him do.

In Bertram Jay the elements were surprisingly mingled; you would have gone astray, in reading him, if you had counted on finding the complements of some of his qualities. He would nevertheless not have struck you in the least as incomplete, for in every case in which you did n't find the complement you would have found the contradiction. He was in the Royal Engineers and tall, lean and high-shouldered. He looked every inch a soldier, yet there were people who considered he had missed his vocation in not becoming a priest. He took a public interest in the spiritual life of the army. Other persons still, on closer observation, would have felt his most appropriate field to be neither the army nor the church, but simply the world — the social successful worldly world. If he had a sword in one hand and a Bible in the other he had a Court Guide concealed somewhere about his person. His profile was hard and handsome, his eyes both cold and kind, his dark straight hair imperturbably smooth and prematurely streaked with grey. There was nothing in existence that he did n't take seriously. He had a first-rate power of work and an ambition as minutely "down on paper" as a German plan of invasion. His only real recreation was to go to church, but he went to parties when he had time. If he was in love with Rose Tramore this was distracting to him only in the same sense as his religion, and it was included in that department of his extremely subdivided life. His religion indeed was of an encroaching annexing sort. Seen from in front he looked diffident and blank, but he was capable of exposing himself in a way — to speak only of the paths of peace — wholly inconsistent with shyness. He had an unnatural passion for open-air speaking, since he was not generally thought to be great at it unless he could help himself out with a hymn. In conversation he kept his eyes on you with a colourless candour, as if he had not understood what you were saying and, in a fashion that made many people turn red, waited before answering. This was only because he was considering their remarks in more relations than they had intended. He had in his face no expression whatever save the one just mentioned, and was in his profession already very distinguished.

IV

He had seen Rose Tramore for the first time on a Sunday of the previous March, at a house in the country at which she was staying with her father, and five weeks later had made her, by letter, a proposal of marriage. She showed her father the letter of course, and he left her in no doubt of the joy it would give him that she should send Captain Jay about his business. "My dear child," he said, "we must really have some one who will be better fun than that." Rose had declined the honour, very considerately and kindly, but not simply because her father urged it. She did n't herself wish to detach this flower from the stem, though when the young man wrote again, to express the hope that he *might* hope — so long was he willing to wait — and ask if he might n't still sometimes see her, she answered even more indulgently than at first. She had shown her father her first letter but did n't show him this one; she only told him what it contained, submitting to him also that of her correspondent. Captain Jay moreover wrote to Mr. Tramore, who replied sociably, but so vaguely that he almost neglected the subject under discussion — a communication that made poor Bertram ponder long. He could never get to the bottom of the superficial, and all the proprieties and conventions of life were profound to him. Fortunately for him old Mrs. Tramore liked him — he was satisfactory to her long-sightedness; so that a relation was established under cover of which he still occasionally presented himself in Hill Street — presented himself nominally to the mistress of the house. He had had scruples about the veracity of his visits but had finally disposed of them; he had scruples about so many things that he had had to invent a general way, to dig a central drain. Julia Tramore happened to meet him when she came up to town, and she took a view of him more tender than her usual estimate of people encouraged by her mother. The fear of agreeing with that lady was a motive, but there was a stronger one, for this particular case, in the fear of agreeing with her niece, who had rejected him. His situation might be held to have improved when Mr. Tramore was taken so gravely ill that with regard to his recovery those about him left their eyes to speak for their lips; and in the light of the poor gentleman's recent death it was doubtless better than it had ever been.

He was only a quarter of an hour with the girl, but this gave him time to take the measure of it. After he had spoken of her bereavement very much as an especially mild missionary might have spoken to a beautiful Polynesian, he let her know he had had news from her companions of the very strong step she was about to take. This led to their spending together ten minutes which, to her mind, threw more light on his character than anything that had ever passed between them. She had always felt with him as if she stood on an edge and looked down into something decidedly deep. To-day the impression of the perpendicular shaft was there, but it was rather

an abyss of confusion and disorder than the large
bright space in which she had figured everything as
ranged and pigeon-holed, presenting the appearance
of the labelled shelves and drawers at a chemist's.
He discussed without an invitation to discuss, he
appealed without a right to appeal. He was nothing
but a suitor tolerated after dismissal, but he took
strangely for granted a participation in her affairs.
He assumed all sorts of things that made her draw
back. He implied that there was everything now to
assist them in arriving at an agreement, since she
had never pronounced him positively objectionable; but that this symmetry would be spoiled if she
should n't be willing to take a little longer to think of
certain consequences. She was greatly disconcerted
when she saw what consequences he meant and at
his reminding her of them. What on earth was the
use of a lover if he was to speak only like one's grandmother and one's aunt? He struck her as much in
love and as particularly careful at the same time as
to what he might say. He never mentioned her
mother; he only alluded, indirectly but earnestly, to
the "step." He disapproved of it altogether, took
an unexpectedly prudent politic view of it. He evidently also believed she would be dragged down —
in other words would n't be "asked out." It was his
idea that her mother would so contaminate her
that he should — if he did n't look out — find himself interested in a young person discredited and virtually unmarriageable. All this was more obvious
to him than the consideration that a daughter should
be merciful. Where was his religion if he understood

mercy so little, and where his talent and his courage if he were so miserably afraid of trumpery social penalties? Rose's heart sank when she reflected that a man supposed to be first-rate had n't guessed that rather than not do what she could for her mother she would give up all the Royal Engineers in the world. She became aware that she probably would have been moved to place her hand in his on the spot if he had come to her saying "Your idea's the right one; put it through at every cost." She could n't discuss this with him, though he impressed her as having too much at stake for her to treat him with mere disdain. She sickened at the disclosure that a gentleman could see so much in mere vulgarities of opinion, and though she uttered as few words as possible, conversing only in sad smiles and headshakes and in intercepted movements toward the door, she happened to use in some unguarded lapse from her reticence the expression that she was disappionted in him. He caught at it and, seeming to drop his fieldglass, pressed upon her with nearer tenderer eyes.

"Can I be so happy as to believe then that you had thought of me with some confidence and some faith?"

"If you did n't suppose so what 's the sense of this visit?" Rose lucidly asked.

"One can be faithful without reciprocity," said the young man. "I regard you in a light which makes me want to protect you even if I 've nothing to gain by it."

"Yet you speak as if you thought you might keep me for yourself."

"For *yourself*. I don't want you to suffer."

"Nor yet to suffer yourself by my doing so," said Rose looking down.

"Ah if you would only marry me next month!" he broke out inconsequently.

"And give up going to mamma?" She waited to see if he would say "What need that matter? Can't your mother come to us?" But he said nothing of the sort; he only answered —

"She surely would be sorry to interfere with the exercise of any other affection which I might have the bliss of believing you now to be free, in however small a degree, to entertain."

Rose was sure her mother would n't be sorry at all; but she contented herself with replying, her hand on the door: "Good-bye. I shan't suffer. I'm not afraid."

"You don't know how terrible, how cruel, the world can be."

"Yes, I do know. I know everything!"

The declaration sprang from her lips in a tone that made him look at her as he had never yet looked till now, as if he saw something new in her face, as if he had never known her. He had n't displeased her so much but that she would have liked to give him this impression, and since she felt she might be doing so she lingered an instant for the purpose. It enabled her to see, further, that he turned red, then to become aware that a carriage had stopped at the door. Captain Jay's eyes, from where he stood, fell on this arrival, and the nature of their glance made Rose step forward to look. Her mother sat there, brilliant, conspicuous, in the eternal victoria, and the footman was already sounding the knocker. It had been no part of the arrangement that she should come to fetch her; it had been out of the question — a stroke in such bad taste as would have put Rose all in the wrong. The girl had never dreamed of it, but somehow, suddenly, perversely, she was glad of it now; she even hoped her grandmother and her aunt were looking out upstairs.

"My mother has come for me. Good-bye," she repeated; but this time her visitor had got between her and her flight.

"Listen to me before you go. I'll give you a life's devotion," the young man pleaded. He really barred the way.

She wondered whether her grandmother had told him that if her flight were n't prevented she would forfeit money. Then it strongly came over her that this would be what he was occupied with. "I shall never think of you — let me go!" she cried with passion.

Captain Jay opened the door, but she did n't see his face and in a moment was out of the house. Aunt Julia, who was sure to have been hovering, had fled before the profanity of the knock.

"Heavens, dear, where did you get your impossible mourning?" the lady in the victoria asked of her daughter as they drove away.

V

LADY MARESFIELD had given her boy a push in his fat-looking back and had said to him "Go and speak to her now; it's your best chance." She had for a long time wanted this scion to make himself audible to Rose Tramore, but the opportunity was not easy to come by. The case was complicated. Lady Maresfield had four daughters, of whom only one was married. It so happened moreover that this one, Mrs. Vaughan-Vesey, the only person in the world her mother was afraid of, was the most to be reckoned with. The Honourable Guy was in appearance all his mother's child, though he was really a simpler soul. He was large and pink; large, that is, as to everything but his eyes, which were diminishing points, and pink as to all else but his hair, which was comparable, faintly, to the hue of the richer rose. He had also, it must be conceded, very small neat teeth, which made his smile look like a young lady's. It was not his design to resemble any such person, but he was perpetually smiling, and he smiled more than ever as he approached Rose Tramore, who, looking altogether, to his mind, as a pretty girl should, and wearing a soft white opera-cloak over a softer black dress, leaned alone against the wall of the vestibule at Covent Garden while, a few paces off, an old gentleman engaged her mother in conversation. Madame Patti had been singing and they were

465

all waiting for their carriages. To their ears at present came a vociferation of names and a rattle of wheels. The air, through banging doors, entered in damp warm gusts, heavy with the stale, slightly sweet taste of the London season when the London season is overripe and spoiling.

Guy Mangler had only three minutes to reaffirm an interrupted acquaintance with our young lady. He reminded her that he had danced with her the year before, and he mentioned that he knew her brother. His mother had lately been to see old Mrs. Tramore, but this he did n't mention, not being aware of it. That visit had produced on Lady Maresfield's part a private crisis, engendered visions and plans. One of these conceptions was that the grandmother in Hill Street had really forgiven the wilful girl much more than she admitted. Another was that there would still be some money for Rose when the others should come into theirs. Still another was that the others would come into theirs at no distant date, the old lady was so visibly going to pieces. There were several more besides, as for instance that Rose had already fifteen hundred a year from her father. The figure had been betrayed in Hill Street — it was part of the proof of Mrs. Tramore's decrepitude. Then there was an equal amount that her mother had to dispose of and on which the girl could absolutely count, though of course it might involve much waiting, as the mother, a person of gross insensibility, evidently would n't die of cold-shouldering. Equally definite, to do it justice, was the conception that Rose was in truth remarkably good-looking and that what she had undertaken to do showed, and would show even should it fail, cleverness of the right sort. Cleverness of the right sort was just the quality that Lady Maresfield prefigured as indispensable in a young lady to whom she should marry her second son, over whose own deficiencies she flung the veil of a maternal theory that *his* cleverness was of a sort that was unfortunately wrong. Those who knew him less well were content to wish he might n't conceal it for any such scruple. This enumeration of his mother's views does n't exhaust the list, and it was in obedience to one too profound to be uttered even by the historian that, after a very brief delay, she decided to move across the crowded lobby. Her daughter Bessie was the only one with her; Maggie was dining with the Vaughan-Veseys and Fanny was not of an age. Mrs. Tramore the younger showed only an admirable back — her face was to her old gentleman — and Bessie had drifted to some other people; so that it was comparatively easy for Lady Maresfield to say to Rose in a moment: "My dear child, are you never coming to see us?"

"We shall be delighted to come if you'll ask us," Rose smiled.

Lady Maresfield had been prepared for the plural number and was a woman whom it took many plurals to disconcert. "I'm sure Guy's longing for another dance with you," she rejoined with the most unblinking irrelevance.

"I'm afraid we're not dancing again quite yet," said Rose, glancing at her mother's exposed shoulders but speaking as if they were muffled in crape.

Lady Maresfield leaned her head on one side and seemed almost wistful. "Not even at my sister's ball? She's to have something next week. She'll certainly write to you."

Rose Tramore, on the spot, looking bright but vague, turned three or four things over in her mind. She remembered that the sister of her interlocutress was the proverbially rich Mrs. Bray, a bankeress or a breweress or a builderess who had so big a house that she couldn't fill it unless she opened her doors, or her mouth, very wide. Rose had learnt more about London society during these lonely months with her mother than she had ever picked up in Hill Street. The younger Mrs. Tramore was a mine of *commérages* and had no need to "go out" to bring home the latest intelligence. At any rate Mrs. Bray might serve as the end of a wedge. "Oh I dare say we might think of that," Rose said. "It would be very kind of your sister."

"Guy'll think of it, won't you, Guy?" asked Lady Maresfield.

"Rather!" Guy responded with an intonation as fine as if he had learnt it at a music hall; while at the same moment the name of his mother's carriage was bawled through the place. Mrs. Charles had parted with her old gentleman; she turned again to her daughter. Nothing occurred but what always occurred, which was exactly this absence of any occurrence — the maintained state of the universal lapse. She didn't exist even for a second to any recognising eye. The people who looked at her — of course there were plenty of those — were only the people who

468

did n't exist for hers. Lady Maresfield surged away on her son's arm.

It was this noble matron herself who wrote, the next day, enclosing a card of invitation from Mrs. Bray and expressing the hope that Rose would come and dine and let her ladyship take her. She should have only one of her own girls — Charlotte Vesey was to take the other. Rose handed both the note and the card in silence to her mother, the card superscribed only "Miss Rose Tramore." "You had much better go, dear," her mother said; in answer to which Miss Rose Tramore tore up the documents, looking with clear meditative eyes out of the window. Her mother always said "You had better go" — there had been other incidents — and Rose had never even once taken account of the observation. She would make no first advances, only plenty of second ones, and, condoning no discrimination, would treat no omission as venial. She would keep all concessions till afterwards, and then would make them one by one. Fighting society was quite as hard as her grandmother had said it would be; but there was a tension in it that made the dreariness vibrate — the dreariness of such a winter as she had just passed. Her companion had cried at the end of it and she herself had cried all through; only her tears had been private, while her mother's had fallen once for all, at luncheon on the bleak Easter Monday — produced by the way a silent survey of the deadly square brought home to her that not another creature but the pair in that room was not out of town and not having tremendous fun. Rose felt it useless to attempt

to explain merely by her mourning this severity of
solitude; for if people did n't go to parties (at least
a few did n't) for six months after their father died,
this was the very time other people took for coming
to see them. It was not too much to say that during
this first winter of Rose's heroic campaign she had
no communication whatever with the world. It
had the effect of making her take to reading the
new American books: she wanted to see how girls
got on by themselves. She had never read so much
before, and there was a lawful indifference in it
when topics failed with her mother. They often
failed after the first days, and then while she bent
over instructive volumes this lady, dressed always as
if for impending revels, sat on the sofa and watched
her. Rose felt no scruple for her detachments, since
she could remember that a little before her companion had not even a girl who was taking refuge
in queer researches to look at. She was moreover
used to that companion's attitude by this time and
had her own description of it: it was the attitude
of waiting for the carriage. If they did n't go out
it was n't that Mrs. Charles was n't ready in time,
and Rose had even an alarmed prevision of their
some day — it took for granted the day of fruition
— always arriving first. Mrs. Charles's talk at
such moments was abrupt, inconsequent and personal. She sat on the edge of sofas and chairs and
glanced occasionally at the fit of her gloves — she
was perpetually gloved, and the fit was a thing it
was melancholy to see wasted — as people do who are
expecting guests to dinner. Rose used almost to fancy

herself at times a perfunctory husband on the other side of the fire.

What she was not yet used to — there was still a charm in it — was the poor woman's extraordinary tact. During the period they were together they never had a discussion; a circumstance all the more remarkable since if the girl had a reason for sparing her companion — that of being sorry for her — Mrs. Charles had none for sparing her child. She only showed in doing so a happy instinct — the happiest thing about her. She took in perfection a course which represented everything and covered everything; she utterly abjured all authority. She testified to her abjuration in hourly ingenious touching ways. On this system nothing had to be talked over, which was a mercy all round. The tears on Easter Monday had been merely a nervous gust, to help show she was not a Christmas doll from the Burlington Arcade; and there was no lifting up of the repentant Magdalen, no uttered remorse for the former abandonment of children. Of the way she could treat her children her demeanour to this one was an example; it was an uninterrupted appeal to her elder daughter for direction. She took the law from Rose in every circumstance, and if you had noticed the pair without knowing their history you would have wondered what tie was fine enough to make maturity so respectful to youth. No mother was ever so filial as Mrs. Charles, and there had never been such a difference of position between sisters. Not that the elder one fawned, which would have been fearful; she only renounced — whatever she had to renounce. If the amount was not much she at any rate made no scene over it. Her hand was so light that Rose said of her secretly, in vague glances at the past, "No wonder people liked her!" She never characterised the force that had made of old against the parental respectability more definitely than as "People." They were people, it was true, for whom gentleness must have been everything and who did n't demand a variety of interests. The desire to "go out" was the one passion that even a closer acquaintance with her charge revealed to Rose Tramore. She marvelled at its strength, in the light of the poor lady's history: there was comedy enough in this unquenchable flame on the part of a woman who had known such misery. She had drunk deep of every dishonour, but the bitter cup had left her still with a passion for lighted candles, for squeezing up staircases and hooking herself to the male elbow. Rose had a vision of the future years in which this passion would grow with renewed exercise — of its victim, in a long-tailed dress, jogging on and on and on, jogging further and further from her sins, through a century of *The Morning Post* and down the fashionable avenue of time. She herself would then be very old — she herself would then be dead. Mrs. Charles would cover a span of life for which such an allowance of sin as that represented by the dim dreadfulness might be judged trifling. The girl could laugh indeed now at that theory of her being dragged down. If one thing was more present to her than another it was the desolation of their propriety. As she glanced at her fellow outcast it sometimes seemed to her that if she had been a bad woman she would have been worse than that. There were compensations for being "cut" which Mrs. Charles could surely have been viewed as too much neglecting.

The lonely old lady in Hill Street — Rose thought of her that way now — was the one person to whom she was ready to say that she would come to her on any terms. She wrote her this three times over and knocked still oftener at her door. But Granny answered no letters — if Rose had remained in Hill Street it would have been her own function to answer them; and from the barred threshold the butler, whom the girl had known ten years, considered her, when he told her his mistress was not at home, quite as he might have considered a young person who had come about a place and of whose eligibility he took a negative view. That was Rose's one pang, her probably appearing so heartless. Her Aunt Julia had gone to Florence with Edith for the winter, on purpose to promote this appearance; for Miss Tramore was still the person most scandalised by her secession. Edith and she doubtless often talked over by the Arno the destitution of the aged victim in Hill Street. Eric never came to see his sister, because, being full both of family and of personal feeling, he thought she really ought to have stayed with his grandmother. If she had been sole owner of that relative she might have done what she liked, but he could n't forgive such a want of consideration for property of his. There were moments when Rose would have been ready to take her hand from the plough and insist on resuming her rights, if only the fierce voice of the old house had allowed people to look her up. But she read ever so clearly that her grandmother had made this a question of loyalty to eighty years of virtue. Mrs. Tramore's forlornness didn't prevent her drawing-room from being a very public place, in which Rose could hear certain words reverberate: "Leave her alone — it's the only way to see how long she'll hold out." The old woman's visitors were people who didn't wish to quarrel, and the girl was conscious that if they hadn't let her alone — that is if they had come to her from her grandmother — she might perhaps not have held out. She had no friends quite of her own; she had not been brought up to have them — it wouldn't have been easy in a house that two such persons as her father and his mother divided between them. Her father disapproved of crude intimacies, and all the intimacies of youth were crude. He had married at five-and-twenty and could testify to such a truth. Rose felt she shared even Captain Jay with her grandmother; she had seen what *he* was worth. Moreover she had spoken to him at that last moment in Hill Street in a way which, taken with her former refusal, made it impossible he should come near her again. She hoped he went to see his protectress: he could be a sort of male military granddaughter and administer comfort.

It so happened, however, that the day after she threw Lady Maresfield's invitation into the waste-paper basket she received a visit from a certain Mrs. Donovan, whom she had occasionally seen in Hill Street. She vaguely knew this lady for a busybody, but she was in a situation which even busybodies

might alleviate. Mrs. Donovan was poor but honest
— so scrupulously honest that she was perpetually
returning visits she had never received. She was
always clad in weather-beaten sealskin and had an
odd air of being prepared for the worst, which was
borne out by her denying she was Irish. She was of
the old English Donovans.

"Dear child, won't you go out with me?" she
asked.

Rose looked at her a moment and then rang the
bell. She spoke of something else, without answering the question, and when the servant came she said:
"Please tell Mrs. Tramore that Mrs. Donovan has
come to see her."

"Oh that'll be delightful; only you mustn't tell
your grandmother!" the visitor exclaimed.

"Tell her what?"

"That I come to see your mamma."

"You don't," said Rose.

"Sure I hoped you'd introduce me!" cried Mrs.
Donovan, compromising herself in her embarrassment.

"It's not necessary. You knew her once."

"Indeed and I've known every one once," the
visitor confessed.

Mrs. Charles, when she came in, was charming
and exactly right; she greeted Mrs. Donovan as if
she had met her week before last, giving her daughter
such a fine further view of her happy instincts that
Rose again had the idea that it was no wonder
"people" had liked her. The girl grudged Mrs.
Donovan so fresh a morsel as a description of her

mother at home, rejoicing that she would be vexed at having to keep the story out of Hill Street. The elder inmate retreated, but in the best order, before Mrs. Donovan went, and Rose was touched by guessing her reason — the thought that since even this circuitous personage had been moved to come the two might, if left together, invent some remedy. Rose waited to see what Mrs. Donovan had in fact invented.

"You won't come out with me then?"

"Come out with you?"

"My daughters are married. You know I'm a lone woman. It would be an immense pleasure to me to have so charming a creature as yourself to present to the world."

"I go out only with my mother," said Rose after a moment.

"Yes, but sometimes when she's not inclined?"

"She goes everywhere she wants to go," Rose continued, uttering the biggest fib of her life and only regretting it should be wasted on Mrs. Donovan.

"Ah but do you go everywhere *you* want?" the visitor sociably asked.

"One goes even to places one hates. Every one does that."

"Oh what *I* go through!" this social martyr cried. Then she laid a persuasive hand on the girl's arm. "Let me show you at a few places first and then we'll see. I'll bring them all here."

"I don't think I understand you," Rose made answer, though in Mrs. Donovan's words she perfectly saw her own theory of the case reflected. For a quarter of a minute she asked herself whether she might n't after all do so much evil that good might come. Mrs. Donovan would take her out next day and be thankful enough to annex such an attraction as a pretty girl. Various consequences would ensue and the long delay be shortened; her mother's drawing-room would in due course resound with the clatter of teacups.

"Mrs. Bray's having some big thing next week; come with me there and I'll show you what I mane," Mrs. Donovan pleaded.

"I see what you 'mane,'" Rose said, brushing away her temptation and getting up. "I'm much obliged to you."

"You know you're wrong, my dear," said her interlocutress with angry little eyes.

"I'm not going to Mrs. Bray's."

"I'll get you a kyard; it'll only cost me a penny stamp."

"I've got one," the girl smiled.

"Do you mean the penny stamp?" Mrs. Donovan, especially at departure, always observed all the forms of amity. "You can't do it alone, my darling," she declared.

"Shall they call you a cab?" Rose asked.

"I'll pick one up. I choose my horse. You know you require your start," her visitor went on.

"Excuse my mother," was Rose's only reply.

"Don't mention it. Come to me when you need me. You'll find me in the Red Book."

"It's awfully kind of you."

Mrs. Donovan lingered a moment on the threshold. "Who will you *have* now, my child?" she appealed.

"I won't have any one!" Rose turned away, blushing for her. "She came on speculation," she said afterwards to Mrs. Charles.

Her mother looked at her a moment in silence. "You may do it if you like, you know."

Rose made no direct answer to this observation; she remarked instead: "See what our quiet life allows us to escape."

"We don't escape it. She has been here an hour."

"Once in twenty years! We might meet her three times a day."

"Oh I'd take her with the rest!" sighed Mrs. Charles; while her daughter recognised that what her companion wanted to do was just what Mrs. Donovan was doing. Mrs. Donovan's life was her ideal.

On a Sunday ten days later Rose went to see one of her old governesses, of whom she had lost sight for some time and who had written her that she was in London, unoccupied and ill. This was just the sort of relation into which she could throw herself now with inordinate zeal; the idea of it, however, not preventing a foretaste of the queer expression in the good lady's face when she should mention with whom she was living. While she smiled at this picture she threw in another joke, asking herself if Miss Hack could be held in any degree to constitute the nucleus of a circle. She would come to see her in any event — come the more the further she was dragged down. Sunday was always a difficult day with the two ladies — the afternoons made it so flagrant that their company wasn't sought. Her mother, it is true, was comprised in the habits of two or three old gentlemen — she had for a long time avoided male friends of less than seventy — who disliked each other enough to make the room, when they were there at once, crack with pressure. Rose sat for a long time with Miss Hack, doing fond justice to the truth that there could be troubles in the world worse than her own; and when she came back her mother was alone, but with a story to tell of a long visit from Mr. Guy Mangler, who had desperately awaited her return. "He's regularly in love with you; he's coming again on Tuesday," Mrs. Charles mentioned.

"Did he say so?"

"That he's coming back on Tuesday?"

"No, that he's in love with me."

"He did n't need, when he stayed two hours."

"With you? It's you then he's in love with, mamma!"

"That will do as well," laughed Mrs. Charles. "For all the use we shall make of him!" she added in a moment.

"We shall make great use of him. His mother sent him."

"Oh she 'll never come!"

"Then *he* shan't," said Rose. Yet he was admitted on the Tuesday, and after she had given him his tea Mrs. Charles left the young people alone. Rose wished she had n't — she herself had another view. At any rate she disliked her mother's view, which she had easily guessed. Mr. Mangler did nothing but say how charming he thought his hostess

of the Sunday and what a tremendously jolly visit
he had had. He did n't add in so many words "I
had no idea your mother was such a good sort"; but
this was the spirit of his simple discourse. Rose
liked it at first—a little of it gratified her; then she
judged there was too much of it for any taste. She
had to reflect that one does what one can and that
Mr. Mangler probably thought himself particularly
tasteful. He wished to convey that he desired to
make up to her for the injustice of society. Why
should n't her mother receive gracefully, she asked
(not audibly) and who had ever said she did n't?
Mr. Mangler had many words — that is he had the
same ones many times — about the disappointment
of his own parent over Miss Tramore's not having
come to dine with them the night of his aunt's ball.

"Lady Maresfield knows why I did n't come" —
Rose made short work with it at last.

"Ah now, but *I* don't, you know; can't you tell
me?" asked the young man.

"It does n't matter if your mother 's clear about it."

"Oh but why make such an awful mystery of it
when I 'm dying to know?"

He talked about this, chaffed her about it for the
rest of his visit: he had at last found a topic after his
own heart. If her mother considered that he might be
the agent of their redemption he was an engine, to this
end, of the most primitive construction. He stayed
and stayed: he struck Rose as on the point of bringing out something for which he had not quite, as he
would have said, the cheek. Sometimes she thought
he was going to begin: "By the way, mamma told

me to propose to you." At other moments he seemed charged with the admission: "I say, of course I really know what you're trying to do for her," nodding at the door: "therefore hadn't we better speak of it frankly, so that I can help you with mamma, and more particularly with my sister Char, who's the difficult one? The fact is, you see, they won't do anything for nothing. If you'll accept me they'll call, but they won't call without something 'down.'" Mr. Mangler departed without their speaking frankly, and Rose Tramore had a hot hour during which she almost entertained, vindictively, the project of "accepting" the limpid youth until after she should have got her mother into circulation. The cream of the vision was that she might break with him later. She could read that this was what her mother would have liked — yet in spite of these possibilities the door the next time he came was closed to him, and the next and the next.

In August there was nothing to do but to go abroad with the sense on Rose's part that the battle was still all to fight; for a round of country visits was not in prospect, and English watering-places constituted one of the few subjects on which the girl had heard her mother express herself with disgust. Lean Continental autumns had been indeed for years one of the various forms of Mrs. Charles's atonement, and Rose could easily see that such fruit as they had borne was bitter. The stony stare of Belgravia could be practised at Homburg, and somehow it was inveterately mere men who brooded beside her at the *table d'hôte* at Cadenabbia. Gentlemen had never been of

any use to Mrs. Charles for getting back into society
— they had only helped her so effectually to get out
of it. She once dropped, to her daughter, in a moral-
ising mood, the remark that it was astonishing how
many of them one could know without its doing one
any good. Fifty of them — even very clever ones
— represented a value inferior to that of one stupid
woman. Rose wondered at the off-hand way in which
she could talk of fifty clever men; it seemed to herself
that the whole world could n't contain such a number.
She had a sombre sense that mankind must be dull
and mean. These cogitations took place in a cold
hotel during an eternal Swiss rain, and they had a
flat echo in the transalpine valleys while the talked-
out couple, deprecating the effect of exclusiveness they
sought so little to produce, went vaguely down to the
Italian lakes and cities. Rose guided their course at
moments with an aimless ferocity; she moved abruptly,
feeling vulgar and hating her life, though replacing
it by no vision of better profit either inward or outward. She had set herself a task and clung to it, but
had now the sense of wading through desert sands.
She had succeeded in not going to Homburg waters,
where London was trying to wash away some of its
stains; that would be too staring an advertisement
of their situation. The main difference in situations
to her was thus the difference of being the more or
the less pitied, at the best an intolerable danger; so
that the places she preferred were the "unworldly"
ones. She wanted to triumph with contempt, not
with submission.

One morning in September, coming with her

mother out of the marble church at Milan, she noticed that a gentleman who had just passed her on his way into the cathedral and whose face she had not caught had raised his hat with a suppressed ejaculation. She involuntarily glanced back; the gentleman had paused, again uncovering, and Bertram Jay stood saluting her in the Italian sunshine. "Oh good-morning!" she said and walked on, pursuing her course; her mother was a little in front. She overtook in a moment this source of complications and seemed to feel admonished — it was a gust of cold air — that men were worse than ever. Captain Jay had apparently moved off to the church. Her mother turned as they met, and suddenly, as she looked back, an expression of peculiar sweetness came into the lovely eyes. It made Rose's take the same direction and rest a second time on Captain Jay, who was planted, contrary to her supposition, just where he had stood a minute before. He immediately came forward, asking Rose with great gravity if he might speak to her a moment, Mrs. Charles meanwhile delicately hovering, but with an offish tendency. He had the expression of a man who wished to say something very important; yet his next words were simple enough and consisted of the remark that he had n't seen his young friend for a year.

"Is it really so much as that?" His young friend seemed to doubt.

"Very nearly. I'd have looked you up, but in the first place I've been very little in London, and in the second I believed it would n't do me any good."

"You should have put that first," said the girl. "It would n't have done you any good."

He was silent a little over this, in his customary deciphering way; but the view he took of it did n't prevent his enquiring, as he slowly followed her mother, if he might n't walk with her now. She answered with as near an approach as she could make to a bold bad laugh that it would do him less good than ever, but that he might please himself. He replied without the slightest show of levity that it would serve him more than if he did n't, and they strolled together, with Mrs. Charles well before them, across the big amusing piazza, where the front of the cathedral reigns as builded lustre. He asked a question or two and explained his own presence: having a month's holiday, the first clear time for several years, he had just popped over the Alps. He wondered if Rose had recent news of her grand-mother, and it was the only tortuous thing she had ever heard him say.

"I've had no communication of any kind from her since I parted with you under her roof. Has n't she mentioned that?" said Rose.

"I have n't seen her."

"I thought you were such great friends."

Bertram Jay just blinked. "Well, not so much now."

"What has she done to you?" Rose demanded.

He fidgeted a little, as from thought of something that superseded her question; then with mild violence brought out the enquiry: "Miss Tramore, are you really happy?"

She was startled by the words, for she on her side had quickly calculated, guessing that he had broken with her grandmother and that this pointed to a reason. It suggested at least that he would n't now be a mere mouthpiece for that ancestral hardness. She turned off his question — said it never was a fair one, since you gave yourself away however you answered it. When he repeated "You give yourself away?" as if he did n't understand, she remembered how little he must have read the funny American books. This brought them to a silence, for she had enlightened him only by another laugh, and he was evidently preparing another question, which he wished carefully to disconnect from the former. Presently, just as they were coming near Mrs. Tramore, it arrived in the words "Is the lady your mother?" On Rose's assenting, with the addition that she was travelling with her, he said: "Will you be so kind as to introduce me?" They were so close to this bland apologist that she probably heard, but she floated away with a single stroke of her paddle and an inattentive poise of her head. It was a striking exhibition of the famous happy instinct, for Rose waited before answering, which was exactly what might have made her mother wish to turn; and indeed when at last the girl spoke she only said to her companion: "Why do you ask me that?"

"Because I aim at the pleasure of making her acquaintance."

Rose had stopped, and in the middle of the square they stood confronted. "Do you remember what you said to me the last time I saw you?"

"Oh don't speak of that!"

"It's better to speak of it now than to speak of it later."

Bertram Jay looked round him as to see if any one would hear; but the bright foreignness gave him a sense of safety, and he brought out all distinctly: "Miss Tramore, I love you more than ever!"

"Then you ought to have come to see us," declared the girl, who quickly walked on.

"You treated me the last time as if I were positively offensive to you."

"So I did, but you know my reason."

"Because I protested against the course you were taking? I did, I did!" the young man rang out as if he still a little stuck to that.

His tone made her own quite profane. "Perhaps you do so yet?"

"I can't tell till I've seen more of the details of your life," he replied with eminent honesty.

She took it in, then her light laugh at the nature in it filled the air. "And it's in order to see more of them and judge that you wish to make my mother's acquaintance?"

He coloured at this and hedged, but presently broke out with a confused "Miss Tramore, let me stay with you a little!" which made her stop again.

"Your company will do us great honour, but there must be a rigid condition attached to our acceptance of it."

"Kindly mention it," said Captain Jay, staring at the front of the cathedral.

"You don't take us on trial."

486

"On trial?"

"You don't make an observation to me — not a single one, ever, ever! — on the matter that, in Hill Street, we had our last words about."

He appeared to be counting the thousand pinnacles of the church. "I think you really must be right," he remarked at last.

"There you are!" cried Rose Tramore, and swiftly turned her back.

He caught up with her, he laid his hand on her arm to stay her. "If you're going to Venice let me go to Venice *with* you!"

"You don't even understand my terms."

"I'm sure you're right then: you must be right about everything."

"That's not in the least true, and I don't care a fig whether you're sure or not. Please let me go."

He had barred her way, he kept her longer. "I'll go and speak to your mother myself!"

Even in the midst of something deeper she was amused at the air of audacity accompanying this declaration. Poor Captain Jay might have been on the point of marching up to a battery. She showed moreover all her irony. "You'll be disappointed!"

"Disappointed?"

"She's much more proper than grandmamma, because she's much more amiable."

"Dear Miss Tramore — dear Miss Tramore!" the young man murmured helplessly.

"You'll see for yourself. Only there's another condition," Rose went on.

"Another?" he cried with discouragement and alarm.

"You must understand thoroughly, before you throw in your lot with us even for a few days, what our position really is."

"Is it very bad?" he said artlessly.

"No one has anything to do with us, no one speaks to us, no one looks at us."

"Really?" he stared.

"We've no social existence, we're utterly ignored."

"Oh Miss Tramore!" her friend distressfully gasped. And he added quickly, vaguely, with a want of presence of mind of which he as quickly felt ashamed: "Do none of your family yet —?" The question collapsed; the hot bright creature was too much for him.

"We're extraordinarily happy," she threw out.

"Now that's all I wanted to know!" he returned with extravagant cheer, walking on with her briskly to be presented.

He had not put up at their inn, but he insisted on coming that night to their *table d'hôte*. He sat next Mrs. Charles and afterwards accompanied them gallantly to the opera, given at a third-rate theatre where they were almost the only ladies in the boxes. The next day they went together by rail to the Charterhouse at Pavia, and while he strolled with his younger companion as they waited for the homeward train he said to her candidly: "Your mother's remarkably pretty." She remembered the words and the feeling they gave her: they were the first note of new era. The relief was quite that of an anxious

488

encumbered matron who has "brought out" her child and is thinking but of the marriage-market. Men might be of no use, as Mrs. Charles said, yet it was from this moment Rose dated the rosy dawn of her confidence that she should work her *protégée* off; and when later, in crowded assemblies, the phrase, or something like it behind a hat or a fan, fell repeatedly on her anxious ear, "Your mother *is* in beauty!" or "I've never seen her look better!" she had a faint vision of the yellow sunshine and the afternoon shadows on the dusty Italian platform.

Mrs. Charles's behaviour at this period was a revelation of her native gift for delicate situations. She needed no fine analysis of this one from her daughter — it was one of the things for which she had a scent; and there was a kind of loyalty to the rules of games in the silent sweetness with which she smoothed the path of Bertram Jay. It was clear that she was in her element in fostering the exercise of the affections, and if she ever spoke, at this pass, without thinking thirteen times, it is presumable she would have exclaimed with some gaiety "Oh I know all about *love!*" Rose could see how she understood that their companion would be a help, and this in spite of his being no dispenser of patronage. The key to the gates of fashion had not been placed in his hand, and no one had ever heard of the ladies of his family, who lived in some vague hollow of the Yorkshire moors; but none the less he might administer a muscular push. Yes indeed, men in general were broken reeds, but Captain Jay's presence was not so much the plant itself as the strong straight stick driven in for the plant to grow on. Respectability was the woman's maximum, as honour was the man's, but this distinguished young soldier inspired more than one kind of confidence. Rose had a high ironic relish for the use to which his respectability was put, even though there mingled with this freedom not a little compassion. She saw that after a couple of days he decidedly liked her mother, yet still did n't suspect his abasement. He took for granted he "saw through" her; notwithstanding which he would have trusted her with anything except Rose herself. His trusting her with Rose would come very soon. He never spoke to her daughter about her qualities of character, but two or three of them — and indeed these were all the poor lady had, and they made the best show — were what he had in mind in praising her appearance. When he remarked "What attention Mrs. Tramore seems to attract everywhere!" he meant "What a beautifully simple nature it is!" and when he said "There's something extraordinarily harmonious in the colours she wears," it signified "Upon my word I never saw such a sweet temper in my life!" She lost one of her boxes at Verona and made the prettiest joke of it to Captain Jay, who himself did all the fuming. When Rose saw this she said to herself "Next season we shall have only to choose." Rose knew what was in the box.

By the time they reached Venice — they had stopped at half a dozen little old romantic cities in the most frolicsome æsthetic way — she liked their comrade better than she had ever liked him before. She did him the justice to recognise that if he was n't quite honest with himself he was at least wholly honest with Rose Tramore. She reckoned up everything he had been since he joined them, and put upon it all an interpretation so favourable to his devotion that, catching herself in the act of glossing over one or two displays that had not struck her at the time as disinterested, she exclaimed beneath her breath "Look out, my dear — you're falling in love!" But if he prized correctness was n't he quite right? Could any one possibly prize it more than she? And if he had protested against her throwing in her lot with her mother this was not because of the benefit conferred but because of the injury received. He exaggerated the injury, but that was the privilege of a lover perfectly willing to be selfish on behalf of his mistress. He might have wanted her grandmother's money for her, but if he had given her up on first becoming sure she would throw away her chance of it (oh this was *her* doing too!) he had given up her grandmother as much: not keeping well with the old woman, as some men would have done; not waiting to see how the perverse experiment would turn out and appeasing her, if it should promise tolerably, with a view to future operations. He had had a pious, evangelical lurid view of what the girl he loved would find herself in for. She could see this now — she could see it from his present bewilderment and mystification, and she liked him and pitied him, with the kindest smile, for the original want of the finer wit as well as for the actual meekness. No wonder he had n't known what she was in for, since he now did n't even know what he was in for himself. Were n't there moments when

491

he thought his companions almost unnaturally good, too good, as the phrase was, to be true? He had lost all power to verify that sketch of their isolation and *déclassement* to which she had treated him on the great square at Milan. The last thing he noticed was that they were neglected, and he had never, for himself, had such an impression of society.

It could scarcely be enhanced even by the apparition of a large fair hot red-haired young man, carrying a lady's fan in his hand, who suddenly stood before their little party as, on the third evening after their arrival in Venice, it partook of ices at one of the tables before the celebrated Café Florian. The lamp-lit Venetian dusk appeared to have revealed them to this gentleman as he sat with other friends at a neighbouring table, and he had in unsophisticated glee sprung up to shake hands with Mrs. Charles and her daughter. Rose recalled him to her mother, who looked at first as though she did n't remember him, then, however, bestowing a sufficiently gracious smile on Mr. Guy Mangler. He gave with youthful candour the history of his movements and indicated the whereabouts of his family: he was with his mother and sisters; they had met the Bob Veseys, who had taken Lord Whiteroy's yacht and were going to Constantinople. His mother and the girls, poor things, were at the Grand Hotel, but he was on the yacht with the Veseys, where they had Lord Whiteroy's cook. Was n't the food in Venice filthy and would n't they come and look at the yacht? She was n't very fast, but she was awfully jolly. His mother might have come if she would, but she would n't at first, and now, when she wanted to, there were other people who naturally would n't turn out for her. Mr. Mangler sat down; he alluded with artless resentment to the way, in July, the door of his friends had been closed to him. He was going to Constantinople, but he did n't care — if *they* were going anywhere: meanwhile his mother hoped awfully they would look her up.

Lady Maresfield, if she had given her son any such message, which Rose disbelieved, entertained her hope in a manner compatible with her sitting half an hour, surrounded by her little retinue, without glancing in the direction of Mrs. Charles. The girl at the same time felt this to be scarce good proof of their humiliation; inasmuch as it was rather she who on the occasion of their last contact had held off from Lady Maresfield. She was a little ashamed now of not having answered the note in which this affable personage ignored her mother. She could n't help noting indeed a faint movement on the part of some of the other members of the group; she made out an attitude of observation in the high-plumed head of Mrs. Vaughan-Vesey. Mrs. Vesey perhaps might have been looking at Captain Jay, for as this gentleman walked back to the hotel with our young lady (they were at the Britannia, and young Mangler, who clung to them, went in front with Mrs. Charles) he revealed to Rose that he had some acquaintance with Lady Maresfield's eldest daughter, though he did n't know, and did n't particularly want to know, her ladyship. He expressed himself with more acerbity than she had ever heard him use

— Christian charity so generally governed his speech — about the young booby who had been prattling to them. They separated at the door of the hotel. Mrs. Charles had got rid of Mr. Mangler, and Bertram Jay was in other quarters.

"If you know Mrs. Vesey why did n't you go and speak to her? I'm sure she saw you," Rose said.

Captain Jay replied even more circumspectly than usual. "Because I did n't want to leave you."

"Well, you can go now; you're free," our young woman pursued.

"Thank you. I shall never go again."

"That won't be civil," said Rose.

"I don't care to be civil. I don't like her."

"Why don't you like her?"

"You ask too many questions."

"I know I do," the girl acknowledged with secret pleasure.

Captain Jay had already shaken hands with her, but at this he put out his hand again. "She's too worldly," he murmured while he held Rose Tramore's a moment.

"Ah you dear!" Rose exclaimed almost audibly as, with her mother, she turned away.

The next morning, on the Grand Canal, the gondola of our three friends encountered a stately barge which, though it contained several persons, seemed pervaded mainly by one majestic presence. During the instant the gondolas were passing each other it was impossible either for Rose Tramore or for her companions not to become conscious that this distinguished identity had markedly inclined itself —

a circumstance commemorated the next moment, almost within earshot of the other boat, by the most spontaneous cry that had issued for many a day from the lips of Mrs. Charles. "Fancy, my dear, Lady Maresfield has bowed to us!"

"We ought to have returned it," Rose answered; but she looked at Bertram Jay, who was opposite to her. He blushed, and she blushed, and during this moment was born a deeper understanding than had yet existed between these associated spirits. It had something to do with their going together that afternoon, without her mother, to look at certain out-of-the-way pictures as to which Ruskin had inspired her with a desire to see sincerely. Mrs. Charles hinted at the wish to stay at home, and the motive of this wish — a finer shade than any even Ruskin had ever found a phrase for — was not translated into misrepresenting words either by the mother or the daughter. At San Giovanni in Bragora the girl and her companion came upon Mrs. Vaughan-Vesey, who, with one of her sisters, was also endeavouring to do the earnest thing. She did it to Rose, she did it to Captain Jay as well as to Gianbellini; she was a handsome long-necked aquiline person, of a different type from the rest of her family, and she did it remarkably well. She secured our friends — it was her own expression — for luncheon the next day on the yacht, and made it public to Rose that she would come in the afternoon to invite her mother. When the girl returned to the hotel Mrs. Charles mentioned before Captain Jay, who had come up to their sitting-room, that Lady Maresfield had called.

"She stayed a long time — at least it seemed long!" laughed Mrs. Charles.

The poor lady could have her revenge of laughter now; yet there was some grimness in her colloquy with her daughter after Bertram Jay had gone. Before this happened Mrs. Vesey's card, scrawled over in pencil and referring to the morrow's luncheon, had been brought up to her.

"They mean it all as a bribe," said the principal recipient of these civilities.

"As a bribe?" Rose repeated.

"She wants to marry you to that boy; they've seen Captain Jay and they're frightened."

"Well, dear mamma, I can't take Mr. Mangler for a husband."

"Of course not. But oughtn't we to go to the luncheon?"

"Certainly we'll go to the luncheon," Rose stoutly said; and when the thing really came to pass on the morrow she could feel for the first time that she was taking her mother out. This appearance was somehow brought home to every one else, and it was the great agent of her success. For it is of the essence of this simple history that, in the first place, that success dated from Mrs. Vesey's Venetian *déjeuner*, and in the second reposed, by a subtle social logic, just on the monstrosity that had at first put it out of the question. There is always a place for chance in things, and Rose Tramore's chance had turned up in the fact that Charlotte Vesey was, as some one had said, awfully modern, an immense improvement on the exploded science of her mother, and capable of seeing

what a "draw" there would be in the comedy, if
properly brought out, of the reversed positions of
Mrs. Charles and Mrs. Charles's diplomatic daughter.
With a first-rate managerial eye she perceived that
people would flock into any room — and all the
more into one of hers — to see Rose bring in her
dreadful mother. She treated the cream of English society to this thrilling spectacle later in the autumn, when she once more "secured" both perform-
ers for a week at Brimble. It made a hit on the spot,
the very first evening — the girl was felt to play her
part so well. The rumour of the performance spread;
every one wanted to see it. It was an entertainment
of which, that winter in the country, and the next
season in town, persons of taste, and of the first
fashion, desired to give their friends the freshness.
The thing was to make the Tramores come late,
after every one had arrived. They were engaged for
a fixed hour, like the American imitator and the
Patagonian contralto. Mrs. Vesey had been the
first to say the girl was awfully original, but this
became the general view.

Charlotte Vesey had with her mother one of the
few quarrels in which Lady Maresfield had really
stood up to such an antagonist — the elder woman
having to recognise in general in whose veins it was
that the blood of the Manglers flowed — on account
of this very circumstance of her attaching more importance to Miss Tramore's originality ("Her originality be hanged!" her ladyship had gone so far as
unintelligently to exclaim) than to the prospects of the
unfortunate Guy. Mrs. Vesey actually lost sight of

these pressing problems in her admiration of the
way the mother and the daughter, or rather the
daughter and the mother — it was slightly confusing
— unfailingly "drew." They were absolutely to be
depended on. It was Lady Maresfield's version of
the case that the brazen girl — she was shockingly
coarse — had treated poor Guy with the last perfidy.
At any rate it was made known, just after Easter, that
Miss Tramore was to be married to Captain Jay.
The marriage was not to take place till the summer,
but Rose felt that before this the field would practically be won. There had been some bad moments,
there had been several warm corners and a certain
number of cold shoulders and closed doors and stony
stares; but the breach was effectually made — the
rest was only a question of time. Mrs. Charles
could be trusted to keep what she had gained, and
it was the dowagers, the old dragons with promin-
ent fangs and glittering scales, whom the trick had
already mainly caught. By this time there were
several houses into which the liberated lady had
crept alone. Her daughter had been expected with
her, but they could n't turn her out because the girl
had stayed behind, and she was fast acquiring a new
identity, that of a parental connexion with the heroine of one of the most romantic of stories. She was
at least the next best thing to her daughter, and Rose
foresaw the day when she would be valued principally
as a memento of one of the prettiest episodes — so
charmingly modern — in the annals of English society. At a big official party in June Rose had the
joy of positively introducing Eric to his mother. She

was a little sorry it was an official party — there were some other such queer people there; but Eric called, observing the shade, the next day but one.

No observer, probably, would have been acute enough to fix exactly the moment at which the girl ceased to take out her mother and began to *be* taken out, as a young person not "brazen" should. A later phase was more distinguishable — that at which Rose forbore to inflict on her companion a duality that might become oppressive. She began to economise her value, going only when the particular effect was required. Her marriage was delayed by the period of mourning consequent upon the death of her grandmother, who, the younger Mrs. Tramore averred, was killed by the rumour of her own new birth. She was the only one of the dragons who had not been tamed. Julia Tramore, for that matter, knew the truth on this head — she was determined such things should n't kill *her*. She would live to do something about it all — she hardly knew what. The provisions of her mother's will were published in the *Illustrated News;* from which it appeared that everything that was not to go to Eric and to Julia was to go to the fortunate Edith. Miss Tramore makes no secret of her own intentions as regards this favourite. Edith is not pretty, but Lady Maresfield is waiting for her; she is determined Char Vesey shall not get hold of her. Mrs. Vesey however takes no interest in her at all. Mrs. Vesey is whimsical, as befits a woman of her fashion; but there are two persons she is still very fond of — the delightful Bertram Jays. The fondness of this pair, it must be added,

499

is not wholly expended in return. They are extremely united, but their life is more domestic than might have been expected from the preliminary signs. It owes a part of its concentration to the fact that Mrs. Tramore has now so many places to go to that she has almost no time to come to her daughter's. She is, under her son-in-law's roof, a brilliant but a rare apparition, and the other day he remarked upon the circumstance to his wife.

"If it had n't been for you," she unsparingly replied — she is mistress of an odd deep irony — "mamma might have had her regular place at our fireside."

"Gracious goodness, how did I prevent it?" cried Captain Jay with all the consciousness of virtue.

"You ordered it otherwise, you goose!" And she says in the same spirit, whenever her husband commends her (which he does sometimes extravagantly) for the way she launched her mother: "Nonsense, my dear — practically it was *you!*"

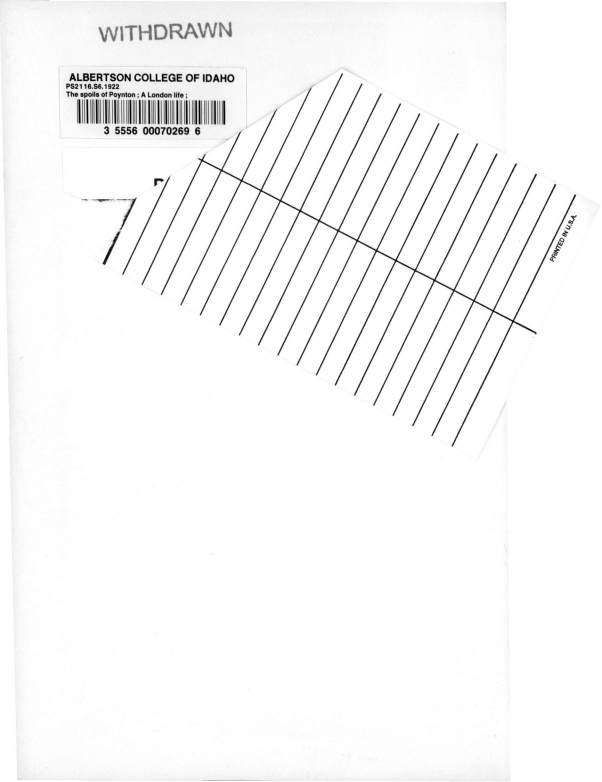

PRINTED IN U.S.A.